A WHISPER FROM THE PAST

The letters were brittle and yellow... full of old words of love written years ago from hearts that were dust... full of old joys that had once been raptures and dim old griefs that had once been agonies. Pat lingered, going back to the window where the full moon was beginning to weave beautiful patterns of vine leaves on the garret floor. The spookier the garret was the more she loved it.

The letters in her hands made her think of Hilary's letter that day. Like all his letters it had a certain flavour. It *lived*. You could almost hear Hilary's voice speaking through it... see the laughter in his eyes. Pat had one of her moments of wishing passionately that Hilary was somewhere about... that they could join hands as of old and run across the old stone bridge over Jordan. Surely they had only to slip over the old bridge to find themselves in the old fairyland. They would go back to Happiness and the Haunted Springs, following the misty little brook through the old fields where the moonlight loved to dream. Surely Happiness kept their old days for them and they would find them there.

Pat shivered. The rising wind moaned rather eerily around the lofty window. She felt suddenly, strangely lonely... right there in dear Silver Bush she felt lonely... *homesick*.

MISTRESS PAT

L. M. Montgomery

BANTAM BOOKS
NEW YORK · TORONTO · LONDON · SYDNEY · AUCKLAND

RL 6, IL age 6 and up

MISTRESS PAT

*A Bantam Book / published by arrangement with
the author's estate*

PRINTING HISTORY

*Copyright 1935 by McClelland and Stewart Limited
Canadian Favourites edition 1977
Bantam edition / August 1989*

ISBN 0-553-28048-1

Published simultaneously in the United States and Canada

Bantam Books are published by Bantam Books, a division of
Bantam Doubleday Dell Publishing Group, Inc. Its trademark,
consisting of the words "Bantam Books" and the portrayal
of a rooster, is Registered in U.S. Patent and Trademark Office
and in other countries. Marca Registrada. Bantam Books,
666 Fifth Avenue, New York, New York 10103.

PRINTED IN CANADA
COVER PRINTED IN U.S.A.

U   0 9 8 7 6 5 4 3 2 1

Contents

The First Year

THERE were hundreds of trees, big and little, on the Silver Bush farm and every tree was a personal friend of Pat's. It was anguish to her when one of them, even some gnarled old spruce in the woods at the back, was cut down. Nobody had ever been able to convince Pat that it was not murder to cut a tree down . . . justifiable homicide perhaps, since there had to be fires and lumber, but homicide nevertheless.

And no tree was ever cut in the grove of white birches behind the house. *That* would have been sacrilege. Occasionally one blew down in an autumn storm and was mourned by Pat until time turned it into a beautiful mossy log with ferns growing thickly all along it.

Everybody at Silver Bush loved the birch grove, though to none of them did it mean what it meant to Pat. For her it *lived*. She not only knew the birches but they knew her: the fern-sweet solitudes, threaded with shadows, knew her: the wind in the boughs always made her a glad salutation. From the first beginnings of memory she had played in it and wandered in it and dreamed in it. She could not remember the time it had not held her imagination in thrall and dominated her life. In childhood it had been peopled by the leprechauns and green folk of Judy Plum's stories: and now that those dear and lovely beliefs had drifted away from her like faint and beckoning wraiths their old magic still haunted the silver bush. It could never be to Pat just the ordinary grove of white-skinned trees and ferny hollows it was to other people. But then, Pat, so her family always said, was just a little different from other people, too. She had been different when she was a big-eyed child . . . different when she was a brown, skinny little imp in her early teens . . . and still differ-

1

ent, now that she was twenty and ought, so Judy Plum felt, to be having beaus.

There *had* been a boy or two in Pat's past but Judy considered them mere experiments. Pat, however, did not seem to want beaus, in spite of Judy's sly hints. All she really wanted, or seemed to want, was to "run" Silver Bush and take care of mother... who was a bit of an invalid... and see that as few changes as possible came into existence there. If she could have been granted a fairy wish it would be that she might wave a wand and make everything remain exactly the same for at least a hundred years.

She loved her home with a passion. She was deeply loyal to it... to its faults as well as its virtues... though she would never admit it had any faults. Every small thing about it gave her the keenest joy. If she went away for a visit she was homesick until she could return to it.

"Silver Bush isn't her house... it's her religion," Uncle Brian had once said teasingly.

Every room in it meant something... had some vital message for her. It had the look that houses wear when they have been loved for years. It was a house where nobody ever seemed to be in a hurry... a house from which nobody ever went away without feeling better in some way... a house in which there was always laughter. There had been so much laughter at Silver Bush that the very walls seemed soaked in it. It was a house where you felt welcome the moment you stepped into it. It took you in... rested you. The very chairs clamoured to be sat upon, so hospitable was it. And it was overrun by beautiful cats... fat, fluffy fellows basking on the window sills or huddles of silk-soft kittens sleeping on the warm sandstone slabs in the old family graveyard beyond the orchard. People came from all over the Island to get a Silver Bush cat. Pat hated to give them away but of course something had to be done, since the kitten crop never failed.

"Tom Baker was here for a kitten to-day," said Judy. "'What brade is it?' sez he, solemn-like. That fam'ly av Bakers never did be having too much sinse. 'Oh, oh, no brade at all,' sez I. 'Our cats do be just common or garden cats,' sez I. 'But we give thim a good home and talk to thim now and thin as inny self-respicting cat likes to be talked to,' sez I, 'wid a bit av a compliment thrown in once in a while. And so they do their bist for us in the matter av kittens as well as all ilse. Sure and I do be forgetting what a rat looks like,' sez I. I was faling a bit unwilling to give him the kitten. They'll trate it well, I'm having no manner av doubt, but they'll niver rimimber to pass the time av day wid it."

"Our cats own us anyway," said Cuddles lazily. "Aunt Edith says it's absurd the way we spoil them. She says there are lots of poor Christians don't have the life our cats have and she thinks it awful that we let them sleep at the foot of our beds."

"Oh, oh, see there now, ye've sint Gintleman Tom off mad," said Judy reprovingly. "Cats always do be knowing what ye're saying av thim. And Gintleman Tom's that sensitive."

Cuddles idly watched Gentleman Tom . . . Judy's lank, black cat who was so old that he had forgotten to die, Sid said . . . stalk indignantly off through the ferns of the path. She and Pat and Judy were spending the hours of the late summer afternoon in the silver bush. They had fallen into the habit of doing their odd jobs there, where bird music occasionally dripped through the leafy silence or a squirrel chattered or wood winds wove their murmurous spells. Pat went there to write her letters and Cuddles studied her lessons. Often mother brought her knitting and sewing. It was a lovely place to work in . . . though Cuddles seldom worked while there. She generally left that to Pat and Judy. The latter was sitting on a mossy log, stoning cherries for preserving and the former was making new apple-green curtains for the dining room. Cuddles, observing that it was a poor place that couldn't support one lady, put her hands on the grass behind her and leaned back on them, looking up at the opal-hued sky between the tree-tops.

"Bold-and-Bad won't leave us," she said. "*He* isn't so touchy."

"Oh, oh, ye cudn't be hurting that cat's falings, by rason that he hasn't got inny," said Judy, with a somewhat scornful glance at the big grey cat sitting on the log by Pat, blinking eyes of pale jade with a black line down their centre at a dog with a sleek, golden-brown back who was happily gnawing a rather malodorous bone behind the log, occasionally pausing to gaze up in Pat's face adoringly and wistfully. Then Pat would stroke his head and pull his pointed ears, whereat Bold-and-Bad would look more remote than ever. Bold-and-Bad always considered "the dog McGinty," as Judy called him, an interloper. Hilary Gordon had left him with Pat nearly two years ago, when he went away to college in

Toronto. At first McGinty had nearly broken his heart but he knew Pat loved him and eventually he perked up a bit and gave Bold-and-Bad as good as he sent. An armed truce existed between them, for Bold-and-Bad had not forgotten what Pat did to him the day he scratched McGinty's nose. McGinty would always have been friends but Bold-and-Bad was simply not having any.

"Oh, oh, what wid all these cherries to be stoned afore supper I do be wishing we had a ghost like they had at Castle McDermott in the ould days," said Judy, with an exaggerated sigh. "That was a ghost now...a rale useful, industrious cratur. The odd jobs he'd do ye wudn't be belaving... stirring the porridge and peeling the pittaties and scouring the brasses...he wasn't above turning his hand to innything. Sorra the day the ould lord lift a bit av money on the kitchen dresser for him, saying the labourer was worthy av his hire. He niver come agin...his falings having been hurt be the same. Oh, oh, it cost the McDermott the kape av another maid. Ye niver know where ye are whin ye're daling wid the craturs. Sure and that's the disadvantage av ghosts. Some wud have been offinded if they hadn't been thanked. But a ghost like that wud be rale handy once in a while at Silver Bush, wudn't it now, Cuddles, darlint?"

Luckily Judy did not see Pat and Cuddles exchanging smiles. They had begun to share with each other their amused delight in Judy's stories, which had replaced the credulity of early childhood. There had been a time when both Pat and Cuddles would have believed implicitly in the industrious McDermott ghost.

"Judy, if that yarn is a gentle hint for me to get busy and help you stone those cherries I'm not going to take it," said Cuddles with a grin. "I hate sewing and preserving. Pat is the domestic type...I'm not. When I'm here I just like to squat on the grass and listen to you talking. I've got my blue dress on and cherry juice stains. Besides, I've got pains in my stomach...I really have...every now and then."

"If ye *will* ate liddle grane apples ye must put up wid pains in yer stomach," said Judy, as remorselessly as cause and effect. "Though whin I was a girleen it wasn't thought rale good manners to talk av yer insides so plain, Cuddles."

"You keep on calling me Cuddles," said Cuddles sulkily. "I've asked you all to stop it and not one of you will. Away from home I'm Rae...I like that, but here at Silver Bush everybody 'Cuddles' me. It's so ... so babyish ... now that I'm thirteen."

"So it is, Cuddles dear," agreed Judy. "But I'm too old to be larning new names. I'm guessing ye'll always be Cuddles to me. And such a tommyshaw as we had finding a name for ye at that! Do ye be minding, Pat? And how upset ye was bekase I wint hunting in the parsley bed for a new baby the night Cuddles was born? Oh, oh, that was the tarrible night at Silver Bush! We niver thought yer mother wud live through it, Patsy dear. To think it do be thirteen years ago!"

"I remember how big and red the moon was that night, rising over the Hill of the Mist," said Pat dreamily. "Oh, Judy, did you know that the lightning struck the middle Lombardy on the Hill of the Mist last week? It killed it and it has to be cut down. I don't see how I can stand it. I've always loved those three trees so. They've been there ever since I can remember. Now, McGinty, don't do it. I know it's a temptation when his tail hangs down so ... that's right, Bold-and-Bad, tuck it up. And while I think about it, Bold-and-Bad, you needn't ... you really needn't ... bring any more mice to my bedside in the early morning hours, I'll take your word for it that you caught them."

"The yells av him whin he's carrying one upstairs!" said Judy. "It'd break his heart if he cudn't be showing it off to somebody."

"I thought you said a moment ago he hadn't any feelings," giggled Cuddles.

Judy ignored her and turned to Pat.

"Will we be having a cherry pudding to-morrow, Patsy?"

"Yes, I think so. Oh, do you remember how Joe loved cherry puddings?"

"Oh, oh, there's not much I do be forgetting about Joe, Patsy dear. Was it Shanghai his last letter was from? I'm not belaving thim yellow Chinese know innything about making cherry puddings. Or plum puddings ather. We'll have one av thim for Christmas when Joe will be home."

"I wonder if he really will," sighed Pat. "He has never been home for Christmas since he went away. He's always planned to come but something always prevents."

"Trix Binnie says Joe has had his nose tattooed and that's the reason he doesn't come home," said Cuddles. "She says Captain Dave Binnie saw him last year in Buenos Ayres and didn't know him, he looked so awful. Do you think there's any truth in it?"

"Not if a Binnie do be telling it," said Judy contemptuously. "Don't be worrying, Cuddles."

"Oh, I'm not. I rather hoped **it** was. It would be so interesting. If he *is* tattooed I'm **going** to get him to do me when **he** comes home."

There was simply nothing to be said to this. Judy turned again to Pat.

"He's to be captain by Christmas, didn't he say? Oh, oh, but that b'y has got on! He'll be a year younger than yer Uncle Horace was whin he got his ship. I do be minding the time *he* come home that summer and brought his monkey wid him."

"A monkey?"

"I'm telling ye. The baste took possession. Yer liddle grandmother was nearly out av her wits. And poor ould Jim Appleby... he was niver known to be sober... just a bit less drunk than common was all ye cud be saying at the bist av times... he come down to Silver Bush to buy some pigs and yer Uncle Horace's monkey was skipping along the top av the pig-pen fince quite careless-like. Yer grandfather said ould Jim turned white... all but his nose... and he sez, sez he, 'I've got 'em! Ma always said I'd git 'em and I have. But I'll niver be touching a drop agin.' He kipt his word for two months but he was that cross and cantankerous his family were rale glad whin he forgot about the monkey. Mrs. Jim did be saying she wished Horace Gardiner wud kape his minagerie widin bounds. If Jim comes it's a rale re-union we'll have, Patsy."

"Yes. Winnie and Frank will be over and we'll all be together again. We must plan it all out some of these days. I do love planning things."

"Aunt Edith says it's no use making plans because something always happens to upset them," said Cuddles gloomily.

"Niver ye be belaving it, me jewel. And innyhow what if they do be upset? Ye've had the fun av planning. Don't be letting yer Aunt Edith make a...a...what did Siddy be calling it now?"

"A pessimist."

"Oh, oh, doesn't that sound just like her! Innyway, don't be letting her make ye that. Aven if Joe doesn't get home, the darlint, there'll be Winnie and Frank and yer Aunt Hazel's liddle gang, and the turkeys we'll be having for dinner are roosting on the fence behind the church barn this blessed minute growing as hard as they kin. And Pat there is saving up all the resates and menoos in the magazines. Oh, oh, there'll be the great preparations I'm thinking and me fine Edith won't be spiling it wid her sighs and sorrows. She do be having a grudge at life, that one. Patsy, do ye be minding the time ye were dancing naked here by the light av the moon and me lady Edith nabbed ye?"*

"Dancing naked? And you won't even let me wear shorts round home," moaned Cuddles.

"And they broke my heart by sending me to Coventry," went on Pat, as if Cuddles had not spoken. "They never knew how cruel they were. And the night you came home, Judy, and I smelt the ham frying!"

"Sure, minny's the good liddle bite we've had in the ould days, Patsy. But there's as minny ahead as behind I'm hoping. And maybe, Miss Cuddles...as I shud be after calling Rachel...if ye won't be stoning inny cherries will ye be above making some blueberry muffins for supper? Patsy is wanting to finish her hemstitching and Siddy's that fond av thim."

"I'll do that," agreed Cuddles. "I like blueberry things. Oh, and I'm going up to the Bay Shore next week to pick blueberries with Winnie. She says I can sleep out in a tent right down by the shore. I want to sleep out some night here in Silver Bush. We could have a hammock swung between those two big trees there. It would be heavenly. Judy, did Uncle Tom ever have any love affairs when he was young?"

"Oh, oh, the way ye do be jumping from one thing to another!" protested Judy. "No doubt he had his fun girling like the rest av the b'ys. I'm not knowing why it niver turned sarious. What put him into yer head?"

"He's asked me to mail a letter for him at Silverbridge three times this summer. He said they were too nosy at the North Glen post office. It was addressed to a lady."

Pat and Judy exchanged knowing glances. Judy repressed her excitement and spoke with careful carelessness.

"Did ye be noticing the name av the lady, Cuddles darlint?"

*See "Pat of Silver Bush."

"Oh, Mrs. Something-or-other," said Cuddles with a yawn. "I forget the name. Uncle Tom looked so red and sheepish when he asked me I just wondered what he was up to."

"Yer Uncle Tom must be close on sixty," reflected Judy. "It do be the time some min take a second silly spell about the wimmen. But wid Edith to kape him straight he can't go far. Sure and I do be minding how crazy he was to go to the Klondike whin the big gold rush was on . . . nather to hold nor bind. But me lady Edith nipped that in the bud and I'm thinking he's niver ralely forgiven her for it. Oh, oh, we've all had our bits av drames that niver come true. If I cud just have a run over to the Ould Country now and see if Castle McDermott is as grand as it used to be. But it'll niver niver come to pass."

"'Each mortal has his Carcassonne,'" quoted Pat dreamily, recalling a poem Hilary Gordon had marked for her once.

But Cuddles, always the more practical, said coolly, "And why can't it, Judy? You could take a couple of months off any summer, now that I'm old enough to help Pat. The fare second class wouldn't be too much and you could see all your relatives there and have a gorgeous time."

Judy blinked as if somebody had struck her.

"Oh, oh, Cuddles darlint, it sounds rale rasonable whin ye put it that way. It's a wonder I niver thought av it. But I'm not so young as I once was . . . I do be getting a bit ould for gallivanting round."

"You're not too old, Judy. Just you go next summer. All you have to do is to make up your mind."

"Oh, oh, make up yer mind, sez she. That takes a bit av doing, Cuddles dear . . . as well as a bit av thinking av."

"Don't think about it . . . just go," said Cuddles, rolling over on her stomach and pulling McGinty's ears. "If you think too much about it you'll never do it."

"Oh, oh, whin I was thirteen I was be way av being nearly as wise as you are. I've larned foolishness since," said Judy sarcastically. "It's not running off to Ireland I'll be as if it was a jaunt to Silverbridge. And me frinds there have grown ould . . . I doubt if they'd know me, grey as an owl that I am. There do be a new McDermott at the castle, I'm ixpicting, talking rale English. The ould lord had a brogue so thick ye cud stir it."

"It's perfectly thrilling to think you ever lived in a castle,

Judy . . . and waited on a lord. It's even more exciting than remembering that mother's fourth cousin married into the English nobility. I wonder if we'll ever see her. Pat, let's you and I go over some day and call on our titled friend."

"I'm afraid she's not even aware of our existence," grinned Pat. "A fourth cousin is pretty far removed and she went to England to live with her aunt when she was a little girl. Mother saw her once, though."

"Oh, oh, that she did," said Judy. "She visited at the Bay Shore whin she was tin and they all come over here one day to play wid the young fry here. They had a day av it. She's a barrownite's wife now . . . Sir Charles Gresham . . . and his aunt do be married to an earl."

"Is he a belted earl?" demanded Cuddles. "A belted earl sounds so much more earlish than an unbelted one."

"Oh, oh, he's iverything an earl shud be. I do be forgetting what he was earl of but it was a rale aristocratic name. It was all in the papers whin yer cousin was married. Lady Gresham wasn't young but she made a good market be waiting. Oh, oh, niver shall I be forgetting the aunts at the Bay Shore whin the news come. They cudn't be inny prouder than they always were, so they got rale humble. 'It's nothing to us av coorse,' sez yer Great-aunt Frances. 'She's a great leddy now and she wudn't be acknowledging inny kin to common people like us.' Oh, oh, to be hearing Frances Selby calling herself common people!"

"Trix Binnie says she doesn't believe that Lady Gresham is any relation at all to us," said Cuddles, picking up a yellow kitten, with a face like a golden pansy, that came skittering through the ferns, and tucking it under her chin.

"She wudn't! But yer fourth cousin she is and it was her uncle the Bishop they did be blaming for staling the silver at the Bay Shore the night he slipt there."

"Stealing the silver, Judy?" Pat had never heard of this though Judy had been recounting her family legends to her all her life.

"I'm telling ye. Ye know that illigant silver hair-brush and comb in the spare room at the Bay Shore, to say nothing av the liddle looking glass and the two scent bottles. That proud av it they was. They niver did be putting it out for common people but a Bishop was a Bishop and whin he wint up to bed there it was all spread out gorgeous like on the bury top. Oh, oh, but it wasn't there the nixt morning, though. Yer Great-great-aunt Hannah was on the hoof thin... it was long afore she got bed-rid... and she was just about wild. She just set down and wrote and asked the Bishop what he'd done wid it. Back he wrote, 'I am poor but honest. The silver is in the box av blankets. It was too luxurious for a humble praste like mesilf to use and I was afraid some av me medicine might fall on it.' Oh, oh, the silver was on top av the blankets all right enough and yer poor Great-great-aunt was niver the same agin, after as much as accusing the Bishop av staling it. Patsy darlint, spaking av letters, was there inny news in the one ye got from Jingle this morning if a body may ask?"

"A very special bit of news," said Pat. "I saved it to tell you this afternoon when we'd be out here. Hilary sent in the design for a window to some big competition... and it won the prize. Against a hundred and sixty competitors."

"It's the cliver lad Jingle is... and it'll be the lucky girl that do be getting him."

Pat ignored this. She didn't want Hilary Gordon for anything but a friend but she did not exactly warm to the idea of that "lucky girl" whoever she was.

"Hilary always had a liking for windows. Whenever he saw one that stood out from the ordinary run he went into raptures over it. That little dormer one in old Mary McClenahan's house... Judy, do you remember the time you sent us to her to witch McGinty back?"

"And she did, didn't she now?"

"She knew where he was to be found anyhow," Pat sighed. "Judy, life was really more fun when I believed she was a witch."

"I'm telling ye." Judy nodded her clipped grey head mysteriously. "The less ye do be belaving the colder life do be. This bush now... it was nicer whin it was packed full av fairies, wasn't it?"

"Yes... in a way. But their magic still hangs round it, though the fairies are gone."

"Oh, oh, ye belaved in thim once, that's why. If ye don't belave in fairies they can't exist. That do be why grown folks can niver be seeing thim," said Judy sagely. "It's pitying the children I am that niver have the chanct to belave in fairies. They'll be the poorer all their lives bekase av it."

"I remember one story you told me... of the little girl who was playing in a bush like this and was lured away to fairyland by exquisite music. I used to tiptoe through here in the 'dim' and listen for it. But I don't think I really wanted to hear it...I was afraid that if I went to fairyland I'd never come back. And no fairy country could ever satisfy me after Silver Bush."

The look came into Pat's brook-brown eyes which always made people feel she was remembering something very lovely. Pat was not the beauty of the Gardiner family but there was magic in her face when that look came. She rose and folded up her sewing and went down to the house, followed by McGinty. The robins were beginning to whistle and the clouds over the bush were turning to a faint rose. The ferns and long grasses of the path were gold in the light of the westering sun. Away to the right long shadows were creeping over the hill pasture. And down beyond the low fields was the blue mist that was an August sea.

Sid was in the yard trying to make an obstinate calf drink. Cuddles' two pet white ducks were lying by the well. They were to be offered up for Thanksgiving dinner but Judy had not dared to hint this to Cuddles as yet. Father was mowing the early oats. Mother, her nap over, was down in the garden among the velvety Sweet Williams. A squirrel was running saucily over the kitchen roof. It was going to be a dear quiet evening, such as she loved best, with every one and everything at Silver Bush happy. Pat loved to see things and people happy; and she herself had the gift, than which there is none more enviable, of finding great pleasure in little things. The bats would be coming out at the rising of the moon and the great, green spaciousness of the farm would be all around the house that always seemed to her more a person than a house.

"Pat's just as crazy as ever about Silver Bush, isn't she?" said Cuddles. "I think she'd die if she had to leave it. I don't believe she'll ever get married, Judy, just because of that. I love Silver Bush, too, but I don't want to live here *all* my life. I want to go away... and have adventures... and see the world."

"Sure and it wudn't do if iverybody wanted to stay at home," agreed Judy. "But Patsy has always had Silver Bush in her heart... right at the very core av it. Whin she was no more than five she was asking yer mother one fine day where God was. And yer mother sez gentle-like, 'He is iverywhere, Patsy.' 'Iverywhere?' sez Pat, her eyes that pitiful. 'Hasn't He got inny home? Oh, mother, I'm so sorry for Him.' Did ye iver hear av such a thing as being sorry for God! Well, that was me liddle Pat. Cuddles dear"... Judy lowered her voice like a conspirator, although Pat was well out of sight and hearing... "Jem Robinson has been hanging round a bit, hasn't he now? He's a rale nice lad and only one year more to go at college. Do ye be thinking Pat has inny notion av him?"

"I'm sure she hasn't, Judy. Though she says the only thing she has against him is that his face needs side-whiskers and he was born a generation too late. I heard her say that to Sid. What did she mean, Judy?"

"The Good Man Above do alone be knowing," groaned Judy. "Sure, Cuddles darling, it's all right to be a bit particular-like. The Silver Bush girls have niver been like the Binnies. 'Olive has a beau for ivery night in the wake,' sez Mrs. Binnie to me onct, boastful-like. 'So she do be for going in for quantity afore quality,' sez I. But what if ye're too particular? I'm asking ye."

"I'm not old enough to have beaus yet," said Cuddles, "but just you wait till I am. It must be thrilling, Judy, to have some one tell you he loves you."

"Ould Tom Drinkwine did be telling me that onct upon a time but niver a thrill did I be faling," said Judy reflectively.

2

"All the months are friends of mine but apple month is the dearest," chanted Pat.

It was October at Silver Bush and she and Cuddles and Judy picked apples in the New Part of the orchard every afternoon... which wasn't so very new now, since it was all of twenty years old. But the Old Part was very much older and the apples in it were mostly sweet and fed to the pigs. Sometimes Long Alec Gardiner thought it would be far better to cut it down and get some real good out of the land but Pat couldn't be made to hear reason about it. She loved the Old Part far better than the New. It had been planted by Great-grandfather Gardiner and was shadowy and mysteri-ous, with as many old spruce trees as apple trees in it, and one special corner where generations of beloved cats and kittens had been buried. Besides, as Pat pointed out, if you cleared away the Old Part it would leave the graveyard open to all the world, since the Old Part surrounded it on three sides. This argument had weight with Long Alec. He was proud, in his way, of the old family burial plot, where nobody was ever buried now but where so many greats and grands of every degree slept... for the Gardiners of Silver Bush came of old P. E. Island pioneer stock. So the Old Part was spared and in spring it was as beautiful as the New Part, when the gnarled trees were young and bridal again for a brief space in the sweet spring days and the cool spring nights.

It was such a mellow and dreamy afternoon and Silver Bush seemed mellow and dreamy, too. Pat thought the old farm had a mood for every day in the year and every hour in the day. Now it would be gay... now melancholy... now friendly... now austere... now grey... now golden. To-day it was golden. The Hill of the Mist had wrapped a scarf of blue haze about its brown shoulders and was mysteriously lovely still, in spite of the missing Lombardy. Behind it a great castle of white cloud, with mauve shadows, towered up. There had been a delicate, ghostly rain the night before and the scent of the little hollow in the graveyard, full of frosted ferns, was distilled on the air. How green the pastures were for autumn! The kitchen yard was full of the pale gold of aspens and the turkey house was almost lost in a blaze of crimson sumacs. The white birches which some forgotten bride had planted along the Whispering Lane, that led from Silver Bush to Swallowfield, were amber, and the huge maple over the well was a flame. When Pat paused every few minutes just to look at it she whispered,

> "*The scarlet of the maples can shake me like a cry
> Of bugles going by.*'"

"What might ye be whispering to yersilf, Patsy? Sure and ye might be telling us if it's inny joke. It seems to be delighting ye."

Pat lifted eyebrows like little slender wings.

"It was just a bit of poetry, Judy, and you don't care much for poetry."

"Oh, oh, po'try do be all right in its place but it won't be kaping the apples if there's a hard frost some av these nights. We're a bit behind wid the picking as it is. And more work than iver to look forward to, now that yer dad has bought the ould Adams place for pasture and going into the live stock business."

"But he's going to have a hired man to help him, Judy."

"Oh, oh, and who will be looking after the hired man I'm asking ye. He'll be nading a bite to ate, I'm thinking, and mebbe a bit av washing and minding done. Not that I'm complaining av the work, mind ye. But ye can niver tell about an outsider. It's been minny a long day since we had inny av the brade at Silver Bush and it'll be a bit av a change, as ye say yersilf."

"I don't mind changes that mean things *coming* as much as changes that mean things *going*," said Pat, pausing to aim a wormy apple at two kittens who were chasing each other up the tree trunks. "And I'm so glad dad has bought the old Adams place. The little stone bridge Hilary and I built over Jordan and the Haunted Spring will belong to us now... and Happiness."

"Oh, oh, to think av buying happiness now!" chuckled Judy. "I wasn't after thinking it cud be done, Patsy."

"Judy, don't you remember that Hilary and I called the little hill by the Haunted Spring Happiness? We used to have such lovely times there."

"Oh, I'm minding. It was just me liddle joke, Patsy dear. Sure and it tickled me ribs to think av inny one being able to buy happiness. Oh, oh, there do be a few things God kapes to Himsilf and that do be one av thim. Though I did be knowing a man in ould Ireland that tried to buy off Death."

"He couldn't do that, Judy," sighed Pat, recalling with a shiver the dark day when Bets, the lovely and beloved friend of her childhood, had died and left a blank in her life that had never been filled.

"But he *did*. And thin, whin he wanted Death and prayed for him Death wudn't come. 'No, no,' sez Death, 'a bargain is a bargain.' But this hired man now... where is he going to slape? That's been bothering me a bit. Wud yer dad be wanting me to give up me snug kitchen chamber for him and moving somewhere up the front stairs?"

Judy couldn't keep the anxiety out of her voice. Pat shook her slim brown hands, that talked quite as eloquently as her lips, at Judy reassuringly.

"No, indeed, Judy. Dad knows that kitchen chamber is your kingdom. He's going to fit up that nice little loft over the granary for him. Put a stove and a bed and a bit of furniture in it and it will be very comfortable. He can spend his evenings there when he's home, don't you think? What's been worrying *me*, Judy, was that he might want to hang around the kitchen and spoil our jolly evenings."

"Oh, oh, we'll manage." Judy was suddenly in good cheer. She would have surrendered her kitchen chamber without a word of protest had Long Alec so decreed but the thought had lain heavy on her heart. She had slept so cosily in that chamber for over forty years. "All I'm hoping is that yer dad won't be hiring Sim Ledbury. He's been after the place I hear."

"Oh, surely dad wouldn't want a Ledbury round," said Cuddles.

"Ye can't pick and choose, Cuddles dear. That do be the trouble. Hired hilp is be way av being scarce and yer dad must be having a man that understands cows. Sim do be thinking he does. But a Ledbury wid the freedom av me kitchen will be a hard pill to swallow and him wid a face like a tombstone and born hating cats. Gintleman Tom took just the one look at him the day he was here and thin made himsilf scarce. If we can be getting a man who'll be good company for the cats ye'll niver hear a word av complaint from me about him, as long as he's willing to do a bit av work for his wages. Yer dad has got his name up for niver being put out at innything so he cud be imposed upon something shameful. But we'll all be seeing what we'll see and now we've finished wid this tree I'm going in to bake me damsons."

"I'm going to stay out till the sunshine fails me. I think, Judy, when I grow *very* old I'll just sit and bask in the sunshine all the time . . . I love it so. Cuddles, what about a run back to the Secret Field before sunset?"

Cuddles shook a golden-brown head.

"I'd love to go but you know I twisted my foot this morning and it hurts me yet. I'm going over to sit on Weeping Willy's slab in the graveyard for a while and just dream. I feel shimmery to-day . . . as if I was made of sunbeams."

When Cuddles said things like that Pat had a vague feeling that Cuddles was clever and ought to be educated if it could be managed. But it had to be admitted that so far Cuddles seemed to share the family indifference to education. She went in unashamedly for "a good time" and pounced on life like a cat on a mouse.

Pat slipped away for one of her dear pilgrimages to the

Secret Field... that little tree-encircled spot at the very back of the farm, which she and Sid had discovered so long ago and which she, at least, had loved ever since. Almost every Sunday evening, when they walked over the farm, talking and planning... for Sid was developing into an enthusiastic farmer... they ended up with the Secret Field, which was always in grass and always bore a wonderful crop of wild strawberries. Sid had promised her he would never plough it up. It was really too small to be worthwhile cultivating anyhow. And if it were ploughed up there might never be any more of Judy's famous wild strawberry shortcakes or those still more delicious things Pat made and which she called strawberry cream pies.

It was nice to go there with Sid but it was even nicer to go alone. There was nothing then to come between her and the silent, rapt communion she seemed to hold with it. It was the loneliest and loveliest spot on the farm. Its very silence was friendly and seemed to come out of the woods around it like a real presence. No wind ever blew there and rain and snow fell lightly. In summer it was a pool of sunlight, in winter a pool of frost... now in autumn a pool of colour. Musky, spicy shadows seemed to hover around its grey old fences. Pat always felt that the field knew it was beautiful and was happy in its knowledge. She lingered in it until the sun set and then went slowly back home, savouring every moment of the gathering dusk. What a lovely phrase "gathering dusk" was... almost as lovely as Judy's "dim", though the latter had a certain eerie quality that always gave Pat a rapture.

At the top of the hill field she paused, as always, to gloat over Silver Bush. The light shone out from the door and windows of the kitchen where Judy would be preparing supper, with the cats watching for a "liddle bite" and McGinty cocking a pointed ear for Pat's footstep. Would it be as nice when that unknown creature, the all-too-necessary hired man, would be hanging round, waiting for his supper? Of course it wouldn't. He would be a stranger and an alien. Pat fiercely resented the thought of him.

They would have supper by lamplight now. For a while she always hated to have to light the lamp for supper... it meant that the wind had blown the summer away and that winter nights were closing in. Then she liked it... it was so cosy and companionable and Silver Bushish, with Judy's "dim" looking in through the crimson vines around the window.

The colour of home on an autumn dusk was an exquisite thing. The trees all around it seemed to love it. The house belonged to them and to the garden and the green hill and the orchard and they to it. You couldn't separate them, Pat felt. She always wondered how any one could live in a house where there were no trees. It seemed an indecency, like a too naked body. Trees... to veil and caress and beshadow... trees to warn you back and beckon you on. Lombardies for stateliness... birches for maiden grace... maples for friendliness... spruce and fir for mystery... poplars to whisper secrets. Only they never really did. You thought you understood as long as you listened... but when you left them you realized they had just been laughing at you... thin, rustling, silky laughter. All the trees kept some secret. Who knew but that all those white birches, which stood so primly all day, when night and moonlight came, might step daintily out of the earth and pirouette over the meadows, while the young spruces around the Mince Pie Field danced a saraband? Laughing at her fancy, Pat ran into the light and good cheer of Judy's white-washed kitchen with life singing in her heart.

3

"Tillytuck! Did ye iver be hearing the like av that for a name?" said Judy, quite flabbergasted for once. "Niver have I heard such a name on the Island before."

"He's been working on the south shore for years but he really belongs to Nova Scotia, dad says," said Cuddles.

"Oh, oh, that ixplains it. Minny a quare name I've known coming out av Novy Scoshy. And what will we be after calling him? If he's a young chap we can be calling him be his given name if he do be having one but if he's a bit oldish it'll have to be Mr. Tillytuck, since hired hilp is getting so uppish these days, and it'll be the death av me if I do have to be saying 'Mr. Tillytuck' ivery time I open me mouth. *Mister* Tillytuck!"

Judy savoured the absurdity of it.

"He's quite old, dad says. Over fifty," remarked Cuddles. "And dad says, too, that he's a bit peculiar."

"Peculiar, is it, thin? Oh, oh, people do be saying that

I'm a bit that way mesilf, so there'll be a pair av us. Is he peculiar in being worth his salt in the way av work? That do be the question."

"He comes well recommended and dad was almost in despair of getting any one half suitable."

"And is *Mister* Tillytuck married, I'm asking. *Mistress* Tillytuck! Oh, oh."

"Dad didn't say. But he's to be here to-morrow so we'll find out all about him. Judy, what *have* you got in that pot?"

"A bit av soup lift over from dinner. I did be thinking we'd like a liddle sup av it be bed-time. And lave a drop in the pot for Siddy. He's gone gallivanting and it's a cold night and mebbe a long drive home."

There was no trace of disdain in Judy's "gallivanting." Judy thought gallivanting one of the lawful delights of youth.

It was a wild wet November evening, with an occasional vicious swish of rain on the windows. But the fire glowed brightly: Gentleman Tom was curled up on his own prescriptive chair and McGinty slumbered on the rug; Bold-and-Bad on one side of the stove, and Squedunk, a half-grown, striped cat on his promotion, on the other, kept up a lovely chorus of purrs: and Cuddles had a cherry-red dress on that brought out the young sheen of her hair. Cuddles had such lovely hair, Pat thought proudly. Nothing so pallid and washed out as gold, like Dot Robinson's . . . no, a warm golden brown.

Judy's soup had a very tempting aroma. Judy was past-mistress of the art of soup-making. Long Alec always said all she had to do was wave her hand over the pot. Mother was mending by the table. Mother had never been strong since her operation and Pat, who watched her with a jealous love, thought she ought to be resting. But mother always liked to do the mending.

"It will be the last thing I'll give up, Pat. Most women don't like mending. I always did. The little worn garments . . . when you were children . . . they seemed so much a part of you. And now your bits of silk things. It doesn't hurt me really. I like to think I'm a little use still."

"Mother! Don't you dare say anything like that again! You're the very heart and soul of Silver Bush . . . you know you are. We couldn't do without you for a day."

Mother smiled . . . that little slow, sweet, mysterious smile of mother's . . . the smile of a woman very wise and very loving. But then everything about mother was wise and loving. When shrieks of laughter rang out she looked as if she were laughing, too, though mother never did laugh... not really.

"Let's have a jolly evening," Cuddles had said. "If this Tillytuck creature doesn't like staying in the granary loft in the evenings this may be the last evening we'll have the kitchen to ourselves, so let's make the most of it. Tell us some stories, Judy... and I'll roast some clove apples."

"'Pile high the logs, the wind blows chill,'" quoted Pat. "At least put a few more sticks in the stove. That doesn't sound half as romantic as piling high the logs, does it?"

"I'm thinking it might be more comfortable if it isn't be way av being romantic," said Judy, sitting down to her knitting in a corner whence she could give the soup pot an occasional magic stir. "They did be piling the logs in Castle McDermott minny the time and we'd have our faces frying and the backs av us frazing. Oh, oh, give me the modern ways ivery time."

"It seems funny to think of fires in heaven," ruminated Pat, curling up Turk-fashion on the old hooked rug before the stove, with its pattern of three rather threadbare black cats. "But I want a fire there once in a while... and a nice howly, windy night like this to point the contrast. And now for your ghost story, Judy."

"I'm clane run out av ghosts," complained Judy... who had been saying the same thing for years. But she always produced or invented a new one, telling it with such verisimilitude of detail that even Pat and Cuddles were... sometimes... convinced. You could no longer believe in fairies of course, but the world hadn't quite given up all faith in ghosts. "Howsiver, whin I come to think av it, I may niver have told ye av the night me own great-uncle saw the Ould Ould McDermott... the grandfather of the Ould McDermott av me own time... a-sitting on his own grave and talking away to himsilf, angry-like. Did I now?"

"No... no... go on," said Cuddles eagerly.

But the ghost story of the Ould Ould McDermott was fated never to be told for at that moment there came a resounding treble knock upon the kitchen door. Before one of the paralysed trio could stir the door was opened and Tillytuck walked into the room... and, though nobody just then realised it, into the life and heart of Silver Bush. They knew he was Tillytuck because he could be nobody else in the world.

Tillytuck came in and shut the door behind him but not before a lank, smooth-haired black dog had slipped in beside him. McGinty sat up and looked at him and the strange dog sat down and looked at McGinty. But the Silver Bush trio had no eyes just then for anybody but Tillytuck. They stared at him as if hypnotised.

Tillytuck was short and almost as broad as he was long. His red face was almost square, made squarer, if possible, by a pair of old-fashioned mutton-chop whiskers of a faded ginger hue. His mouth was nothing but a wide slit and his nose the merest round button of a nose. His hair could not be seen for it was concealed under a mangy old fur cap. His body was encased in a faded overcoat and a rather gorgeous tartan scarf was wrapped around his neck. In one hand he carried a huge, bulging old Gladstone bag and in the other what was evidently a fiddle done up in a flannel case.

Tillytuck stood and looked at the three wimmen critters out of twinkling little black eyes almost buried in cushions of fat.

"How pleased ye look to see me!" he said. "Only sorter paralysed as it were. Well, I can't help being good-looking."

He went into what seemed an internal convulsion of silent chuckles. Pat jerked herself out of her trance. Mother had gone upstairs...somebody must do...say...something. Judy, probably for the first time in her life, seemed incapable of speech or movement.

Pat scrambled up from the rug and went forward.

"Mr. ... Mr. Tillytuck, is it?"

"The same, at your service. ... Christian name, Josiah," said the newcomer, with a bow that might have been courtly if he had had any neck to speak of. It was not till afterwards that Pat thought what a nice voice he had. "Age, fifty-five...in politics, Liberal...religion, fundamentalist...gentleman-at-large, symbolically speaking. And an Orangeman," he added, looking at a large picture of King William on a white horse, crossing the Boyne, that hung upon the wall.

"Won't you...take off your coat...and sit down?" said Pat rather stupidly. "You see...we didn't expect you to-night. Father told us you would be here to-morrow."

"I got a chance up on a truck to Silverbridge so I thought I'd better take it," rumbled Mr. Tillytuck. He hung his cap up on a nail, revealing a head thatched with thick pepper-and-salt curls. He took off his scarf and coat and the cause of a mysterious bulge at one side was explained . . . a huge, stuffed, white Arctic owl which he proudly set up on the clock shelf. He put his bag in one corner with his fiddle on top of it. Then, with unerring discrimination, he selected the most comfortable chair in the kitchen . . . Great-grandfather Nehemiah Gardiner's old glossy wooden arm-chair with its red cushions . . . sank into it and produced a stubby black pipe from his pocket.

"Any objections?" he rumbled. "I never smoke if ladies object."

"We don't," said Pat. "We're used to Uncle Tom smoking."

Mr. Tillytuck deliberately loaded and lighted his pipe. Ten minutes before no one in the room had ever seen him. And now he seemed to belong there . . . to have been always there. It was impossible to think of him as a stranger or a change. Even Judy, who, as a rule, didn't care what any man thought of her clothes, was thanking her stars that she had on her new drugget dress and a white apron. McGinty had sniffed once at him approvingly and then gone to sleep again, ignoring the new dog entirely. The two grey cats went on purring. Only Gentleman Tom hadn't yet made up his mind and continued to stare at him suspiciously.

Mr. Tillytuck's body was almost as square as his face and was encased in a faded and rather ragged old grey sweater, revealing glimpses of a red flannel shirt which brought a sudden peculiar gleam into Judy's eyes. It was so exactly the shade she would be wanting for the red rosebuds in the rug she meant to hook coming on spring.

"If ye've no objection to the pipe have ye any to the dog?" went on Mr. Tillytuck. "If ye haven't maybe ye wouldn't mind him lying down in that corner over there."

Judy decided that it was time she asserted herself. After all, this was *her* kitchen, not *Mister* Tillytuck's.

"Oh, oh, and is it a well-behaved dog he is, *Mister* Tillytuck, I'm asking ye."

"He is," replied Tillytuck solemnly. "But he's been an unfortunate kind of dog . . . born to ill-luck as the sparks fly upward. Ye may not believe me, Miss . . . Miss . . ."

"Plum," said Judy shortly.

"Miss Plum, that dog has had a hard life of it. He's had mange and distemper once each and worms continual. He got run over by a truck last summer and poisoned by strychnine the summer before that."

"He must have as many lives as a cat," giggled Cuddles.

"He's in good health now," assured Mr. Tillytuck. "He's a bit lame from cutting his foot with a sliver of broken glass last week but he'll soon be over it. And he throws a fit once in a while...epileptic. Foams at the mouth. Staggers. Falls. In ten minutes gets up and trots away as good as new. So ye need never be worrying about him if ye see him take one. He's really a broth of a dog, only kind of sensitive, and fine with the cows. I have a great respect for dogs...always touch my cap when I meet one."

"What is his name?" asked Pat.

"I call him just Dog," responded Mr. Tillytuck. And Just Dog he remained during his entire sojourn at Silver Bush.

"A bit too glib wid yer tongue, *Mister* Tillytuck," thought Judy. But she only said,

"And what may yer mind be in regard to cats?"

"Oh," said Mr. Tillytuck, who seemed quite contented with a whiff of his pipe between speeches, "I have a feeling for cats, Miss Plum. When I wandered in here the other morning I thought I'd like the people here because there was a cat on the window sill. It's a kind of instink with me. So thinks I to myself, 'This place has got a flavour. I could do with a job here.' And how right I was!"

"Where might your last place be?"

"On a fox farm down South Shore way. No names mentioned. I've been there three years. Got on well...liked it well...till the old missus died and the boss married again. I couldn't pull with the new one at all. Everything on the table bought and only enough to keep the worms quiet at that. A terrible tetchie old woman. Ye couldn't mention the weather to her but she'd quarrel with ye over it. Seemed to take it as a personal insult if you didn't like the day. Then she picked on Dog right along. 'Even a dog has some rights, woman,' I told her. 'You and me ain't going to click,' I told her. 'I'm rather finnicky as to the company I keep,' I told her. 'My dog is better company than a contentious woman,' I told her. 'I'm nobody's slave,' I told her...and give notice. When I can't stay in a place without quarrelling with the folks I just mosey along. Likely I'll be here quite a while. Looks like a snug harbour to me. This arm-chair just fits my kinks. I've had my ups and downs. Escaped from the *Titanic* for one thing."

"Oh!" Cuddles and Pat were all eyes and ears. This *was* exciting. Judy gave her soup a vicious swirl. Was she to have a rival in the story telling art?

"Yes, I escaped," said Mr. Tillytuck, "by not sailing in her." He put his pipe back into his mouth and emitted a rumble which they were to learn he called laughter.

"Oh, oh, so that do be your idea of a joke," thought Judy. "I'm getting yer measure, *Mister* Tillytuck."

"Not but what I've had my traggedies," resumed Mr. Tillytuck. He rolled up his sweater sleeve and showed a long white scar on his sinewy arm. "A leopard gave me that when I was a tamer in a circus in the States in my young days. Ah, that was the exciting life. I have a peculiar power over animals. No animal," said Mr. Tillytuck impressively, "can look me in the eye."

"Oh, oh, and are ye married?" persisted Judy remorselessly.

"Not by a jugful!" exclaimed Mr. Tillytuck, so explosively that every one jumped, even Gentleman Tom. Then he subsided into mildness again. "No, I've neither wife nor progeny, Miss Plum. I've often tried to get married but something always prevented. Sometimes every one was willing but the girl herself. Sometimes nobody was willing. Sometimes I couldn't get the question out. If I hadn't been such a temperance man I might have been married many a time. Needed something to loosen my tongue."

Mr. Tillytuck winked at Pat and Pat had a horrible urge to wink back at him. Really, some people did have a queer effect on you.

"I've always thought nobody understood me quite as well as I understood myself," resumed Mr. Tillytuck. "It isn't likely I'll ever marry now. But while there's life there's hope." This time it was at Judy he winked and Judy felt that she was not half as "mad" as she should be. She gave her soup a final stir and stood up briskly.

"Wud ye be jining us in a sup av soup, *Mister* Tillytuck?"

"Ah, some small refreshment will not be amiss," responded Mr. Tillytuck in a gratified tone. "I am not above the pleasures of the palate in moderation. And ever since I entered this dwelling I've been saying to myself whenever you stirred that pot, 'Of all the smells that I ever did smell I never smelled a smell that smelled half as good as that smell smells.'"

Pat and Cuddles proceeded to set the table. Mr. Tillytuck watched them with approbation.

"A pair of high-steppers," he remarked presently in a hoarse aside to Judy. "Some class to *them*. The little one has the wrist of an aristycrat."

"Oh, oh, and so ye've noticed that now?" said Judy, highly gratified.

"Naturally. I'm an expert in regard to weemen. 'There's elegance for you,' I said to myself the moment I opened the door. Some difference from the girls at the fox farm. Just between friends, Miss Plum, they looked like dried apples on a string. One of them was as thin as a weasel and living on lettuce to get thinner. But these two now... Cupid will be busy I reckon. No doubt you've a terrible time with the boys hanging round, Miss Plum?"

"Oh, oh, we're not altogether overlooked," said Judy complacently. "And now, *Mister* Tillytuck, will ye be sitting in?"

Mr. Tillytuck slid into a chair.

"I wonder if you'd mind leaving out the 'mister,'" he said. "I'm not used to it and it makes me feel like a pilgrim and sojourner. Josiah, now... if you wouldn't mind."

"Oh, oh, but I wud," said Judy decidedly. "Sure and Josiah has always been a name I cudn't bear iver since old Josiah Miller down at South Glen murdered his wife."

"I was well acquainted with Josiah Miller," remarked Mr. Tillytuck, taking up his spoon. "First he choked his wife, then he hanged her, then he dropped her in the river with a stone tied to her. Taking no chances. Ah, I knew him well. In fact, I may say he was a particular friend of mine at one time. But after that happened of course I had to drop him."

"Did they hang him?" demanded Cuddles with ghoulish interest.

"No. They couldn't prove it although everybody knew he did it. They kind of sympathised with him. There's an odd woman that *has* to be murdered. He died a natural death but his ghost walked. I met it once on a time."

"Oh!" Cuddles didn't notice Judy's evident disapproval of this poaching on her preserves. "Really, Mr. Tillytuck?"

"No mistake, Miss Gardiner. Most ghosts is nothing but rats. But this was a genuwine phantom."

"Did he . . . did he speak to you?"

Mr. Tillytuck nodded.

"'I see you're out for a walk like myself,' says he. But I made no reply. I have discovered it is better not to monkey with spooks, miss. Interesting things, but dangerous. So irresponsible, speaking romantically. So, as Friend Josiah was right in the road and I couldn't get past him I just walked through him. Never saw him again. Miss Plum, this is soup."

Judy had spent the evening swinging from approval to disapproval of Mr. Tillytuck . . . which continued to be the case during his whole sojourn at Silver Bush. His appreciation of her soup got him another bowlful. Pat was wishing father would come home from Swallowfield. Perhaps Mr. Tillytuck didn't know he had to sleep in the granary. But Mr. Tillytuck said, as he got up from the table,

"I understand my quarters is in the granary. . . so if you'll be kind enough to tell me where it is . . ."

"*Miss Rachel* will be taking the flashlight and showing ye the way," said Judy. "There do be plinty av good blankets on the bed but I'm afraid ye'll find it cold. There do be no fire since we didn't be knowing ye were coming."

"I'll kindle one in a jiffy."

"Oh, oh, thin ye'll be smoked out. That fire has to be lit for an hour afore it'll give over smoking. There do be something out av kilter wid the chimney. Long . . . Mr. Gardiner is maning to have it fixed."

"I'll fix it myself. I worked with a mason for years. Down at the fox farm they had a bad chimney and I built it over in fine shape."

"Did it draw?" asked Judy sceptically.

"Draw! Miss Plum, that chimney drew the cat clean up it one night. The poor animal was never seen again."

Judy subsided. Mr. Tillytuck possessed himself of his bag and his violin and his owl and his dog.

"I'm ready, Miss Gardiner. And as for the matter of names, Miss Plum, the Prince of Wales called me Josiah the whole summer I worked on his ranch in Alberta. A very democratic young man. But if you can't bring yourself to it plain Tillytuck will do for me. And if you've warts or anything like that on your hands" . . . Cuddles guiltily put a hand behind her . . . "I can cure them in a jiffy."

Judy primmed her mouth and took a high tone.

"Thank ye kindly but we do be knowing a few things at

Silver Bush. Me grandmother did be taching me a charm for warts whin I was a girleen and it works rale well. Good-night, *Mister* Tillytuck. I'm hoping ye'll be warm and slape well."

"I'll be in the arms of old Murphy in short order," assured Mr. Tillytuck.

They heard Cuddles' laughter floating back through the rain all the way to the granary. Evidently Mr. Tillytuck was amusing her.

"Certainly he is peculiar," said Pat. "But peculiar people give colour to life, don't they, Judy?"

Cuddles ran in, her face sparkling and radiant from wind and rain.

"Isn't he a darling? He told me he belonged to one of the best families in Nova Scotia."

"Av which statement I have me doubts," said Judy. "I'm thinking he was spaking symbolically, as he sez himself. And it didn't use to be manners, taking yer story right out av yer mouth as ye heard him do to mesilf. But he sames a good-natured simple sort av cratur and likely we can put up wid him as long as our family animals can."

"He thinks you're wonderful, Judy. And he wishes you *would* call him Josiah."

"That I'll not thin. But I'm not saying I won't be laving off the Mister after a day or two. It's too much of a strain. Cuddles dear, to-morry I'll be fixing up a bit av a charm for that liddle wart av yours. I'm knowing it shud av been attinded to long ago but what wid all these comings and goings and hirings it wint out av me head. Oh, oh, I'll not be having any *Mister* Tillytuck wid a side-whisker casting up the fam'ly warts to me!"

"I must write Hilary all about him," laughed Pat. "He would delight in him. Oh, Judy, if Hilary could only drop in some of these November evenings as he used to do things would be perfect. It's over two years now since he went away and it seems like a hundred. Is there any soup left for Sid, Judy?"

"Loads and lashings av it. Was it to the dance at South Glen he was going?"

"Wherever he went he took Madge Robinson," said Cuddles. "He's giving her quite a rush now. All summer it was Sara Russell. I believe Sid is a dreadful flirt."

Pat smiled contentedly. There was safety in numbers. After all, Sid had never seemed really to have a serious notion of any girl since Bets had died. It pleased Pat to think he would be faithful to her sweet memory all his life... as she, Pat, would be. She would never have another intimate girl friend. She liked to think of herself as a happy old maid and **Sid** a happy old bachelor, living gaily together all their lives, loving and caring for Silver Bush, with Winnie and Cuddles and Joe coming home for long visits with their families, and McGinty and the cats living forever and Judy telling stories in the kitchen. One couldn't think of Silver Bush without Judy. She had always been there and of course she always would be.

"Judy," said Cuddles solemnly, turning back in the hall doorway on her way to bed, "Judy, mind you don't go and fall in love with Josiah. I saw him winking at you."

Judy's only reply was a snort.

4

The days of that late autumn seemed to Pat to slip by like a golden river of happiness, even after the last cricket song had been sung. Mother was keeping well... father was jubilant over the good harvest... Cuddles was taking more interest in her lessons... the surplus kittens of the summer's crop had all found excellent homes... and there was enough of dances and beaus to satisfy Pat's not very passionate love of social life. Almost any time she would have preferred to roast apples and bandy lovely ghost stories in Judy's kitchen to going to a party. Cuddles could not understand this: *she* was longing for the day when she would be old enough to go to dances and have "boy-friends."

"I mean to have a great deal of *attention*," she told Judy gravely. "A few flirtations... *nice* ones, Judy... and then I'll fall in love *sensibly*."

"Oh, oh," said Judy with a twinkle, "I'm thinking that can't be done, Cuddles darlint. A sinsible love affair now... it do be sounding a bit dull to me."

"Pat says she's never going to fall in love with anybody. I really believe she does want to be an old maid, Judy."

"I've been hearing girls talk that way afore now," scoffed Judy. But she was secretly uneasy. The Silver Bush girls in any generation had never been flirts but she would have liked Pat to show a little more interest in the young men who came and went at Silver Bush and took her to dances and pictures and corn-roasts and skating parties and moonlight snowshoe tramps. Pat had any number of "boy friends" but friends were all they were or seemed likely to be. Judy was quite elated when Milton Taylor of South Glen began haunting Silver Bush and taking Pat out when she would go. But Pat would not go often enough to please Judy.

"Oh, oh, Patsy dear, he'll have the finest farm in South Glen some day and the nice boy he is! It's the affectionate husband he'd be making ye."

"'An affectionate husband,'" giggled Pat. "Oh, Judy, you're so Victorian. Affectionate husbands are out of date. We like the cave men, don't we, Cuddles?"

Cuddles and Pat exchanged grins. In spite of the difference in their ages they were great chums and Pat had a dreadful habit of telling Cuddles all about her beaus, what they did and what they said. Pat had a nippy tongue when she chose and the youths in question would not have been exactly delighted if they could have overheard her.

"But don't you intend to get married sometime, Pat?" Cuddles asked once.

Pat shook her brown head impatiently.

"Oh . . . sometime perhaps . . . when I have to . . . but not for years and years. Why, Silver Bush couldn't spare me."

"But if Sid brings a wife in sometime . . ."

"Sid won't do that," cried Pat passionately. "I don't believe Sid will ever marry. You know he was in love with Bets, Cuddles. I believe he will always be faithful to her memory."

"Judy says men aren't like that. And every one says May Binnie is making a dead set at him."

"Sid will never marry May Binnie . . . that's one thing I'm sure of," said Pat. The very thought made her feel cold. She and May Binnie had always hated each other.

Tillytuck was almost as much interested in Pat's affairs as was Judy. Every young man who came to Silver Bush got a severe scrutiny, though he knew it not, from Tillytuck's little black eyes. It delighted him to listen to Pat's badinage.

"Gosh, but she knows how to handle the men!" he exclaimed admiringly one night, when the door closed behind Pat and Milton Taylor. "She'll make a fine wife for some one. I admit that I admire her deportment, Judy."

"Oh, oh, we all do know how to be handling the men at Silver Bush, Tillytuck," said Judy loftily.

For it was "Judy" and "Tillytuck" now. Judy would have none of Josiah and "mister" was too formal to keep up for long. They were excellent friends after a fashion. It seemed to Judy, as to everybody, that Tillytuck must have always been at Silver Bush. It was impossible to believe that it was only six weeks since he had dropped in with his owl and his fiddle and Just Dog. The very cats purred louder when he came into the house. To be sure, Gentleman Tom never quite approved of him. But then Gentleman Tom had always been a reserved, taciturn cat who never really took up with any one but Judy.

Tillytuck had his prescriptive corner and chair in the kitchen and he was always slipping in to ask Judy to make a cup of tea for him. The fun of it, to Pat and Cuddles, was that Judy always made it, without a word of complaint. She soon discovered that Tillytuck had a sweet tooth where pies and cake were concerned and when she was in a good humour with him there was usually a triangle of one or a slice of the other waiting for him, to the amusement of the girls who affected to believe that Judy was "sweet" on Tillytuck, much to her scorn. Sometimes she would even sit down on the other side of the stove and drink a cup of tea with him. When she felt compelled to scold him he always soothed her with a compliment.

"See how I can manage the weemen," he would whisper complacently to Pat. "Ain't it the pity I'm not a marrying man?"

"Perhaps you may marry yet," responded Pat with a grave face, dropping a dot of red jelly like a gleaming ruby in the pale yellow centre of her lemon tarts.

"Maybe . . . when I make up my mind whether I want to take pity on Judy or not," Tillytuck answered with a wink. "There's times when I think she'd suit me. She's fond of talking and I'm fond of listening."

Judy ignored nonsense of this kind. She had, so she informed the girl, taken Tillytuck's measure once and for all.

She was, however, very bitter because he never went to church. Judy thought all hired men ought to go to church. It was only respectable. If they did not go who knew but that censorious neighbours would claim it was because they were so overworked at Silver Bush during the week that they did not be having the strength to go to church on Sundays. But Tillytuck was adamantine to her arguments.

"I don't approve of human hymns," he said firmly. "Nothing should be sung in churches but the psalms of David . . . with maybe an occasional paraphrase on special occasions. Them's my principles and I sticks to them. I always sing a psalm before I go to bed and every Sunday morning I read a chapter in my testament."

"And on Waping Willy's tombstone," muttered Judy, who for some mysterious reason resented Tillytuck's habit of going into the graveyard to read the said chapter.

And then . . . Christmas was drawing near and Great Preparations were being made. You could hear the capitals in Tillytuck's voice when he referred to them. They were going to have a real "re-union." Winnie and Frank would come and Uncle Tom and Aunt Edith and Aunt Barbara from Swallowfield and Aunt Hazel and Uncle Rob Madison and their five children and the Bay Shore Great-aunts if their rheumatism let them. In fact, it was to be what Judy called "a regular tommyshaw" and Pat was brimful of happiness and expectation over it all. It would be the first "real" Christmas since she had become the virtual mistress of Silver Bush. The previous one Frank had had bronchitis, so he and Winnie couldn't come, and the one before that Aunt Hazel's family had measles and Hilary was not there for the first time in years, and it hadn't been a Christmassy Christmas at all. But everything would be different this year. And Joe expected to be home for the first Christmas since he went away. Judy's turkeys were fat as fat could be and there was to be a goose because dad liked goose and a couple of ducks because Uncle Tom liked ducks. As for the rest of the bill of fare, Pat was poring over cook-books most of her spare time. Many and old were the cook-books of Silver Bush, full of clan recipes that had stood the test of time. Most of them had nice names linked up with all kinds of people who had invented the recipes . . . many of them people who were dead or in far lands. It gave Pat a thrill to thumb them over . . . Grandmother Selby's jellied cabbage salad . . . Aunt Hazel's ginger cookies . . . Cousin Miranda's beef-steak pie . . . the Bay Shore pudding . . . Great-grandmother Gardiner's fruit cake . . . Old Joe Pingle's mince pie . . . Uncle Horace's raisin gravy. Pat never could find out who Old Joe Pingle was. Nobody, not even Judy, seemed to know. But Uncle Horace had brought the recipe for raisin gravy home from his first voyage and told Judy he had killed a man for it... though nobody believed him.

Judy was planning to get a new "dress-up dress" for the occasion. Her old one, a blue garment of very ancient vintage, was ralely a liddle old-fashioned.

"And besides, Patsy dear, I'd be nading it if I took a run over to ould Ireland some av these long-come-shorts. I can't be getting the thought out av me head iver since Cuddles put it in. Sure and if I wint I'd want to make a rale good apparance afore me ould frinds, not to spake av a visit to Castle McDermott. What wud ye think av a nice wine-colour, Patsy? They tell me it's rale fashionable, this fall. And mebbe sating as a bit av a change from silk."

Pat, although the thought of Judy going to Ireland, even if only for a visit, gave her a nasty sensation, entered heartily into the question of the new dress and went to town with Judy to help in the selection and bully the dressmaker into making it exactly as Judy wanted it. Uncle Tom was in town that day and they saw him dodging out of a jeweller's shop, trying hastily to secrete a small, ornately wrapped parcel in his pocket before he encountered them. Not succeeding, he muttered something about having to see a man and shot down a side street.

"Uncle Tom is awfully mysterious about something these days," said Pat. "What do you suppose he has been buying in that shop? I'm sure it couldn't have been anything for Aunt Edith or Aunt Barbara."

"Oh, oh, Patsy dear, I'm belaving yer Uncle Tom has a notion av getting married. I know the signs."

Pat experienced another disagreeable sensation. Change at Swallowfield was almost as bad as change at Silver Bush. Uncle Tom and the aunts had *always* lived there... always would. Pat couldn't fit an Aunt Tom into the picture at all.

"Oh, Judy, I can't think he would be so foolish. At his age! Why, he's sixty!"

"Wid me own eyes, Patsy, I saw him rading a letter one day and stuffing it into his pocket like mad whin he caught me eye on him. And blushing! Whin a man av his age do be blushing there's something quare in the wind. Do ye be minding back in the summer Cuddles telling us she was after mailing letters from him to a lady?"

Pat sighed and put the disagreeable matter out of her

mind. She wasn't going to have the afternoon spoiled. There were many things to buy besides Judy's satin dress. Pat loved shopping. It was so fascinating to go into the big department store and pick things to buy... pretty things that just wanted to be taken away from all the glitter and too-muchness to be made part of a real home. They had to have some new overdrapes for the dining-room and new covers for the Big Parlour cushions and a set of little glass dishes to serve the chilled fruit cocktails Pat had decided on for the first course of the Christmas dinner. Judy was a little dubious about trying to put on too much style... "cocktails" had a quare sound whin all was said and done and Silver Bush had always been a great timperance place....

"Oh, Judy darling, it isn't that kind of cocktails at all. Just bits of fruit... and juice... and a red maraschino cherry on top. You'll love them."

Judy surrendered. If Patsy wanted quality dishes she must have them. Anyhow, Judy was sure the Binnies never opened a dinner with cocktails and it was always well to be a few frills ahead of them. Judy enjoyed every minute of her excursion to town and brought home a wine-coloured satin of a lustre to dazzle even Castle McDermott. It dazzled Tillytuck to whom Judy proudly displayed it that night.

"A bit too voluptuous" was all he would say. And got no pie that night. Tillytuck confessed to himself as he took his way to the granary that this was one of the times he had failed in tact. If he had known that Judy had in the pantry a cold roast duck and a dish of browned potato which she had intended to share with him by way of a "liddle bite" he would have had a still poorer opinion of his tact. As it was, Cuddles discovered it and she and Pat and Judy did justice to it before they went to bed, Sid coming in at the last to pick the bones and listen to Judy's story about a lost diamond ring that had been found in a turkey's crop cut open by accident.

"And that do be minding me... did I iver be telling ye av the first time yer Aunt Hazel dressed a turkey for dinner whin she was a slip av a girleen? Oh, oh, there niver was such a disgrace at Silver Bush. It tuk us years to live it down."

"What happened, Judy?"

"Ye'll niver be telling her I told ye? Well, thin, she tuk a great notion to be dressing and stuffing the turkey for dinner one time and nobody was to interfere wid it. We didn't be ixpicting any company that day just having the turkey for ourselves we were, not being binnies as sells ivery blessed thing off the farm they can and living on potatoes and point. But unixpicted company come... quality folks from town no less... a mimber of Parlymint and his lady wife. I did be thanking me stars we had the turkey but oh, oh, what happened whin yer dad cut a slice off the Lrist, maning to give all white mate to the lady visitor!"

"Judy, what *did* happen? Don't be so mysterious."

"Mysterious, is it? Well, it's hating to tell it av Silver Bush I am. Not but what yer dad laughed till he was sick afterwards. Well, thin, to tell the worst, yer Aunt Hazel had niver taken out the turkey's crop and whin yer dad carved off that slice kernels av whate and a bunch av oats fell down all over the plate. I wasn't there av coorse... I niver wud be setting at the table whin there was quality company... and it did be well I wasn't for niver wud I have been the same agin. It was bad enough to hear yer grandmother telling av it. She niver hilt up her head quite so high agin, poor ould leddy. Oh, oh, it's only something to be laughing over now, though we did be thinking it was a tragedy thin."

Cuddles screamed over the tale but Pat felt a little troubled. It *was* a dreadful thing to have happened at Silver Bush even if it had been a quarter of a century before. Nothing worse could have been told of the Binnies.

"I do hope nothing disgraceful will happen at our Christmas dinner," she said anxiously.

"Niver worry, Patsy dear. There do be no paycock's feathers in the house now. Sure and I burned thim all the day after *that*. Yer Uncle Horace said I was a superstitious ould woman and was rale peeved bekase he had brought thim home. So there'll be nothing to bring us bad luck but still I'll be thankful whin it's all well over. As Tillytuck was remarking yisterday, there do be a certain amount av nervous strain over it all."

"Tillytuck told me to-day that his grandfather was a pirate," said Cuddles. "Also that he was through the Halifax horror when that ship loaded with munitions blew up in the days of the war. Do you really think, Judy, that Tillytuck has had all the adventures that he says he has?"

Judy's only reply was a sardonic laugh.

5

Christmas was drawing nearer and there was so much to be done. Pat and Cuddles worked like beavers and Judy flew about, or tried to, in three directions at once. A big box of goodies had to be packed and sent to Hilary... poor Hilary who must spend his Christmas in a dreary Toronto boarding-house. Mince meat and Christmas cake must be concocted. Judy had to go for fittings of the new dress and nearly died of them. The silver and brasses had to be cleaned: everything must be made spick and span.

"The things in this house *are* nice," said Cuddles, as she rubbed at the spoons. "I wonder why. They're not really so handsome but they're *nice*."

"They're loved, that's why," said Pat softly. "They've been loved and cared for for years. I love everything in this house *terribly*, Cuddles."

"I believe you love them too much, Pat. I love them, too, but you seem to worship them."

"I can't help it. Silver Bush means everything to me and it seems to mean more every year of my life. I do want this Christmas to go off well... everything just right... all the folks enjoying themselves. Judy, do you think six mince pies will be enough? It would be disgraceful if we didn't have enough of everything."

"Loads and lashings," assured Judy. "Mrs. Tom Robinson do be thinking we're tarrible extravagant. 'A fat kitchen makes a lean will,' she did be sighing to me the other day whin she was in, borrying the quilt clamps off av me. 'Oh, oh,' sez I, 'we're not like the Birtwhistles at the bridge,' sez I. 'After they do be having a bit av company,' sez I, 'not a dab av butter will be et in that house till all the extry bills are made up,' sez I. She tuk it wid her chin up but she was faling it all right. Ould Mrs. Birtwhistle was her mother's cousin. Oh, oh, I'm knowing too much about all the folks in these parts for inny av thim to be giving me digs in me own kitchen. A lean will indade! Plaze the Good Man Above it'll be a long time afore there's inny nade to talk av wills at Silver Bush."

"But Aunt Edith says we do live too high at Silver Bush," said Cuddles. "She says we really ought to be more frugal."

"Frugal! I hate that word," said Pat. "It sounds so... so porridgy. I do hope Joe will get home in time. We must give a party for him if he does, some night between Christmas and New Year's. I love to give parties. It's so nice to see people coming to Silver Bush in pretty dresses, all smiling and happy. I hope everybody will have a good appetite Christmas Day. I love to feed hungry people."

"Oh, oh, and what are women for if it's not to fade the world?" said Judy complacently. "Sure and it do be giving me pleasure just to see a cat lapping his milk. It's glad I am you girls do be having the rale Silver Bush notions av hospitality. I'm minding the fuss yer Aunt Jessie did be making once bekase company came unixpicted like and she had nothing to give thim to ate. Niver was Silver Bush in inny such predicament I'm telling ye."

"There ain't so much fun here as the Jebbs' though," said Tillytuck, who was sandpapering an axe-handle in his corner and thought Judy needed taking down a bit. "They were always quarrelling there. Two would start and then all the rest would join in. It was interesting. You folks here never quarrel. I never saw such a harmonious family."

"I should think we wouldn't quarrel," said Pat indignantly. "It would be terrible to have quarrels at Silver Bush. I hope we never, never will have."

"You'll be a fortunate family then," said Tillytuck. "There ain't many families but have a ruction once in a while."

"I think I would *die* if any of us quarrelled," said Pat. "We leave that to people like the Binnies."

Hope died hard in the matter of Joe but the days passed without any word of him or his ship. It was over three years since Joe had been home and Pat always knew, when she surprised a certain look in mother's eyes, that she was longing for her sailor boy. It would shadow mother's Christmas a bit if Joe didn't get home in time for it.

Pat had hoped for a fine Christmas day, clear and crisp, with a crackle of frost and unspoiled fields of snow and caps of lovely white fur on the posts down the lane: but she felt dubious as she took her last look from the kitchen door late on Christmas Eve. She and Judy had stayed up to make the stuffing for "the birds" but Judy was now folding weary hands for slumber in the kitchen chamber and Tillytuck had gone to sleep, perchance to snore, in the granary loft. A snarling, quarrelsome wind was fighting with the white birches and wailing around the barns. It did not sound like a fine day on the morrow but one must hope for the best, as Judy said. Pat shut out the chill of the winter night and paused a moment in the warm old kitchen to gloat over things in general. Everything she loved best was safe under her roof. The house seemed breathing softly and contentedly in its sleep. Life was very sweet.

Pat's hopes for a fine day were vain. Christmas morning dawned on a dreadful combination of fog and rain. Rain by itself, Pat always thought, was an honest thing . . . fog lovely and eerie . . . but together they were horrible. Tillytuck agreed with her.

"It's fogging, Judy," he said dolefully when he came in for breakfast. "Fogging hard. I can put up with a rainy day but I can't come these half-and-halfs, like a woman who never knows her own mind. No, sir."

"Oh, oh, and I'm not knowing what's to be done, wid people tramping all over me clane floor in dirty boots," said Judy viciously.

"We'll just have to do as they do in Nova Scotia, Judy." Judy bit.

"Oh, oh, and what is it they do in Novy Scoshy, if a body may ask?"

"They do the best they can," said Tillytuck solemnly, as he went out with the milking pails. Tillytuck mostly did the milking now. Judy had surrendered the chore unwillingly. She was afraid, when Long Alec insisted on it, that he thought she was growing too old for it. And she never could be brought to believe that Tillytuck stripped the cows properly. Besides, wasn't he ruining the young barn cats by milking into their mouths? That was no way to be training cats. Ye wudn't be catching Gintleman Tom or Bold-and-Bad or Squedunk at inny such capers.

After breakfast the blue and gold and purple and silver parcels were distributed and every one was pleased. Pat had been afraid Sid might not like the rather gorgeous silk pyjamas she had got him but Sid did.

"They're the very niftiest pyjamas I ever saw in my life," vowed Cuddles.

"And where have you seen so many pyjamas, miss?" demanded Long Alec, thinking to "get a rise" out of Cuddles.

"On the bargain counters," retorted Cuddles . . . and the laugh was on dad. It did not take much to make the Silver Bush people laugh. Laughter came easily to them.

"Isn't she the cliver one," said Judy . . . and then stiffened in horror.

Tillytuck was proudly uncovering his Christmas present for "the missus." A Jerusalem cherry! A pretty thing, to be sure, with its glossy green leaves and ruby red fruit, and mother was delighted with it. But Judy beat a sudden retreat to the kitchen, followed by Pat.

"Judy, what is the matter? You're never going to be sick to-day!"

"Patsy darlint, it's well if there's nothing worse than me being sick happens here this blissed day. Were ye seeing what that Tillytuck did be giving to yer mother? A Jerusalem cherry no less! Sure and didn't I come all out wid gooseflesh whin I saw it."

"But what about it, Judy? It's a pretty thing. I thought it lovely of Tillytuck to remember mother."

"Oh, oh, don't ye be knowing a Jerusalem cherry brings bad luck? There was one brought into this house thirty years ago and yer Uncle Tom slipped on the stairs and bruk three ribs that very night. I'm telling ye. Patsy darlint, can't ye be contriving to set the thing outside somewhere till the dinner be over at laste?"

Pat shook her head.

"We couldn't do that. It would offend Tillytuck. Anyway, I know mother wouldn't hear of it. You mustn't be superstitious, Judy. A pretty thing like a Jerusalem cherry can't bring bad luck."

"I'm hoping ye're right, Patsy, but we'll be seeing what we'll see. 'Fogging, Judy,' sez he. No wonder it do be fogging, and him wid that Jerusalem thing in his granary that blissed minute! But wid all there is to see to I'm not to stand bithering here."

"I'm going to see about the spare room right off so that it will be all in order if any one comes early," said Pat briskly. "May I have that new hooked rug you've got stored away in the attic to lay by the bed . . . the one with the great soft, plushy roses?"

"Av coorse. I mint it for yer hope chist but the way ye're snubbing the min right and lift there'll be lashings av time for *that*. Put plinty av blankets on the bed, Patsy darlint. If the Bay Shore aunts come they may be staying all night. Style widout comfort is not the way av Silver Bush. Yer Aunt Helen at Glenwood now . . . ye do be knowing yersilf what

style she puts on . . . silk spreads and liddle lace and ribbing
cushions . . . but I've always been hearing that people who
slipt there vowed they were cold in bed. The minister slipt
there one night and so cold he was he started prowling for a
blanket in the night and fell down the back stairs. That was
be way av being a disgrace. I'm telling ye."

Cuddles had already made the spare room bed and was
infuriated because Pat insisted on making it over again.

"You'll be as bad as Aunt Edith before you're thirty, Pat.
She imagines nobody can do anything right but herself. And
Judy's no better, no matter what she thinks. She's been
teaching me to make gravy for weeks but now when I want to
make it to-day she won't let me. You all make me weary."

"Don't be cross, Cuddles. You made the bed as nicely as
any one could but the extra blankets have to be put on.
Cuddles, do you know I love to make up beds and think of all
the tired people who will lie in them. I couldn't bear it if any
one should be cold in bed in Silver Bush. Will you get some
of the silver polish and do the mirrors? I want them to shine
like diamonds . . . especially the one in the hall."

The hall mirror was one that had been brought out from
France by Great-great-grandmother, Marie Bonnet. It was a
long, softly gleaming thing in a ruddy copper frame and Pat
loved it. Cuddles had an affection for it, too, because she
thought she looked nicer in it than in any other mirror at
Silver Bush.

"Sure and it was always the flattering one," said Judy, as
Cuddles rubbed at the frame. "Minny's the pretty face that's
looked into it."

"I wonder," said Pat dreamily . . . passing carelessly through
the hall just to make sure Cuddles was doing the polishing
right . . . "if one came here some moonlit night one couldn't
see all the shadowy faces that once looked into it looking out
again."

"Oh, oh, ye'd nade the enchanted mirror of Castle
McDermott for that," chuckled Judy. "That looking glass
wasn't like other looking glasses. There did be a curse on it. I
was always afraid av it. Be times it did be saming like a frind
and thin agin like an inimy. And I was always wanting to look
in it, in spite av me fear, jist to be seeing if innything looked
out av it."

"And did anything ever, Judy?"

"Niver a bit av it, girl dear. The looking glass wasn't for

common folks like mesilf. Niver did I be seeing innything worse than me own frickled face. But there did be thim that did."

"What did they see, Judy?"

"Oh, oh, there's no time for that now. It's me raisin gravy I must be seeing to this blissed minute."

Pat shut the hall door and set her back against it resolutely.

"Judy, not one step do you stir from this hall till you've told us what was seen in the McDermott mirror, if there's no raisin gravy made this Christmas."

"Oh, oh" . . . Judy surrendered . . . "it's mebbe as well to tell it whin Tillytuck can't be claiming to have stipped out av the glass. Did ye be hearing him the other avening whin I was telling av the dance one Saturday night in South Glin that they kipt up too late . . . past the stroke av twilve . . . and the Bad Man Below intered? Sez me Tillytuck solemnly, 'I rimimber it only too well. I was at that dance.' 'Indade,' sez I, sarcastic-like, 'ye must be an aged man, Tillytuck, for the dance was all av eighty years ago.' But he carried it off wid a grin. Ye can't shame that man. But I can't be rimimbering all the tales av the looking glass now. There was a Kathleen McDermott once who was no better than she shud be and me fine lady whips out one night to meet her gintleman lover and run away wid him. But me grand gintleman was killed on his way to her and Kathleen hurried back home thinking no one wud know. But the doors were closed agin her. The McDermott had looked in the glass and seen it all. Bridget McDermott saw *her* soldier husband dying in India the night he was killed. But nobody iver knew what Nora McDermott saw for the pore liddle soul dropped the lamp she was holding and her dress caught fire and she was dead in two hours."

"Oh!" Cuddles shivered deliciously. "Why did they keep such a terrible thing in the castle?"

"Sure, it *belonged* there," said Judy mysteriously. "Ye wudn't have thim move it. And it was be way av being frindly as often as not. Eileen McDermott knew her man was alive, shipwrecked on a South Say island, whin iveryone else was sure for a whole winter that he was drowned. She saw him in the glass. And the McDermott av me own time saw a minuet danced in it one night and niver was inny the worse av it. And now I'm getting back to me kitchen. I've wasted enough time palavering wid ye."

"Half the fun of making preparations for anything is in talking things over," reflected Cuddles, giving the mirror a final whisk. It held no ghosts. But Cuddles felt secretly satisfied with what she saw in it.

6

Eventually everything was in readiness. The table beautifully set. . . . Pat made Cuddles take off the tablecloth three times before it was smooth enough to suit her . . . the house full of delicious odours, everybody dressed up except Judy.

"I'm not putting on me dress-up dress till me dinner is out of the way. I'm not wanting spots on it. Whin the last dish is washed I'll slip up and put it on in time for supper. They'll see me in all my grandeur thin. Yer table do be looking lovely, Patsy, but I'm thinking it wud look better if that cherry thing didn't be sitting in the middle av it."

"I thought it would please Tillytuck. He's sensitive, you know. And if it is going to bring us bad luck it will anyhow, so what matter where it sits?"

"Sez she, laughing in her slave at the foolish ould woman. Oh, oh, we'll be seeing, Patsy. Joe hasn't come after all and I've me own opinion as to what previnted him."

Pat looked about happily. Everything was just right. She must run and tie Sid's neck-tie for him. She loved to do that . . . nobody else at Silver Bush could suit him. What matter if a cold rain were falling outside? Here it was snug and warm, the smiling rooms full of Christmas magic. Then the old brass knocker on the front door began to go tap-a-tap. The first guests had arrived . . . Uncle Brian and Aunt Jessie, who hadn't been asked at all but had just decided to run down in the free and easy clan fashion and bring rich old Cousin Nicholas Gardiner from New Brunswick, who was visiting them and wanted to see his relatives at Silver Bush. Pat, as she let them in, cast one wild glance through the dining room door to see if three more places could be crowded into the table without spoiling it and knew they couldn't. The Jerusalem cherry had begun its dire work.

Soon everybody had come . . . Frank and Winnie, Aunt Hazel and Uncle Robert Madison and all the little Madisons, the two stately Great-aunts, Frances and Honor from the Bay

Shore farm, Uncle Tom and Aunt Barbara and Aunt Edith . . . the latter looking as disapproving as usual.

"Raisin gravy," she sniffed, as she went upstairs. "Judy Plum made that on purpose. She knows I can't eat raisin gravy. It always gives me dyspepsia."

But nobody seemed to have dyspepsia at that Christmas table. At first all went very well. A dear, gentle lady, with golden-brown eyes and silvery hair, sat at the head and her smile made every one feel welcome. Pat had elected to help Judy wait on the table but every one else sat down. The children sat at a special table in the Little Parlour as was the custom of the caste, and the cocktail course passed off without a hitch . . . three extra cocktails having been hurriedly concocted by Cuddles who, however, forgot to put a maraschino cherry on them. Of course Aunt Edith got one of the cherryless ones and blamed Judy Plum for it, and Great-aunt Frances got another and felt slighted. Old Cousin Nicholas got the third and didn't care. He never et the durn things anyhow. Uncle Tom ate his, although Aunt Edith reminded him that maraschino cherries were apt to give old people indigestion. "I'm not so aged yet," said Uncle Tom stiffly. Uncle Tom did look surprisingly young, as Pat and Judy were quick to note. The once flowing, wavy black beard, which had been growing smaller all summer, was by now clipped to quite a smart little point and he had got gold-rimmed eyeglasses in place of the old spectacles. Pat thought of those California letters but put the thought resolutely away. Nothing must mar this Christmas dinner . . . though Winnie was telling a story that would have been much better left untold. Judy almost froze in her tracks with horror as Winnie's clear voice drifted out to the kitchen.

"It was just after Frank and I were married, you know. I hadn't really got settled down. Unexpected company came to supper one night and I sent Frank off to the store to get some sliced ham for an emergency dish. I thought it seemed *rather* pink when I was arranging it on the plate . . . *so* nicely, with curly little parsley sprays. It *did* look artistic. Frank helped everybody and then took a bite himself. He laid down his fork and looked at me. I knew something was awfully wrong but *what?* I stopped pouring the tea and snatched up a mouthful of ham. What do you think?" Winnie looked impishly around the table. "That ham was *raw!*"

Shouts of laughter filled the dining room. Under cover of

the noise Pat dashed out to the kitchen where she and Judy had a silent rage. They had laughed themselves when Winnie had first told the tale at Silver Bush. But to tell it to all the world was a very different thing.

"Oh, oh, the disgrace av having Edith and Mrs. Brian hear av it!" moaned Judy. "But niver be hard on her, Patsy. I do be knowing too well what loosened her tongue. And were ye noticing that Cuddles put the slim grane chair out av the Liddle Parlour for yer Uncle Brian and it cracked in one leg? Ivery time I've gone in I've seen the crack widening a bit and the Good Man Above only knows if it'll last out the male. And here's Tillytuck sulking bekase he slipped on the floor and fell on his dog. He's been vowing I spilled a liddle gravy right in his corner, the great clumsy. But it's time to be taking in the soup."

And then, as if it had been waiting for Judy's words as a cue, the Jerusalem cherry showed what it could really do when it gave its mind to it. It seemed as if everything happened at once. Tillytuck, made sulkier still by Judy's speech, opened the door and stalked furiously out into the rain. Uncle Tom's wet, dripping Newfoundland, who had followed the Swallowfield folks over, dashed in. Just Dog simply couldn't stand that, after being fallen on. He flew at the intruder. The two dogs rolled in a furry avalanche right against Pat who had started for the dining room door bearing a trayful of soup plates full of a delicious brew that Judy called chicken broth. Down went poor Pat in a frightful mêlée of dogs, broken plates and spilled soup. Hearing the din, every one except Cousin Nicholas rushed out of the dining room. Aunt Hazel's two year old baby began to shriek piercingly. Aunt Edith took a heart attack on the spot. Judy Plum, for the first and only time in her life, lost her head but lost it to good purpose. She grabbed a huge pepper-pot from the dresser and hurled the contents full in the faces of the writhing, snarling dogs. It was effective. The Newfoundland tore loose, dashed wildly through the dining room, ruining Aunt Jessie's new blue georgette dress as he collided with her, tore through the hall, tore upstairs, ran into a delicately papered pastel wall, tore down again, and escaped through the front door which Billy Madison had presence of mind enough to open for him. As for Just Dog, he had bolted through the cellar door, which had been left open, and struck the board shelf across the steps. Just Dog, shelf, three tin pails, two stewpans, and a dozen glass jars of Judy's baked damson preserves all crashed down the cellar steps together!

It seemed that Pandemonium reigned at Silver Bush for the next quarter of an hour. Aunt Edith was gasping for breath and demanding a cold compress. She had to be taken upstairs by Aunt Barbara and ministered to.

"Excitement always brings on that pain in my heart," she murmured piteously. "Judy Plum *knows* that."

Uncle Tom and Uncle Brian were in kinks of laughter. Aunt Frances and Aunt Honor *looked* "This is not how things are done at the Bay Shore." And poor Pat scrambled dizzily up from the floor, dripping with soup, crimson with shame and humiliation. It was Cuddles who saved the situation. Cuddles was superb. She didn't lose her wits for a second.

"Everybody go back and sit down," she ordered. "Buddy, stop yelling . . . stop it, I say! Pat, slip up and get into another dress. Judy, clean up the mess. There is plenty of soup left. . . . Pat had only half the servings on the tray and Judy hid a potful away in the pantry. I'll have it ready in a jacksniff. Shut the cellar door and keep that dog down there until he gets the pepper out of his eyes."

Judy always declared she had never been as proud of any one at Silver Bush as she was of Cuddles at that time. But just at the moment poor Judy was feeling nothing but the bitterest humiliation. Never had such a shameful thing happened at Silver Bush. Wait till she got hold of Tillytuck! Wait till she could get her hands on that Jerusalem cherry.

In a surprisingly short time the guests were back at the table, where Cousin Nicholas had been placidly eating crackers through all the hullabaloo. Cuddles and Judy between them served the soup. Pat came down, clothed and in her right mind once more. Two cats, whose nervous systems had been shattered, fled to the peace and calm of Judy's kitchen chamber. The Jerusalem cherry bided its time. The goose-duck-turkey course was a grand success and Judy's raisin gravy was acclaimed the last word in gravies. The dessert was amazing, though Cousin Nicholas did manage to upset a jug of sauce over the tablecloth. Judy came in and calmly mopped it up. Judy had got her second wind now and was prepared for anything.

Pat sat down for the dessert and there was laughter. People were to seek Pat from birth till death because she gave them the gift of laughter. Though she had a secret worry gnawing at her heart. Aunt Jessie had eaten only three spoonfuls of her pudding! Wasn't it good? And Winnie... somehow... wasn't looking just right. She had suddenly become very quiet and rather pale.

To Judy's thankfulness the cracked chair lasted the dinner out, though it creaked alarmingly every time Uncle Brian moved. Then came "the grand dish-washing," as Judy called it, in the kitchen. Judy and Pat and Cuddles tackled it gaily. Things weren't so bad, after all. The guests were enjoying a good clan pi-jaw in the Big Parlour and the children were sitting around Tillytuck in the Little Parlour, looking up fascinated, while he told them stories. "Tarrible lies," Judy vowed they were. But then Tillytuck had once said, "What a dull fellow I'd be if I never told anything but the truth." Anyhow, he was keeping "the young ones" quiet and that was something.

7

The dishes disposed of, Pat and Judy began to think of the supper. Judy determinedly set the Jerusalem cherry on the side-board and hid the slim chair in the hall closet. A fresh cloth... the one with daisies woven in it... was brought out and Pat began to feel cheered up. After all, the guests were enjoying themselves and that was the main thing. Even Aunt Edith had come down, pale and heroic and forgiving. Just Dog crawled out of the cellar and coiled himself up in his own corner. Silver Bush rang with gay voices, firelight shimmered over pretty dishes, delicious things were brought from pantry and cellar: and Pat thought proudly that the supper table, with its lighted candles, looked even prettier than the dinner table. And its circle of faces was happy and wise and kind.

"What's the matter with Win?" asked Cuddles, who had decided to help wait with Judy and Pat and have her supper with them in the kitchen later on. "She's yellow and pea-green... is she sick?"

On the very heels of her question Frank came out hurriedly and whispered something to Pat who gave an ejaculation of dismay.

"I didn't think it wise for her to come," said Frank. "But

she was so anxious to... and you know... we didn't expect
...*this*... for two weeks."

Pat pushed him aside and ran to the telephone. Confusion reigned again at Silver Bush. Winnie was being taken
upstairs to the Poet's room. Pat and Judy were dashing madly
from place to place. Mother couldn't stay at the table. Cuddles was left to wait on it alone and did it well. As Tillytuck
was wont to aver, she had her head screwed on right. But it
was a rather flat meal. No laughter. And nobody had much
appetite now, except Cousin Nicholas. A doctor and a nurse
arrived in the pouring rain and as soon as possible the guests
departed... except Cousin Nicholas, who hadn't caught on to
the situation at all and announced his intention of staying a
few days at Silver Bush.

As soon as they had gone, Judy, with a set face, marched
into the dining room and carried the Jerusalem cherry out to
Tillytuck, uncorking the vials of her wrath.

"Take this *thing* out av the house immajetly if not sooner,
Josiah Tillytuck. It's done enough harm already and now, wid
what's ixpicted upstairs, I'm not having it here one minute
longer."

Tillytuck obeyed humbly. What was the use of being
peevish with the women?

A strange quiet fell over Silver Bush... an expectant
quiet. The supper dishes were washed and put away and Judy
and Pat and Cuddles sat down before the kitchen fire to
wait... and eat russet apples in place of their forgotten
supper. Their irrepressible gaiety was beginning to bubble up
in spite of everything. After all, it *was* something to get a
good laugh.

Tillytuck was smoking in his corner with Just Dog at his
feet. McGinty was as near Pat as he could get and Bold-and-
Bad and Squedunk ventured downstairs. Dad and Cousin
Nicholas were raking over clan history in the Little Parlour.
Sid was reading a murder mystery in the dining-room. Things
seemed quite normal again... were it not for muted sounds
overhead and the occasional visits of the white-capped nurse
to the kitchen.

"Oh, oh, what a day!" sighed Judy.

"It's been dreadful," assented Pat, "but it will be a story
to laugh at some day. That is why things don't always go
smoothly I suppose. There'd be no interesting history. I only
wish Hilary had been here to-day. I must write him a full

account of it. What a sight I must have been, drowned in soup and dogs! Well, eight of our good soup plates go to the dump and the slim chair is done for...and we'll have no damson preserves till next fall...but after all, that's all the real damage."

"I'm hoping it may be," said Judy, with an ear cocked ceilingward. "What did ye do wid yer cherry, Tillytuck? If ye put it in the granary the place'll burn down to-night."

"I hove it into the pig-pen," said Tillytuck sourly.

"Oh, oh, God hilp the poor pigs thin," retorted Judy.

"I'll never forget Aunt Frances' face," giggled Cuddles.

"Oh, oh, Aunt Frances, is it? Niver be minding her, Cuddles dear. Things have happened at the Bay Shore, too. Don't I be minding one time I was over there hilping them out at a big time and whin yer Aunt Frances was jist in the act av setting a big bowl of red currant preserves on the table she did be giving the awfullest yell ye iver heard and falling over backward wid the bowl. Talk av soup! She did be looking as if she was lying murdered in her blood. At first ivery one thought she'd had a fit. But thin they come to find out a wee divil av a b'y had slipped down under the table and grabbed holt av her leg. Oh, oh, minny's the time I've laughed over it. Her dress was clane ruint, and her timper.... Patsy darlint!"

"Judy...what is it?"

"Oh, oh, nothing much," said Judy in a despairing tone. "Only I niver rimimbered to put me dress-up dress on after all! It wint clare out av me head after the dog-fight...and me puddling round afore all the company in me old drugget."

"Never mind, Judy," comforted Pat, seeing Judy was really upset. "Nobody would notice it. And you might have got spots on it and then what about Castle McDermott?"

"Yer Aunt Edith wud be thinking I'd nothing but drugget to wear," groaned Judy. "Though she hadn't got all the basting thrids out of her own dress, if ye noticed. It's meself isn't used to dog-fights in me kitchen"... with a malevolent glance at Tillytuck. "It's minny a year since I saw one...the last was in South Glin church all av tin years ago. Oh, oh, that was a tommyshaw! Billy Gardiner always brought his dog to church. It was be way av being winked at for iverybody knew poor Billy was only half there, and they did be setting in a back pew, the dog behaving himself fine, though he did be giving a tarrible howl whin a lady visitor from town got up one day to sing a solo. Sure, nobody blamed the dog. But this day I'm telling ye av, another dog wandered in, the door being open, and Billy's dog wint for him. The strange dog flew up the aisle wid Billy's dog after him. He was caught jist under the pulpit! Oh, oh!" Judy rocked with laughter at the recollection, forgetful of her unworn splendours.

"What did they do, Judy?"

"Do, is it? Elder Jimmy Gardiner and Elder Tom Robinson aich grabbed a dog and carried it out be the scruff av the neck. Picture to yersilves, girls dear . . . a solemn ould elder wid a long beard and a most unchristian ixpression walking down the aisle, one on one side av the church and one on the other, houlding a dog at arm's length."

"Ah," said Tillytuck, "I was in the church that day. I remember it well."

This was too much for Judy. She got up and went into the pantry. Sid came out to say that Cousin Nicholas wished to go to bed and wanted a hot water bottle to take with him. Pat convoyed him to the spare room. Tillytuck, realising that he was out of favour, went off to the granary.

Pat had just come down when there was a knock at the door. Who on earth could it be at this time of night? Cuddles opened it . . . and in out of the starless dripping night stepped Joe! Captain Joe, tall and bronzed and changed, after years of typhoons on China seas, but unmistakably Joe.

"Flew here," said Joe laconically. "Flew from Halifax. Got into Charlottetown at dusk and hired a motor to bring me out. Thought I'd make it in time for supper anyhow. Everything happened to that car that could happen . . . and finally a broken axle. Nevertheless, here I am . . . and why are you all up as late and looking so solemn?"

Pat told him. Joe whistled.

"Not little Winnie! Why, I always think of her as a kid herself. What a night for the stork to fly! Anything in the pantry, Judy?"

His old grin robbed the question of insult. Joe *knew* there would be something in the pantry. Judy had a whole turkey stowed away, as well as the pot of soup. By the time mother had come down and hugged Joe and hurried anxiously back upstairs Judy had another table spread and they all sat down to it, even forgiven Tillytuck, whom Cuddles haled in from the granary.

"Ah, this is worth coming home for," said Joe. "Cuddles, you're almost grown up. Any beau yet, Pat?"

"Oh, oh, ye'd better be asking her that," said Judy. "Don't ye think it's time we had another widding at Silver Bush? She snubbed Elmer Moody last wake so bad he wint off vowing he'd niver set foot in Silver Bush agin."

"He breathes through his mouth," said Pat airily.

"Listen at her. Some fault to find wid ivery one av the poor b'ys. And what about yersilf, Joe? Do ye be coming home to find a wife?"

Joe blushed surprisingly. Pat only half liked it. She had heard rumours of several girls Captain Joe had been writing to occasionally. None of them were quite good enough for Joe. But it was the old story . . . change . . . change. Pat hated change so. And little, cool, unexpected breaths of it were always blowing across everything, even the jolliest of times, bringing a chill of foreboding.

"And you're not tattooed after all, Joe," said Cuddles, half disappointedly.

"Only my hands," said Joe, displaying a blue anchor on one and his own initials on the other.

"Will you tattoo mine on mine?" asked Cuddles eagerly.

Before Joe could answer an indignant old man suddenly erupted into the kitchen, wrapped in a dressing gown. It was Cousin Nicholas and Cousin Nicholas was distinctly in a temper.

"Cats!" he snarled. "Cats! I had just fallen into a refreshing slumber when a huge cat jumped on my stomach . . . on my stomach, mark you. I detest cats."

"It . . . must have been Bold-and-Bad," gasped Pat. "He does so love to get into the spare room bed. I'm so sorry, Cousin Nicholas . . ."

"Sorry, miss! I never can get to sleep again after I am once wakened up. Will your sorrow cure that? I came down to ask you to find that cat and secure him. *I* don't know where the beast is . . . probably under the bed, plotting more devilment."

"Peevish . . . very peevish," muttered Tillytuck quite audibly. Cuddles meowed and Cousin Nicholas glared at her.

"The manners of Silver Bush are not what they were in my day," he said crushingly. "I had a very hard time to get to sleep at all. There was too much going and coming upstairs. Is anybody sick?"

"Yes . . . but it don't be catching," said Judy reassuringly.

Pat, trying not to laugh, hurried upstairs and discovered Bold-and-Bad crouching in the corner of the hall, evidently trying to figure out how many lives he had left. For once in his life Bold-and-Bad was cowed. Pat carried him down and shut him up in the back porch, not without a pat or two... for she was not overly attracted to Cousin Nicholas.

That irate gentleman was finally persuaded to go back to bed. Evidently some idea of what was going on had filtered through his aged brain, for, as Pat assisted his somewhat shaky steps up the stairs, he whispered,

"Mebbe I shouldn't mention it to a young girl like you... but is it a baby?"

Pat nodded.

"Ah, then," said Cousin Nicholas, peering suspiciously about him, "you'd better watch that cat. Cats suck babies' breaths."

"What an opinion our Cousin Nicholas will have of Silver Bush," said Pat, half mournfully, half laughingly, when she returned to the kitchen. "Even our cats and dogs can't behave. And you, Cuddles.... I'm ashamed of you. Whatever made you meow at him?"

"I wasn't meowing at *him*," said Cuddles gravely. "I was just meowing."

"Oh, oh, ye naden't be worrying over what ould Nicholas Gardiner thinks av our animals," sniffed Judy. "I wasn't saying innything before for he's your cousin and whin all is said and done blood do be thicker than water. But did ye iver hear how me fine Nicholas got his start in life? Whin his liddle baby brother died ould Nicholas... only he was jist eliven thin... earned fifty cents be letting all the neighbourhood children in to see the wee dead body in the casket for a cint apace. That did be the foundation av *his* fortunes. He turned that fifty cints over and over, it growing wid ivery turn, and niver a bad spec did he make."

"Judy, is that really true? I mean... haven't you mixed up Cousin Nicholas with some one else?"

"Niver a bit av it. The Gardiners don't all be angels, me jewel. Sure and that story was laughed over in the clan for years. Aven his mother laughed wid the bist av thim. She was a Bowman and he got his quare ways from her. So he's more to be pitied than laughed at."

"Yes, indeed," agreed Pat. "Think of never knowing the delight of loving a nice, prowly, velvety cat."

"He's awfully rich though, isn't he?" said Cuddles.

"Oh, oh, wid one kind av riches, Cuddles darlint. But

it's better to be poor and fale rich than to be rich and fale poor. Hark!"

Judy suddenly held up her hand.

"What's that?"

"Sounds like a cat on the porch roof," said Sid.

Pat dashed upstairs, returning in a few minutes flushed with excitement.

"Come here, *Aunt* Cuddles," she laughed.

8

Joe and Sid and dad went to bed. Tillytuck, mildly remarking that he had had enough passionate scenes for one day, betook himself to the granary. But Pat and Cuddles and Judy decided to make a night of it. It was three now. They sat around the fire and lived over that fateful Christmas Day. They roared with laughter over the look of Cousin Nicholas.

"Sure and he naden't have been making such a fuss over a poor cat," said Judy. "Well do I remimber what happened to a man in Silverbridge years ago. He jumped into his bid one night and found a dead man atwane the shates."

"Judy!"

"I'm telling ye. It was his own brither but if Tillytuck was here he'd be saying he was the dead man. And now let's be having another liddle bite. I'm faling as if I hadn't had a dacent male for wakes, what wid dog-fights and ould cousins and people flying like birds. It's thankful I am that I frog-marched me Tillytuck out wid that Jerusalem cherry afore Joe did be starting from Halyfax."

"To think that mother is a grandmother and we're aunts," said Cuddles. "It makes me feel awfully old. I'm glad it's a girl. You can dress them so cute. They're going to name it Mary Laura Patricia after its two grandmothers and call it Mary. Frank put the Patricia in for you, Pat, because he said if it hadn't been for you that child would never have been born. What did he mean?"

"Just some of his nonsense. He persists in thinking I gave up a career so that Winnie could get married. I'm glad they're calling it mother's name. But I always think a second name seems woeful and reproachful because it is never mentioned often enough to give it personality. As for a third name, it's nothing but a ghost."

"Tillytuck was really quite excited over it, wasn't he?"

"Can you imagine Tillytuck ever being a baby?" said Pat dreamily.

"Oh, oh, he was, and mebbe somebody's pride and joy," sighed Judy sentimentally. "It do be tarrible what we come to wid the years. Sure and another Christmas is over and we can't be denying it was merry in spots."

And then it was morning. The rain was over; the whole world was soaked and sodden but in the east was a primrose brightening and soon the Hill of the Mist was like a bare, brown breast in the pale early sunshine. The house, after all the revel and excitement, had a dishevelled, cynical, ashamed look. Pat longed to fall upon it and restore it to serenity and self-respect.

Winnie, white and sweet, was asking them with her pretty laugh what they thought of her little surprise party. Sid was declaring to indignant Cuddles that the baby had a face like a monkey. Mother was played out and condemned to a day in bed. And Judy stole out to see if the pigs had survived the Jerusalem cherry.

9

"Oh, oh, I do be tasting spring to-day," said Judy one early May morning. It had been a long cold winter, though a pleasant one socially, with dances and doings galore. They had two dances at Silver Bush for Joe . . . one the week after he came home and one on the night before he went away again. Tillytuck had been the fiddler on both occasions and Cuddles had danced several sets and thought she was nearly grown up. It was a family joke that Cuddles had cut Pat out in the good graces of Ned Avery and had been asked to go with him to a dance at South Glen. But mother would not allow this. Cuddles, she said, was far too young. Cuddles was peeved.

"It seems to me you're always too young or too old to do anything you like in this world," she said scornfully. "And you won't let Joe tattoo my initials on my arm. It would be *such a* distinction. Nobody in school is tattooed *anywhere*. Trix Binnie would just be wild with envy."

"Oh, oh, since whin have the Gardiners taken to caring what a Binnie thought av innything?" sniffed Judy.

Spring was late in coming that year. Judy had a saying that "it wudn't be spring till the snow on the Hill av the Mist melted and the snow on the Hill av the Mist wudn't melt till spring." There were fitful promises of it . . . sudden lovely days followed by bitter east winds and grey ghost mists, or icy north-west winds and frosts. But on this particular day it did seem as if it had really come to stay. It was a warm day of entrancing gleams and glooms. Once a silver shower drifted low over the Hill of the Mist . . . over the Long House . . . over the Field of the Pool—over the silver bush . . . and away down to the gulf. Then the day made up its mind to be sunny. The distances were hung with pale blue hazes and there was an emerald mist on the trees everywhere. The world was sweet and the Pool was a great sapphire. Cuddles found some white and purple violets down by the singing waters of Jordan and young ferns were uncoiling along the edge of the birch grove. Pat discovered that the little clump of poet's narcissus on the lawn was peeping above ground. It gave her a pang to remember that she had got it from Bets . . . Bets who had loved the springs so but no longer answered to their call. Pat looked wistfully up the hill to the Long House . . . the Long Lonely House once more, for the people who had moved into it when the Wilcoxes went away had gone again and the house was untenanted, as it had been when Pat was a child and used to wish its windows could be lighted up at night like other houses. Now she no longer felt that way about it, though she still felt a thrill of pleasure when the sunset flame kindled its western windows into a fleeting semblance of life and colour, and still shivered when it looked cold and desolate on moonlit winter nights. She resented the thought of any one living there when Bets, sweet, beloved Bets, had gone, never to return. When it was empty she could pretend Bets was still there and would come running down the hill, as in the old fair and unforgotten days, on some of these spring evenings that seemed able to call anything out of the grave.

When Judy "tasted" spring it was time to begin housecleaning and as Tillytuck was away for the day on "the other farm" as the "old Adams place" was now called, Judy and Pat took the opportunity to clean the granary chamber . . . a task which Judy performed rather viciously, for Tillytuck was temporarily out of favour with her, partly because Just Dog had killed three of her chickens the day before and chewed up one leg of Siddy's khaki pants, and partly because . . .

"He did be coming home drunk agin last night and slipt in the stable."

Judy's "agin" seemed to imply that Tillytuck came home drunk frequently. As a matter of fact this was only his second offence and Tillytuck was such an excellent worker that Long Alec winked at his very occasional weakness.

"Not that he'd be giving in he was tight.... Oh, no. He wud only say the moon seemed a bit unsteady-like. And he was after warning me not to be getting inny notion av marrying into me head aven if he did be liking to talk to me. Me! But wud it be inny use getting mad wid the likes av him? It ann'ys him more to be laughing at him. He did be trying to get up the granary stips... me watching him through the liddle round windy and having me own fun... but he cudn't trust his legs, so he paraded to the stable, walking very stiff and pompous. Oh, oh, the dear knows what we'll be finding in his din... a goat's nest, I wudn't be wondering."

"Tillytuck says he's going to get a radio," said Cuddles, who was not in school, as it was Saturday.

"Oh, oh, a radio, is it? I'm relaved to hear it. Mebbe if he gets one he won't be rading such trash as this." Judy indignantly held up a book she had discovered on Tillytuck's table. "Do ye be seeing it... *The Mistakes av Moses*. It do be a rank infidel book he borryed off ould Roger Madison av Silverbridge and whin I rated him for rading it he sez, 'I like to see both sides av a question,' sez he. Him and his curiosity!"

Judy tossed the offending volume out of the window into the pig-pen and ostentatiously washed her hands.

"You can't stick Tillytuck on the catechism though," said Pat. "And he really is a great hand to read his Bible."

"But he has his doubts about the story of Jonah and the whale," said Cuddles. "He told me so."

"Does he be talking to children av such things?" Judy was horrified. "It's telling him me opinion av that I'll be. Don't ye be hading him, Cuddles. We've niver hild wid infidelity at Silver Bush and if Moses did be making a mistake or two it's me considered opinion that he knew more about things in gineral than Josiah Tillytuck and ould Roger Madison put together."

"You're just a bit peeved with Tillytuck because he tried to cap your stories," suggested Cuddles slyly. For there had been quite a scene in the kitchen two evenings previously when Judy had told a tale of some lady on the south side who put rat poison by mistake for baking powder in the family pancakes and Tillytuck had said he had eaten one of them.

"It isn't a chanct I do be having wid Tillytuck," said Judy passionately. "I stick to the truth but he do be making things up as he goes along."

"But you made candy for him afterwards, Judy."

"Oh, oh, so I did," admitted Judy with a deprecating grin. "He gets round a body somehow wid his palaver. There do be times whin he cud wheedle the legs off an iron pot. Niver be laughing at an ould woman, Cuddles dear. Tillytuck and I do be understanding each other rale well, for all av our tiffs. If he likes to think I'm dying about him he's welcome to it. He hasn't minny pleasures. And now we've finished the chamber so we'll . . ."

"The pigs are in the graveyard, Judy," cried Cuddles.

"I'll pig thim," ejaculated Judy viciously as she whirled down the granary stairs in horror. But after all cud ye be blaming the poor pigs? They had niver been thimsilves since they et the Jerusalem cherry.

In the afternoon they tackled the garret. Pat always loved cleaning in general and the garret in particular. It was delightful to make Silver Bush as clean and sweet as the spring . . . a new curtain here . . . a new wall-paper there . . . a spot of paint where it would do most good. Little changes that didn't hurt . . . much. Though Pat was always sorry for the old wall-papers and missed them.

When you came to the garret you always found so many things you had almost forgotten and all the family ghosts got a good rummaging.

"Sure, houseclaning and diggin' a well do be the only two things I know av that ye begin at the top and work down wid," said Judy. "Well, the garret do be done and that do be making the fortieth time I've been at the claning av it. Forty-one years this very May, Patsy dear, since I tuk up wid Silver Bush, hoping to put the summer in if Long Alec's mother was suited wid me . . . and here I do be still."

"And will be for forty more years I hope," said Pat with a hug. "But we haven't quite finished, Judy. I want to see what's in that old black chest in the corner. It hasn't been turned out properly for years."

"Oh, oh, there's nothing much there but the relics av ould dacency," said Judy.

"We really should examine it. The moths may have got into it."

"Sure and it's always aisy to find an excuse for what ye want to do," said Judy slyly. "But we'll ransack it if ye wait till I get supper. We'll come up here in the dim and see what's in it."

Accordingly, after supper Pat betook herself to the garret, which was growing shadowy, although the outside world was still in the glow of sunset. It was a spring sunset . . . pale golds and soft pinks and ethereal apple greens shading up to silvery blue over the birches. Pat ached with the loveliness of it, being one of those.

> *"who feel the thrill*
> *Of beauty like a pang."*

Violet mists were veiling the distant hills. The little green-skirted maples over at Swallowfield were dancing girls with the dark spruces behind them, like grim, old-maid duennas. Sid had ploughed the Mince Pie field that day and it lay in beautiful, red, even furrows. From the Field of the Pool there sounded the dreamy trill of a few frogs through the brooding spring evening and there was some indefinable glamour over everything. Things were a little "queer" as they had sometimes seemed in childhood on certain evenings.

"This makes me think of the night you told me Cuddles was coming," she said to Judy, who came up the stairs, panting a little. "Oh, Judy dear, just look at that sunset."

"Innything spacial about it?" asked Judy a little shortly . . . because she didn't like the idea of being out of breath after only two flights of stairs.

"There's something special about every sunset, Judy. I never saw a cloud just that colour and shape before . . . see . . . the one over the tall fir-tree."

"I'm not denying it's handsome. Sure and I wudn't be like ould Rob Pennock at the South Glen. His wife was rale ashamed av his insinsibility. 'He doesn't know there's such a thing as a sunset,'—she sez to me once, impatient-like."

"How terrible it must be not to see and *feel* beauty," said Pat softly. "I'm so glad I can find happiness in all lovely little things . . . like that cloud. It seems to me that every time I look out of a window the world gives me a gift. Look at those old dark firs around the pool. Judy, does it ever seem to you that the Pool is drying up? It seems to me that it isn't as deep as it used to be."

"I'm fearing it is," acknowledged Judy. "It's a way thim pools has. There was one below Swallyfield whin I was here first...and now it's nothing but a grane dimple wid some ferns and bracken in it."

"I don't know how I'll bear it if it dries up. I've always loved it so."

"What don't ye be loving around the ould place, Patsy dear?"

"The more things and people you love the more happiness you get, Judy."

"Oh, oh, and the more sorrow too. Now, whativer made me go and say that! It jist slipped out."

"It's true, I suppose," said Pat thoughtfully. "It's the price you pay for loving, I guess. If I hadn't loved Bets so much it wouldn't have hurt me so terribly when she died. But it was worth the hurt, Judy."

"It always do be," said Judy gently. "So niver ye be minding me silly talk av the sorrow."

"Well, how about the black chest, Judy?"

"Cuddles wants us to be waiting till she can come. She said she wudn't be long...she had a bit av Lating to look over. She do be getting int'rested in her books at last. Joe did be giving her a bit av advice now and thin."

"I hope we'll be able to afford to give her a real good education, Judy. We never do seem to have much money, I admit."

"Too hospitable, I'm supposing some do be thinking. Mrs. Binnie says we throw out more wid a spoon than the min can bring in wid a shovel...Binnie-like. *Our* min like the good living. And what if we don't be having too much money, Patsy dear? Sure and we have lashings av things no money cud be buying. There'll be enough squazed out for Cuddles whin the time comes, niver fear. The Good Man Above will be seeing to that."

The drone of the separator came up from the yard below where Tillytuck was operating under the big maple over the well and singing a Psalm sonorously, with McGinty and some cats for an audience. It struck Pat that Tillytuck had a remarkably good voice. And he was setting the saucer for the fairies, just as Judy always did.

"I used to think the fairies really came and drank it. I wish I could believe things like that now, Judy."

"It do be fun belaving things. I often wonder, Patsy dear, at all the skiptics do be losing. As for the saucer av milk, the dog McGinty gets it now mostly. Look at him sitting there and thumping his bit av a tail ivery time Tillytuck gets to the end av a verse. He may not be having inny great ear for music but he do be knowing how to get round Tillytuck."

"Judy, I'm almost sure dear little dogs like McGinty must have souls."

"A liddle bit av one mebbe," said Judy cautiously. "I niver cud hould wid the verse 'widout are dogs,' Patsy dear, though niver be telling the minister or Tillytuck I said it. Whiniver I see the dog McGinty I think av Jingle. Wasn't it a letter from him ye got to-day? And is there inny word av him coming home this summer?"

"No," Pat sighed. She had been hoping Hilary would come. "He has to work in vacation, Judy."

"I s'pose his mother doesn't be thinking inny more about him than she iver did?"

"I don't know. He never mentions her name now. Of course she is quite willing to send him all the money he needs . . . but he's terribly independent, Judy. He is determined to earn all he can for himself. And as for coming home . . . well, you know, since his uncle died and his aunt went to town he really has no home to come back to. Of course I've told him a dozen times he is to look upon Silver Bush as home. Do you remember how I used to set a light in this very window when I wanted him to come over?"

"And he niver failed to come, did he, Patsy? I'm almost belaving if ye set a light in this windy to-night he'd see it and come. Patsy dear," . . . Judy's voice grew wheedling and confidential . . . "do ye iver be thinking a bit about Jingle . . . ye know. . . ."

Pat laughed, her amber eyes full of roguish mirth.

"Judy darling, you've always had great hopes of making a match between Hilary and me but they're doomed to disappointment. Hilary and I are chums but we'll never be anything else. We're *too* good chums to be anything else."

"Ye seem so set on turning ivery one else down," sighed Judy. "And I always did be liking Jingle. It's not a bad thing to be chums wid yer husband, I'm tould."

"*Why* are you so set on my having a 'real' beau, Judy? Any one would think you wanted to get rid of me."

"It's better ye're knowing than that, me jewel. Whin ye lave Silver Bush the light av ould Judy Plum's eyes will go wid ye."

"Then just be glad I mean to stay, Judy. I never want to leave Silver Bush. . . . I want to stay here always and grow old with my cats and dogs. I love the very walls of it. Look, Judy, the Virginia creeper has got to the roof. It's lucky we have so many vines here, for the house does need painting terribly and dad says he can't afford it this year."

"Yer Uncle Tom is painting Swallyfield . . . white, wid grane trimmings, it's to be. He started to-day."

"Yes." A shadow fell over Pat's face. Every one in North Glen knew by this time that Tom Gardiner was writing to a lady in California, though not even the keenest of the gossips had found out anything more, not even her name. "Swallowfield really needs painting but it has needed it for years. And now Uncle Tom seems to have a mania for sprucing things up. He's even going to have that dear old red door stained and grained. I've always loved that red door so much. Judy, you don't think there is anything in that story of his going to be married, do you?"

"I wudn't be saying. And me fine Aunt Edith wudn't be liking it," said Judy in a tone which indicated that for her, at least, there would be balm in Gilead if Tom Gardiner really up and married at last. "There do be another story round, Patsy, that Joe do be ingaged to Enid Sutton. Is there inny truth in *it*?"

"I can't say. He saw a good deal of her when he was home. Well, she is a very nice girl and will suit Joe very well."

Pat felt herself very magnanimous in thus according approval to Joe's reputed choice. If it had been Sid . . . Pat shivered a little. But Sid wouldn't be thinking of marrying for years yet.

"Oh, oh, if it iver comes to a widding I hope Enid will be having better luck wid her dress than her mother had. There was a dressmaker in town making it . . . the Suttons houlding thimsilves a bit above the Silverbridge dressmaker . . . and she was sick, but she sint word she'd have the dress ready for the widding day widout fail. Whin the morning come, she did be phoning up she had sint it be the train but whin the train come in niver a widding dress was on it. And, what's more, that dress niver turned up . . . niver, Patsy dear. The poor liddle bride was married in a blue serge suit and tears."

"Whatever became of the dress, Judy?"

"The Good Man Above knows and Him only. It was shipped be the ixpress agent at Charlottetown and that was the last iver seen or heard av it. White sating and lace! But at that I do be thinking she was luckier than the bride at Castle McDermott."

"What happened to her?"

"Oh, oh, it was a hundred years afore me time there but the story was tould me. She wint to the wardrobe and put her hand in to fetch out her widding dress and . . ." Judy leaned forward dramatically in the gathering gloom . . . "*and it was grasped by a bony hand.*"

"Whose?" Pat shivered deliciously.

"Oh, oh, *whose?* That did be the question, Patsy dear. No good Christian, I'm telling ye. The poor bride fainted and the widding had to be put off and the groom was killed on the way home, being thrown from his horse. Minny's the time I did be seeing the wardrobe whin I was working there but niver wud the McDermotts allow that door to be opened agin. The story wint that the widding dress was still hanging there. Oh, oh!" Judy sighed. "I belave I'll have to be paying a visit to ould Ireland this fall. I do be having a hankering for it I haven't had for years."

Cuddles came running up the stairs, preceded by Bold-and-Bad who covered three steps at a leap.

"Oh, I hope I'm in time. I've finished that Latin. No wonder Latin died. *Did* people ever really talk that stuff? Talk it just as you and I do? I can't believe it. Joe made me promise I'd lead my class in it and if I did he'd tattoo my arm next time he came no matter what fuss *you* made. So I'm going to do it or bust."

"The young ladies av Castle McDermott niver did be talking av busting," said Judy reproachfully.

"Oh, I suppose they talked a brogue you could cut with a knife," retorted Cuddles. "Well, let's get at the old chest. It's such fun to rummage through old boxes. You never know what you may come across. It's like living for a while in yesterday."

10

They dragged the old black chest out of its corner to the window. Bold-and-Bad, deciding that it was not a thing likely to do a cat any good, crept off into the darkness under the eaves and imagined himself a Bengal tiger. The black chest was full of the usual miscellany of old garret chests. Ancient lace and velvet and flower-trimmed hats, bundles of banished Christmas cards, limp ostrich feathers, faded family photographs, strings of birds' eggs, discarded dresses with the pointed basques and polonaises and puffed sleeves of other vintages, old school-books, maps the Silver Bush children had drawn, packets of yellow letters, a "rat" worn in the days of pompadours, old faded things once beautiful. They had oceans of fun over them.

"What on earth is this?" demanded Cuddles, holding up an indescribable mass of crushed wire. Judy gave a snort of laughter.

"Oh, oh, that do be yer Aunt Helen's ould bustle. I rimimber how yer dad yelled whin she brought it home. It's the dashing lady she was and always the first in the clan to be out in a new fashion. She wint to a concert that night at the Bridge wid her beau and they say he was crimson to the ears, he was that ashamed av it. But in a few wakes' time iverybody did be wearing thim. He shud have been thankful she didn't wear it like Maggie Jimson at the South Glin did whin her sister as was working up in Bosting sint her one home . . . a rale fancy one all covered wid blue sating."

"How did she wear it, Judy?"

"Outside her dress," said Judy solemnly. "They say the folks who were in church that day were niver the same agin. Oh, oh, but the fashions do be changing always. Only kissing stays in. Mebbe this ould bustle will be took down some av these days and displayed on the parlour mantel-piece be way av an heirloom."

"Look at this!" Cuddles held up a huge brown velvet hat with a draggled and enormous shaded-green ostrich feather on it. "Fancy living up to a hat like that!"

"Oh, oh, that was yer Aunt Hazel's hat wid what they called a willow plume and rale nice it did be looking over her pompydore. Though I niver fancied velvet hats mesilf iver since the mouse jumped out av Mrs. Reuben Russell's one Sunday at the Bridge church. *That* was a tommyshaw."

"If Tillytuck was here he'd say he was the mouse," giggled Cuddles.

Pat pounced on an article.

"Judy, if here isn't my old little cheese hoop! I've often wondered where it disappeared to. I wanted to keep it always in remembrance of those dear little cheeses you used to make me in it . . . one for myself every year. You don't remember Judy making cheese, Cuddles, but I do. It was such fun."

"And here do be one av yer Great-grandmother Gardiner's ruffled caps," said Judy. "Minny's the time I've done it up for her . . . she always said that nobody cud be giving the frills the right quirk like young Judy. Oh, oh, I was young Judy thin and I'd larned the trick at Castle McDermott. Ould lady Gardiner always made her caps hersilf . . . it's the beautiful himstitcher she was. She was a rale fine ould lady, if some folks did be thinking her a bit too uppity. Did I iver be telling ye av the night she was knaling be her bed be an open windy, saying her prayers and her thoughts in hiven . . . I'm s'posing . . . and a big cat crawled through the windy and lit on her back suddent-like wid a pair av claws that tuk hold?"

"Oh!" Cuddles shrieked in delight. "What did Great-grand say?"

"Say, is it?" Judy looked cautiously around. "It was thirty-nine years ago and I've niver told a living soul afore. She said a word beginning wid D and inding wid N."

Pat doubled up with laughter. Stately old Great-grandmother Gardiner whose picture hung in the Big Parlour with her white cap encircling her saintly face! Really, the things Judy knew about respectable people were dreadful.

"This ould rag was a dress yer grandmother wore in her day." Judy held up a faded affair with manifold flounces. "Striped silk jist like ribbing grass. Mebbe it's the very one. . . . I'm not saying it is but it might be . . . she wore jist the twicet."

"Why didn't she wear it again?" asked Cuddles.

"Oh, oh, if it's the one . . . mind ye. I'm not saying it is . . . yer grandmother and her cousin, Mrs. Tom Taylor, were great rivals, it did be said, in the matter av dresses and both av thim fond av gay colours. And whin yer grandmother come to church quite gorgeous-like in her striped dress Mrs. Tom turned quite grane and said nothing but wint to town nixt day and bought a dress av the same piece and give it to her ould scrubwoman at the Bridge. The poor ould soul was pleased as Punch and got it made up at oncet and wore it to church the nixt Sunday. Oh, oh, 'twas ràle cruel av Mrs. Tom and there was a judgmint on her, for her own father died and she did have to be wearing black for two years. It was rale bitter, for black didn't set her. But niver wud yer grandmother put the striped dress on her back agin."

"How foolish of her," said Cuddles loftily.

"Oh, oh, it's the foolish folks as does all the int'risting things," chuckled Judy. "There'd not be minny stories to tell if ivery one was wise. And if here isn't Siddy's ould Teddy bear! Niver a night wud he go to slape widout it. It's mesilf sewed thim shoe-buttons in for eyes whin Ned Binnie picked the first ones out and poor Siddy's liddle heart was broken."

"They're saying in school Sid has a case on Jenny Madison," said Cuddles.

"Sid has a new 'case' every two months," said Pat lightly. "What a pretty dress this must have been in its time, Judy... a sort of silvery stuff with lace frills in the sleeves."

"Silvery, is it? If ye cud see it as I see it! That was a dress yer Aunt Lorraine had for her first liddle party the summer I come here. Ye niver cud imagine innything bluer than her eyes. I can see her dancing in the orchard be moonlight yet to show it off to us afore she wint. She's been churchyard dust for forty years. Her first liddle party was her last. Ye'll rimimber her tombstone av white marble wid a baby's head and wings sticking out behint its ears. Sure I niver thought it suitable for a girl's tombstone but I've been tould it wasn't a baby but a cherub, whativer that may be. I'm not forgetting the day I took Siddy through the South Glin churchyard whin he was six. He did be looking at the cherub and thin at me. 'Where is the rist av it, Judy?' he sez, solemn like."

"Are these her letters?" asked Cuddles, holding up a yellowed packet.

"I'm thinking those are yer Great-aunt Martha's. She did be dying young, too, but she had a beau as was a great letter-writer. Her father didn't hould wid him and some say Martha died av a broken heart and some from wearing too thin stockings in the winter time. Ye can be taking the romantic or the sinsible explanation, whichiver's suiting ye bist."

"Why didn't her father approve of her beau?"

"I'm not thinking he had much agin the young man himself but he was after having an uncle who was hanged for taking part in some rebellion and cut down and recovered. He niver talked agin. Some said his throat had been injured . . . but there was some as thought he'd seen something as scared him out av talking foriver. Anyhow, her father wasn't wanting inny half-hanged person in his fam'ly."

"Now, here's something!" exclaimed Pat, fishing up a silver 'chain' bracelet. "It's a bit black but it could be cleaned."

"The padlock and kay's missing, Patsy dear, so it wudn't be much use. That was yer Aunt Hazel's, too. They did be all the rage thin. I had a hankering after one mesilf but whin I heard the story av Sissy Morgan's chain bracelet up at the Bay Shore it tuk the fascination out av thim for me."

"What was that?"

"Oh, oh, her beau was a capting and afore he wint on the v'yage that proved his last he locked a chain bracelet on her arm . . . a gold one it was, no less . . . and tuk the kay wid him, making her promise she'd niver marry inny one ilse unless he come back and unlocked the bracelet. Sissy promised light enough. The Morgans wud promise innything. But she was pretty, that Sissy, and the capting was crazy about her. He was swept over-board in a storm and the kay wint to the bottom av the Atlantic wid him. Liddle Sissy tuk on a bit but the Morgans soon get over things and in a year she did be wanting rale bad to marry Peter Snowe. But she was scared to bekase av her promise about the bracelet. Her dad wanted the match bekase Peter was rale well to do but Sissy stuck to it she dassn't and siveral tommyshaws they had over it all. Oh, oh, but there was the funny squeal to it."

"What was the sequel?"

"Oh, oh, sequel, is it? Well, Sissy was slaping sound in her bed one moonlight night and whin she woke the bracelet was unlocked . . . just that. She didn't be seeing nothing or nobody but it was unlocked."

"I don't think that is funny, Judy," said Cuddles with a little shiver. "That was . . . horrible."

"Oh, oh! Sure and it was funny thin whin Peter Snowe wudn't have her after all . . . said he wasn't taking inny ghost's lavings. The rist av the min samed to be having the same faling and she died an ould maid in the ind av it."

"Why, here's Joe's silver spoon," pounced Pat. "This *is* a

find. We never knew what became of it. How in the world did it get here? Won't mother be pleased!"

The little silver spoon with the dents where Joe had cut his teeth... Joe who was half way to China now. Pat sighed and rose.

"Well, that is all. I wonder if we should burn those old letters. In a way I'd like to read them... there's something fascinating in old letters... they seem to open ghostly gates... but I suppose Aunt Martha wouldn't have liked it."

Pat picked the packet up. An old dim, flattened four-leaved clover slipped from it. Who had found luck with it? Not Aunt Martha at all events. The letters were brittle and yellow... full of old words of love written years ago from hearts that were dust... full of old joys that had once been raptures and dim old griefs that had once been agonies.

"We must drag the chest back into its corner. Look at Bold-and-Bad peering out of it."

Bold-and-Bad's eyes were glowing in his lair, giving that uncanny expression cats' eyes often do... as if they were merely transparent, letting the burning fires behind them become visible.

"They did be saying that Martha's beau's uncle's looked like that be times," Judy whispered as she went downstairs.

It was rather too spooky. Cuddles fled in Judy's wake. But Pat still lingered, going back to the window where the full moon was beginning to weave beautiful patterns of vine leaves on the garret floor. The spookier the garret was the more she loved it. The letters in her hands made her think of Hilary's letter that day. Like all his letters it had a certain flavour. It *lived*. You could almost hear Hilary's voice speaking through it... see the laughter in his eyes. Every time you re-read one of his letters you found something new in it. To-day's had enclosed a sketch of his prize design for a house on the side of a hill. There was something about it faintly reminiscent of Silver Bush. Pat had one of her moments of wishing passionately that Hilary was somewhere about... that they could join hands as of old and run across the old stone bridge over Jordan. Surely they had only to slip over the old bridge to find themselves in the old fairyland. They would go back to Happiness and the Haunted Spring, following the misty little brook through the old fields where the moonlight loved to dream. They would linger there, lapped round by exquisite silence. Shadowy laughter would echo faintly about them. Cool elusive night smells would be all around. Little white sheep would be out on the hills. Surely Happiness kept their old days for them and they would find them there. Pat shivered. The rising wind moaned rather eerily around the lofty window. She felt suddenly, strangely lonely... right there in dear Silver Bush she felt lonely... *homesick*. It was uncanny. She ran downstairs and left the garret to its ghosts.

11

When Judy read an item from "Events of the Week" in a Charlottetown paper to the Silver Bush girls one evening they were only mildly and pleasantly excited over it. The Countess of Medchester, the paragraph stated, was visiting friends in Ottawa on her way home from Vancouver to England.

"That do be the lady married to the earl as is uncle av yer cousin, Lady Gresham," said Judy proudly. "Oh, oh, it do be giving me a bit av a thrill, as Cuddles says, to rade that item and riflict that we do be in a manner connected wid her."

"Even though she doesn't know of our existence," laughed Pat. "I don't suppose Lady Gresham brags to her friends of her very distant relationship to certain unimportant people on a Canadian farm."

"Likely she thinks we're Indians," grinned Cuddles. "Still, as Judy says, there's a thrill in it."

"Whin ye see May Binnie nixt time ye can be saying... to yersilf, av coorse... 'Ye don't be having a fourth cousin in the English aristocracy, *Miss* Binnie.' And *that*'ll be a satisfaction."

"*I* shall say it to Trix," said Cuddles.

"Indeed, you won't," cried Pat. "Don't make yourself ridiculous, Cuddles. We're of no more importance in the Countess of Medchester's eyes... supposing she ever heard of us... than the Binnies. And who cares? Look at that froth of cherry bloom behind the turkey house. I'm quite sure there's nothing lovelier on the grounds of Medchester Castle... if there is a castle."

"Av coorse there's a castle," said Judy, carefully cutting out the item. "An earl cudn't be living in innything humbler. I'm pinning this up on the wall be me dresser to show

66   L. M. Montgomery

Tillytuck. He's niver quate belaved me whin I tould him av yer being third cousin to Lady Gresham. . . ."

"Fourth, Judy, fourth."

"Oh, oh, I might have made a bit av a mistake in the figure but does it be mattering? Innyhow, *this* will convince him. He was be way av being a bit cranky this morning whin he come in for breakfast though he cudn't be putting a name to the rason . . . like the cintipede that had rheumatism in one av his legs but cudn't tell which. He was putting on some frills wid me but *this* will be one in the eye for him. A rale countess wid a maid to button her boots! Oh, oh! I had a faling last night there did be something strange in the air."

When the letter came that day . . . being left in the mailbox at the road just like any common epistle and carried up to the house in Tillytuck's none too clean hand . . . Judy felt there was something stranger still in the air. A heavy cream-tinted envelope with a dainty silver crest on the flap, addressed in a black distinctive hand to Mrs. Alex Gardiner, North Glen, P. E. Island, and post-marked Ottawa. The crest and the post-mark had a very queer effect on Judy. She gave a gasp and looked at Gentleman Tom. Gentleman Tom winked knowingly.

"Anybody dead?" said Tillytuck.

Judy ignored him and called for Pat in an agitated voice. Pat came in from the garden, her arms full of the plumes of white lilac, McGinty ambling at her heels. Cuddles came running across the yard, the spring sunlight shining on her golden-brown head. Judy was standing in the middle of the kitchen floor holding the letter at arm's length.

"Judy, what is it?"

"Ye may well ask," said Judy. "Will ye be looking at the crest? And the post-mark?"

Pat took the letter.

"I feel a thrill . . . several thrills," whispered Cuddles.

"Thrills, is it? Sure and ye'll be having thrills wid a vengeance if that do be what I'm thinking it is."

"It's for mother," said Pat slowly. Mother was away for a visit at Glenwood. "I suppose we'd better open it. It may be something requiring prompt attention."

Judy handed Pat the paring knife. She had a presentiment that the letter should not be torn open like an ordinary epistle. Pat slit the envelope, took out the letter . . . likewise crested . . . and glanced over it. She turned red . . . she turned pale . . . she stared at the others in silence.

"What is it?" whispered Cuddles. "Quick . . . I've got such a queer prickly feeling in my spine."

"It's from the Countess of Medchester," said Pat in a hollow voice. "She says she promised Lady Gresham she would see her *cousins* before she returned to England . . . she's coming to Charlottetown to visit friends and she wants to come out here . . . *here* . . . next Saturday. Saturday!"

Poor Pat repeated the word as if Saturday meant the end of the world.

For a moment nobody spoke . . . could speak. Even Tillytuck seemed to have passed into a state of coma. In the silence Gentleman Tom reached over and dug a claw into his leg but Tillytuck did not even wince.

Cuddles was the first to recover.

"Have the Countess of Medchester *here*," she gasped. "We *can't.*"

But Judy had got her second wind. She was an expert in dealing with situations without precedent.

"Oh, oh, mebbe we can't . . . but we will. What's a countess whin all is said and done? Sure, she'll ate and drink and wash behind her ears like inny common person. What time av day will she be here, Patsy?"

"The forenoon . . . she's leaving on the night boat. That means she'll be here for dinner, Judy!"

"She will be in a good place for the same thin, I'm telling ye. It will be a proud day for Silver Bush and no countess was iver ating a better male than we can be putting up. But 'twill take some planning, so kape up yer pecker, Patsy, and let's be getting down to brass tacks. We've no time for blithering. Sure and yer countesses can't be ating lilac blossoms."

Pat came up gasping. She felt ashamed of herself. It was positively Binnie-like to be flabbergasted like this.

"You're right, of course, Judy. Let me see . . . this is Tuesday. The floors in the dining room and the Big Parlour must be done over . . . they're simply terrible. I'll paint them to-day and stain them to-morrow. I wish I could do something to the front door. The paint is all peeling off. But I daren't meddle with it. We must just leave it open and trust she won't notice it. Then, Cuddles, we have to go to Winnie's one day this week to help her get her sewing done. We should have gone last week but I wanted to wait till this week to see their big crab-apple tree in bloom. We'll go Thursday. That will give us Friday to prepare. We must take her to the Poet's room because the ceiling isn't cracked there as it is in the spare room and we must put the spread mother embroidered on the bed. Sid can go for mother Friday evening. It *is* a shame to have her visit cut short when it's her first for years . . . but of course she'd like to be here."

"Oh, oh, and there'll be two great ladies together thin," said Judy. "I'll match yer mother agin inny countess in the world. Sure and a Bay Shore Selby cud hould up her hid wid inny av the quality."

Pat was herself again. Tillytuck was lost in admiration of her. From that moment Silver Bush was a place of excited but careful planning and overhauling and cleaning and decorating and discussing. Even Tillytuck had his say.

"The dinner's the thing," he told them. "A good meal is never to be sneezed at, speaking symbolically."

Every one agreed with this. The dinner must be such as even the wife of a belted earl could not turn up her nose at. Pat did endless research work among all her recipe books. Cuddles cut school to help. What was Latin and the chance of tattooing compared to this?

It was decided to have fried chicken for dinner . . . Judy's fried chicken was something to dream about.

"Wid sparrow grass. Sure and sparrow grass is a sort av hardy vegetable. Ye'll be making the sauce ye larned at the Short Coorse, Patsy dear. And will ye be having time to hemstitch the new napkins?"

"Cuddles and I are going to sit up all night to do them. I think we'll have iced melon balls and ice-cream for dessert and a lemon cocoanut cake. We mustn't attempt too much."

"Not to be ostentatious," agreed Judy who dearly loved a big word now and then.

"And, after all, she may be on a diet," grinned Cuddles. Cuddles had regained all her insouciance. Trix Binnie would be sunk when she heard of it all, positively sunk.

"I hope she'll think Silver Bush nice," breathed Pat. That was all she really cared about.

"She cudn't be hilping it," said Judy. "Let's be hoping it will be fine on Saturday. If it rains . . ."

Judy left it to the imagination what it would be like to entertain a countess in a rainstorm.

"It *must* be fine," was Pat's ultimatum.

"Do you think it wouldn't be a good thing to... to pray for fine weather?" suggested Cuddles, who felt that no chances should be taken.

Judy shook her head solemnly.

"Girls dear, I wudn't. Ye can niver be telling what comes av such praying. Well do I rimimber the day in South Glen church whin the minister, ould Mr. McCary, did be praying for rain wid all his might and main. Whin the people were going home from church down comes a thunderstorm and drinches iverybody to the skin. Ould James Martin and ould Thomas Urquhart were together and Thomas sez, sez he, 'I do be wishing he hadn't prayed till we got home. Thim McCarys niver cud be moderate,' sez he. So ye'd better be laving it to nature, girls dear. And thank the Good Man Above there'll be no Jerusalem cherries around. Whin she comes, Patsy dear, av coorse I'll kape in the background but don't ye be thinking I'd better have me dress-up dress on, in case she might catch a glimpse av me coming or going?"

"Of course, Judy. And oh, Judy, do you think you could coax Tillytuck to leave off that terrible old fur cap of his for one day? If she saw him going through the yard!"

"Niver be worrying over Tillytuck. He'll be away to town that day wid the calves yer dad sold. And none too well plazed about it. Him thinking he wanted a glimpse av a countess! And trying to be sarcastic. He sez to me, sez he, 'Kape a stiff upper lip, Judy. After all, yer grandmother was a witch and that's a sort of aristocracy, symbolically spaking.' 'I'm not nading to stiffen me upper lip,' sez I. 'I do be knowing me place and kaping it, spaking the plain truth and no symbols.' Tillytuck do be getting a bit out av hand. He was after smoking his pipe in the graveyard to-day, setting on Waping Willy's tombstone as bould as brass."

"Aunt Edith and Aunt Barbara are terribly excited," said Pat. "I wanted them to come over for dinner but they wouldn't. Aunt Edith vetoed it. However, she very kindly offered to lend us her silver soup spoons. She said a countess could tell at a glance if the spoons were solid or only plated. I'm so glad our teaspoons are solid... only they're so old and thin."

"Oh, oh, they do be all the more aristocratic for that," comforted Judy. "The countess will be saying to hersilf, 'There's *fam'ly* behind *thim*. Nothing av the mushroom in *thim,'* she'll be saying. And spaking av the Swallowfield folks, have ye noticed innything odd about yer Uncle Tom's beard?"

"Yes . . . it has almost disappeared," sighed Pat. "It's nothing more than an imperial now."

"Whin it disappears altogether we'll be hearing some news," said Judy with a mysterious nod.

But Pat had no time just then to be worrying over Uncle Tom's vanishing whiskers. By Wednesday night Silver Bush was ready for the countess . . . or for royalty itself. On Thursday Sid took Pat and Cuddles over to the Bay Shore to help Winnie with her spring sewing. They really sewed all the forenoon. In the afternoon Winnie said, "Never mind any more for a while. Come out in the wind and sun. We don't often have such an afternoon to spend together."

They prowled about the garden, picking flowers, drinking in the crab-apple blossoms, watching the harbour and making nonsense rhymes. In the midst of their fun they heard the telephone ring in the house.

12

Pat went in to answer it, as Winnie had her Christmas baby in her arms. When Pat heard Judy's voice she knew that something tremendous had occurred for Judy never used the telephone if she could help it.

"Patsy dear, is it yersilf? I do be having a word for you. *She's here.*"

"Judy! Who? Not the countess?"

"I'm telling ye. But I can't be ixplaining over the phone. Only come as quick as ye can, darlint. Siddy and yer dad have gone to town."

"We'll be right over," gasped Pat.

But how to get right over? Frank was away with the car. There was nothing for it but the old buggy and the old grey mare. It would take them an hour to get to Silver Bush. And Uncle Brian must be 'phoned to and asked to bring mother right home. Between them Pat and Cuddles got the mare harnessed and after several hundred years . . . or what seemed like it . . . they found themselves alighting in the yard of Silver Bush . . . which looked as quiet and peaceful as usual with Just Dog sleeping on the door-stone and three kittens curled up in a ball on the well platform.

"I suppose the countess is in the Big Parlour," said Pat. "Let's slip into the kitchen and find out everything from Judy first."

"How do you talk to countesses?" gasped Cuddles. "Pat, I think I'll go and hide in the barn loft."

"Indeed you won't! You're not a Binnie! We'll see Judy and then we'll slip upstairs and get some decent clothes on before we beard the lion in her den."

Pat had on her blue linen afternoon dress... which, incidentally, was the most becoming thing she owned. Cuddles wore her pretty green sweater with its little white embroidered linen collar, above which her wind-tossed hair gleamed, the colour of sunlight on October beeches. Both girls ran, giggling with nervousness, up the herring-bone brick walk to the kitchen door and rushed in unceremoniously. Then they both stopped in their tracks. Cuddles' eyes wirelessed to Pat, "Do you really live through things like this or do you just die?"

Judy Plum and the Countess of Medchester were sitting by the table, whereon were the remnants of a platterful of baked sausages and potatoes. At the very moment of the girls' entry Judy was pouring cream from her "cream cow" into her ladyship's cup and the latter was helping herself to a piece of the delightful thing Judy called "Bishop's bread." Gentleman Tom was attending meticulously to his toilet in the centre of the floor and Bold-and-Bad was coiled on the countess' lap, while McGinty was squatted by the legs of her chair. Tillytuck was sitting in his corner... fortunately minus the fur cap, which, however, hung on his chair back. Judy was in her striped drugget but with a beautiful white apron starched stiff as a board. She was as completely at her ease as if the countess had been a scrubwoman. And as for Lady Medchester, Pat, amid all her dumfounderment, instantly got the impression that she was enjoying herself hugely.

"And here," said Judy, with incredible nonchalance, "are the girls I've been telling ye av... Mrs. Long Alec's daughters. Patricia and Rachel."

The countess instantly got up and shook hands with Patricia and Rachel. She had mouse-coloured hair and a square, reddish face, but the smile on her wide mouth was charming.

"I'm so glad you've come before I have to go," she said. "It would have been dreadful to go back home and have to tell Clara that I hadn't seen any of her cousins at all. She has always had such a dear recollection of some wonderful days she spent on Prince Edward Island when a child. It was too bad to come down on you like this. But I got a cable from England last night which made it imperative I should leave to-night, so I had to come this afternoon. Your Judy..." she flashed a smile at Judy... "made me delightfully welcome and showed me around your lovely home... and, last but not least, has given me a most delicious meal. I was *so* hungry."

Somehow they found themselves all sitting around the table. Pat realized thankfully that Judy had had sense enough to put the best tablecloth on it and the silver spoons. But why on earth hadn't she got supper in the dining room? And what was the silver teapot doing on the dresser while the old brown crockery one graced the table?

And there was Tillytuck sitting in his shirt sleeves! Was there really anything to do but die? What was one to say? Pat wildly thought of an article in a recent magazine on "How to Start a Conversation With People You Have Just Met," but none of the gambits seemed to fit in here exactly. However, they were not necessary. The countess kept on talking in a frank, friendly, charming way that somehow included everybody, even Tillytuck. Pat, with a reckless feeling that nothing mattered now anyhow, flung conventionality to the winds. Cuddles was never long rattled by anything and in a surprisingly short time they were all chatting gaily and merrily. The countess insisted on their having some tea and Bishop's bread with her... she was on her third cup herself, she said. Judy trotted to the pantry and brought back some forgotten orange biscuits. Lady Medchester wanted to hear all about mother and was only sorry she couldn't see her way clear to taking a Silver Bush kitten back with her to England.

"You see one of your cats has already quite made up his mind to like me," she laughed, looking down at the placidly heaving, furry flanks of Bold-and-Bad.

"And that cat don't condescend to every one, speaking symbolically, ma'am," said Tillytuck.

Pat had a confused impression that it was quite proper to say "ma'am" to a queen but hardly the way to address a countess. A countess! *Was* this stout, comfortable lady, in the plain, rather sloppy tweed suit, really a countess? Why... why... she seemed just like anybody else. She had the oddest resemblance to Mrs. Snuffy Madison of South Glen! Only Mrs. Snuffy was the better looking!

And there was no mistaking it . . . she was enjoying the bread and biscuits.

"Cats don't," said Lady Medchester, smiling at Tillytuck out of her hazel eyes and giving the wistful McGinty a nip of sausage. "That is why their approval, when they do bestow it, is really so much more of a compliment than a dog's. Dogs are so much easier pleased, don't you think?"

"You've said a mouthful, ma'am," said Tillytuck admiringly.

Cuddles, who, up to now, had contrived to keep a perfectly demure face, narrowly escaped choking to death over a gulp of tea. Pat, glancing wildly around, suddenly encountered Lady Medchester's eyes. Something passed between them . . . understanding . . . comradeship . . . a delicious enjoyment of the situation. After that Pat didn't care what anybody did or said . . . which was rather fortunate, for a few minutes later, when Lady Medchester happened to remark that she had had friends on the *Titanic*, Tillytuck said sympathetically, "Ah, so had I, ma'am . . . so had I."

"The ould liar!" said Judy under her breath. But everybody heard her. This time it was Lady Medchester who narrowly escaped disaster over a bit of biscuit. And again her twinkling eyes sought Pat's.

"Couldn't you stay till mother comes?" asked Pat, as the countess rose, gently and regretfully displacing her lapful of silken cat.

"I'm so sorry I can't. I've really stayed too long as it is. I have to catch that boat train. But it has been delightful. And I can tell Clara that at least I've seen Mary's dear girls. You'll be coming to England some day I'm sure, and when you do you must look me up. I'm so sorry to put this beautiful cat down."

"You've got hairs all over your stomach, ma'am," said Tillytuck. "Dogs ain't like that now."

If looks could have slain Judy would have been a murderess. But the countess put her hands on Pat's shoulders, kissed her cheek and bowed her head, shaking with laughter.

"He's priceless," she whispered. "Priceless. And so is your Judy. Darlings, I only wish I could have stayed longer."

The countess picked up a little squashy hat with a gold and brown feather on it that looked like a hand-me-down from the Silverbridge store, adjusted a silver fox stole which

Pat knew must have cost a small fortune, kissed Cuddles, made a mysterious visit into the pantry with Judy, donned a pair of antiquated gauntlets and went out to her car. Before she got in she looked around her. Silver Bush had cast over her the spell it cast over all.

"A quiet, beautiful place where there is time to live," she said, as if speaking to herself. Then she waved her hand to Judy... "We had such a pleasant little chat, hadn't we?"... and was gone.

"Oh, oh, but Silver Bush has been honoured this day," said Judy as they went back in.

"Judy, tell us everything... I'm simply bursting. And how did you come to have supper in the kitchen?"

"Oh, oh, don't be blaming me," entreated Judy. "It do be a long story that'll take some telling. Niver did I live through such an afternoon in me life. Tillytuck, do ye be wanting a liddle bite? Not that ye desarve it... but there's some av the pittaties and sausages lift if ye care for them."

"What's good enough for a countess is good enough for me," said Tillytuck, sitting down to the table with avidity. "She's a fine figure of a woman that, though maybe a bit broader in the beam than you'd expect of a countess, symbolically speaking. I found something alluring about her."

"Come out to the graveyard," whispered Judy to the girls. "We won't be disturbed there and I can be telling ye the tale. Sure and 'twill be one for the annals of Silver Bush."

"Uncle Brian has just phoned that mother was away to a picnic with some friends of Aunt Helen's and he couldn't locate her."

"It doesn't matter now," sighed Pat. "Why, oh, why, do things never happen as you plan? But I don't care... she was lovely... and she enjoyed herself...."

"Oh, oh, that she did," agreed Judy, settling herself on Weeping Willy's tombstone, while Pat and Cuddles and McGinty squatted on Wild Dick's, "and nothing could or magnificent about her. But whin she drove in, girls dear, I didn't be knowing for a minute whither I stud on me heels or me hid. I did be taking her up to the Poet's room to wash her hands... oh, oh, I did all the honours, aven to slipping in that extry nice cake av soap ye brought home the other day, the one wrapped up in shiny paper... and the bist av the embridered towels. I cudn't manage the new sprid but if ye'd heard her ladyship rave over the beautiful patchwork quilt!

Thin I dashed up to me room for a squint in me book av Useful Knowledge. But niver a word cud I find about intertaining the nobility so I had to be falling back on what I cud rimimber av the doings at Castle McDermott. It do be a pity I niver thought av slipping into me dress-up dress. But I was a bit excited-like. Whin I'd finished ixplaining to her that I'd phoned for ye nothing wud do her but I must show her all round the place. She said she wanted to see a rale Canadian farm at close range. It did be suiting me for I didn't be knowing if it was manners to lave her all alone and to sit wid a countess in the Big Parlour was a fearsome thought. I did be taking her all through the orchard and the silver bush and the cats' burying ground. And thin all through the graveyard and telling her all the ould stories...and didn't she laugh over Waping Willy! Thin whin we wint back to the house she wanted to see me kitchen...and me not knowing how Just Dog wud behave. Whin we got in it she sez to me, just like one old frind to another, 'Cud ye let me have a cup av tay, Judy...and what is that delicious odour I smell?' Well, girls dear, ye know just what it was...me bit av baked sausage and pittaties I had in the oven for Tillytuck and mesilf, ivery one ilse being away. 'Will ye be giving me a taste av it?' she sez, wheedling-like. 'Right here in the kitchen, Judy, where the scint av lilacs is coming in through that windy, Judy,' sez she, 'and the very same white kittens that hung on me nursery wall more years ago than I'll admit aven to you, Judy,' sez she. Sure and I cudn't stand up to a countess so she had her way. I got out the bist silver taypot and one av the parlour chairs for her. But she plunked hersilf down on ould Nehemiah's and sez, sez she, 'I want me tay right out av that ould brown pot. There's nothing like it for flavour,' sez she. And nothing wud do but I must sit down wid her and take a share av the sausages and pittaties. But I wasn't after ating minny, girls dear...me appetite wasn't wid me. Siven av thim sausages disappeared and I et only the one av thim. Think av it, me drinking tay wid a countess, and crooking me liddle finger rale illigant whin I happened to think av it! Madam Binnie'll niver be belaving it. And wud ye be belaving it, girls dear? She was at Castle McDermott hersilf whin she was a girleen and tould me all about the ould place. It did be making me fale I must be going to see it afore long. Prisently Bold-and-Bad comes along asking 'have ye room for a cat?' and jumps up in her lap. Oh, oh, ye saw for yersilves she was a different brade from Cousin Nicholas. Well, we did be sitting there colloguing, her and me and the cats, rale cosy and frindly, whin I heard a tarrible noise in the back porch. It didn't sound like innything on earth but I did be knowing it was Tillytuck gargling his throat, him thinking it was a bit sore this morning. I did be glancing at the countess a bit apprehensive-like but she was admiring me crame cow and taking no notice apparently. I was fearing whin he finished wid his throat he'd be breaking out into a Psalm but niver did I think he'd have the presumption to come in. I was clane flabbergasted whin I saw him standing in the dureway. I did be giving him the high sign to take himsilf off but he paid no attintion and was all for setting down on her ladyship's hat which she had tossed on a chair careless-like. I got it away just in time, girls dear, and down he plumped. Wud ye belave it, her ladyship smiled at him in that nice way she has and passed a remark about the weather. And didn't Tillytuck tell her rain was coming bekase he had rheumatism in his arms! And thin tilting back on the hind-legs av his chair, wid his thumbs tucked into his bilt, casual-like, he wint on to tell her one av his 'traggedies' . . . how the lion had got out av his cage and clawed him. 'It was a lippard last time,' I cudn't hilp saying, sarcastic-like. But her ladyship tuk his measure and I cud see she was lading him on, and him thinking he was showing me how to hobnob wid the quality. Thin Just Dog started to throw one av his fits but Tillytuck whisked him out so quick I'm not thinking her ladyship tuk it in. What wid it all, me nerves were getting a bit jumpy and niver was there a more welcome sound to me ears than the ould Russell mare's trot up the lane."

"Did you give the countess a swig out of your black bottle, Judy?" asked Sid, who had arrived home and come to find out why nobody had got supper ready for him. "If she left anything in the pantry I'd be glad of a bite."

"Why did you take her into the pantry just as she was leaving, Judy?" asked Pat.

"Oh, oh, I'd promised to give her a jar av me strawberry jam. But she'll niver be getting it home safe . . . there do be something in an ocean v'yage it can't be standing . . . she'll be firing it overboard afore she's half way across. She said to me in the pantry, Patsy dear, that ye did be having a lovely smile and a grand sinse av fun. Sure and I'm putting that bit av biscuit she lift on her plate in me glory box for a kapesake. It was her third so there did be no insult in her laving it. Well, it do be all over and whether I'll slape a wink to-night or not the Good Man Above only knows."

Judy was snoring soundly enough in the kitchen chamber when Pat and Cuddles went to bed. Young Joe Merritt had been around Silver Bush that night, wanting Pat to go to a picture with him but Pat had refused. Judy, as usual, wanted to know why poor Joe was always being snubbed. Wasn't he be way av being a rale nice young man and a cousin av the Charlottetown Merritts at that?

"I haven't a fault to find with him, Judy," said Pat gravely, "but our taste in jokes is entirely different."

"Oh, oh, that's sarious," agreed Judy... and crossed Joe Merritt's name from her list of possibles.

"Pull up the blind and let the night in, Cuddles. And don't light the lamp yet. When you light it you make an enemy of the dark. It stares in at you resentfully. Just now it's kind and friendly. Let's sit here at the window and talk it all over. It would be wicked to go to sleep too soon on such a night."

"Sleep! I'll never sleep again in this world," sighed Cuddles luxuriously, squatting on the floor and snuggling against Pat's knee while she proceeded to devour some water-cress sandwiches. They were getting in the habit of these delightful little gossips by their window, with only the trees and the stars to listen. To-night the scent of lilacs drifted in and the night was like a cup of fragrance that had spilled over. A wind was waking far off in the spruces on the hill. The robins were still whistling and the silver bush was an elusive, shadowy world breathing mystery. Bold-and-Bad padded in and insinuated himself into Cuddles' lap, where he lay and purred, tensing and flexing his claws happily. One lap was quite as good as another to Bold-and-Bad.

"I've had too many thrills to-day to be sleepy... some just awful and some wonderful. Wasn't Lady Medchester lovely, Pat? And *not* because she was a countess. She had such a finished air somehow. She wasn't a bit handsome... did you notice how much she looked like Mrs. Snuffy Madison? ... and her clothes were really shabby. Except the fox stole of course. But her hat... well, it looked as if Tillytuck *had* sat on it. But for all that there was something about her that we can't ever get, Pat, in a hundred years."

"*She* wouldn't care what the Binnies thought," said Pat mischievously.

"Don't . . . I'm blushing. And I'm never going even to mention it to Trix. Have a sandwich, Pat? You must be empty. We neither of us had anything since dinner but a biscuit and a scrap of Bishop's bread. I was only pretending to eat under Lady Medchester's eyes. Puss, do stop digging your claws into me. I'm sure Lady Medchester will have an amusing tale to tell when she gets home. The stately halls of England will resound to mirth over Judy and Tillytuck."

"Tillytuck perhaps . . . but not Judy. People laugh *with* Judy, not *at* her. Our countess liked Judy. Did you notice what a lovely voice she had? It somehow made me think of old mellow things that had been loved for centuries . . . after I got capable of thinking at all, that is. Cuddles, I'll never forget the sight as we bounced into the kitchen . . . Judy Plum and the Countess of Medchester *tête-à-tête* at our kitchen table, with Tillytuck for audience. Nobody will ever believe it. It *will* be something to tell our grandchildren . . . if we ever have any."

"*I* mean to have some," said Cuddles coolly.

"Well," said Pat, leaning out of the window to catch a glimpse of that loveliest of created things . . . a young moon in an evening sky, . . . "there's one thing the Countess of Medchester will never know she missed . . . my lemon cocoanut cake and Judy's fried chicken. I must write Hilary an account of this."

The Second Year

PAT never could discover how Lady Medchester's visit to Silver Bush got into the Charlottetown papers. But there it was in "Happenings of the Week." "The Countess of Medchester, who has been spending a few days with friends in Charlottetown, was a visitor at Silver Bush, North Glen, on Thursday last. Lady Medchester is a distant connection of Mr. and Mrs. Alexander Gardiner. Her ladyship is delighted with our beautiful Island and says that it resembles the old country more than any place she has yet seen in Canada."

The Silver Bush people did not like the item. It savoured too much of a certain publicity they scorned... "putting on dog," as Sid slangily expressed it. No doubt it reduced the Binnies to speechless impotence for a time and everybody in South Glen church the next Sunday gazed at the Gardiner family with almost the awe they would have accorded to royalty itself. But that did not atone for what Pat felt was a breach of good taste. Even Tillytuck thought it "rather crude, symbolically speaking." Nobody happened to notice that Judy, who might have been expected to be the most indignant of all, had very little to say and fought shy of the subject. Eventually it was forgotten. After all, there were much more important things to think of at Silver Bush. Countesses might come and countesses might go but wandering turkeys had to be reclaimed at night and Madonna lilies divided and perennial seeds sown, and a new border of delphiniums planned for down the front walk. Lady Medchester's visit slipped into its proper place in the Silver Bush perspective... a gay memory to be talked and laughed over on winter nights before the fire.

Meantime, Uncle Tom had stained and grained his once

79

red front door and had painted his apple house sage green with maroon trim. And everybody in Silver Bush and Swallowfield was wondering more or less uneasily why he had done it. Not but what both needed attention. The apple house had long been a faded affair and the red of the door was badly peeled. Nevertheless they had been that way for years and Uncle Tom had not bothered about them. And now, right in the pinch of hard times, when the hay crop was poor and the potato bugs unusually rampant and the turnips practically non-existent, Uncle Tom was spending good money in this unneccessary fashion.

"He do be getting younger every day," said Judy. "Oh, oh, it's suspicious, I'm telling ye."

"I opine there's a female in the wind, speaking symbolically," said Tillytuck.

It was the one cloud on Pat's horizon that summer. Some change was brewing and change at Swallowfield was nearly as bad as change at Silver Bush. Everything had been the same there for years. Aunt Edith and Aunt Barbara had held sway in the house, agreeing quite amicably in the main, and both bossing Uncle Tom for his soul's and body's good. And now both were uneasy. Tom was getting out of hand.

"It has to do with those California letters . . . I'm sure it has," Aunt Barbara told Pat unhappily. "We know he gets them . . . the post-office people have told it . . . but we've never seen one of them. We don't know where on earth he keeps them . . . we've looked everywhere. Edith says if she can find them she'll burn them to ashes but I don't see what good that would do. We haven't an idea who she is . . . Tom must mail his answers in town."

"If Tom brings a . . . a wife in here . . ." Aunt Edith choked over the word . . . "you and I will have to go, Barbara."

"Oh, don't say that, Edith." Aunt Barbara was on the verge of tears. She loved Swallowfield almost as much as Pat loved Silver Bush.

"I will say it and I do say it," repeated Aunt Edith inflexibly. "Can you think for one minute of us staying here, under the thumb of a new mistress? We can get a little house at the Bridge, I suppose."

"I can't believe Uncle Tom will really be so foolish at his age," said Pat.

"I have never been a man," said Aunt Barbara somewhat

superfluously, "but this I do know... a man can be a fool at *any* age. And you know the old proverb. Tom is fifty-nine."

"I sometimes think," said Aunt Barbara slowly, "that you... that we... didn't do quite right when we broke off Tom's affair with Merle Henderson, long ago, Edith."

"Nonsense! What was there to break off?" demanded Aunt Edith crisply. "They weren't engaged. He had a school-boy's fancy for her... but you know as well as I do, Barbara, that it would never have done for him to have married a Henderson."

"She was a clever, pretty little thing," protested Aunt Barbara.

"Her tongue was hung in the middle and her grand-mother was insane," said Aunt Edith.

"Well, Dr. Bentley says everybody is a little insane on some points. I do think we shouldn't have meddled, Edith."

Aunt Barbara's "we" was a concession to peace. Both of them knew it had been Edith's doings alone.

Pat sympathised with them and her heart hardened against Uncle Tom when she found him waiting for her at the old stile, half way along the Wispering Lane, where the trees screened them from the sight of both Swallowfield and Silver Bush. Pat was all for sailing on with a frosty nod but Uncle Tom put a shy hand on her shoulder.

"Pat," he said slowly, "I'd... I'd like to have a little talk with you. It's... it's not often I have the chance to see you alone."

Pat sat down on the stile ungraciously. She had a horrible presentiment of what Uncle Tom wanted to tell her. And she wasn't going to help him out... not she! With his vanishing beard and his front doors and his apple barns he had kept everybody on the two farms jittery all summer.

"It's... it's a little hard to begin," said Uncle Tom hesitatingly.

Pat wouldn't make it any easier. She gazed uncompromisingly through the birches to a field where winds were weaving patterns in the ripening wheat and making sinuous shadows like flowing amber wine. But for once in her life Pat was blind to beauty.

Poor Uncle Tom took off his straw hat and mopped a brow that had not been so high some thirty-odd years back.

"I don't know if you ever heard of a... a... a lady by the name of Merle Henderson," he said desperately.

Pat never had until Aunt Edith had mentioned her that day but...

"I have," she said drily.

Uncle Tom looked relieved.

"Then... then perhaps you know that once... long ago... when I was young... ahem, younger... I... I... in short... Merle and I were... were... in short..." Uncle Tom burst out with the truth explosively... "I was desperately in love with her."

Pat was furious to find her heart softening. She had always loved Uncle Tom... he had always been good to her... and he did look so pathetic.

"Why didn't you marry her?" she asked gently.

"She... she wouldn't have me," said Uncle Tom, with a sheepish smile. Now that the plunge was over he found himself swimming. "Oh, I know Edith thinks *she* put the kibosh on it. But not by a jugful. If Merle would have married me a regiment of Ediths wouldn't have mattered. I don't wonder Merle turned me down. It would have been a miracle if she had cared for me... then. I was nothing but a raw boy and she... she was the most beautiful little creature, Pat. I'm not romantic... but she always seemed like a... like an ethereal being to me, Pat... a... a fairy, in short."

Pat had a sudden glimpse of understanding. To Uncle Tom his vanished Merle was not only Merle... she was youth, beauty, mystery, romance... everything that was lacking in the life of a rather bald, more than middle-aged farmer, domineered over by two maiden sisters.

"She had soft, curly, red-brown hair... and soft, sweet red-brown eyes... and such a sweet little red mouth. If you could have heard her laugh, Pat... I've never forgotten that laugh of hers. We used to dance together at parties... she was as light as a feather. She was as slim and lovely as... as that young white birch in moonlight, Pat. She walked like... like spring. I've never cared for anybody else... I've loved her all my life."

"What became of her?"

"She went out to California... she had an aunt there... and married there. But she is a widow now, Pat. Two years ago... you remember?... the Streeters came home from California for a visit. George Streeter was an old pal of mine. He told me all about Merle... she wasn't left well off and she's had to earn her own living. She's a public speaker... a lecturer . . . oh, she's very clever, Pat. Her letters are wonderful. I . . . I couldn't get her out of my head after what George told me. And so . . . I . . . well, I wrote her. And we've been corresponding ever since. I've asked her to marry me, Pat."

"And will she?" Pat asked the question kindly. She couldn't hurt Uncle Tom's feelings . . . poor old Uncle Tom who had loved and lost and went on faithfully loving still. It *was* romantic.

"Ah, that's the question, Pat," said Uncle Tom mysteriously. "She hasn't decided . . . but I think she's inclined to, Pat . . . I think she's inclined to. I think she's very tired of facing the world alone, poor little thing. And this is where I want you to help me out, Patsy."

"Me!" said Pat in amazement.

"Yes. You see, she's in New Brunswick now, visiting friends there. And she thinks it would be a good idea for her to run across to the Island and . . . and . . . sorter see how the land lays, I guess. Find out maybe if I'm the kind of man she could be happy with. She wanted me to go over to New Brunswick but it's hard for me to get away just now with harvest coming on and only a half-grown boy to help. Read what she says, Patsy."

Pat took the letter a bit reluctantly. It was written on thick, pale-blue paper and a rather heavy perfume exhaled from it. But the paragraph in reference to her visit was sensibly expressed.

"We have probably both changed a good deal, honey boy, and perhaps we'd better see each other before coming to a decision."

Pat with difficulty repressed a grin over the "honey boy."

"I still don't quite see where I come in, Uncle Tom."

"I . . . I want you to invite her to spend a few days at Silver Bush," said Uncle Tom eagerly. "I can't invite her to Swallowfield . . . Edith would—would have a conniption . . . and anyhow she wouldn't come there. But if you'd write her a nice little note . . . Mrs. Merle Merridew . . . and ask her to Silver Bush . . . she went to school with Alec . . . do, now, Patsy."

Pat knew she would be letting herself in for awful trouble. Certainly Aunt Edith would never forgive her. Judy would think she had gone clean crazy and Cuddles would think it a huge joke. But it was impossible to refuse poor Uncle Tom, pleading for what he believed his chance for happiness again. Pat did not yield at once but after a consultation with mother she told Uncle Tom she would do it. The letter of invitation was written and sent the very next day and during the following week Pat was in swithers of alternate regret, apprehension, and a determination to stand by Uncle Tom at all costs.

There was a good deal of consternation at Silver Bush when the rest of the family heard what she had done. Dad was dubious . . . but after all it was Tom's business, not his. Sid and Cuddles, as Pat had foreseen, considered it a joke. Tillytuck stubbornly refused to express any opinion. It was a man's own concern, symbolically speaking, and wimmen critters had no right to interfere. Judy, after her first horrified, "God give ye some sinse, Patsy!" was just a bit intrigued with the romance of it . . . and a secret desire to see how me fine Edith wud be after taking it.

Edith did not take it very well. She descended on Pat, dragging in her wake poor Aunt Barbara who had been weeping all over the house but still thought they ought not to meddle in the matter. Pat had a bad quarter of an hour.

"How *could* you do such a thing, Pat?"

"I couldn't refuse Uncle Tom," said Pat. "And it doesn't really make any difference, Aunt Edith. If I hadn't asked her to come here he would have gone to New Brunswick to see her. And she may not marry him after all."

"Oh, don't try to be comforting," groaned Aunt Edith. "Marry him! Of course she'll marry him. And she is a *grandmother.* George Streeter said so . . . and thinks she is still a girl. It's simply terrible to think of it. I don't see how I'm going to stand it. Excitement always brings on a pain in my heart. Everybody knows that. *You* know it, Pat."

Pat did know it. What if it all killed Aunt Edith? But it was too late now. Uncle Tom was quite out of hand. He felt that the situation was delicious. Life had suddenly become romantic again. Nothing that Edith could and did say bothered him in the least. He had even begun negotiating for the purchase of a trim little bungalow at Silverbridge for "the girls" to retire to.

"Him and his bungalow!" said Aunt Edith in a contempt too vast to be expressed in words. "Pat, you're the only one who seems to have any influence . . . *any* influence . . . over that infatuated man now. Can't you put him off this notion in some way? At least, you can try."

Pat promised to try, by way of preventing Aunt Edith from having a heart attack, and went up to the spare room to put a great bowl of yellow mums on the brown bureau. If she were to have a new aunt she must be friends with her. Alienation from Swallowfield was unthinkable. Pat sighed. What a pity it all was! They had been so happy and contented there for years. She hated change more than ever.

2

Mrs. Merridew was coming on the afternoon train and Uncle Tom was going to meet her with the span.

"I suppose I ought to have an automobile, Pat. She'll think this turn-out very old-fashioned."

"She won't see prettier horses anywhere," Pat encouraged. And Uncle Tom drove away with what he hoped was a careless and romantic air. Outwardly he really looked as solemn as his photograph in the family album but at heart he was a boy of twenty again, keeping tryst with an old dream that was to him as of yesterday.

Tillytuck persisted in hanging around although Judy hinted that there was work waiting on the other place. Tillytuck took no hints. "I'm always interested in courtings," he averred shamelessly.

It seemed an endless time after they heard the train blow at Silverbridge before Uncle Tom returned. Sid unromantically proffered the opinion that Uncle Tom had died of fright. Then they heard the span pausing by the gate.

"Here comes the bride," grunted Tillytuck, slipping out by the kitchen door.

Pat and Cuddles ran out to the lawn. Judy peered from the porch window. Tillytuck had secreted himself behind a lilac bush. Even mother, who had one of her bad days and was in bed, raised herself on her pillows to look down through the vines.

They saw Uncle Tom helping out of the phaeton a vast lady who seemed even vaster in a white dress and a large, white, floppy hat. A pair of very fat legs bore her up the walk to the door where the girls awaited her. Pat stared unbelievingly. Could this woman, with feet that bulged over her high-heeled shoes, be the light-footed fairy of Uncle Tom's old dancing dreams?

"And this is Pat? How *are* you, sugar-pie?" Mrs. Merridew gave Pat a hearty hug. "And Cuddles...darling!" Cuddles was likewise engulfed. Pat found her voice and asked the guest to come upstairs. Uncle Tom had spoken no word. It was Cuddles' private opinion that his vocal cords had been paralysed by shock.

"Can that be all one woman?" Tillytuck asked the lilac bush. "I don't like 'em skinny...but..."

"Think av *that* in Swallowfield," Judy said to Gentleman Tom. "Oh, oh, it's widening his front dure as well as painting it Tom Gardiner shud have done."

Gentleman Tom said nothing, as was his habit, but McGinty crawled under the kitchen lounge. And upstairs mother was lying back on her pillows shaking with laughter. "Poor Tom!" she said. "Oh, poor Tom!"

Mrs. Merridew talked and laughed all the way upstairs. She lifted her awful fat arms and removed her hat, showing snow-white hair lying in sleek moulded waves around a face that might once have been pretty but whose red-brown eyes were lost in pockets of flesh. The red sweet mouth was red still...rather too red. Lipstick was not in vogue at Silver Bush...but the lavish gleam of gold in the teeth inside detracted from its sweetness. As for the laugh that Uncle Tom had remembered, it was merely a fat rumble...yet with something good-natured about it, too.

"Oh, honey, let's sit outside," exclaimed Mrs. Merridew, after she had got downstairs again. They trailed out to the garden after her. Uncle Tom, still voiceless, brought up the rear. Pat did not dare look at him. What on earth was going on in his mind? Mrs. Merridew lowered herself into a rustic chair, that creaked ominously, and beamed about her.

"I love to sit and watch the golden bees plundering the sweets of the clover," she announced. "I adore the country. The city is so artificial. Don't you truly think the city is so artificial, sugar-pie? There can be no real interchange of souls in the city. Here in the beautiful country, under God's blue sky"...Mrs. Merridew raised fat be-ringed hands to it... "human beings can be their real and highest selves. I am sure you agree with me, angel."

"Of course," said Pat stupidly. She couldn't think of an earthly thing to say. Not that it mattered. Mrs. Merridew could and did talk for them all. She babbled on as if she were on the lecture platform and all her audience needed to do was sit and listen. "Are you interested in psychoanalysis?" she asked Pat but waited for no answer. When Judy announced supper Pat asked Uncle Tom to stay and share it with them. But Uncle Tom managed to get out a refusal. He said he must go home and see to the chores.

"Mind, you promised to take me for a drive this evening," said Mrs. Merridew coquettishly. "And, oh, girls, he didn't know me when I got off the train. Fancy that . . . when we were sweethearts in the long ago."

"You were . . . thinner . . . then," said Uncle Tom slowly.

Mrs. Merridew shook a pudgy finger at him.

"We've both changed. You look a good bit older, Tom. But never mind . . . at heart we're just as young as ever, aren't we, honey boy?"

Honey boy departed. Pat and Cuddles and Mrs. Merridew went in to supper. Mrs. Merridew wanted to sit where she could see the beauty of the delphiniums down the garden walk. Her life, she said, was a continual search for beauty.

They put her where she could see the delphiniums and listened in fascinated silence while she talked. Never had any one just like this come to Silver Bush. Fat ladies had been there . . . talkative ladies had been there . . . beaming, good-natured ladies had been there. But never any one half so fat and talkative and beaming and good-natured as Mrs. Merridew. Pat and Cuddles dared not look at each other. Only when Mrs. Merridew gave utterance to the phrase, "a heterogeneous mass of potentiality," as airily as if she had said "the blue of delphiniums" Cuddles kicked Pat under the table and Judy, in the kitchen, said piteously to Tillytuck, "Sure and I used to be able to understand the English language."

The next morning Mrs. Merridew came down to breakfast, looking simply enormous in a blue kimono. She talked all through breakfast and all through the forenoon and all through dinner. In the afternoon she was away driving with Uncle Tom but she talked all through supper. During the early evening she stopped talking, probably through sheer exhaustion, and sat on the rustic chair on the lawn, her hands folded across her satin stomach. When Uncle Tom came over she began talking again and talked through the evening, with the exception of a few moments when she went to the piano and sang, *Once in the Dear Dead Days Beyond Recall*. She sang beautifully and if she had been invisible they would all have enjoyed it. Tillytuck, who was in the kitchen and couldn't see her, declared he was enraptured. But Judy could only wonder if the piano bench would ever be the same again.

"She simply can't forget she isn't on the lecture plat-form," said Pat.

There was no subject Mrs. Merridew couldn't talk about. She discoursed on Christian Science and vitamines, on Bol-shevism and little theatres, on Japan's designs in Manchuria and television, on theosophy and bi-metallism, on the colour of your aura and the value of constructive thinking in contrast to negative thinking, on the theory of re-incarnation and the Higher Criticism, on the planetesimal hypothesis and the trend of modern fiction, on the best way to preserve your furs from moths and how to give a cat castor oil. She reminded Pat of a random verse conned in schooldays and she wrote it of her in her descriptive letter to Hilary.

> *"Her talk was like a stream that runs*
> *With rapid flow from rocks to roses,*
> *She passed from parrakeets to puns,*
> *She leaped from Mahomet to Moses."*

"I do be thinking she ain't mentally sound," groaned Judy. "There was a quare streak in the Hindersons I do be rimimbering. Her grandmother was off be spells and her Great-uncle had his coffin made years afore he died and kipt it under the spare-room bed. Oh, oh, the talk it made."

"I knew the man when I was a boy," said Tillytuck. "His wife kept her fruit cake and the good sheets in it."

Judy went on as if there had been no interruption.

"And yet, in spite av iverything, girls dear, I do be kind av liking her."

In truth, they all "kind of liked" her . . . even mother, who, nevertheless, was compelled by Pat to stay in bed most of the time that she might not be talked to death. Mrs. Merridew was so entirely good-natured and her smile *was* charming. The floors might creak as she walked over them but her spirit was feather-light. She might have a liking for snacks of bread and butter with an inch of brown sugar spread on top of it but there wasn't a scrap of malice in her heart. Judy might speculate pessimistically on what would happen if she fell downstairs but she adored McGinty and was hail-fellow-well-met with all the cats. Even Gentleman Tom succumbed to her spell and waved his thin, stiff tail when she tickled him behind the ears. Judy, who had implicit confidence in Gentleman Tom's insight into human nature, admitted that maybe Tom Gardiner wasn't quite the fool she had been thinking him. For Mrs. Merridew, in spite of her avoirdupois, was "rale cliver round the house." She insisted on helping with the chores and washed dishes and polished silver and swept floors with astonishing deftness, talking ceaselessly and effortlessly all the time. In the evenings she went driving with Uncle Tom or sat with him in the moonlight garden. Nobody could tell what Uncle Tom was thinking, not even Pat. But the aunts had subsided into the calm of despair. They had not called on Mrs. Merridew. . . they would not countenance her in any way. . . but it was their opinion that she had Tom hypnotised.

Pat was sitting on a log in the silver bush one evening. . . her own dear, dim silver bush, full of moon-patterned shadows . . . having crept away to be by herself for a little while. Mrs. Merridew was in the kitchen eating doughnuts, telling Judy how travel broadened the mind, and encouraging her to take her trip to Ireland. Judy's kitchen was certainly not what it used to be just now and Pat was secretly relieved to feel that Mrs. Merridew's visit was drawing to a close. Even if she came back to North Glen it would be to Swallowfield, not to Silver Bush.

Some one came along the path and sat down beside her with a heavy sigh. Uncle Tom! Somehow Pat understood what was in his heart without words . . . that "all that was left of his bright, bright dream" was dust and ashes. Poor mistaken Uncle Tom, who had imagined that the old magic could be recaptured.

"She's expecting me to propose to her again, Patsy," he said, after a long silence.

"Must you?" asked Pat.

"As a man of honour I must . . . and that to-night," said Uncle Tom solemnly. . . and said no more.

Pat decided that silence was golden. After a time they got up and went back to the house. As they emerged from the bush the shadow of a fat woman was silhouetted on the kitchen blind.

"Look at it," said Uncle Tom, with a hollow groan. "I never imagined any one could change so much, Patsy. Patsy . . ." there was a break in Uncle Tom's voice . . . "I . . . I . . . wish I had never seen her *old*, Patsy."

When they went in Mrs. Merridew whisked Uncle Tom off to the Little Parlour. But the next day something rather mysterious happened. Mrs. Merridew announced at breakfast that she must catch the ten-fifteen train to town and would Sid be kind enough to drive her down to Silverbridge? She bade them all good-bye cheerily and drew Pat aside for a few whispered sentences.

"Don't blame me, sugar-pie. He told me you knew all about it . . . and I really did intend to take him before I came, darling. But when I saw him . . . well, I knew right off I simply couldn't. Of course it's rotten to let any one down like that but I'm so terribly sensitive in regard to beauty. He was so old-looking and changed. He wasn't a bit like the Tom Gardiner I knew. I want you to be specially good to him and cheer him up until he is once more able to tune his spirit into the rhythm of the happiness vibrations that are all around us. He didn't say much but I knew he was feeling my decision very deeply. Still, after a little he'll see for himself that it is all for the best."

She climbed into the waiting car, waved a chubby, dimpled hand at them and departed.

"I hope the springs av that car will be lasting till they get to the station," said Judy. "And whin's the widding to be, Patsy?"

"Never at all," smiled Pat. "It's all off."

"Thank the Good Man Above for that," said Judy devoutly. "Oh, oh, it was a rale noble act av ye to ask her here, Patsy, and ye've had yer reward. If yer Uncle Tom had got ingaged to her be letter he'd have had to have stuck to it, no matter what he filt like whin he saw her. And it isn't but what I liked her, Patsy, and it's sorry for her disappointmint I am . . . but she wud niver have done for a wife for Tom Gardiner. It's well he had the sinse to see it, aven at the last momint."

Pat said nothing. Uncle Tom said nothing . . . neither then nor at any other time. His little flyer in romance was over. The negotiations for the Silverbridge bungalow were abruptly dropped. The aunts both persisted in thinking that Pat had "influenced" Uncle Tom and were overwhelmingly grateful to her. In vain Pat assured them she had done nothing.

"Don't tell *me*," said Aunt Edith. "He was simply *fascinated* from the moment she came. He went around like a man in a dream. But *something* held him back from the last fatal step and that something was *you,* Pat. She'll be furious that he's slipped through her fingers again of course."

Still Pat held her tongue. They would never believe Mrs. Merridew had actually refused Tom and that he thanked heaven for his escape.

Life at Swallowfield and Silver Bush settled back into its customary tranquillity.

"I must write all about it to Hilary," said Pat, sitting down at her window in the afterglow. The world was afloat in primrose light, pale and exquisite. The garden below was alive with robins, and swallows were skimming low across the meadows. The hill field was a sea of wheaten gold and beyond it velvety dark spruces were caressing crystal air. How lovely everything was! How everything seemed to beckon to her! What a *friendly* farm Silver Bush was! And how beautiful it was to have a quiet evening again, with a "liddle bite" and a glorious gab-fest with Judy later on in prospect. And oh, how glad she was that there was to be no change at Swallowfield. Hilary would be glad to hear it, too.

"I wish I could slip that sunset into the letter and send it to him," she thought. "I remember when I was about six saying to Judy, 'Oh, Judy, isn't it lovely to live in a world where there are sunsets?' I still think it is."

3

During the autumn and winter after the shadow of a new bride at Swallowfield had vanished from Pat's sky life went on at Silver Bush delightfully. It was a very cold winter . . . so cold that there was not only frost but feathers on the windows most of the time . . . and there was much snow and wild wind in birch and spruce. And never a thaw, not even in January, although Tillytuck was loath to give up hope of one.

"I've never seen a January without a thaw yet and I've seen hundreds of them," he asserted . . . and wondered grumpily why everybody laughed. But he saw one that year. The cold continued unbroken. The stones around Judy's flower beds always wore white snow caps and looked like humpy little gnomes. Pat was glad the garden was covered up. It always hurt her to see her beautiful garden in winters when there was little snow... so forsaken looking, with mournful bare flower stalks sticking up out of the hard frozen earth and bare, writhing shrubs that you never could believe could be mounds of rosy blossoms in June. It was nice to think of it sleeping under a spotless coverlet, dreaming of the time when the first daffodil would usher in spring's age of gold.

And there was beauty, too, everywhere. Sometimes Pat thought the winter woods with their white reserve and fearlessly displayed nakedness seemed the rarest and finest of all. You never knew how beautiful a tree really was until you saw it leafless against a pearl-grey winter sky. And was there ever anything quite so perfect as the birch grove in a pale-rose twilight after a fine calm fall of snow?

In the stormy evenings Silver Bush, snug and sheltered, holding love, laughed defiance through its lighted windows at the grey night full of driving snow. They all crowded into Judy's kitchen and ate apples and candy, while happy cats purred and a wheezy little dog who, alas, was growing old and a bit deaf, snored at Pat's feet. Wild and weird or gay and thrilling were the tales told by Judy and Tillytuck in a rivalry that sometimes convulsed the Silver Bush folks. Judy had taken to locating most of her yarns in Ireland and when she told a gruesome tale of the man who had made a bargain with the Bad Man Below and broke it Tillytuck could not possibly claim to have known or been the man.

"What was the bargain, Judy?"

"Oh, oh, it was for his wife's life. She was to live as long as he niver prayed to God. But if he prayed to God she wud die and *he* was to belong to Ould Satan foriver. Sure and she lived for minny a year. And thin me fine man got a bit forgetful-like and one day whin the pig bruk its leg he sez, sez he, in a tragic tone, 'Oh God!' sez he. And his wife did be dying that very night."

"But that wasn't a prayer, Judy."

"Oh, oh, but it was. Whin ye cry on God like that in inny trouble it do be a prayer. The Bad Man Below knew it well."

"What became of the husband, Judy?"

"Oh, oh, he was *taken away*," said Judy, contriving to convey a suggestion of indescribable eeriness that sent a shiver down everybody's back. Satisfied with the effect she remarked deprecatingly,

"But listen to me prating av ould days. I'd be better imployed setting me bread."

And while Judy set the bread Tillytuck would spin a yarn of being chased by wolves one moonlit night while skating and told it so well that every one shuddered pleasantly. But Judy said coldly,

"I did be rading that very story, Tillytuck, in Long Alec's ould Royal Rader in me blue chist."

"I daresay you read something like it," retorted Tillytuck unabashed. "I never claimed to be the only man chased by wolves."

Then they all had "a liddle bite" and went to bed, snuggled warm and cosy while the winds ravened outside.

Dwight Madison took to haunting Silver Bush that winter and it was quite plain that he had, as Sid said, "a terrible ailment called serious intentions." Pat tried to snub him. Dwight wouldn't *be* snubbed. It never occurred to Dwight that any girl would want to snub him. Aunt Hazel was hot in his favour but Judy, for a wonder, was not. He was a too deadly serious, solemn, in-earnest young man for Judy.

"De ye be calling *that* a beau?" she demanded after his first visit in a tone that implied she would rather call it something the cats had brought in. Pat said she thought he snored and Cuddles remarked that he looked like spinach. After that, there was no more to be said and Long Alec, who rather favoured Dwight because he had prospects from a bachelor uncle, concluded that modern girls were hard to please. Aunt Hazel was quite cool to Pat for a time.

Bold-and-Bad had pneumonia in March but got over it, thanks, it was believed, to Tillytuck's ministrations. Tillytuck sat up with him two whole nights in the granary chamber, keeping him covered with a blanket in a box by the open window. Twice during each night Judy ploughed out to him through the snow to carry him a hot cup of tea and "a liddle bite." Gentleman Tom did not have pneumonia but he had a narrow escape of his own, which Judy related with gusto.

"Girls dear, niver did I be hearing av such a thing. Ye'll be rimimbering that whin we had the rolled roast for dinner Sunday I did be taking out the string afore I tuk it to the table and throwing it into the wood-box? Oh, oh, and this afternoon whin I come in didn't Gintleman Tom be sitting there be the stove, wid something hanging from his mouth like a rat's tail. Whin I looked closer I saw it was a bit av string and

I tuk hould av it and pulled it. I did be pulling out over a yard av it. The baste had swallied it till he was full av it and cudn't quite manage the last two inches and it did be that saved his life for niver cud he have digested it. But, girls dear, if ye cud have seen the look on his face whin I was pulling at the string! And from this out it's burning ivery roast string at once I'll be doing for we don't want inny more av our cats committing suicide in that fashion."

"Another joke for you to write to Hilary, Pat," said Cuddles slyly.

But at last they were throwing open the windows to let in the spring and Pat learned all over again how lovely young cherry trees were, waving whitely in green twilights, and the scent of apple blossoms in moonlight, and the colonies of blue grape-hyacinths under the dining-room windows. But there were some clouds on her horizon, no bigger than a man's hand yet fraught with worrisome possibilities. She could not settle down in perfect peace, even after house-cleaning was, as Tillytuck said, "all done though not quite finished." There was a lick of paint to be administered here and there, some curtains to be mended, the early carrots to be thinned out and dozens of delightful little things like that to be attended to. But ever and anon what Hawthorne calls "a dreary presentiment of impending change," crept across her happiness like a hint of September coolness stealing athwart the languor of an August afternoon. For one thing, trees were dying everywhere as a result of the bitter winter or because of some disease. The cross little spruce tree at the garden gate, which had grown up into a cross big tree, died, and although Pat had liked it the least of all the trees she grieved over its death. It was heartrending to walk through the woods at the back and see a friend here and there turning brown or failing to leaf out. Even the huge spruce in Happiness was dying and one of Hilary's "twin spires."

For another thing, Judy was by now quite keen on going to Ireland for a visit in the fall. Pat hated the very thought but she knew she must not be selfish and horrid. Judy had served Silver Bush long and faithfully and deserved a holiday if any one ever did. Pat choked down her dismay and talked encouragingly. Of course Judy must go. There was nothing in the world to prevent her. Cuddles was going to try the Entrance in July and if she passed would likely be away at Queen's next year, but somebody could be got in to help Pat during Judy's absence. Judy would stay all winter of course. It would not be worth going for less and a winter crossing of the Atlantic was not advisable. The Atlantic! When Pat thought of the Atlantic rolling between her and Judy she felt absolutely sick. But Cuddles was "thrilled" about it all.

"Thrilled, is it?" said Judy rather sourly. "Ye'll be having thrills wid a vengeance if ould Mrs. Bob Robinson comes here in me place. She's the only one we can be getting, it sames. Oh, oh, what'll me poor kitchen be in her rajame?"

"But think of all the fun you'll have when you come back, putting it to rights, Judy."

"Oh, oh, ye've got the right philosophy av it," agreed Judy brightening up. "Did I be telling ye I had a letter from me cousin in Ireland to-day?"

They had been very curious about that letter. A letter for Judy was a phenomenon at Silver Bush And Judy had been curiously affected by it. If it had been possible for her to turn pale she would have done so. She had taken the letter and stalked off to the graveyard to read it. All the rest of the day she had been strangely quiet.

"I sint her a scratch av me pin back a bit. I hadn't been hearing from her for over twinty years and thinks I to mesilf, 'Maybe she's dead but at innyrate I'll find out.' And to-day along comes her answer. Living and flourishing and that glad to think av me visiting her. And me ould Uncle Michael Plum do be living yet at ninety-five and calling his son av sivinty a saucy young felly whiniver he conterdicts him! It did be giving me a quare faling, Patsy. I'm thinking I know what it's going to be like on the resurrection day, no less."

"Hilary is going across this month," said Pat. "He has won the Bannister scholarship and is going to spend the summer in France, sketching French country houses."

Pat did not tell them everything about the matter. She did not tell them that Hilary had asked her a certain question again. If she could answer it as he wished he would spend the summer in P. E. Island instead of in France. But Pat was sure she couldn't answer it as he wished. She loved him so dearly as a friend but that was all.

"I'm putting into this letter," she concluded, "a little corner of the orchard, a young fir all overgrown with green tassel tips, that moonlit curve you remember in Jordan . . . a bit of wild plum spray . . . a wind that has blown over spice ferns . . . the purr of a little cat and the bark of a little dog who

desires to be remembered to you...and always my best
friendly love. Isn't that enough, Hilary, darling? Come home
and enjoy these things and let us have one more summer of
our old jolly companionship."

Her heart glowed with the thought of it. There never
was such a chum and playfellow in the whole world as Hilary.
But Hilary couldn't see it that way: and so he was going to
France. Perhaps Hilary knew more about some things than
Pat ever told him. Cuddles wrote to him occasionally and told
him more of Pat's goings-on than Pat ever dreamed of. Hilary
knew of all the would-be's who came to Silver Bush and it
may be that Cuddles coloured her accounts a trifle highly.
Certainly Hilary somehow got the impression that Pat had
developed into a notable flirt, with no end of desperate lovers
at her feet. Even when Cuddles wrote about Dwight Madison
she did not mention his goggling eyes or the fact that he was
an agent on commission for farm implements. Instead she
said he was President of the Young Men's Bible Class and that
dad thought him a very sensible young man who would have
oodles of money when his bachelor uncle died. If it had not
been for that dramatic epistle of Cuddles...who honestly
thought she was doing Pat a good turn by trying to make
Hilary jealous...Hilary might have come to the Island that
summer after all. He was too used to being turned down by
Pat as a lover to be discouraged by that alone.

Then there was the rumour that Sid was engaged to
Dorothy Milton. Jealousy went through Pat like a needle
whenever she heard it. Vainly she tried to comfort herself by
thinking that, at any rate, Sid could not marry until the other
place was paid for and a new house built on it. The old house
had been torn down and the lumber in it used to build a new
stable. Pat had felt sad over that, too. It had been Hilary's
home and they had signalled back and forth on cool blue
summer nights. As for Dorothy Milton, she was a nice girl
undoubtedly and would be a very suitable wife for Sid if he
had to marry some day. Pat told herself this a hundred times
without making much impression on something that would
not be reconciled. She was hurt, too, that, if it were true, Sid
had not told her. They were such chums in everything else.
He consulted her in everything else. Sid was taking over the
running of the farm more and more, as Long Alec devoted
himself to stock-raising on the other place. Every Sunday
evening Pat and Sid would walk over the entire farm and note

the crops and fences and plan for the future. It was Sid's ambition to make Silver Bush the best farm in North Glen and Pat was with him heart and soul. If only things could go on forever like this! When Pat read her Bible chapter one night she found the verse, "Meddle not with them that are given to change," and underscored it three times. Solomon, she felt, had gone to the root of things.

Cuddles was another of Pat's problems... or rather Rae, as she must henceforth be called. On her birthday she had gathered all the family around her and told them without circumlocution that they were not to call her Cuddles any more. She would simply not take any notice of anything that was said to her unless she was called Rae. And she stuck to it. It was hard at first. They all hated to give up the dear, absurd old name that was linked with so many sweet memories of Cuddles when she was an adorable baby, when she was a new school-girl, when she was in her arms-and-legs stage, when she was just stepping daintily into her teens. But Cuddles stood to her guns and they got into the new habit sooner than they would have thought possible... all except Judy. Judy did try her best but she could never do better than "Cud-Rae," which was so ridiculous that Rae eventually yielded a point and let Judy revert to the old name.

The Silver Bush folks had suspected for some time that Rae was going to be the beauty of the family and at last they were sure of it. Martin Madison, who had three ugly daughters, said contemptuously that Rae Gardiner was only two dimples and a smile. But there was more to her than that. Tillytuck considered that he had put it in a nutshell when he said she had all the other North Glen girls skinned a mile. There was some "glamour" about her that they didn't have. She really had a headful of brains and talked of being a doctor... more to horrify Judy than anything else since she had really no especial hankering for a "career." And she was clever enough to conceal her cleverness, especially from the youths who began to come to Silver Bush... boys of the generation after Pat, whom they regarded as quite elderly. Rae was very popular with them: she had a come-and-find out air about her that intrigued them and she had practised a faraway, mysterious smile so faithfully before her mirror that it drove them quite crazy guessing what she was thinking of. None of them interested her at all, not being in the least like the pictures of the movie stars she kept pinned on the wall at the head of her bed. But, she coolly told Pat, they would do for getting your hand in.

Rae was full of life. Her every step was a dance, her every gesture full of grace and virility. She went about looking for thrills and always found them. Pat, looking at the exquisite oval of her little unwritten face, sighed and wondered what life had for this dear sister. She was far more worried over Rae's future than her own and mothered her to what Rae considered an absurd degree. It *was* provoking when you were feeling romantic and ethereal to be cautioned to put on your overshoes! And to be told you were a snob because you complained of Tillytuck saying queer things in the kitchen when you were entertaining a Charlottetown boy and his sister in the Little Parlour.

"I'm *not* a snob, Pat. You know very well Tillytuck is always saying odd things. Of course they're great fun and *we* laugh at them but *strangers* don't understand. And that Little Parlour door *won't* stay shut. I'll *never* forget the look on Jerry Arnold's face last night when he heard Judy and Tillytuck in one of their arguments."

Rae came to an end of breath and italics which gave Pat a chance to say bitingly,

"Jerry Arnold's father was a junk man twenty years ago."

"Who is being the snob now?" retorted Rae. "Jerry is going to have money. Oh, you needn't look at me like that, Pat. I've no notion of ever marrying Jerry Arnold . . . he isn't my style" . . . (was this . . . could this, be little Cuddles who was a baby day before yesterday?) . . . "but when I *do* marry I'm going to marry a rich man. I admit I'm worldly. I like money. And you know, Pat, we've never had quite enough of that at Silver Bush."

"But think of the other things we've had," said Pat softly. Rae, sweet, absurd little Rae, was not to be taken too seriously. "Not much money I admit but everything else that matters. And besides we've always got to-morrow."

"That sounds very fine but what does it mean?" Rae had taken up a pose of being hard-boiled this spring. "No, my Patricia, one has to be practical in this kind of a world. I've thought it all over carefully and I've decided that I'll marry money . . . and have a good time the rest of my life."

"Have you any one in mind?" enquired Pat sarcastically.

Rae's blue, black-lashed eyes filled with laughter.

"No, darling. There's really plenty of time. Though Trix

Binnie is married... married at seventeen. Just think of it... only two years older than I am. Her face while she was being married was simply a scream. Jerry Arnold says she looked exactly like a kitten that had caught its first mouse."

"Well, we had an excellent view of May's shoulder blades for the space of a quarter of an hour," said Pat, who had been so furious over the Binnies presuming to invite the Gardiners to the wedding that it took Rae a whole evening to persuade her to go to church.

"Those raw-boned girls certainly shouldn't wear backless dresses," said Rae, with a complacent glance over her own shoulder. "Trix really didn't care a bit for Nels Royce, but when she failed in the Entrance last year there was really nothing else for her. It was so funny to hear Mrs. Binnie pretending Trix wouldn't have gone to Queen's even if she had passed. 'I wouldn't have Trix teaching school. I ain't going to have *my* daughter a slave to the public.'"

Pat howled. Rae's mimicry of Mrs. Binnie was inimitable.

"I'm sure May is furious because Trix is married before her," continued Rae. "I suppose she has finally given up hope of Sid, now that he is really engaged to Dorothy Milton."

"Do you suppose... he really is?" asked Pat.

"Oh, yes. She's got her ring. I noticed it last night at choir practice. I wonder when they'll be married."

Pat shivered. She suddenly felt like a very small cat in a very big world. The gold was fading out of the evening sky. A great white moth flew by in the dusk. The spruce wood on the hill had turned black. The moon was rising over the Hill of the Mist. Far down the sea shivered in silver ecstasy. Everything was beautiful but there was something in the air... another chill of change. Rae had suddenly grown up and Sid belonged to them no longer.

Then one of her April changes came over her. After all, the world was full of June and Silver Bush was still the same. She sprang up.

"It's a waste of time to go to bed too early on moonlight nights. And all the wealth of June is ours, no matter how poor we may be according to your worldly standards, darling. Let's get out the car and run over to Winnie's."

Pat had learned to run the car that spring. Judy had been much upset about it and talked gloomily of a girl at the Bridge who had tried to run her father's car, put her foot on the accelerator instead of the brake and had gone clean through a haystack . . . or so Judy had heard. Pat managed to acquire the knack without any such disaster, although Tillytuck averred that on one occasion he saved his life only by jumping over the dog-house, and Judy still came out in gooseflesh when she saw Pat backing the car out of the garage.

"Times do be changed," she remarked to Gentleman Tom. "Here's Patsy and Cuddles dashing off in the car whin they shud be thinking av their bed. Cat dear, is it that I do be getting ould whin I can't get used to it?"

Gentleman Tom put a leg rather stiffly over his shoulder. Perhaps he, too, felt that he was getting old.

4

They heard about the Long House at Winnie's. It was to have new tenants. They had rented the house for the summer . . . not the farm, which was still to be farmed by John Hammond, the owner, who had bought it from the successor of the Wilcoxes.

Pat heard the news with a feeling of distaste. The Long House had been vacant almost ever since Bets had died. A couple had bought the farm, lived there for a few months, then sold out to John Hammond. Pat had been glad of this. It was easier to fancy that Bets was still there when it was empty. In childhood she had resented it being empty and lonely, and had wanted to see it occupied and warmed and lighted. But it was different now. She preferred to think of it as tenanted only by the fragrance of old years and the little spectral joys of the past. Somehow, it seemed to belong to her as long as it was

> "Abandoned to the lonely peace
> Of bygone ghostly things."

Judy had more news the next morning. The newcomers were a man and his sister. Kirk was their name. He was a widower and had been until recently the editor of a paper in Halifax. And they had bought the house, not rented it.

"Wid the garden and the spruce bush thrown in," said Judy. "John Hammond do be still houlding to the farm. He was here last night, after ye wint away, complaining tarrible about the cost av his wife's operation. 'Oh, oh, what a pity,' sez I, sympathetic-like. 'Sure and a funeral wud have come chaper,' sez I. Patsy dear, did ye be hearing Lester Conway was married?"

"Somebody sent me a paper with the notice marked," laughed Pat. "I'm sure it was May Binnie. Fancy any one supposing it mattered to me."

It seemed a lifetime since she had been so wildly in love with Lester Conway. Why was it she never fell in love like that nowadays? Not that she wanted to . . . but *why*? Was she getting too old? Nonsense!

She knew her clan was beginning to say she didn't know what she wanted but she knew quite well and couldn't find it in any of the men who wooed her. As far as they were concerned, she seemed possessed by a spirit of contrariness. No matter how nice they seemed while they were merely friends or acquaintances she could not bear them when they showed signs of developing into lovers. Silver Bush had no rival in her heart.

In the evening she stood in the garden and looked up at the Long House . . . it was suddenly a delicate, aerial pink in the sunset light. Pat had never been near it since the day of Bets' funeral. Now she had a strange whim to visit it once more before the strangers came and took it from her forever . . . to go and keep a tryst with old, sacred memories.

Pat slipped into the house and flung a bright-hued scarf over her brown dress with its neck-frill of pleated pink chiffon. She always thought she looked nicer in that dress than any other. Somehow people seldom wondered whether Pat Gardiner was pretty or not . . . she was so vital, so whole-some, so joyous, that nothing else mattered. Yet her dark-brown hair was wavy and lustrous, her golden-brown eyes held challenging lights and the corners of her mouth had such a jolly quirk. She was looking her best to-night with a little flush of excitement staining her round, creamy cheeks. She felt as if she were slipping back into the past.

Judy was in the kitchen, telling stories to a couple of Aunt Hazel's small fry who were visiting at Silver Bush. Pat caught a sentence or two as she went out. "Oh, oh, the ears av him, children dear! He cud hear the softest wind walking over the hills and what the grasses used to say to aich other at the sunrising." Dear old Judy! What a matchless storyteller she was!

"I remember how Joe and Win and Sid and I used to sit on the backdoor steps and listen to her telling fairy tales by moonlight," thought Pat, "and whatever she told you you felt had happened . . . *must* have happened. That is the difference between her yarns and Tillytuck's. Oh, it is really awful to think of her going away in the fall for a whole winter."

Pat went up to the Long House by the old delightful short cut past Swallowfield and over the brook and up the hill fields. It was a long time since she had trodden that fairy path but it had not changed. The fields on the hill still looked as if they loved each other. The big silver birch still hung over the log bridge across the brook. The damp mint, crushed under her feet, still gave out its old haunting aroma, and all kinds of wild blossom filled the crevices of the stone dyke where she and Bets had picked wild strawberries. Its base was still lost in a wave of fern and bayberry. And on the hill the Watching Pine still watched and seemed to shake a hand meaningly at her. At the top was the old gate, fallen into ruin, and beyond it the path through the spruce bush where silence seemed to kneel like a grey nun and she felt that Bets must come to meet her, walking through the dusk with dreams in her eyes.

Past the bush she came out on the garden with the house in the midst. Pat stopped and gazed around her. Everything she looked on had some memory of pleasure or pain. The old garden was very eloquent . . . that old garden that had once been so beloved by Bets. She seemed to come back again in the flowers she had tended and loved. The whole place was full of her. She had planted that row of lilies . . . she had trained that vine over the trellis . . . she had set out that rosebush by the porch step. But most of it was now a festering mass of weeds and in its midst was the sad, empty house, with the little dormer window in its spruce-shadowed roof . . . the window of the room where she had seen the sunrise light falling over Bets' dead face. A dreadful pang of loneliness tore her soul.

"I hate those people who are going to live in you," she told the house. "I daresay they'll tear you up and turn you inside out. That will break my heart. You won't be *you* then."

She went across the garden, along an old mossy walk where the unpruned rosebushes caught at her dress as if they wanted to hold her. Across the lawn, overgrown with grass, to the cherry orchard and around its curve. Then she stopped short in amazed embarrassment.

In a little semicircle of young spruces was a fire of applewood, like a vivid rose of night. Two people were squatted on the grass before it... two people and a dog and a cat. The dog, a splendid white and gold creature, who looked as if he could understand a joke, sat beside the man, and the cat, black, bigger than any cat had a right to be, with pale-green moonlike eyes, was snuggled down beside the girl, his beautiful white paws folded under his snowy breast. Pat, in a surge of unreasonable indignation... Bets had set out that semicircle of trees... muttered a curt "Pardon me... I didn't mean to... intrude."

She, Pat, an *intruder* here! It was bitter.

But before she could turn and vanish the girl had sprung to her feet, run across the intervening space and caught Pat's arm.

"Don't go," she said imploringly. "Oh, don't go. Stop and get acquainted. You must be one of the Gardiner girls from Silver Bush. I've been hearing about you."

"I'm Pat Gardiner," said Pat curtly. She knew she was being silly and bitter but for the moment she could not help it. She almost hated this girl: and yet there was something undeniably attractive about her. You felt that from the very first. She was a little taller than Pat and she wore knicker-bockers and a khaki shirt. She had long, slanted, grey-green eyes with long fair lashes that should have gone with fair hair. But her hair was sloe-black, worn in a glossy braid around her head and waving back from her forehead in a peculiarly virile way. Her skin was creamy with a few freckles... delicious freckles, as if they had been shaken out of a pepper-pot over nose and tips of cheeks. She had a crooked clever mouth with a mutinous tilt. Pat didn't think her a bit pretty but she felt drawn to that face in spite of herself.

"And I'm Suzanne Kirk. Really Suzanne. Christened so. Not Susan putting on frills. Now we know each other... or rather we've known each other for hundreds of years. I recognised you as soon as I saw you. Come and squat with us."

Pat, still a little stiff, let herself be pulled over to the fire. She wanted to be friendly... and yet she didn't.

"This is my brother, David, Miss Gardiner."

David Kirk got up and put out a long lean brown hand. He was quite old... forty, if a day, Pat thought mercilessly... and there were grey dabs in the dark hair over his ears. He was not handsome, yet he was certainly what Judy would have called "a bit distinguished-like." There was a good deal of his sister's charm in his face and though his eyes were grey-blue instead of grey-green, there was the same tilt to his mouth . . . perhaps a little more decided . . . a little cynical. And when he spoke, although he said only, "I am glad to meet you, Miss Gardiner," there was something in his voice that made everything he said seem significant.

"And this is Ichabod," said Suzanne, waving her hand to the dog, who thumped his tail ingratiatingly. "Of course it's an absurd name for a lordly creature like him but David wanted to give him a name no dog had ever had before. I'm *sure* no dog was ever called Ichabod before, aren't you?"

"I never heard of one." Pat felt that she was yielding in spite of herself. It *did* seem as if she had known them before.

"Our cat is called Alphonso-of-the-emerald-eyes. Alphonso, meet Miss Gardiner."

Alphonso did not wave his tail. He merely blinked a disdainful eye and went on being Alphonso-of-the-emerald-eyes. Suzanne whispered to Pat,

"He is a haughty cat of ancient lineage but he likes being tickled under the ear just as well as if he were a cat who didn't know who his grandfather was. He understands every word we say but he never gossips. Pick out a soft spot of ground, Miss Gardiner, and we'll have a nice do-nothing time."

For a moment Pat hesitated. Then she curled up beside Alphonso.

"I suppose I've been trespassing," she said, "but I didn't know you'd come yet. So I wanted to come up and say good-bye to the Long House. I . . . I used to come here a great deal. I have very dear memories of it."

"But you are not going to say good-bye to it . . . and you are going to come here a great deal again. I know we are going to be good friends," said Suzanne. "David and I want neighbours . . . want them terribly. And we're not really moved in yet . . . we're going to sleep in the hay-loft to-night . . . but our furniture is all in there higgledy-piggledy. The only thing in place is that old iron lantern over the front door. I *had* to hang that up and put a candle in it. It's our beacon star . . . we'll light it every night. Isn't it lovely? We picked it up one time we were over in France . . . in an old château some king had built for his beloved. David went for his paper and I mortgaged my future for years and went with him. I've never regretted it. It's funny . . . but all the things I do regret were prudent things . . . or what seemed so at the time. David and I have just been prowling about this evening. We arrived two hours ago in a terrible old rattling, banging, squeaking car . . . a second-hand which we bought last week. It took all our spare cash to buy the house but we don't grudge it. The minute we saw that house I knew we must have it. It is a house of delightful personality, don't you think?"

"I've always loved it," said Pat softly.

"Oh, I knew it had been loved the moment I saw it. I think you can always tell when a house has been loved. But it's been asleep for so long. And lonely. It always hurts me to see a house lonely. I felt that I must bring it back to life and chum with it. I *know* it feels happy because we are going to fix it up."

Pat felt the cockles of her heart warming. Houses meant to this girl what they meant to herself . . . creatures, not things.

"We found this pile of apple boughs here and couldn't resist the temptation to light it. There is no wood makes such a lovely fire as applewood. And we're so happy to-night. We've just been hungry for a home . . . with trees and flowers and a cat or two to do our purring for us. We haven't had a home since we were children . . . not even when David was married. He and his wife lived in a little apartment for the short time the poor darling did live. We're short on relations so we'll have to depend on neighbours. It doesn't take much to make us laugh and although we're quite clever we're not so clever that anybody need be scared of us. We can't be very wild . . . David here was shell-shocked somewhere in France when he was twenty and has to live quietly . . . but we do mean to be good friends with life."

"I was bad friends with it when I came up here," said Pat frankly, letting herself thaw a little more. "You see, I really did resent you . . . anybody . . . coming in here. It seemed to belong to a dear friend of mine who used to live here . . . and died six years ago."

"But you don't resent us any longer, do you? Because now you know we love this place, too. We'll be good to your ghosts and your memories, Miss Gardiner."

"I'm just Pat," . . . letting herself go completely.

"Just as I'm Suzanne."

Suddenly they all felt comfortable and congenial. Ichabod lay down . . . Alphonso really went to sleep. The applewood fire crackled and sputtered companionably. About them was the velvet and shadow of the oncoming night with dreaming moonlit trees beyond. In the spruces little winds were gossiping and far below the river gleamed like a blue ribbon tied around its green hill.

"I'm so glad the view goes with the house," said Suzanne. "You don't know how rich it makes me feel just to look at it. And that old garden is one I've always dreamed. I knew I had to have wistaria and larkspur and fox-gloves and canterbury-bells and hollyhocks and here they all are. It's uncanny. We're going to build a stone fireplace here in this crescent of trees. It just wants it."

"Bets . . . my friend . . . planted those trees. They're hers . . . really . . . but she won't mind lending them to you."

Suzanne reached across Alphonso and squeezed Pat's hand.

"It's nice of you to say that. No, she won't mind, because we love them. You never mind letting people have things when you know they love them. And she won't mind our making an iris glade in the spruce bush. That is another thing I've always dreamed of . . . hundreds of iris with spruce trees around them . . . all around them, so the glade will never be seen save by those you want to see it. And we can go there when we want to be alone. One needs a little solitude in life."

They sat and talked for what might have been an hour or a century. The talk had colour . . . Pat recognised that fact instantly. Everything they talked of was interesting the moment they touched it. Occasionally there was a flavour of mockery in David Kirk's laughter and a somewhat mordant edge to his wit. Pat thought he was a little bitter but there was something stimulating and pungent about his bitterness and she found herself liking that lean, dark face of his, with its quick smiles. He had a way of saying things that gave them poignancy and Pat loved the fashion in which he and Suzanne could toss a ball of conversation back and forth, always keeping it in the air.

"The moon is going behind a cloud . . . a silvery white cloud," said Suzanne. "I love a cloud like that."

"There are so many things of that sort to give pleasure," said Pat dreamily. "Such *little* things . . . and yet so much pleasure."

"I know . . . like the heart of an unblown rose," murmured Suzanne.

"Or the tang of a fir wood," said David.

"Let's each give a list of loveliest things," said Suzanne. "The things that please us most, just as they come into our heads, no matter what they are. *I* love the strange deep shadows that come just before sunset . . . June bugs thudding against the windows . . . a bite of home-made bread . . . a hot water bottle on a cold winter night . . . wet mossy stones in a book . . . the song of wind in the top of an old pine. Now, Pat?"

"The way a cat folds its paws under its breast . . . blue smoke rising in the air on a frosty winter morning . . . the way my little niece Mary laughs, crinkling up her eyes . . . old fields dreaming in moonlight . . . the scrunch of dry leaves under your feet in the silver bush in November . . . a baby's toes . . . the smell of clean clothes as you take them off the line."

"David?"

"The cold of ice," said David slowly. "Alphonso's eyes . . . the smell of rain after burning drouth . . . water at night . . . a leaping flame . . . the strange dark whiteness of a winter night . . . brook-brown eyes in a girl."

It never occurred to Pat that David Kirk was trying to pay her a compliment. She thought her eyes were yellow . . . "cat's eyes," May Binnie had said. She wondered if David Kirk's dead young wife had had brook-brown eyes.

The Kirks walked down the hill with her and she made them go into the kitchen and have some of Judy's orange biscuits with a glass of milk. There was no place else to take them for Rae had callers in the Big Parlour and mother had an old friend in the Little Parlour and Long Alec was colloguing with the minister in the dining-room. But the Kirks were people you'd just as soon take into the kitchen as not. Judy was excessively polite, in spite of Suzanne's shirt and knickerbockers . . . too polite, really. Judy didn't know what to make of this sudden intimacy.

"I want to see lots of you . . . I'm sure we are going to be good friends."

Sid, coming in, spoke to them on the doorstep.

"Do you know them?" asked Pat in surprise.

"Met them in the Silverbridge store this afternoon. The

girl asked me if I knew who lived in the queer old-fashioned place at the foot of the hill."

Pat, who had been feeling very rich, suddenly felt poor... horribly poor. She went out into the garden and looked at Silver Bush... friendly Silver Bush with its lights welcoming all the world. Blossoms cool with night were around her but they meant nothing to her. Squedunk slithered through the delphiniums to rub against her leg and she never even noticed him. The colour had gone out of everything.

"She dared to laugh at you... she dared to call you old-fashioned," she whispered to the house. She shook her brown fist at the darkness. She had never been able to hear Silver Bush disparaged in any way. She had hated Uncle Brian last week because he had said that Silver Bush was settling on its foundations and getting a slant to its floors. And now she hated Suzanne Kirk. Suzanne, indeed! No more of Suzanne for her. To think she had been ready to accept her as a friend... to put her in Bets' place! To think she had hobnobbed with her around the applewood fire and told her sacred things! But never again.

"I... I feel just like a caterpillar somebody had stepped on," said Pat chokily.

In the kitchen the genius of prophecy had descended upon Tillytuck.

"That'll be a match some day, mark my words, Judy Plum."

"Ye wud better go out and look at the moon," scoffed Judy. "Beaus don't be so scarce at Silver Bush that Patsy nades to take up wid *that*. He do be old enough to be her father. We'll have to be rale civil to him though, for they tell me he do be writing a book and if we offind him he might be putting us into it."

Up at the Long House David Kirk was saying to Suzanne, "She makes me think of a woodland brook."

5

Pat snubbed Suzanne when the latter telephoned down to ask her and Sid to their house-warming. She could not go because she had another engagement for the evening... which was quite true, for, knowing that the house-warming was coming off, she had promised to go to a dance in South Glen.

And when Suzanne and David came down the hill path one evening on their way to a moonlit concert which the boarders at the Bay Shore hotel were giving on the North Glen sandshore, and asked Pat to go with them she was entirely gracious and aloof and very sorry she couldn't possibly go . . . with no more excuse than that. Though in her heart she wanted to go. But something in her had been hurt too deeply. She could never forgive a jibe at Silver Bush, as unlucky Lester Conway had discovered years ago, and she took a bitter delight in refusing very sweetly. . . "oh, oh, tarrible polite she was," Judy reported to Tillytuck. Judy was just as well pleased that this threatened friendship with the Long House people seemed unlikely to materialise. "Widowers do be sly. . . tarrible sly," she reflected.

Suzanne was not one of those who could not take a hint and Pat was troubled with no more invitations. The lights gleamed in the Long House at evening but Pat resolutely turned her eyes away from them. Music drifted down the hill when Suzanne played on her violin in the garden under the stars but Pat shut her ears to it.

And yet she felt by times a strange hint of loneliness. Just now and then came a queer, hitherto unknown feeling, expressed by the deadly word "drab" . . . as if life were made of grey flannel. Then she felt guilty. Life at Silver Bush could never be *that*. She wanted nothing but Silver Bush and her own family. . . nothing!

Rae contributed a bit to the comedy of living that summer by having a frightful attack of schoolgirl veal love, the object of which was a young evangelist who was holding revival meetings in Mr. Jonas Monkman's big barn. He did not approve of "organised churches" and these services were in the nature of a free-for-all and, being very lively of their kind, attracted crowds, some of whom came to scoff and remained to pray. For it could not be denied that the young preacher had a very marked power for stirring the emotions of his hearers to concert pitch. He had an exceedingly handsome, marble-white face with rather too large, too soft, too satiny brown eyes and long, crinkly, mahogany-hued hair, sweeping back in a mane from what Rae once incautiously said was "a noble brow," and a remarkably caressing, wooing voice, expressive of everything. The teen-agers went down like ninepins before him. A choir was collected, consisting of everybody in the two Glens who could be persuaded to function. Rae, who sang sweetly, was leading soprano, looking like the very rose of song as she carolled with her eyes turned heavenward . . . or at least towards the banners of cobwebs hanging from the roof of the barn. She went every night, gave up teasing to be allowed to wear knickerbockers around home, and discarded costume earrings because the evangelist referred to jewelry as "gauds . . . all gauds." She was tormented terribly because of her "case" on the preacher, but she gave as good as she got and nobody except Pat thought it was anything but a passing crush. For that matter, all the girls were more or less in love with him and it was difficult to tell where love left off and religion began, as Elder Robinson remarked sarcastically. But Elder Robinson did not approve of the revivals conducted by itinerant evangelists . . . "go-preachers" he called them. And Rae and her ilk considered Elder Robinson a hide-bound old fossil. Even when Jedidiah Madison of Silverbridge, who hadn't been inside of a church for years, wandered into the barn one night and was saved in three minutes Elder Robinson was still incredulous of any good thing. "Let us see if it lasts," he was reported to have said . . . and added that he had just been reading of a very successful evangelist who had turned out to be a bank bandit. Pat had no fear that Mr. Wheeler was a bandit but she detested him and was as puzzled as alarmed over Rae's infatuation.

Tillytuck was likewise hard-boiled and said that the meetings were merely a form of religious dissipation. Judy went one night out of curiosity but could never be prevailed on to go again. Mr. Wheeler played a violin solo that night and she was horrified. No matter if the meeting was held in a barn. It was, or purported to be, Divine Service and fiddles had no place in such. Neither had she any exalted opinion of the sermon. "Oh, oh, not much av a pracher that! Sure and I cud understand ivery word he said." So Pat and Rae were the only ones who went regularly . . . Pat going because Rae was so set on it . . . and very soon it was bruited abroad in the Glens that the Gardiner girls meant to leave the Presbyterian church and join the go-preachers. It blistered Pat's pride to hear it and she was less than civil to Mr. Wheeler when he walked home with them after the meeting. To be sure it was on the way to his boarding house and he always walked by Pat and not by Rae, but Pat was the suspicious older guardian sister to the backbone. It was all very well to laugh at calf love but Rae must be protected. It was a real relief to Pat's mind when, after six hectic weeks, Mr. Wheeler departed for pastures new and Mr. Monkman's barn reverted to rats and silence. Rae continued to blush furiously for several weeks when Sid teased her about her boy-friend. . . . Mr. Wheeler had said that he was glad to find there were still girls in the world who *could* blush . . . but nothing more came of it and Pat's alarm subsided. Rae was asked to sing in the South Glen choir . . . began to experiment with the effect of her eye-lashes on the tenor and wear "gauds" again . . . and everything blew over, save for a little knot of faithful disciples who continued to hold services of their own in their homes and would have nothing further to do with churches of any description.

6

Pat was in a store in town one evening when Suzanne Kirk came up to her and, in spite of Pat's frigid bow, said smilingly,

"May I have a chance home with you, Miss Gardiner? David was to have run in for me but something must have gone wrong with our Lizzie."

"Oh, certainly," said Pat graciously.

"You are sure it won't crowd you?"

"Not in the least," said Pat more graciously still. Inwardly she was furious. She had promised herself a pleasant leisurely drive home through the golden August evening, over a certain little back road where nobody ever went and where there were such delicious things to see. Pat knew all the roads home from town and liked each for some peculiar charm. But now everything was spoiled. Well, she would go by the regular road and get home as soon as she could. She made the car screech violently as she rounded the first corner. It seemed to express her feelings.

"Don't let's go home by this road," said Suzanne softly. "There's so much traffic . . . and it's so straight. A straight road is an abomination, don't you think? I like lovely turns around curves of ferns and spruce . . . and little dips into brooky hollows . . . and the things the car lights pick up as you turn corners, starting out at you in the undergrowth like fairy folk taken by surprise."

"A thunderstorm is coming up," said Pat, more graciously every time she spoke.

"Oh, we'll out-race it. Let us take the road out from that street. David and I went by that last week... it's a dear, lost, bewitching road."

Oh, didn't she know it! Pat turned the car so abruptly in the direction of the back road that she narrowly avoided a collision. How dare Suzanne Kirk, who had called Silver Bush queer, like that road? It was an insult. She hated to have Suzanne Kirk like anything she liked. Well, the road was rough and rutty... and the thunderstorm was an excuse for driving fast. Suzanne Kirk should have a good bumpy drive that would cure her of her liking for back roads.

Pat did not talk or try to talk. Neither, after a few futile attempts, did Suzanne. They were about half way home when the latter said, with a tinge of alarm in her voice,

"The storm is coming up rather quickly, isn't it?"

Pat had been grimly aware of that for some time. It was growing dark. Huge menacing black masses were piling up in the northwest in the teeth of a rapidly rising wind. This was a frightful road to be on in a rain... narrow and twisting, with reedy ditches on either side. Curves and dips and startled fairy folk were all very well in fine weather, but in wind and rain and darkness... and all three seemed to envelop them at once... a wall of black... an ocean of driving rain... a howl of tempest... a blue-white flare of lightning... a deafening crash of thunder... and then disaster. The car had swerved on the suddenly greasy road and the next moment they were in the ditch.

Well, it might have been worse. The car was right-side up and the ditch was not deep. But it was full of soft mud under its bracken and Pat knew she could never get the car back to the road.

"There's nothing to do but stay here till the storm is over and some one comes along," she said. "I'm... I'm sorry I've ditched you, Miss Kirk."

"Never be sorry. This is an adventure. What a storm! It's been brewing all day but I really didn't expect it so soon. What time is it?"

"Eight-thirty. The trouble is this is *such* a back road. Very few people travel on it at any time. And houses are few and far between. But I think that last glare of lightning showed one off to the right. As soon as the rain stops I'll go to it and see if I can get somebody to haul us out ... or at least phone for help."

It was an hour before the storm passed. It was pitch dark by now and the ditch in which they sat so snugly was a rushing river.

"I'm going to try to make that house," said Pat resolutely.

"I'll go with you," said Suzanne. "I won't stay here alone. And I've got a flashlight in my bag."

They managed to get out of the car and out of the ditch. There was no use in hunting for the gate, if there was a gate, but when Suzanne's flashlight showed a place where it was possible to scramble over the fence they scrambled over it and through a wilderness of raspberry canes. Beyond this a barn loomed up and they had to circumnavigate it in mud. Finally they reached the house.

"No lights," said Pat as they mounted the crazy steps to a dilapidated veranda. "I'm afraid nobody lives here. There are several old uninhabited houses along this road and it's just our luck to strike one."

"What a queer, old-fashioned place!" said Suzanne, playing her flashlight over it. She couldn't have said anything more unfortunate. Pat, who had thawed out a trifle, froze up again.

She knocked on the door ... knocked again ... took up a board lying near and pounded vigorously ... called aloud ... finally yelled. There was no response.

"Let us see if it is locked," said Suzanne, trying the latch. It wasn't. They stepped in. The flashlight revealed a kitchen that did not seem to have been lived in for many a day. There was an old rusty stove, a trestle table, several dilapidated chairs, and a still more dilapidated couch.

"Any port in a storm," said Suzanne cheerfully. "I suggest, Miss Gardiner, that we camp here for the night. It's beginning to rain again ... listen ... and we may be miles from an inhabited house. We can bring in the rugs. You take the couch and I'll pick out the softest spot on the floor. We'll be dry at least and in the morning we can more easily get assistance."

Pat agreed that it was the only thing to do. They would probably not worry at Silver Bush. It had not been certain that she would return home that night ... an old Queen's classmate had asked her to visit her. They went back to the car, got the rugs and locked it up. Pat insisted that Suzanne should take the couch and Suzanne was determined Pat should have it. They solved it by flipping a coin.

Pat wrapped a rug around her and curled up on the couch. Suzanne lay down on the floor with a cushion under her head. Neither expected to sleep. Who could sleep with a sploshy thud of rain falling regularly near one and rats scurrying overhead. After what seemed hours Suzanne called softly across the room,

"Are you asleep, Miss Gardiner?"

"No...I feel as if I could never sleep again."

Suzanne sat up.

"Then for heaven's sake let's talk. This is ghastly. I've a mortal horror of rats. There seem to be simply swarms of them in this house. Talk...talk. You needn't pretend to like me if you don't. And for the matter of that, as one woman to another, why don't you like me, Pat Gardiner? Why *won't* you like me? I thought you did that night by the fire. And we liked you...we thought there was something simply dear about you. And then when we called on our way to the concert...why, we seemed to be looking at you through glass! We couldn't get near you at all. David was hurt but I was furious...simply furious. I'm sure my blood boiled. I could hear it bubbling in my veins. Oh, how I hoped your husband would beat you! And yet, every night since, I've been watching your kitchen light and wondering what was going on in it and wishing we could drop in and fraternise. I can't imagine you and I not being friends...*real* friends. We were made for it. Isn't it Kipling who says, 'There is no gift like friendship?'"

"Yes...Parnesius in *Puck*," said Pat.

"Oh, you know *Puck*, too? Now, why can't we give that gift to each other?"

"Did you think," said Pat in a choked voice, "that I could be friends with any one who...who laughed at Silver Bush?"

"Laugh at Silver Bush! Pat Gardiner, I never did. How could I? I've loved it from the first moment David and I looked down on it."

Pat sat up on the creaking couch.

"You...you asked in the Silverbridge store who lived in that *queer* old-fashioned place. Sid heard you."

"Pat! Let me think. Why, I remember...I *didn't* say 'queer.' I said, 'Who lives in that dear, quaint, old-fashioned house at the foot of the hill?' Sid forgot one of the adjectives and was mistaken in one of the others. Pat, I couldn't call Silver Bush 'queer.' You don't know how much I admire it. And I admire it all the more because it *is* old-fashioned. That is why I loved the Long House at first sight."

Pat felt the ice round her heart thawing rapidly. "Quaint" was complimentary rather than not and she didn't mind the "old-fashioned." And she did want to be friends with Suzanne. Perhaps Suzanne was prose where Bets had been poetry. But such prose!

"I'm sorry I froze up," she said frankly. "But I'm such a thin-skinned creature where Silver Bush is concerned. I couldn't bear to hear it called queer."

"I don't blame you. And now everything is going to be all right. We just *belong*, somehow. Don't you feel it? You're all so nice. I love Judy . . . the wit and sympathy and blarney of her. And that wonderful old, wise, humorous face of hers. She's really a museum piece . . . there's nothing like her anywhere else in the world. You'll like us, too. I'm decent in spots and David is nice . . . sometimes he's very nice. One day he is a philosopher . . . the next day he is a child."

"Aren't all men?" said Pat, tremendously wise.

"David more than most, I think. He's had a rotten life, Pat. He was years getting over his shell-shock. It simply blotted out his career. He was so ambitious once. When he got better it was too late. He has been sub-editor of a Halifax paper for years . . . and hating it. His bit of a wife died, too, just a few months after their marriage. And I taught school . . . and hated it. Then old Uncle Murray died out west and left us some money . . . not a fortune but enough to live on. And so we became free. Free! Oh, Pat, you've never known what slavery meant so you don't know what freedom is. I *love* keeping house . . . it's really a lovely phrase, isn't it? *Keeping* it . . . holding it fast against the world . . . against all the forces trying to tear it open. And David has time to write his war book at last . . . he's always longed to. We are so happy . . . and we'll be happier still to have you as a friend. I don't believe you've any idea how nice you are, Pat. And now let's just talk all night."

They talked for a good part of it. And then Suzanne fell suddenly silent. Pat rather envied her the floor. It was level, at least . . . not all bumps and hollows, like the couch. Would it ever stop raining? How the windows rattled! Great heavens, what was that? Oh, only a brick blowing off the chimney and thumping down over the roof. Those rats! Oh for an hour of Gentleman Tom! It was... so nice... to be friends... with Suzanne... she hoped... a great wave of sleep rolled over Pat and engulfed her.

When she wakened the rain had ceased and the outside world was lying in the strange timeless light of early dawn. Pat raised herself on her elbow and looked out. Some squirrels were scolding and chattering in an old apple tree. A little pond at the foot of the slope was softly clear and pellucid, with spruce trees dark and soft beyond it. An old crone of a hemlock was shaking her head rebukingly at some giddy young saplings on the hill. Gossamer clouds were floating in a clear silvery eastern sky that looked as if it had not known a thunderstorm in a hundred years. And a huge black dog was sitting on the doorstep. This was like a place Judy used to tell of in Ireland that was haunted by the ghost of a black dog who bayed at the door before a death. However, this dog didn't look exactly like a ghost!

Suzanne was still asleep. Pat looked around and saw something that gave her an idea. She got to her feet cautiously.

7

When Suzanne wakened half an hour later she sat up and gazed around her in amazement. A most delectable odour came from a sizzling frying pan on the stove in which crisp bacon slices could be discerned. On the hearth was a plateful of golden-brown triangles of toast and Pat was putting a spoonful of tea in a battered old granite teapot.

The table was set with dishes and in the centre was a bouquet of ferns and meadow-queen in an old pickle jar.

"Pat, what magic is this? Are you a witch?"

"Not a bit of it. When I woke up I saw a pile of firewood behind the stove and a frying pan on a nail. I found plates and cups and knives and forks in the pantry. Evidently this house is occupied by times. The owner probably lives on some other farm and camps here for haying and harvest and things like that. I lit the fire and went out to the car. Took a chance with the dog... there is a dog... but he paid no attention to me. I had a package of bacon in the car and a couple of loaves of bread. Mother likes baker's toast, you know. I found some tea in the pantry... and so breakfast is served, madam."

"You're a born home-maker, Pat. This awful place actually looks quite homey and pleasant. I never thought a pickle jar bouquet could be so charming. And I'm hungry... I'm positively starving. Let's eat. Our first meal together... our first breaking of bread. I like that phrase... breaking bread together... don't you? Who is it speaks of 'bread of friendship'?"

"Carman," said Pat, dishing up her bacon.

"What a lovely *clean* morning it is!" said Suzanne, scrambling up. "Look, Pat, there's a big pine down by that pond. I love pines so much it hurts me. And I love crisp bacon and crisper toast. Thank heaven there is plenty of it. I never was so hungry in my life."

They were half through their breakfast when a queer strangled noise behind them startled them. They turned around... and stiffened with horror. In the hall doorway a man was standing... a tall, gaunt, unshaven creature in a motley collection of garments, with an extraordinarily long grey moustache, which didn't seem to belong to his lean, lantern-jawed face at all, hanging down on either side of his chin. This apparition was staring at them, apparently as much taken aback as they were.

"I thought I was over it," he said mournfully, shaking a grizzled head. "I mostly sleeps it off."

Pat rose and stammered out an explanation. The gentleman waved a hand at her.

"It's all right. Sorry you had to sleep on the floor. If I'd been awake I'd have give you my bed."

"We knocked... and called..."

"Just so. Old Gabe's trump couldn't have roused me last night. I was a bit lit up, to state facts. You did right to make yourselves at home. But it's a wonder the dog didn't tear you to pieces. He's a savage brute."

"He wasn't here when we came... and he seemed quite quiet this morning."

"'Zat a fact? Then I've been fooled. Bought him on the grounds that he was a tartar. I keep him here for tramps. My name is Nathaniel Butterbloom and I'm just sorter camping here while I take off the harvest. I live down at Three Corners."

"Won't you sit down and share our breakfast?" said Pat lamely.

"Don't care if I do," said Mr. Butterbloom and sat down

without more ado. "Sorry there ain't no table-cloth. I had one but the rats et it."

Pat, exchanging a grin with Suzanne, poured him a cup of tea and helped him liberally to bacon and toast.

"This *is* a pleasant surprise and that's a fact. I've been scraping up my own meals. When I run out of provisions I fry a kitten," he added mournfully. "That barn out there is overrun with cats. I started out with three cats two years ago but there must be hundreds now."

"It's a wonder they don't keep the rats down," said Suzanne mischievously. "And your roof leaks very badly, Mr. Butterbloom."

"Well," said Mr. Butterbloom placidly, "when it rains I can't get up on the roof to work, can I? And when it's fine it doesn't leak."

"I'm sorry there is no milk for your tea," said Pat.

"There's some in the pantry if the spiders haven't got into it."

"They have," said Pat briefly.

Mr. Butterbloom drank his cup of tea and champed his bacon in silence. Suzanne had just whispered solemnly to Pat, "A **strong** silent man," when he wiped his moustache with the back of his hand and spoke again.

"What mought your names be?"

"This is Miss Kirk . . . and I'm one of the Gardiner girls from North Glen."

"Pleased to meet you both. And so you ain't married women?"

"No . . . no." Suzanne shook her head in demure sadness.

"Neither am I. I've a widder woman keeping house for me at Three Corners. She isn't much of a cook but she rubs my back for me. I have to have my back rubbed for half an hour every night before I can sleep . . . unless I'm lit up. I've heard of the Gardiners. Very genteel. I've never been in North Glen but I courted an old maid in South Glen for a while. I was younger then. She kept me dangling for a year and then up and married a widower. Since then I've sorter lost my enthusiasm for marriage."

He relapsed into silence while he polished off another helping. When the platter was empty he sighed deeply.

"Miss, that *was* a breakfast. After all, I may have made a mistake in not getting married." He fixed a fishy, speculative eye on Suzanne. "I haven't much book-larning but I've a couple of farms, nearly paid for."

Suzanne did not rise to this but she and Pat offered to wash the dishes before leaving.

"Never mind," said Mr. Butterbloom gloomily. "I don't wash dishes. The dog licks 'em clean. If you must be going I'll get out the hosses and haul your buzz-wagon out of the ditch."

He refused an offer of payment sadly.

"Didn't you cook my breakfast? But could you do with a kitten? There's several around just the right age."

Pat explained politely that they had all the cats needful at Silver Bush.

"It's of no consequence. I s'pose"... with a sigh... "it'll come in handy sometime when the cupboard is bare."

When they got out of sight of the house Pat stopped the car so that they might have a laugh. When two people have laughed... really laughed... together they are friends for life.

"Two unchaperoned females spending the night in a house with a drunken man," gasped Suzanne. "Let's pray the writer of 'North Glen Notes' never finds it out."

Nobody but Judy ever knew the whole story. Judy, of course, knew all about Nathaniel Butterbloom.

"A bit av a divil in his day," she said, "but he's too old now to cut up much. Innyhow, ye can be thankful he didn't ask ye to rub his back for him."

8

Pat had gone to her Secret Field, seeking the refreshment of soul she always found there. It was as beautiful and remote and mystic as ever, full of the sunshine of uncounted summers. The trees about it welcomed her and Pat flung herself down among the feathery bent grasses and listened to the silence until she felt at one with it and certain problems that had rather worried her of late dropped into proper focus as they always did in that sweet place, where the fairies still surely lingered if they lingered in the world at all. Under the ancient spell of the Secret Field Pat became a child again and could believe anything.

She went from it to Happiness by a narrow wood lane

where ferns grew waist-high on either side. Pat knew all the little lanes in the woods and was known of them. They had their moods and their whims. One always seemed full of hidden laughter and furtive feet. One never seemed to know just where it wanted to go. In this one it always seemed as if you were in a temple. Overhead in the young, resinous fir boughs a wind was crooning a processional. The aroma drifting under the arches from old sunny hollows and lurking nooks was as the incense of worship, the exquisite shadows that filled the woods were acolytes, and the thoughts that came to her were like prayers.

"If one could only feel always like this," Pat had said once to Judy. "All the little worries swallowed up . . . all the petty spites and fears and disappointments forgotten . . . just love and peace and beauty."

"Oh, oh, but what wud there be lift for heaven, girl dear?" asked Judy.

The lane finally led out to the back fields of the other place and Pat found her way to Happiness and sat down near the Haunted Spring in a little hollow among the ferny cradle-hills. Far down before her, beyond the still, golden pastures, was the sapphire of the gulf. Over the westering hill of spruce a sunset of crimson and warm gold was fading out into apple green. And all this beauty was hers just for the looking. In these silent and remembered places she could think of old, beloved things . . . of sunsets she and Hilary had watched there together . . . Hilary, who at this very moment would be somewhere on the ocean on his way back from his summer in Europe. He had written her most delightful letters but she was glad he would soon be back in Canada. It would be pleasant to think that the Atlantic no longer rolled between them. She wondered a little wistfully why he couldn't have planned to stop off for a few days on the Island on his way to Toronto. She had asked him to. And he had never even referred to the invitation, although he had wound up his letter by saying "my love to Silver Bush." She could see from where she sat her name and his cut on a maple tree and overgrown with lichen. Pat sighed sentimentally. She wished she could be a child again with no worries. To be sure she had thought she had worries then . . . father going west and thinking you were ugly and Joe running away to sea and things like that. But there had been no men then . . . no question of beaus and people who persisted in turning into

lovers when all you wanted of them was to be friends. Jim
Mallory was in love with her now. She had met him at a
dance in Silverbridge and, as Rae told Hilary in her next
letter to him, he fell for her with a crash that could be heard
for miles. He was a really fine fellow... "oh, oh, that's
something like now," Judy said, the first evening he came to
Silver Bush. Pat liked him terribly... almost as much as she
liked Hilary and David. Rae told Judy she believed Pat was
really in love but Judy had grown pessimistic under repeated
disappointments.

"I've no great faith in it lasting," she said.

Pat, when she left home that night, hardly knew herself
whether she wasn't a little bit in love or not. Certainly... the
look in his eyes... the touch of his fingers when he lingered
to say good-night under enchanted moons... she hadn't felt
like that since the days of Lester Conway. But her hour in the
Secret Field and Happiness cleared the matter up for her.
No, liking wasn't enough... little thrills and raptures weren't
enough. There must be something more before she could
dream of leaving Silver Bush. Poor Jim Mallory never had a
chance after that and in a week or two Long Alec was to ask
his wife in a mildly exasperated tone what the dickens the girl
wanted anyways. Was nobody good enough for her?

"No," said mother softly, "just as nobody was good
enough for me till you came, Alec."

"Fiddlesticks!" said Long Alec. But he said it gently.
After all, he was in no hurry to lose Pat.

Rae was another of Pat's little problems. She had passed
her Entrance and wanted to go to Queen's. But just where
was the money to come from? The crop was only fair: there
had been some heavy losses in cattle: it was just barely
possible to pay the interest on the mortgage this year. Dad
wanted Rae to wait for another year and Rae was taking it
hard. But in Happiness Pat decided that Rae must go. They
would borrow the money from Uncle Tom who would be
quite willing to lend it. Long Alec had a horror of borrowing.
It had robbed him of many a night's sleep when he mortgaged Silver Bush to buy the Adams place. But Pat thought
she could bring him round. Rae could pay back the loan in a
year of teaching if she were lucky enough to get the home
school. If not, in two. Everything seemed feasible in Happiness.

If only Judy were not going to Ireland! But Judy was so
set on it now that nothing could turn her from it, even if

anybody could have been selfish enough to try. She meant to sail in November and was already talking of passports and a new trunk.

"Sure and I cudn't be taking my old blue chist. It's a bit ould-fashioned. I tuk it to Australy wid me and thin to Canady but the times have changed since thin and a body must kape up wid thim. And I'll have to be getting a negleege, too, it's like. There do be a pink silk one wid white cherry blossoms all over it, marked down at Brennan's. Do ye be thinking I'm too old for it, girls dear?"

The idea of Judy, in a pink, cherry-blossomed "negleege" was something nobody at Silver Bush could contemplate with equanimity. But not a word was said to dissuade her. Pat assured her there was no longer any age in fashions.

Yes, Judy was going. The fact must be faced. But it no longer blocked up the future. The winter would pass . . . the spring would come . . . and Judy would come with it. Meanwhile, she was not taking Silver Bush to Ireland in her pocket. It would stay where it was, under its sheltering trees, with its fields lying cool and quiet around it. Pat, on her way home, stopped as ever at the top of the hill to gloat over it—this house where her dear ones were lying asleep.

For she had lingered long in Happiness and Silver Bush had gone to bed. There was still a light in Judy's kitchen chamber. Judy was probably hunting through her book of useful knowledge for remedies for seasickness. Though Uncle Tom had slyly suggested that her black bottle was as good an old reliable as any.

Pat was happy. In spite of everything the autumn world was beautiful. Some of its days might bring purple gifts . . . some might bring peace . . . all would bring loveliness.

"Darling Silver Bush!" said Pat. "How could anybody ever think of leaving you if she could help it?"

She remembered how sorry she had been in childhood for the Jamesons of Silverbridge . . . a family who were always moving round. To be sure, they seemed to like it . . . but the very thought of such an existence made Pat shiver.

Long Alec was horrified at first when Pat broached the idea of borrowing the money for Rae's year at Queen's. But she talked him round. It was beginning to be suspected at Silver Bush that Pat could twist dad around her little finger. Rae averred she did it by flattering him but Pat indignantly denied it.

"It would be of no use to try to flatter dad. You know as well as I do, Rae, that dad is impervious to flattery."

"Oh, oh, there do be no such man," muttered Judy with a grin.

Flattery or not, Long Alec yielded and everything was soon arranged. Rae was wild with delight.

"If I'd had to wait till next year I'd have gone straight to the end of the world and jumped off. Emmy's going this year and Dot Robinson and you know we've always been such pals. And I'm going to study, Pat . . . oh, am I going to study? I know everybody says the Silver Bush girls are lookers and popular with the boys but have no brains. I mean to show them. Aunt Barbara says a girl doesn't need brains if she's pretty but that's an idea left over from the Victorians. Nowadays you've got to have brains to capitalise your good looks."

"Did ye be thinking that out for yersilf, darlint?" asked Judy.

"No," said Rae, one of whose charms was honesty. "I saw it in a magazine. Oh, but I'm happy! Pat darling, the world is only sixteen years old to-day. And can't we have a party before I go?"

"Of course. I've got that all planned out."

Pat loved to give parties and welcomed any excuse for one. And this one, being a sort of send-off for Rae, must be a special one.

"We'll have it a week from Friday night. We'll have a platform built in the silver bush for dancing and Chinese lanterns hung on the trees."

"Pat, how lovely! It will be like fairyland. Will there be a moon?"

"There will. I'll see to that," promised Pat.

"Don't make too many fine plans," said Sid warningly. "Remember when you do some of them always go agley."

Pat tossed a defiant brown head.

"What matter? I love making plans. I'll be making plans when I'm eighty. Let's get right to work, Rae, planning out the eats. We'll have some of those new ribbon sandwiches Norma had at her tea last week. They're so pretty."

Brown and golden heads bent together over recipe books. Delicious excitement began to pervade everything. Pat and Rae talked so much about the affair that Long Alec, who was taking a jaundiced view of things just then, growled to Judy that the fools of the world weren't all dead yet.

"Oh, oh, and don't ye think it'll be a rale dull place whin they are?" demanded Judy. "Do ye be thinking..." in a soothing whisper..."ye'd like a bacon-and-pittatie pie for supper?"

Long Alec brightened. After all, crops might be poor and you might be beginning to suspect that you had paid too much for the old Adams place but Judy's bacon-and-potato pies were something to live for. And girls were only young once.

9

Uncle Horace's letter added to the pleasant excitement. Uncle Horace, who had been living as a retired sea-captain in Vancouver, was coming home for a visit for the first time in twenty years. The older folk were naturally the more deeply stirred by this. Judy for a little while was neither to hold nor bind. But Pat and Rae were intrigued, too, at the thought of this mysterious, romantic uncle they had never seen, about whom Judy had told so many yarns... the Horace of the black-ink fruitcake and the monkey and the mutiny off Bombay. The man who, so Judy had said, kept the winds in jars. They *had* believed that once and the charm of it still hung around their thoughts of him.

He had mentioned Wednesday as the probable day of his arrival and on Tuesday Pat subjected Silver Bush to such a furbishing up that Sid asked sarcastically if Uncle Horace were coming to see them or their furniture.

"It's what we are to do wid thim blessed cats do be puzzling me," worried Judy. "Yer Uncle Horace hates cats as bad as ould Cousin Nicholas himsilf cud do."

"Oh, *do* you remember Cousin Nicholas coming downstairs that rainy Christmas night little Mary was born?" giggled Rae.

"Rimimber, is it? Oh, oh, cud I iver be forgetting him, standing there looking like the wrath av God. And now we do be having three to kape out av Horace's way. To be sure, Gintleman Tom won't be bothering him much but Bold-and-Bad and that Squedunk are so frindly. We'll just have to see that the dure av the Poet's room is kipt tight shut and trust the rist to the Good Man Above. It's the lucky thing we've got rid av Popka."

Pat did not know if it were so lucky. It had half-broken her heart to give Popka away to the distant cousin down at East Point. He was such a beautiful cat with his fluffy Maltese coat and white paws, and so affectionate. Why, he used to go over the house at night, visit all the bedrooms and kiss all the sleepers. And the purrs of him! He could outpurr Bold-and-Bad and Squedunk together. It was a shame to give him away. But Long Alec was adamant. Three cats were enough . . . more than enough . . . for any house. He would really like to be sure of an unoccupied chair once in a while. Popka must go . . . and Popka went. Pat and Rae both cried when his new owner bore him away, shrieking piteously in a basket.

Uncle Horace did not come Wednesday, nor on Thursday or Friday. Long Alec shrugged disappointedly. Likely he had changed his mind at the last minute and wouldn't come at all. That was Horace all over.

"But if he does come I want all you folks to mind your p's and q's," said Long Alec warningly. "Horace is a bit peculiar in some ways. He was a regular martinet on board ship I understand. Everything had to be just so, running smooth as oil. And he was just the same about a house. That's why he never married, he told us the last time he was home. Couldn't find a wife neat enough. It's all very well to listen to Judy's yarns of his pranks. He used to be a rip for them, I admit, but nobody else was to play them and accidents had no place in his scheme of things. I don't know what he'll think of your dance. The last time he was home he was badly down on dancing."

"And him the liveliest dancer on the Island forty years ago," marvelled Judy.

"He's reformed since then . . . and the reformed ones are generally the stiffest. Anyhow, all of you do your best to keep things moving smoothly. I don't want Horace to go away thinking things not lawful to be uttered of my household."

Pat and Rae promised, and then forgot all about him in the excitement of the party preparations. Hundreds of last minute things to do. Cream to be whipped . . . floors and furniture to be polished . . . at the very last an extra cake to be made because Pat was afraid they mightn't have enough. Judy declared that the queen's pantry couldn't be better stocked but gave in when Pat insisted.

"Oh, oh, ye do be the mistress here," she said with a touch of grandeur. Pat made an old-fashioned jelly roll that would cut into golden coils with ruby jelly between them. A pretty cake... just as pretty as any new-fangled thing. Where on earth was Rae? Prinking in her room of course... fussing over her hair. And so much yet to be seen to! Pat had always been conscious of a sneaking sympathy with Martha. But she was very happy. Silver Bush looked beautiful. She loved the shining surfaces... the flowers in bowls all over the house... the glitter of glass and silver in the dining-room... everything in the best Gardiner tradition. Sid had strung Chinese lanterns on the trees all around the platform and Tillytuck was to be fiddler, with old Matt Corcoran from the Bridge to spell him. The day of gold would be followed by a night of silver, for the weather was behaving perfectly. And at dusk, pretty girls and girls not so pretty were gazing into mirrors all over the two Glens and Silverbridge and Bay Shore. Judy, with groans that could not be uttered, was donning her wine-hued dress and Tillytuck was struggling into a white collar in the granary loft. Even the cats were giving their flanks a few extra licks. For the party at Silver Bush was easily the event of the season.

Pat, hurrying into a frock of daffodil chiffon, fluffed out her dark-brown cloud of hair and looked in her mirror with pleasure. She was feeling a trifle tired but her reflection heartened her up wonderfully. She had forgotten that she was really rather pretty. "Nae beauty" of course... Pat had never forgotten Great-great-Aunt Hannah's dictum... but quite pleasant to look upon.

And Rae, in her dress of delphinium blue, was a dream.

"Blue is really the loveliest colour in the world," thought Pat. "I'm sorry I can never wear it."

The dress suited Rae. But for that matter any dress did. Rae's clothes always seemed to *belong* to her. You could never imagine any one else wearing them. Once she slipped a dress over that rippling gold-brown head you thought she must have been born in it. Pat reflected with a thrill of pride that she had never seen this darling sister looking so lovely. Her eyes had such starry lights in them behind her long lashes... eyes that were as full of charm as wood violets. To be sure, Rae wouldn't have wanted her eyes compared to wood violets... or forget-me-nots either. That was Victorian. Cornflower blue, now... that sounded so much more up to date. Don Robinson had told her at the last club dance that her eyes were cornflower blue.

The Binnies were the first to come... "spying out the

land," Judy vowed. They heard May's laughter far down the lane. "Ye always hear her afore ye see her, that one," sniffed Judy. May was very gorgeous in a gown of cheap, mail-order radium lace that broke in billows around her feet and afforded a wonderful view of most of the bones in her spine. She tapped Pat condescendingly on the shoulder and said,

"You look dragged to death, darling. If I were you I'd stay in bed all day to-morrow. Ma always makes me do that after a spree."

Pat shrugged away from that hateful, fat, dimpled hand with its nails stained coral. What an intolerable phrase . . . "if I were you"! As if a Binnie ever could be a Gardiner! She was thankful that the arrival of the Russells and Uncle Brian's girls saved her from the necessity of replying. Winnie was looking like a girl again to-night, in spite of her two children. For there was a new baby at the Bay Shore and Judy was going to take care of it during the evening, as she loved to do.

Pat did not dance till late. There were too many things to see to. And even when she was free she liked better to stand a little in the background, where a clump of stately white foxglove spikes glimmered against the edge of the birches, and gloat over the whole scene. Everything was going beautifully. The dreamy August night seemed like a cup of fragrance that had spilled over. The gay lilt of Tillytuck's fiddle rippled through the moonlight to die away magically, through green, enchanted boughs, into the beautiful silences of the silver bush and the misty, glimmering fields beyond. It was really a wonder that Wild Dick didn't rise up out of his grave to dance to it.

The platform, full of flower-like faces and flower-like dresses, looked so pretty. Everybody seemed happy. How sweet darling mother looked, sitting among the young folks like a fine white queen, her gold-brown eyes shining with pleasure. Uncle Tom was as young as anybody, dancing as blithely as if he had never heard of Mrs. Merridew. His beard had grown out in all its old magnificence and the streaks of grey in it did not show in that mellow light. What a lovely dress Suzanne was wearing . . . green crepe and green lace swirling about her feet. Suzanne was not really pretty . . . she said herself that she had a mouth like a gargoyle . . . but she was distinguished looking . . . a friend to be proud of. May Binnie, with all her flashing, full-blown beauty, looked almost comical beside her. Poor Rex Miller was not there. At home, sulking,

Pat thought with a regretful shrug. She had not exactly refused him two evenings before . . . Pat did not often actually have to refuse her lovers . . . she was, as Judy would have said, too diplomatic-like . . . but she had the knack of delicately making them understand a certain thing and thus avoiding for herself and them the awkwardness of a blunt "no."

Where was Sid's Dorothy, with her sweet dark face? She had not come either. Pat wondered why. She hated herself for half hoping Sid and Dorothy had quarrelled. But if that were the reason Sid was dancing so often with May Binnie Pat felt she was already punished for her selfish hope. Of course May was a good dancer . . . of her kind. At any rate, the boys all liked to dance with her. May was never in any danger of being a wallflower.

Amy's new ring flashed on the shoulder of her partner as she drifted by. Amy was engaged. Another change. What a pity people had to grow up . . . and get married . . . and go away. She had always liked Amy much better than Norma. She recalled with considerable relish the time she had slapped Norma's face for making fun of Silver Bush. Norma never dared to do it again.

What an exquisite profile Rae had as she lifted her face to her partner . . . a tall Silverbridge boy. Rae had no lack of partners either. And the way she had of looking at them! Really, the child was getting to be quite a handful. Was there actually anybody standing back in the shadows behind Tillytuck? Pat had fancied several times there was but could never be quite sure. Probably Uncle Tom's hired man.

David hunted her out and insisted on her dancing . . . and sitting out in the silver bush with him afterwards . . . just far enough away from the dancers to make Tillytuck's fiddling sound like fairy music. Pat liked both. David was a capital dancer and she loved to talk with him. He had such a charming voice. Sometimes he was a little bitter but there was such a stimulating pungency about his bitterness. Like choke cherries. They puckered your mouth horribly but still you hankered after them. She would far rather sit here and talk to David than dance with boys who held you closer than you liked and paid you silly compliments, most of which they had picked up from the talkies.

Then a run into the house to see the baby. It was so heavenly to watch a baby asleep, with Judy crooning over it like an old weather-beaten Madonna. Judy was a bit upset on several counts.

"Patsy darlint, there do be some couples spooning on the flat monnymints in the graveyard. Do ye be thinking that dacent now?"

"It's not in the best of taste but we can hardly turn them out of it, Judy. It's only on Wild Dick's and Weeping Willy's. Wild Dick would sympathise with them and as for Weeping Willy... who cares for his feelings? We don't count *him* among our glorious dead... sitting down and crying instead of going bravely to work. Is that all that's worrying you, Judy?"

"It's not worrying I am but there's been a mysterious disappearance. The roll-jelly cake has gone out av the pantry and the bowl av whipped crame in the ice-house is gone. Siddy forgot to lock it. Bold-and-Bad do be licking his chops very suspicious-like but he'd have been laving the bowl at laste. Of coorse I can be whipping up more crame in a brace av shakes. But who cud have took the cake, Patsy? Niver did the like happen before."

"I suppose some of the boys have been playing tricks. Never mind, Judy, there's plenty of cake... you said so yourself."

"But the impidence av thim... coming into me pantry like that. Likely enough it was Sam Birnie. Patsy darlint, Rex Miller isn't here. Ye haven't been quarrelling wid him, have ye now?"

"No, Judy darling. But he won't be coming around any more. I couldn't help it. He was nice... I liked him but... Judy, don't be looking like that....When I asked him a question... any question... I always knew exactly what he'd answer. And he never... really never, Judy... laughs in the right place."

"Mebbe ye cud have taught him to laugh in the right place," said Judy sarcastically.

"I don't think I could. One has to be born knowing that. So I had to wave him gently away... 'symbolically speaking.'"

"Oh, oh, ye'll be doing that once too often, me jewel," predicted Judy darkly.

"Judy, this love business is no end of a bother. 'In life's morning march when my bosom was young' I thought it must be tremendously romantic. But it's just a nuisance. Life would be much simpler if there were nothing of the sort."

"Oh, oh, simple, is it? A bit dull, I'm thinking. I've niver had inny love affairs mesilf to spake av but oh, the fun I've had watching other people's!"

Pat had been able to sidetrack Rex Miller "diplomatically" but she was not so fortunate with Samuel MacLeod...probably because it had never occurred to her that he had any "intentions" regarding her. Samuel...nobody ever called him Sam...it simply couldn't be done...came now and again to Silver Bush to confer with Pat and Rae on the programs of the Young People's Society, of which he was president, but no one, not even Judy, ever looked upon him as a possible beau. And now after supper, having asked Pat to dance...Rae said that dancing with Samuel was almost as solemn a performance as leading the Young People's...he followed it up by asking her to go for a walk in the garden. Pat steered him past the graveyard, which he seemed to mistake for the garden, and got him into the delphinium walk. And, standing there, even more dreadfully conscious of hands and feet than usual, he told her that his heart had chosen her for the supreme object of its love and that if she would like to be Mrs. Samuel MacLeod she had only to say the word.

Pat was so dumbfounded that she couldn't speak at all at first and it was not till Samuel, taking her silence for maidenly consent began gingerly to put a long arm around her, that she came to the surface and managed to gasp out,

"Oh, no...no...I don't think I can...I mean, I'm sure I can't. Oh, it's utterly impossible."

As she spoke there was a smothered giggle on the other side of the delphiniums and Emmy Madison and Dot Robinson scuttled away across the lawn.

"Oh, I'm so sorry," cried Pat. "I never thought anybody was there."

"It doesn't matter," said Samuel, with a dignity that somehow did not misbecome him. "I am not ashamed to have people know that I aspired to you."

In spite of his absurd Victorian phrases Pat found herself for the first time rather liking him. He couldn't help being a South Glen MacLeod. They were all like that. And she made up her mind that she would never entertain Judy or Suzanne by an account of this proposal...though to be sure that wretched Emmy and Dot would spread it all over the clan.

All in all, Pat drew a breath of relief when the last guest had gone and the last lantern candle expired, leaving the silver bush to its dreams and its moonlight. The party had been a tremendous success... "the nicest party I've ever been to," Suzanne whispered before she took the hill road. "And that supper! Come up to-morrow night and we'll have a good pi-jaw about everything."

But when you were hostess there was, as Judy said, "a bit av a strain," especially with the proposal of Samuel thrown in. She turned from the gate and ran up the back walk, crushing the damp mint as she ran. The late August night had grown a bit chilly and Judy's kitchen, where a fire had been lit to brew the coffee, seemed attractive.

Pat halted in the doorway in amazement. There were Uncle Tom and the aunts...mother...Rae...Judy...Tilly-tuck...dad...and Uncle Horace! For of course the stranger could be nobody else.

Pat felt a little bit dazed as he rose to shake hands with her. This was not the Uncle Horace she had pictured...neither the genial old rascal of Judy's yarns nor the typical tar of dad's reminiscences. He was tall and thin and saturnine, with hair of pepper and salt. With his long lean face and shell-rimmed spectacles he looked more like a somewhat dyspeptic minister than a retired sea-captain. To be sure, there was something about his mouth...and his keen blue eyes... Pat felt that she wouldn't have liked to head that mutiny against him.

"This is Pat," said Long Alec.

"Humph! I've been hearing things about you," grunted Uncle Horace as he shook hands.

Pat hadn't a glimmer whether the things were complimentary or the reverse and retreated into herself. Uncle Horace, it seemed, had arrived unexpectedly, walking up from Silverbridge. Finding a party in full swing he had decided not to show himself until it was over.

"Had some fun watching the dance from the bush," he said. "Some pretty girls clothed in smiles...and not much else. I never expected to see P. E. Island girls at a dance with no clothes on."

"No clothes," said Aunt Edith, rather staggered. She had not graced the party but had come over to find out what was keeping Tom so late.

"Well, none to speak of. There were three girls there with no back at all to their frocks. Times have changed since we were young, Alec."

"For the better I should think," said Rae pertly. "It must

have been awful . . . dresses lined and re-lined, sleeves as big as balloons, and rats in your hair."

Uncle Horace looked at her meditatively, as if wondering what kind of an insect she was, fitted his finger-tips carefully together, and went on with his tale. For the first time in her life Rae Gardiner felt squelched.

"When I felt that I needed a little sustenance I slipped into the pantry when the coast was clear and got me a cake. A real good cake . . . roll-jelly . . . I didn't think they made them now. Then I scouted around for some milk and found a bowl of whipped cream in the ice-house. 'Plenty more where that came from,' thought I. Made a pretty decent meal."

"And me blaming Sam Binnie," said Judy. "Oh, oh, I'll be begging his pardon, Binnie and all as he is."

"I kept back in the bush . . . had to," said Uncle Horace. "If I moved I fell over some canoodling couple. There were people in love all over the place."

"Love is in the air at Silver Bush, symbolically speaking," said Tillytuck. "I find it rather pleasant. The little girls' love affairs give a flavour to life."

"But Judy here isn't married yet," said Uncle Horace gravely.

"Oh, oh, I cudn't support a husband," sighed Judy.

"Don't you think it's time?" said Uncle Horace gravely. "We're none of us getting younger, you know, Judy."

"But I'm hoping some av us do be getting a liddle wiser," retorted Judy witheringly.

But she was plainly in high cockalorum. Horace had always had a warm spot in her heart and in her eyes he was still a boy.

"I got a drink out of the old well while you were at supper," said Uncle Horace in a different tone. "There's none like it the world over. I've always understood David and his craving for a drink from the well at Bethlehem. And the ferns along the road from Silverbridge. I've smelled smells all the world over, east and west, and there's no perfume like the fragrance of spice ferns as you walk along a P. E. Island road on a summer evening. Well, young folks like your girls and Judy mayn't mind staying up all night, Alec, but I'm not equal to it any longer. Judy, do you suppose it's possible to have fried chicken for breakfast?"

"How like a man!" Rae telegraphed in disgust to Pat.

Expecting to have fried chicken for breakfast when it was four o'clock after a party! But Judy was actually looking pleased.

"There do be a pair av young roosters out there just asking for it," she said meditatively.

Judy and Pat and Rae had a last word when everybody had gone.

"Oh, oh, but I'm faling like a bit av chewed string," sighed Judy. "Howiver, the party was a grand success and aven Tillytuck sitting down on a shate av fly-paper in the pantry where he did have no business to be and thin strutting pompous-like across the platform wid it stuck to his pants cudn't be called inny refliction on Silver Bush. He did be purtinding to be mad about it but I'm belaving he did it on purpose to make a sinsation. Oh, oh, ye cud have knocked me down wid a feather whin I was after clearing up the supper dishes. I did be hearing a thud . . . and there was me fine Horace full lingth on the floor ye rubbed up so well, Patsy. 'Tarrible slippy floor ye've got, woman,' was all he said. Ye niver cud be telling if Horace was mad or if he wasn't."

"I like him," said Pat, who had made up her mind about him when he talked of the well and the ferns.

"Pat, what on earth were you and Samuel MacLeod doing in the garden?" asked Rae.

"Oh, just moonlighting," answered Pat, demure as an owl.

"I never saw anything so funny as the two of you dancing together. He looked like a windmill in a fit."

"Don't ye be making fun av the poor boy," said Judy. "He can't be hilping his long arms and legs. At that, it do be better than being sawed off. And while he cudn't be said to talk he does be managing to get things said."

"He gets them said all right," thought Pat. But she heroically contented herself with thinking of it.

10

Uncle Horace did not prove hard to entertain. When he was not talking over old times with dad or Uncle Tom or Judy he was reading sentimental novels . . . the more sentimental the better. When he had exhausted the Silver Bush library he borrowed from the neighbours. But the book David Kirk lent him did not please him at all.

"They don't get married at the last," he grumbled. "I don't care a hoot for a book where they don't get properly married... or hanged... at the last. These modern novels that leave everything unfinished annoy me. And the heroines are all too old. I don't like 'em a day over sixteen."

"But things are often unfinished in real life," said Pat, who had picked up the idea from David.

"All the more reason why they should come right in books," said Uncle Horace testily. "Real life! We get enough real life living. *I* like fairy tales. I like a nice snug tidy ending in a book with all the loose ends tucked in. Judy's yarns never left things in the air. That's why she's always been such a corking success as a story-teller."

Uncle Horace was no mean story-teller himself when they could get him going... which wasn't always. Around Judy's kitchen fire in the cool evenings he would loosen up. They heard the tale of his being wrecked on the Magdalens on his first voyage... of the shark crashing through the glass roof of his cabin and landing on the dinner table... of the ghost of the black dog that haunted one of his ships and foreboded misfortune.

"Did you ever see it yourself?" asked David Kirk with a sceptical twist to his lips.

Uncle Horace looked at him witheringly.

"Yes... once," he said. "Before the mutiny off Bombay."

His listeners shivered. When Tillytuck and Judy told tales of seeing ghosts nobody minded or believed it. But it was different with Uncle Horace someway. Still, David stuck to his guns. Sailors were always superstitious.

"You don't mean to say that you really believe in ghosts, Captain Gardiner?"

Uncle Horace looked through David and far away.

"I believe what I see, sir. It may be that my eyes deceived me. Not everybody can see ghosts. It is a gift."

"A gift I wasn't dowered with," said Suzanne, a trifle too complacently. Uncle Horace demolished her with one of those rare looks of his. Suzanne afterwards told Pat that she felt as if that look had bored a hole clean through her and shown her to be hollow and empty.

The next excitement was Amy's wedding to which everyone at Silver Bush and Swallowfield went through a pouring rain, except Judy and mother. Uncle Horace would not go in the car. It transpired that he had never been in a car and was determined he never would be. So he went with Uncle Tom in the phaeton and got well drenched for his prejudices. It rained all day. But Uncle Horace came back in high good humour.

"Thank goodness there's a bride or two left in the world yet," he said as he came dripping into the kitchen where Rae, who had reached home before him, was describing to a greedy Judy how Amy's bridal veil of tulle was held to her head in the latest fashion by a triple strand of pearls, with white gardenias at the back. Judy didn't feel that what-do-you-call-'ems could be so lucky as orange blossoms but she knew without asking that the wedding feast would have been more fashionable than filling and she had a "liddle bite" ready for everybody as they came in. Pat was last of all, having lingered to help Aunt Jessie and Norma. She looked around at the bright, homely picture with satisfaction. It was dismal to start anywhere in rain: but to come home in rain was pleasant . . . to step from cold and wet into warmth and welcome. The only thing she missed was the cats. Since Uncle Horace's coming they had been religiously banished. Gentleman Tom spent his leisure in the kitchen chamber, Tillytuck kept a disgruntled Bold-and-Bad in the granary and Squedunk was a patient prisoner in the church barn. Only when Uncle Horace was away were they allowed to sneak back into the kitchen.

But that night, while everybody slumbered in the comfort of Silver Bush a poor, foot-sore, half-dead little cat came crawling up the lane. It was Popka, cold, tired, hungry on the last lap of his hundred mile journey from East Point. When he reached the well-remembered doorstone he paused and tried to lick his wet fur into some semblance of decency before meowing faintly and pitifully for admittance. But the door of Silver Bush remained cruelly closed. Not even Judy in the kitchen chamber heard that feeble cry. Poor Popka dragged himself around to the back and there discovered the broken pane in the cellar window which Judy had been lamenting for a week. In the kitchen he found a saucer of milk under the table which an over-stuffed Bold-and-Bad had left when Judy had smuggled him in for his supper. Heartened by this Popka looked happily about him. It was home. The kitchen was warm and cosy . . . there were several inviting cushions. But Popka craved the comfort of contact with some of his human friends. On four weary legs he climbed the stairs. Alas, every door but one was closed to him. The door of the Poet's room was half open. Popka slipped in. Ah, here was companionship. Popka jumped on the bed.

Pat, going downstairs before any one else, saw a sight through the door of the Poet's room that both horrified and delighted her. Popka, her dear, lamented Popka, was curled into a placid vibrant ball on Uncle Horace's stomach. Pat slipped in, gently lifted Popka and gently departed, leaving Uncle Horace apparently undisturbed. But when Uncle Horace came down to breakfast his first words were,

"Who came in and took my cat?"

"I did," confessed Pat. "I thought you hated cats."

"Used to," said Uncle Horace. "Couldn't bear 'em years ago. Wiser now. Found out they made life worth living. Been wondering why you didn't have any round. Used to be too much cat here if anything. Missed 'em. Tell you tonight how I come to make friends with the tribe."

That night around the kitchen fire, while Popka purred on his knee and Bold-and-Bad winked at him from the lounge, Uncle Horace told of the mystery of the black cat with the bows of ribbon in its ears.

"It was the last voyage I made on this side of the world. We sailed from Halifax for China and the first mate had his young brother with him . . . a lad of seventeen. He'd fetched his favourite cat along with him . . . Pills was his name. The cat's I mean, not the boy's. The boy's name was Geordie. Pills was black . . . the blackest thing you ever saw, with one white shoe, and cute as a pet fox. Both that cat's ears had been punched and he was togged out with little bows of red ribbon tied in 'em. That proud he was of them, too! Once when Geordie took them out to put fresh ones in and didn't do it for a day Pills just sulked till he had his ribbons back. Every one on board made a pet of him, except Cannibal Jim . . ."

"Cannibal Jim? Why was he called that?" asked Rae.

Uncle Horace frowned at her. He did not like interruptions.

"Don't know, miss. Never asked him. It was his own business. I'd never liked cats before myself but I couldn't help liking Pills. I got just as fond of him as the others and felt as tickled as could be when he favoured me by coming to sleep in my cabin at night. 'Twasn't everybody he'd sleep with. No, sir! That cat picked his bedfellows. There were only three people he'd sleep with . . . Geordie and me and the cook. Turn and turn about. He never got mixed up. One night the cook took him when it was my turn but that cat threw fits till the cook let him go and in less than a minute he was kneading his paws on my stomach. Next night was the cook's regular turn but Pills punished him by acting up again and went and slept in a coil of rope on deck. He wouldn't sleep with Geordie or me out of our turn but the cook had to be dealt with. Well, right in the middle of the Indian Ocean Pills disappeared... clean disappeared. We kept hoping for days he'd turn up but he never did. I'd hard work to keep the crew from mobbing Cannibal Jim, for every one believed he'd thrown Pills overboard, though he swore till all was blue he'd never touched him. And now for the part you won't believe. Six months later that cat walks into his own old home in Halifax and curled up on his own special cushion. That's a fact, explain it as you like. He was mighty thin and his feet were bleeding but Geordie's mother knew him at once by the bows in his ears. She took it into her head the ship was lost and that somehow the cat had survived and got home. She nearly went crazy till she found out different. I went to see Pills when I got back and he knew me right off... draped himself around my legs and purred like mad. There wasn't any doubt in the world that it was Pills."

"But, Uncle Horace, how *could* he have got home?"

"Well, the only explanation I could figure out was this. The day before we missed Pills we'd been hailed by a ship, the *Alice Lee*, bound for Boston, U. S. A. They had sickness on board and had run out of some drug, I forget what, and the captain wanted to know if we could let him have some. We could, so he sent a boat across with two men in it. I concluded that one of them swiped the cat. Afterwards Geordie recalled that Pills had been sitting, perky and impudent, on a coil of rope as the men came over the side. He was never seen again but he wasn't missed till the next day. It was Geordie's turn for him that night but Geordie thought cook had him and being sorry for cook, who was looking like a lopsided squirrel with toothache, made no fuss. He didn't get worried till the next afternoon. The men all maintained that no sailor would ever steal another ship's cat, especially a black one, and blamed Cannibal Jim, as I've said. But I never believed even Cannibal Jim would play fast and loose with luck that way. We certainly had nothing but squalls and typhoons the rest of the voyage and finally a man overboard.

But the most puzzling thing was that Pills took six months to get home. I went west that year and took to voyaging the Pacific so I never fell in with any of the *Alice Lee*'s crew again but I did find out that she got to Boston two months after she'd passed us. Suppose Pills was on her. That left four months to be accounted for. Where was he? I'll tell you where he was. Travelling the miles between Boston and Halifax on his own black legs."

Tillytuck snorted incredulously.

"Either that or he swum it," said Uncle Horace sternly. "I find it easier to believe he walked. Don't ask me how he knew the road. I tell you that I saw, then and there, that cats had forgotten more than human beings ever knew and I made up my mind to cultivate their society. When this little fellow hopped up on me last night I just told him to pick out a soft spot on my old carcase and snuggle down."

By the time Uncle Horace's visit drew near its close they had all decided that they liked him tremendously, even if he did disapprove of their clothes and avert his eyes in horror from the pale green and pink and orchid silk panties on the line Monday mornings. They thought, too, that Uncle Horace liked them, though they couldn't feel sure of it. Pat was sure, however, that he must approve of Silver Bush. Everything went smoothly until the very last day... and *it* was really dreadful. In the first place Sid upset Judy's bowl of breakfast pancake batter on the floor and Winnie's baby crawled into it. Of course Uncle Horace had to appear at the very worst moment before the baby could be even picked up, and probably thought that was how they amused babies at Silver Bush. Then Rae put an unopened can of peas on the stove to heat for dinner. The can exploded with a bang, the kitchen was full of steam and particles of peas, and Uncle Horace got a burn on the cheek where the can struck him. To crown all, Rae dared him to go to Silverbridge in the car with her after supper and Uncle Horace, though he had never been in a car, vowed no girl should stump him and got in. Nobody knew what went wrong... Rae was considered a good driver... but the car, instead of going down the lane dashed through the paling fence, struck the church barn, and finished up against a tree. No harm was done except a bent bumper and Rae and Uncle Horace proceeded on their way. Uncle Horace did not seem disturbed. He said when he came home he had sup-

posed it was just Rae's way of starting and he thought he'd get
a car of his own when he went back to the coast.

"Sure and some av ye must have seen a fairy, wid all the
bad luck we've had to-day," gasped Judy when he was safely
off to bed.

"To-day simply hasn't happened. I cut it out of the
week," said Pat ruefully. "After all our efforts to make a good
impression! But did you ever see anything funnier than his
expression when that can hit him?"

"Yes... his expression when I sideswiped the church
barn," said Rae.

They both shrieked with laughter.

"I am afraid Uncle Horace will think we are all terrible
and you in particular, Rae."

But Uncle Horace did not think so. That evening he told
Long Alec he wanted to pay the expenses of Rae's year at
Queen's.

"She's a gallant girl and easy on the eye," he said. "I've
neither chick nor child of my own. I like your girls, Alec.
They can laugh when things go wrong and I like that. Any
one can laugh when it's all smooth sailing. I'll not be east
again, Alec, but I'm glad I came for once. It's been good to
see old Judy again. Those plum tarts of hers with whipped
cream! My stomach will never be the same again but it was
worth it. I'm glad you keep up all the old traditions here."

"One does one's best," said Long Alec modestly.

But Judy in the kitchen was shaking her grey bob
sorrowfully at Gentleman Tom.

"Young Horace don't be young inny longer. All the divilmint
has gone out av him. And looking so solemn! There was a
time the solemner he looked the more mischief he was
plotting. Oh, oh!" Judy sighed. "I'm fearing we do all be
getting a bit ould, cat dear."

The Third Year

RAE was off to Queen's and Pat was very lonely. Of course Rae came home every Friday night, just as Pat had done in her Queen's year, and they had hilarious week ends. But the rest of the time was hard to endure. No Rae to laugh and gossip with . . . no Rae to talk over the day with at bedtime . . . no Rae to sleep in the little white bed beside her own. Pat cried herself to sleep for several nights, and then devoted herself to Silver Bush more passionately than ever.

Rae, after her first homesick week, liked town and college very much, though she was sometimes cold in her boarding house bed and the only window of her room looked out on the blank brick wall of the next house instead of a flower garden and green fields and misty hills.

And Judy was getting ready for her trip to Ireland. She was to go in November with the Patterson family from Summerside, who were revisiting the old sod, and all through October little else was talked of at Silver Bush. Pat, though she hated the thought of Judy going, threw herself heart and soul into the preparations. Judy must and should have this wonderful trip to her old home after her life of hard work. Everybody was interested. Long Alec went to town and got Judy her steamer trunk. Judy looked a bit strange when he dumped it on the walk.

"Oh, oh, I *know* I do be going . . . but I can't belave it, Patsy. That trunk there . . . I can't fale it belongs to me. If it was the old blue chist now. . . ."

But of course the old blue chest couldn't be taken to Ireland. And Judy at last believed she was going when a paragraph in the "North Glen Notes" announced that Miss Judy Plum of Silver Bush would spend the winter with her relatives in Ireland. Judy looked queerer than ever when she saw it. It seemed to make everything so irrevocable.

"Patsy darlint, it must be the will av the Good Man Above that I'm to go," she said when she read it.

"Nothing like a change, as old Murdoch MacGonigal said when he turned over in his grave," remarked Tillytuck cheerfully.

Everybody gave Judy something. Uncle Tom gave a leather suit-case and mother a beautiful brush and comb and hand mirror.

"Oh, oh, niver did I be thinking I'd have a t'ilet set av me own," said Judy. "Talk av the silver backed ones the Bishop stole! And wid me monnygram on the back av the looking glass! I do be hoping me ould uncle will have sinse enough lift to take in the grandeur av it."

Pat gave her a "negleege" and Aunt Barbara gave her a crinkly scarf of cardinal crepe which she had worn only once and which Judy had greatly admired. Even Aunt Edith gave her a grey hug-me-tight with a purple border. Pat nearly went into kinks at the thought of Judy in such a thing but Judy was rather touched.

"Sure and it was rale kind av Edith. I hadn't ixpicted it for we've niver been what ye might call cronies. Mebbe I'll see some poor ould lady in Ireland that it'll set."

Judy's travelling dress exercised them all but one was finally got that pleased her. Also a grey felt hat with a smart, tiny scarlet feather in it. Judy tried the whole outfit on one night in the kitchen chamber and was so scared by her stylish reflection in the cracked mirror that she was for tearing everything off immediately.

"Oh, oh, it doesn't look like *me*, Patsy. It does be frightening me. Will I iver get back into mesilf?"

But Pat made her go down to the kitchen and show herself to everybody. And everybody felt that this hatted and coated and scarlet-feathered Judy *was* a stranger but everybody paid her compliments and Tillytuck said if he'd ever suspected what a fine-looking woman she really was there was no knowing what might have happened.

"I hope nothing will prevent Judy from going," said Rae. "It would break her heart to be disappointed now. But when I think of coming home Friday nights and Judy not here! And that horrid old Mrs. Bob Robinson, with her pussy cat face!" Rae blinked her eyes fiercely.

"Mrs. Robinson isn't really so bad, Rae," protested Pat half-heartedly. "At any rate she is the best we can get and it's only for the winter."

"I tell you she's an inquisitive, snooping old thing," snapped Rae. "*You* didn't see her going down the walk after you'd hired her, giving her chops a sly lick of self-satisfaction every three steps. I did. And I know she was thinking, '*I'll* show them what proper housekeeping is at Silver Bush.'"

One burning question had been . . . who was to be got in to help Pat for the winter? From several candidates Mrs. Bob Robinson of Silverbridge was finally chosen, as the least objectionable. Tillytuck didn't take to her and nicknamed her Mrs. Puddleduck at sight. It was not hard to imagine why for Mrs. Robinson was very short and very plump and very waddly. The Silver Bush family could never again think of her as anything but Mrs. Puddleduck. Tillytuck's nicknames had a habit of sticking.

To Judy, of course, Mrs. Puddleduck was nothing but a necessary evil.

"She do be more up to date than mesilf I'm not doubting" . . . with a toss of her grey head. "They do be saying she took that domestic short course last year. But will she be kaping our cats continted I'm asking ye?"

"They say she's a very careful, saving woman," said Long Alec.

"Oh, oh, careful, is it? I'm not doubting it." Judy waxed very sarcastic. "She do be getting that from no stranger. Her grandfather did be putting a sun-dial in his garden and thin built a canopy over it to pertect it from the sun. Oh, oh, careful! Ye've said it!"

"She'll never make such apple fritters as yours, Judy, if she took fifty short courses," said Sid, passing his plate up for a second helping.

Then there was the matter of the passport. They had quite a time convincing Judy that she must have a photograph taken for it.

"Sure an' wud ye want to be photygraphed if ye had a face like that, Rae, darlint," she would demand, pointing to the kitchen mirror which never paid any one compliments. But when the picture came home Judy, in her new hat, with the crinkled crepe scarf about her throat looked so surprisingly handsome that she was delighted. She kept the passport in the drawer of the kitchen cupboard and took frequent peeps at it when nobody was about.

"Did I iver be thinking a hat cud make such a difference? I can't be seeing but that I do be ivery bit as good-looking as Lady Medchester, and her a blue-blood aristocrat!"

Had it not been for Judy's going that October would have been a perfectly happy month for Pat. It was a golden, frostless autumn and when the high winds blew it fairly rained apples in the orchards and the ferns along the Whispering Lane were brown and spicy. There were gay evenings up at the Long House with Suzanne and David... hours of good gab-fest by the light of their leaping fire. David developed a habit of walking down the hill with Pat which Judy did not think at all necessary. Pat had come down that hill many a night alone.

"Thim widowers," she muttered viciously... but took care that Pat did not hear her. Judy had soon discovered that Pat resented any criticism of David Kirk.

Then McGinty died. They had long expected it. The little dog had been feeble all summer: he had grown deaf and very wistful. It broke Pat's heart when she met his pleading eyes. But to the very last he tried to wag his tail when she came to him. He died with his golden brown head pillowed on her hand. Judy cried like a child and even Tillytuck and Long Alec blew their noses. McGinty was buried beside Snicklefritz in the old graveyard and Pat had to write and tell Hilary that he was gone.

"I feel as if I could never love a dog again," she wrote. "I miss him so. It is so hard to remember that he is dead. I'm always looking for him. Hilary, just before he died he suddenly lifted his head and pricked his ears just as he used to do when he heard your step. I think he *did* hear something because all at once that heart-breaking look of longing went out of his eyes and he gave such a happy little sigh and cuddled his head down in my hand and... it seems too harsh to say he died. He just ceased to be. I wish you had come home, Hilary. I'm sure it was you his eyes were always asking for. Do you remember how he always came to meet us those Friday evenings when we came home from college? And he was with you that night so long ago when you saved me from dying of sheer terror on the base-line road. He was only a little, loving-hearted dog but his going has made a terrible hole in my life. It's another change... and Rae is gone... and Judy is going. Oh, Hilary, life seems to be just change... change... change. Everything changes but Silver Bush. It is always the same and I love it more every day of my life."

Hilary Gordon frowned a bit when he read this. And he frowned still more over a certain paragraph in a letter Rae had written.

"I do wish you'd come home this summer, Jingle. If you don't soon come Pat will up and marry that horrid David Kirk. I know she will. It's really mysterious the influence that man has gained over her. It's David this and David that... she's always quoting him. So far as I can see he doesn't do anything but talk to her... and he *can* talk. The creature is abominably clever."

Hilary sighed. Perhaps he should have gone to the Island last summer. But he was working his way through college... for accept help from the mother who had neglected him all his life he would not... and summer visits home... to Hilary "home" meant Silver Bush... could not be squeezed into his budget.

2

The first day of November came when Judy must pack. It was mild and calm and sunny but there had been hard frost the night before, for the first time, and the garden had suffered. Pat hated to look at her flowers. The nasturtiums were positively indecent. She realised that the summer was over at last.

Judy's trunk was in the middle of the kitchen floor. Pat helped her pack. "Don't forget the black bottle, Judy," Sid said slyly as he passed. Judy ignored this but she brought down her book of Useful Knowledge.

"I must be taking this, Patsy. There do be a lot av ettiket hints in it. Or do ye be thinking they're a trifle out av date? The book is by way av being a bit ouldish. I wudn't want me cousins in Ireland to be thinking I didn't know the latest rules. And, Patsy darlint, I'm taking me ould dress-up dress as well as the new one. I did be always loving that dress. The new one is rale fine but I haven't been wearing it long enough to fale acquainted wid it. Do ye rimimber how ye always hated to give up any av yer ould clothes, Patsy? And, Patsy dear, here's the kay av me blue chist. I'm wanting ye to kape it for me whin I'm gone and if innything but good shud be happening to me over there... not that I'm thinking it will... ye'll be finding me bit av a will in the baking powder can in the till."

"Judy, just imagine it... this time next week you'll be in the middle of the Atlantic."

"Patsy dear," said Judy soberly, "there's a favour I'd be asking ye. Will ye be saying that liddle hymn ivery night whin ye say yer prayers... the one where it does be mintioning 'those in peril on the say.' It'd be a rale comfort to me on the bounding dape. Well, me trunk's packed, thank the Good Man Above. Sure and I knew a woman that tuk four trunks wid her whin she wint to the Ould Country. I'm not knowing how she stud it. Iverything do be ready but what if something 'll be previnting me from going at the last minute, Patsy? I'm that built up on it I cudn't be standing it."

"Nothing will happen to prevent you, Judy. You'll have a splendid trip and a lovely visit with all your cousins."

"I'm hoping it, girl dear. But I've been seeing so minny disappointments in life. And, Patsy dear, kape an eye on Gintleman Tom, will ye and see that Mrs. Puddleduck don't be imposing on him. I'm not knowing how the poor baste will be doing widout me."

"Don't worry, Judy. I'll look after him... if he doesn't go and disappear as he did the last time you were away from home."

Pat lingered a little while that evening on the back-stair landing looking out of the round window. There was a promise of gathering storm. A peevish wind was tormenting the boughs of the aspen poplar. Scudding clouds seemed to sweep the tips of the silver birches. Soon the rain would be falling on the dark autumn fields. But even a wild wet night like this would have been delightful at Silver Bush if her heart had been lighter. Judy would be gone by this time tomorrow night and Mrs. Puddleduck would be reigning in her stead. No Judy to come home to... no Judy to give you "liddle bites"... no Judy to stir pea soup... no Judy to slip in on cold nights with the eiderdown puff off the Poet's bed.

"And what," said Gentleman Tom on the step above, "is a poor cat to do?"

Long Alec took Judy to the station next morning through a drizzling rain. She was going to Summerside to spend the night at Uncle Brian's and take the boat train with the Pattersons the next day. Everybody stood at the gate and waved her off, smiling gallantly till the car was out of sight. Pat turned back to the kitchen where Mrs. Puddleduck was already making a cake and looking quite at home.

"I hate her," thought Pat, wildly and unjustly.

Dinner... the first meal without Judy... was a sorry affair. The soup of Mrs. Puddleduck was not the soup of Judy Plum.

"She doesn't know how to stir the brew," Tillytuck whispered to Pat.

Rae came home that night but supper was a gloomy affair. Mrs. Puddleduck's cake, in spite of her domestic short course, rather looked as if somebody had sat down on it: Long Alec was very silent: Tillytuck went straight to his granary roost as soon as the meal was over. Nothing pleased him and he did not pretend to be pleased.

"I feel old, Pat... as old as Methuselah," said Rae drearily, as they peeped into the kitchen before going to bed.

"I feel middle-aged, which is far worse," moaned Pat.

Mrs. Puddleduck was sitting there, knitting complacently at a sweater. No cat was in sight, not even Gentleman Tom.

"I wish I could be a cat for a little while, just to bite you," whispered Rae to the fat back of the unconscious Mrs. Puddleduck, who really was quite undeserving of all this hatred and, in fact, thought quite highly of herself for "helping the Gardiners out" while Judy Plum was gallivanting off to Ireland.

Saturday was dark and dour but a pleasant letter from Hilary helped Pat through the forenoon. Dear Hilary! What letters he could write! Hilary as a friend, even in faraway Toronto, was worth all the beaus in the Maritimes.

In mid-afternoon it began to rain again, battering everything down in the desolate garden. Tillytuck and Mrs. Puddleduck were already at loggerheads because when she complained that Just Dog had barked all night he had indulged in one of his silent fits of laughter and said blandly, "If you'd told me he'd purred I'd have been more surprised."

Sid took the girls over to the Bay Shore to help Winnie paper a room. The air was as full of flying leaves as of rain, and floods ran muddily down the gutters of the road. It was just as bad when they returned at night.

"I suppose Judy is on board ship now. They were to sail from Halifax at five o'clock," sighed Rae. "There's Tillytuck playing his fiddle. How can he have the heart? But I suppose he's trying to get on the good side of Mrs. Puddleduck. That man has no soul above snacks."

"I don't know how we'll ever get through the winter," said Pat.

They ran up the wet walk and opened the kitchen door... then stood on the threshold literally paralysed with amazement. Tillytuck's fiddle was purring under his hands. Mother was mending by the table whereon was a huge platterful of fat doughnuts. Long Alec lay on the sofa, snoozing blissfully with Squedunk on his chest and Bold-and-Bad and Popka curled up at his feet. Gentleman Tom, with the air of a cat making up his mind to forgive somebody, was sitting on the rug, with his tail stretched out uncompromisingly behind him.

And Judy... *Judy*... in her old drugget dress was sitting beside the stove stirring the contents of a savoury pot! Her knitting was on her lap and she looked like anything but a heart-broken woman.

For a moment the girls stared at her unbelievingly. Then with a shriek of "Judy!!!" they hurled themselves upon her. Wet as they were she hugged them with a fierce tenderness.

"Judy... Judy... *darling*... but why... why...?"

"I just cudn't be going, that do be all, me jewels. I was knowing it in me heart as soon as I lift. Poor Alec hadn't a word to throw to a dog. Ye cud have been scraping the blue mould off av him be the time we got to the station. But thinks I to mesilf, 'I'd look like a nice fool backing out now, after all thim prisents,' thinks I. So I did be sticking it out till I got into me bed at yer Uncle Brian's that night... the second bist spare room it was... oh, oh, they trated me fine, I'll be saying that for thim. But niver the wink wud I be slaping. I kipt thinking av me kitchen here, wid Mrs. Puddleduck reigning in me stid... and of all the things that might be happening to me, roaming abroad. Running inty an iceberg maybe... or maybe dying over there. Not that I'd be minding the dying so much but being buried among strangers. And thin if innything but good shud be happening to some av ye here! Thinks I, 'Perhaps they'll be larning to like Mrs. Puddleduck better'n me and her as smooth as crame.' I cud see ye all, snug and cosy, wid the beaus slipping along in the dim. Thinks I, 'There do be all the turkeys to be fattened for Christmas and the winter hooking to be done and mebbe Joe coming home to be married,'... and I cudn't be standing it. So at breakfast I up and told Brian I'd been after changing me mind and I'd just be going back to Silver Bush instead av to Ireland wid the Pattersons."

"Judy, you said the other day it would break your heart if anything prevented you from going..."

"Oh, oh, yesterday and to-day do be two different things," said Judy complacently. "Whin ye thought I was all ixcited over me trip I was just talking to kape me spirits up. It's the happy woman I am to think I'll slape in me own snug bed to-night wid Gintleman Tom curled up at me fate. Brian brought me home this afternoon and whin I stepped over the threshold of me kitchen I wudn't have called the quane me cousin. Oh, oh, ye shud have been seeing Madam Puddleduck's face! 'I thought this was how it wud be,' sez she, as spiteful as a fairy that had just got a spanking."

"Judy, where *is* Mrs. Puddleduck?"

"Safe back at the Bridge where she belongs. Sure and she wasn't for staying long whin she saw me back. Oh, oh, she'll be saying plinty besides her prayers to-night. I wint inty me pantry thinking I'd see fine things in the way av Sunday baking, what wid her domestic short course and all. But all I did be seeing was a cake looking like nothing on earth and a pie wid a lot of hen tracks on it. Tillytuck tells me he did be ating a pace av it and niver will his stomach be the same agin. Oh, oh, domestic science, sez I! I did be putting it in the pig's pail and frying up a big batch av doughnuts."

"Praise the sea but keep on land is a good proverb, symbolically speaking," said Tillytuck. After which he ate nine doughnuts.

Everybody was shamelessly glad and showed it, much to Judy's secret delight and relief. They shut out the rain and the cold wind. Never had the old kitchen held a more contented, more congenial bunch of people. Grief and loneliness had gone where old moons go and even King William looked jubilant in his never-ending passage of the Boyne.

Outside it might be a dank and streaming November night but here was the eternal summer of the heart.

"Isn't it nice to look *out* into a storm?" said Rae. "Listen to that wind roaring. I love it. Judy, I'm glad you're not on the Atlantic."

"I do be just where I want to be, Cuddles darlint, and faling rale high and hilarious. Sure and I do be good frinds wid Silver Bush agin. It's been looking at me reproachful-like for a long time. I'm knowing now I cud niver be laving it. It's got into the marrow av me. So here I am, wid enough fine clothes to do me for the rist av me life and all the fun av getting ready. Oh, oh, 'twill be a stirring tale...the story av how Judy Plum wint to Ireland and got back so quick she met hersilf going. And now we'll begin planning a bit for Christmas."

Judy crept in that night to see if the girls were warm...the darling, thoughtful old thing.

"You're such a *dependable* old sport, Judy," said a drowsy Pat, sitting up and hugging her. "It seems unbelievably lovely that you're here...*here*...and not far away on the billow."

Judy was not acquainted with Wilson Macdonald's couplet,

"*For this is wealth to know my foot's returning
Is always music to a friend of mine,*"

but she felt that she was a very rich woman with only one small cloud on her perfect joy.

"Patsy darlint, do ye think I ought to be giving thim back...the prisents, I mane?"

"Certainly not, Judy. They were given to you and they are yours."

Judy gave a sigh of relief.

"It's rale glad I am to hear ye say so, Patsy. It wud have been bitter hard to give up that illigant t'ilet set. But I'm thinking I'll give yer Aunt Edith's hug-me-tight back to her. Niver will I let her be saying I come be it under false pretences."

Just as a great wave of sleep was breaking over Pat a sad premonitory thought drifted across her mind.

"And yet...for all she didn't go...I feel as if things were going to change."

3

When Rae came home from Queen's in the spring, the happy possessor of a teacher's licence, she got the home school and settled down for a summer of good fun before school should open. "Fun" to Rae at this stage meant beaus and, as Judy said, they were standing in line. Pat couldn't quite get used to the idea of "little Cuddles" being really old enough to have beaus but Rae herself had no doubts on that point. And she admitted quite candidly that she liked having them. Not that she ever flirted, in spite of the Binnies. "College has improved Rae Gardiner some," Mrs. Binnie was reported to have said, "but it ain't cured her of being boy-crazy."

Rae just *looked*. "Come," said that look. "I know a secret you would like to know and no one can tell it to you but me."

She was not really as pretty as Winnie or as witty as Pat but there was magic in her . . . what Tillytuck called "glamour, symbolically speaking." "The little monkey has a way with her," said Uncle Tom. And the youth of both Glens knew it. It did not matter how much or how severely she snubbed them, this creature of cruelty and loveliness held them in thrall. Long Alec complained that Silver Bush was literally overrun and that they never had a quiet Sunday any more. But Judy would listen to no such growling. "Wud ye be wanting yer girls to be like John B. Madison's," she enquired sarcastically. "Six av thim there and niver a beau to divide between thim."

"There's reason in all things," protested Long Alec, who liked to have an undisturbed Sunday afternoon nap.

"Not in beaus," said Judy shrewdly. "And I'm minding that the yard at the Bay Shore used to be full of rigs on Sunday afternoons, young Alec Gardiner's among them. Don't be forgetting you were once young, Long Alec. We'll all have a bit av quiet fun be times watching the antics. Were ye hearing what happened to Just Dog last Sunday afternoon whin one av the young Shortreed sprouts . . . Lloyd I'm thinking his name was . . . was sitting on the front porch steps, looking kind av holy and solemn, for all the world like his ould Grandfather Shortreed at prayer mating. Sure and the poor baste . . . not maning Lloyd . . . met up wid a rat in the stone dyke behind the church barn and cornered it. But me Mr. Rat put up a fight and clamped his teeth in Just Dog's jaw. Such howling ye niver did be hearing as he tore across the yard and through me kitchen and the hall and out past the young fry on the steps and through me bed av petunias. Roaring down the lane he wint, the rat still houlding on tight. The girls wint into kinks and Tillytuck come bucketing out, rale indignant, and saying, the divil himsilf must have got inty the modern rats. 'Oh, oh,' sez I, 'don't be spaking so flippant av the divil, *Mr.* Tillytuck. He's an ancient ould lad and shud be rispicted,' sez I. Lloyd Shortreed looked rale shocked."

"And no wonder. I don't hold with such goings-on in my house on Sunday."

"Sure and who cud be hilping it?" protested Judy. "It was Just Dog's doings intirely, going rat-hunting on Sunday. Before that the young fry were all quiet and sober-like. As for Tillytuck and his langwidge, iverybody do be knowing him. It's well known he didn't larn it at Silver Bush. Just Dog did be coming back later on wid no rat attached, rale meek and chastened-like. Lloyd hasn't been back since and good riddance. The Shortreeds do be having no sinse av humour."

"Lloyd's a very decent fellow," said Long Alec shortly.

"And that cliver wid his needle," added Judy slyly. "He did be piecing a whole quilt whin he was but four years ould and he's niver been able to live it down. His mother brings it out and shows it round whiniver company comes."

Long Alec got up and went out. He knew he was no match for Judy.

They celebrated Rae's home-coming by another party to which all Rae's college friends came. Rae loved dancing. Her very slippers, if left to themselves, would have danced the whole night through. But Pat's feet were not as light as they had been at the last party. Sid was not there. Sid was a very remote and unhappy boy. There had been a social sensation in North Glen early in the winter. Dorothy Milton, who had been engaged to Sid for two years, ran away with and married her cousin from Halifax, a dissipated, fascinating youth who "travelled" for a Halifax firm. Sid would have nothing of sympathy from his family. He would not talk of the matter at all. But he had been hard and bitter and defiant ever since and Pat felt hoplessly cut off from him. He worked feverishly but he came and went among his own like a stranger.

"Patience," said mother. "It will wear away in time. Poor Dorothy! I'm sorrier for her than for Sid."

"I'm not," sobbed Pat fiercely. "I hate her . . . for breaking Sid's heart."

"Oh, oh, iverybody's heart gets a bit av a crack at one time or another," said Judy. "Siddy isn't the first b'y to be jilted and he won't be the last, as long as the poor girls haven't got the sinse God gave geese."

But Judy didn't like to look at Sid's eyes herself.

When the party was over Pat and Rae went by a mossy, velvety path to their tent in the bush, amid a growth of young white, wild cherry trees. They had achieved their long-cherished dream of sleeping out in the silver bush and the reality was more beautiful than the dream, even when the wind blew the tent down on them one night and Little Mary was half smothered before they could find her. There was another new baby at the Bay Shore and Little Mary had been committed to the care of Aunt Pat until her mother should be about. They all loved Little Mary but Aunt Pat adored and spoiled her. To see Little Mary running about the garden on her dear chubby legs, pausing now and then to lift a flower to her small nose, or following Judy out to feed the chickens, or chasing kittens in the old barns, where generations of furry things had frisked their little lives and ceased to be, gave Pat never-ending thrills. And the questions she would ask . . . "Aunt Pat, why weren't ears made plain?" . . . "Aunt Pat, have f'owers little souls?" . . . "Where do the days go, Aunt Pat. Dey mus' go *somewhere*" . . . "Does God live in Judy's blue chest, Aunt Pat?" Once or twice the thought came to Pat that to marry and have a dimpled question mark like this of your very own might even make up for the loss of Silver Bush.

Judy came through the scented darkness to see if they were all right and gossip a little about various things. Judy had been to a funeral that day . . . a very unusual dissipation for her. But old William Madison at the Bridge had died and Judy had worked a few months for his mother before coming to Silver Bush.

"Sure and iverything wint off very well. It was the grand funeral he had and he'd have been rale well plazed if he cud have seen it. He had great fun arranging it all, I'm told. Oh, oh, and he died very politely, asking thim all to ixcuse him for the bother he was putting thim to. His ould Aunt Polly was rale vexed because she didn't be getting the sate at the funeral she thought she shud have but nobody else had inny fault to find wid the programme. It do be hard to plaze ivery one. Polly Madison is one av the Holy Christians... holier than inny av thim, I'm hearing."

For the "go-preacher's" disciples had formed themselves into a "Holy Christian church" and were cruelly referred to in the Glens as the Holy Christians.

"I hear they're going to build a church," said Pat.

"That they are... but they're not calling it a church. It do be 'a place av meeting.' The same Aunt Polly do be giving the land for it. And Mr. Wheeler is coming back to be their minister... or their shepherd as they do be saying, not approving av ministers or av paying thim salaries ather. He'll be living on air no doubt. Aunt Polly says he is very spiritual but I'm thinking it's only the way he has av lifting his eyes and taffying her up. Innyway her husband don't be houlding wid new-fangled religions. 'Are ye prepared to die?' the go-preacher asked him rale solemn-like, I'm tould. But ould Jim Polly was always a hard nut to crack. 'Better be asking if I'm prepared to live,' sez he. 'Living comes first,' sez he."

Pat had detected a sudden movement of Rae's when Judy mentioned Mr. Wheeler's name, and felt her worry increase. Suppose he made up to Rae again!

4

Mr. Wheeler did return and did "make up to" Rae. That is, he fairly haunted Silver Bush and made himself quite agreeable socially... or tried to. The Gardiners no longer went to any of his services and the Holy Christians thought he might find more spiritual ways of spending his time than playing violin duets with Rae Gardiner and mooning about the garden with Pat until the very cats were bored. For Pat decidedly put herself forward to entertain him when he came and contrived to be present during most of the duets. To be sure, Rae laughed at and made constant fun of him. But she never seemed her usual saucy, indifferent self in his presence. She was quiet and subdued, with never a coquettish look, and Pat was not exactly easy. The creature *was* handsome in his way, with his dark eyes and crinkly sweep of hair, and his voice in which there were echoes of everything. Aunt Polly's daughter, who taught in South Glen, was reputed to have said that he had a certain Byronic charm. Byronic charm or not Pat wasn't going to have any nonsense and she played gooseberry with amiable persistence whenever he appeared. He looked a great deal at Rae and dropped his voice tenderly when he spoke to her: but he showed no aversion to talking with Pat . . . "currying favour," Tillytuck said.

Judy teased Rae sometimes about him.

"Sure and he'd be easy to cook for, Cuddles darlint. They're telling me he niver ates innything but nuts and bran biscuits. No wonder he's not nading a salary. But how about kaping a wife?"

"You do say such ridiculous things," said Rae rather snappishly. "What is it to me whether he can keep a wife or not?"

Tillytuck was not quite easy in his mind about it. He considered Mr. Wheeler a dangerous creature and wondered why Long Alec tolerated his presence at all. As he entirely disapproved of the Holy Christians he decided he would take up with church-going again as a token of his disapproval. He took several weeks to accumulate enough courage to go, being afraid, as he told Judy, of making too much of a sensation. But when he finally did go and nobody took any particular notice of it he was secretly furious.

"There wasn't a good-looking woman in church," he grumbled, "and no great shakes of a minister. He runs to words and I don't believe his views on the devil are sound. Sort of flabby. I like a devil with some backbone."

"Suppose you do be going to the Holy Christians," said Judy disdainfully, as she sliced up her red cabbage for pickling. "I'm hearing they have wrestling matches wid That Person quite frequent."

"The people of this place are having too much truck with Holy Christians as it is," said Tillytuck sourly, "and the time will come when they'll see it."

"There'll be no harm come to Silver Bush from that poor lad," said Judy. "And ye'll all be getting a rale surprise some day."

"You've got wheels in your head," scoffed Tillytuck.

Pat, at that moment, was working in the garden, at peace with herself and all the world. Somehow, she always felt safe from change in that garden. Just now it seemed to be taking pleasure in itself. Its flowers were guests not prisoners . . . its blue delphiniums, its frail fleeting loveliness of poppies, its Canterbury bells, delicious mauve flecked with purple, its roses of gold and snow, its lilies of milk and wine.

Westward the sun was sinking low over a far land of shining hills. The air was sweet with a certain blended fragrance that only the Silver Bush garden knew. The whole lovesome place was full of soft amethyst shadows.

What fairy things the seeds of immortelles were! What a lovely name "bee balm" was! It was on evenings like this long ago she had listened for Joe's whistle as he came home from work. There was never any whistle now... Sid never whistled. Poor Sid! Would he never get over fretting for that hateful Dorothy? He was running around, here, there and everywhere, with all kinds of girls, rumour said. They saw very little of him at Silver Bush. At work all day... and off in the evenings till late. Mother's eyes were very sad sometimes. Judy advised patience... he would come back to himself yet. Pat found it hard to be patient. At times she felt like shaking Sid. Why should he shut her out of his life as he did? That was always one of the little shadows in the background.

There was a hint of September coolness blowing across August's languor... another summer almost gone. The years were certainly beginning to spin past rather quickly. Well, to grow old with Silver Bush would not be hard, Pat reflected, with the philosophy of one who is as yet very far from age.

Suddenly Pat scowled. There was that wretched Mr. Wheeler coming up the lane. Thank goodness, Rae had gone to Winnie's. Now for another evening of boredom. When would he take the hint that his attentions to Rae weren't welcome to her or anybody else? Her lovely garden evening would be quite spoiled. And he had been here only last night. Really, he was becoming an intolerable nuisance. Would it be violating Silver Bush traditions too flagrantly to give him a hint of it?

Pat's greeting was a trifle distant and she went on coolly snipping off delphinium seeds. Bold-and-Bad, who had been prowling among the shrubs, made a few spiteful remarks. You couldn't hoodwink Bold-and-Bad.

Mr. Wheeler stood looking down at her. Pat had an old sunburned felt hat of Sid's on her head which she would not have thought... if she had thought about it at all... likely to attract masculine admiration. And she wore an ancient brown crepe dress which burrs and stick-tights could no longer injure. She did not know how its warm hues brought out the creaminess of her skin... the gloss of her hair... the fire of her amber eyes. She was really looking her best and when, after a rather overlong silence, she raised her eyes to her caller's she found his dark, soulful orbs... the adjectives were Aunt Polly's daughter's... gazing down at her with a strange expression in their depths. An incredible idea came to Pat... and was instantly dismissed. Nonsense! She wished he wouldn't stand so close to her. She knew at once what he had had for supper. How overfull his red lips were! And when had his finger-nails been cleaned last? *Why* didn't somebody come along? People were always somewhere else when you wanted them and when you didn't you simply fell over them.

"You are smiling... you have such a fascinating smile. What are you thinking of, Patricia," he said in a low, caressing tone.

Merciful goodness, suppose she told him what she was thinking! Pat had hard work to avert a grin. And then the bolt fell, straight out of the blue.

Mr. Wheeler helped himself to one of her hands and looked at it.

"Little white hand," he murmured. "Little white hand that holds my heart."

Pat's hands were brown and not particularly little. She tried to pull it away. But he held on and put his arm around her. Worse and more of it, as Tillytuck would say. Suppose Judy were looking out of the kitchen window!

"Please, don't be so... foolish," said Pat coldly.

"I'm not foolish. I am wise... very wise... wise with the wisdom of countless ages." His voice was getting lower and tenderer with every word. "I've been wanting this opportunity for weeks. It has been so hard to find you alone. Dearest, sweetest of angels, have you any idea how much I love you... have loved you for a thousand lives?"

"I never thought of such a thing... I always thought it was Rae," was all poor Pat could gasp.

Mr. Wheeler smiled patronisingly.

"You couldn't have thought that, my darling. Miss Rachel is a charming child. But it is you, my sweet... and always has been since the first moment I drowned my soul in your beautiful eyes. I think I must have dreamed you all my life... and now my dream has come true." He tried to draw her closer. "You belong to me... you know you do. We will have such a wonderful life together, my queen."

Pat recovered herself. She wrested her hand from his clasp, feeling quite furious over her ridiculous position.

"You must forget all this nonsense, Mr. Wheeler," she said decisively. "I hadn't the slightest idea you felt that way about me. And..." Pat was growing angry, "just how did you come to imagine that I would marry *you*?"

Mr. Wheeler dropped her hand and looked down at her, with something rather unpleasant in his eyes.

"You have encouraged me to think so." His voice had lost a good deal of its smooth oiliness. "I cannot believe you do not care for me."

"Please try," said Pat in a dangerous tone. It flicked on the raw. A dark flush spread over Mr. Wheeler's face. He seemed all at once to be quite a different person.

"You have shown me very plainly that you liked my society, Miss Gardiner... almost *too* plainly. I consider that I had every right to suppose that my proposal would be welcome... very welcome. You have flirted with me shamelessly... you have lured me on, for your own amusement I must now suppose. I should have known it... I was well warned... I was told what you were...."

Pat, looking into his angry eyes, felt as she had felt one day when she had turned over an old, beautiful mossy stone in the Whispering Lane and seen what was underneath.

"I think you had better go, Mr. Wheeler," she said icily.

"Oh, I'm going... I'm going... and rest assured I shall never darken the doors of this place again."

Mr. Wheeler stalked off, his conceit considerably slimmed down, and Pat, still in a swither of various emotions, rushed into the kitchen, displaced a chairful of indignant cats, and gave tongue.

"Oh, oh, and what were you and His Riverince colloguing in the garden about that sint him down the lane at the rate av no man's business?" demanded Judy.

"Judy, I'm feeling so many different things I don't know which I'm feeling most. That horrible creature actually asked me... *me*, Pat Gardiner... to marry him! And he'd been eating onions, Judy!"

"Sure and weren't ye by way av knowing he was a vegetarian," said Judy coolly. "I've been ixpicting this for some time..."

"Judy! What made you expect it?"

"The way he had av looking at ye, whin ye weren't looking at him."

"Oh, Judy... the worst of it is... he thinks I encouraged

him! I feel I'm disgraced. And when he found I wouldn't
marry him...he was horrid. He hasn't *any* manners, not
even bad ones."

"The higher a monkey climbs the more he shows his
tail," quoted Judy. "Niver be taking it to heart, Patsy. Ye're
rid av him now for good."

"I really think so, Judy. I've an idea he meant it when he
said he would never darken our doors again."

"Sure now and that will be our loss," said Judy sarcastically. "He's kipt out considerable av the sunshine this summer. And...I'm not sticking up for him, Patsy...I did
always be thinking he was no rale gintleman under the
skin...but you *did* be always sticking round..."

"I did it to keep him away from Rae. I...I...thought
he'd take the hint. I never dreamed he'd think I was in love
with him...*him*! Judy, it's really a ridiculous and tiresome
world by spells. I'm going up to the Long House...I've got
to have something to take the taste of the Reverend Wheeler
out of my soul and to talk nice scandal with David and
Suzanne may do it."

"I'm wondering how Cuddles will be taking this," muttered
Judy after Pat had gone out. "I'm thinking iverybody but ould
Judy Plum is blind as a bat round here. Well, we're rid av the
go-pracher, glory be. But I'm not knowing if I like that Kirk
man much better. He's got his eye on her. He's not
hurrying...whin it's yer second you do be more careful-like.
But I do be knowing the signs. Oh, oh, it's a wonder me bit
av corned ham wasn't being biled too much whin I was
listening to Patsy's troubles. But it's done to the quane's taste
and I'm setting it in the ice-house to cool. Beaus may come
and beaus may go but we must be having our liddle comforts."

Pat, up at the Long House, soon forgot her anger and
humiliation in the company of David and Suzanne. They
talked and laughed together around the fireplace the Kirks
had built in Bet's crescent of trees while Ichabod sat close to
David and Alphonso shared his favours between the girls and
the evening star looked over cloudy purple ramparts in the
west. It seemed to Pat that every evening she spent there she
grew wiser and maturer in some mysterious way. Their talk
was so different...so rich...so stimulating...so brimming
over with ideas. The ghosts of the past were laid. She had
begun to think of the Long House as the home of Suzanne
and David rather than as the home of Bets.

"She is growing older and I'm growing younger. Perhaps we'll meet," David was thinking.

"Their souls are the same age," Suzanne was thinking.

But nobody knew what Alphonso-of-the-emerald-eyes or Ichabod thought.

The Fourth Year

PAT looked out of the Little Parlour window a bit wistfully one evening in late November. Another summer was ended. How quickly summers passed now! There was a hard grey twilight after a little snow and there was a threat of still more snow in the dour air. The shadows . . . chilly, hostile shadows . . . seemed to be raining out of the silver bush. A biting wind was lashing everything as if determined to take its ill-temper out on the world. A few forlorn yellow leaves blew crazily over the lawn. An empty nest swung lonesomely in the wind from a bough of the big apple tree on which the pale yellow-green apples always stayed so long after the leaves were gone. The apples were no good and were never picked but the tree always looked so exquisite in its spring blossom that Pat wouldn't have it cut down. It had been what Pat called a peevish day and even the loveliness of a tall, dark spruce tree near the dyke, powdered with feathers of snow, did not give her the shiver of delight such things usually did. She thought it was the kind of a day that would make people quarrel if people ever quarrelled at Silver Bush. But November had been a vexing month all through . . . one day glorious . . . the next day savage. You never knew just where you were with it. And Pat did not like this evening . . . she felt as if some long finger of change which was always reaching out to her was at last just on the point of touching her.

She was restless. She would have liked to go up to the Long House but the Kirks were away. She wished Rae would come home. . . . Rae must have called somewhere after school. Though Rae hadn't been exactly the same for the past two months. Pat couldn't lay her finger just on the point of difference but she felt it in her sensitive soul. Rae sometimes snapped now... she who had always been so sunshiny. And sometimes Pat thought that when she looked meaningly at Rae in the presence of others, to share the savour of some subtle joke, Rae averted her eyes without any answering twinkle. And at times it almost seemed as if she had taken up a pose of being misunderstood. What was wrong? Weren't things going well in school? From all Pat could find out they were but she couldn't rid herself of the feeling that Rae had some secret trouble... for the first time an unshared trouble. Nothing was really changed... and yet Pat had moments of feeling that everything was changed. Once she asked Rae if anything was worrying her and Rae snapped out so savage a "Nonsense!" that Pat held her peace. Surely it couldn't be the fact that Mr. Wheeler had suddenly stopped coming to Silver Bush and was reputed to have a wild case on a visiting girl from New Brunswick that accounted for the mournful mauve smudges under Rae's blue eyes some mornings.

Pat reassured herself by reflecting that this would pass. And meanwhile Silver Bush made everything bearable. Pat loved it more with every passing year and all the little household rites that meant so much to her. Always when she came home to Silver Bush its peace and dignity and beauty seemed to envelop her like a charm. Nothing very terrible could happen there.

Judy's cheery philosophy never failed, but Pat could not mention even to Judy the vague chill of change between herself and Rae. In the evenings when they foregathered in the kitchen and Tillytuck played on his fiddle she sometimes felt that she must only have imagined it. Rae was the gayest of them all then... "a bit too gay," Judy thought, though she never said so. Things did be often arranging themselves if you just let them alone. Judy was more worried over a reckless look she sometimes caught in Sid's brown eyes and over certain bits of gossip that came her way occasionally.

Pat lighted the lamp as Sid and Rae came in. Rae flung her school-books on a chair and said nothing. But Sid had a chuckle and a bit of news.

"Your go-preacher has gone, Pat. The Holy C's are blaming you for it. They say you flirted with him and made a fool of him and he can't stand the place now. Aunt Polly is especially down on you. She adores that shepherd."

Sid spoke banteringly and Pat had some laughing rejoinder ready when a smothered sound, between a gasp and a cry, made them look at Rae.

"Great Scott, sis, you'll singe your eyelashes if you let your eyes blaze like that," said Sid.

Rae took no notice of him. She was looking at Pat.

"So this is your doing . . . you have driven him away," she said in a low, tense tone . . . such a tone as Pat had never heard Rae use before . . . seventeen-year-old Rae whom Pat still thought of as a child. Pat almost laughed . . . but laughter suddenly fell dead on her lips. Why, the poor darling was in earnest! And how pretty she looked in her golden-brown dress with her flushed cheeks and overbright eyes! Her head positively shone like a lamp in the dark corner. She was so sweet . . . and absurd . . . and deadly serious. This last realization should have warned Pat but didn't.

"Rae, dearest, don't be foolish," she said gently.

"Oh, don't be foolish," mocked Rae furiously. "That's *your* attitude I know . . . has been right along. *I* am a mere baby of course . . . *I* have no rights . . . no feelings . . . no feelings *at all* . . . no claim to be considered a human being. 'Don't be foolish,' says the wise Patricia. That really *is* a clever idea!"

Rae's voice trembled with passion. She rushed out of the Little Parlour and up the stairs like a golden whirlwind. There were three doors on the way to her room and she banged them all.

"Whew!" whistled Sid. "I always knew she had a bad case on Wheeler but I didn't think it went that deep."

"Sid . . . you don't think she cared really!"

"Oh, calf love no doubt. We all survive it. But it hurts at the time." Sid laughed a bit bitterly.

Pat went up to her room. Rae was pacing up and down it like a caged animal. She turned a stormy young face on her sister.

"Leave me alone, can't you? You've done me enough harm, haven't you? You took him from me . . . deliberately. I saw you trying to attract him. What chance had I? Well, I forgave you. But now he's gone . . . he's gone . . . and I'll never see him again . . . and I can't stand it. I hate you . . . I hate you . . . I hate everything."

"Please don't let's quarrel," said Pat helplessly. In a desperate effort to be calm she picked up her best pair of silk stockings and began to polish the mirror with them, not in the least knowing what she held in her hand. It was the last straw for Rae.

"Who is quarrelling? Don't try to put the blame on me."

"Oh, Rae, Rae . . . don't twist everything I say to mean something else."

"Oh, don't try to twist things, she says. Who twisted things this summer . . . all summer . . . to make him think me a child? It's *such* an interesting thing to watch the man you love making love to another woman and that woman your own sister who is deliberately trying to attract him, just for her own amusement!"

"Rae . . . never . . . never! I *did* try to save you from . . . from . . ."

"Save me! From what? You may well hesitate. You know you made him think I cared for Jerry Arnold. Jerry Arnold! A pipsqueak like that! It was Lawrence Wheeler I loved all the time and you knew it. He loved me, too, till you came between us. Yes, he did. The first time we met we felt . . . we *knew* . . . we had loved each other in a thousand former lives."

For the life of her Pat couldn't help smiling. She recognized the phrase. Hadn't Lawrence Wheeler of the soulful eyes said it to *her*?

"Suppose we talk . . . or try to . . . as if we were grown up," she suggested kindly.

"Oh, but I'm not grown up . . . I'm only a child." Rae was pacing feverishly up and down the room. "A child can't see . . . can't love . . . can't suffer. *Can't suffer!* Oh, what I've gone through these past two months! And nobody saw . . . nobody understood . . . nobody has ever tried to understand me. *You* didn't. *You* care for nothing but Silver Bush. You acted as you did just because you're so crazy to keep Silver Bush always the same. My own sister to use me like that!"

Pat lost her patience and her temper, too. The idea of a scene like this over a creature like Larry Wheeler!

"This has gone far enough," she said frostily.

"I agree with you," Rae was frost instantly also.

"When you come to your senses," said Pat, "you'll realise perhaps just what a goose you've made of yourself over a go-preacher with cow's eyes."

"Don't you think you're really being a little vulgar, my dear Patricia?" said Rae, with eyes of blue ice. "*I* am of no consequence of course . . . but there is such a thing as good taste. You seem to have forgotten that, along with several other things. *Never mention Lawrence Wheeler's name to me again.*"

Pat clamped her teeth together to keep from saying things she would have been terribly sorry for afterwards. The urge to say them passed.

"We've both lost our tempers, Rae, and said foolish things. We'll feel differently in the morning."

"Oh, will we? I'll never feel differently... and I'll never forgive you, Pat Gardiner... never. You and that old widower of yours!"

"Who is being vulgar now?" Pat was furious again. "At least Mr. Kirk is a gentleman!"

"And Lawrence Wheeler isn't, I suppose?"

"You can suppose what you like. You've dragged his name up again. He was simply too sloppy for anything. I never dreamed that *you* ... Rae Gardiner of Silver Bush ... could take him seriously. And he'd been eating onions before he proposed to me."

"Oh, so he proposed to you. I didn't know you had lured him on that far. I thought even you had enough self-respect to stop short of that."

"We have had enough of this," said Pat, her voice trembling.

"I think so, too. But let me tell you this, Pat Gardiner. Since you are so bent on 'saving' people you'd better look after Sid a bit. He's dangling around May Binnie again. I've known it for weeks but I didn't say anything about it because I knew it would worry you. I had a little consideration for *you*. But you've been so intent on running my life that it has ceased to matter to you what Sid does, I suppose."

"Rae dearest... we're both upset... we're both saying things we shouldn't... let's forget this. We mustn't let any one know we've quarrelled...."

"I don't care if all the world knows it." Rae marched out of the room. She did not come back. That night she slept in the Poet's room... if she slept at all. Pat didn't. It was the first time since the night before mother's operation that she had lain awake all night. Surely she and Rae couldn't have quarrelled... after all their years of comradeship and love ... all their secrets kept and shared together. It must be a horrid dream. The Binnie girls were always quarrelling... one expected nothing better of them. But such things simply couldn't happen at Silver Bush. Was there any truth in what

Rae had said about Sid and May? There couldn't be. It was nothing but idle gossip. She knew Sid better than that. Of course May Binnie was pretty, with the obvious, indisputable prettiness of rich black hair, vivid colour, laughing, brilliant, bold eyes. But Sid could never care for her after Bets... or even after sweet foolish mistaken Dorothy. Pat brushed the teasing thought away. It was so easy to start gossip in the Glens. Nothing mattered just now but the quarrel with Rae.

Then it was dawn. Very early dawn is a dreary thing. Nothing is quite human. The world is "fey." And there was no Rae in the little bed beside hers. Pat had always loved to watch Rae waking up... she had such a pretty way of doing it. And the morning sunshine always poured in on her head, making it like a warm pool of gold on the pillow. But there was no Rae this morning... no sunshine. Pat sat up and looked out of the window. The different farmsteads were beginning to take form in the pale grey light on the thin snow. The little row of sheep tracks leading from the church barn across the Mince Pie field might have been made by Pan. A chilly foolish little wind of dawn was sighing around the eaves. A flock of tiny snowbirds settled on the roof of the granary. The haystacks in the Field of Farewell Summers looked gnome-like in the pale greyness. Pat gazed drearily at the blown clouds and the wide white fields and the lonely star of morning. Everything seemed so much the same... and everything was so horribly changed.

Pat looked like the ghost of herself at breakfast but Rae came down, cool, gay, smiling, her face apparently as blithe as the day. She tossed an airy word to Pat, bantered Sid, complimented Judy on her muffins and went off to school with a parting pat for Bold-and-Bad.

Pat tried to feel relieved. It had blown over. Rae was ashamed of her outburst and wanted to ignore it. She was just going to act as if nothing had happened.

"I won't remember it either," vowed Pat. But there was a sore spot in her heart, even after she had talked it all over with Judy... Judy who had suspected all along that Rae was nursing some secret sorrow that loomed large in the eyes of seventeen.

"Judy, it was dreadful. We both lost our tempers and said blistering things... things that can never be forgotten."

"Oh, oh, it do be amazing how much we can be forgetting in life," said Judy.

"But it was so... so ugly, Judy. There has never been a quarrel at Silver Bush before."

"Oh, oh, hasn't there been now, darlint? Sure there was lashings av thim whin yer dad and his gang were growing up. The rafters would ring wid their shouting at each other... and Edith giving her opinion av iverybody ivery once in so long. This will be passing away just as they did. Did ye iver be hearing the rason ould Angus MacLeod av the South Glin didn't hang himsilf? He made up his mind to, all bekase life did be getting too tejus. And thin he had a fight wid his wife... the first one they'd iver had. It livened him up so he wint out and used the rope to tie up a calf and niver was timpted agin. As for poor liddle Cuddles, that sore and hurt and thinking it do be going to hurt foriver... just ye be taking no notice, Patsy... be yersilf and iverything will be just the same only more so."

"Mother must know nothing of it... I won't have mother hurt," said Pat firmly.

"If she can be kaping it from her she do be cliverer than I'm thinking," Judy told Gentleman Tom when Pat had gone out. "And I'm fearing this quarrel do be a bit more sarious than I've been pretinding. Whin two people don't be caring over-much for aich other a quarrel niver amounts to much betwane thim. It's soon made up. But whin they love aich other like Patsy and Cuddles it do be going so dape it's rale hard to be forgetting it. I'm wishing Long Alec had chased that go-pracher off Silver Bush wid a shot-gun the first time he iver showed his cow-eyes here. Whatever cud inny girl be seeing in him? Didn't he nearly sit down on Gintleman Tom the first time he called!"

2

December was a hard month for Pat. Life seemed to drag itself along like a wounded animal. Winter set in early. It snowed continuously for three weeks. Little storm demons danced in the yard and whirled along the lanes. Everywhere were huge banks of snow, white in the sun, pale blue in the shadows. There were quaint caps of it on the unused chimneys. It was piled deep in the Secret Field when Pat went to it on snowshoes. One felt that spring could never come again, either to Silver Bush or one's heart. On a rare fine day the world seemed made of diamond dust, cold, dazzling, splendid, heartless. There was the beauty of winter moonlight on frosted panes and chill harpings of wind beneath cold, unfriendly stars. At least, Pat felt they were unfriendly. Things were *not* the same. Always between her and Rae was the coldness and shadow of a thing that must not be spoken of... that must be forgotten but could not be forgotten. Rae chattered continuously of surface things but in regard to everything else she preserved a silence more dreadful than anger. There was always that false gaiety, good-humoured and polite! To Pat that politeness of Rae's was a terrible thing. They might have been strangers... they *were* strangers. Rae seemed to have locked her heart against her sister forever.

Just before Christmas Rae announced carelessly that she had been awarded a scholarship... a three months' course in nature study at the O. A. C. in Guelph and meant to take advantage of it. The trustees had granted her leave of absence and Molly MacLeod of South Glen was to take the school for the three months.

"That is splendid," said Pat, who knew Rae must have been aware of the possibility of this for weeks and had never said a word about it.

"Isn't it?" Rae was brightly enthusiastic. She was very busy during the following days preparing for her going and talking casually of her plans. She was all radiance and sparkle and teased Judy mercilessly because Judy was afraid she would learn to smoke cigarettes at Guelph. But she never consulted Pat about anything and when Pat, at Christmas, gave her a crimson kimono with darker crimson 'mums embroidered on it, remarking that she thought it would be nice for Guelph, Rae merely said, "How ripping of you! It's perfectly gorgeous." But she never told Pat that Uncle Horace had sent a check for a new coat and when she bought a stunning one of natural leopard with cuffs and collar of seal, she showed it to Judy and mother and the aunts but not to Pat... merely left it lying on her bed where Pat could see it if she chose. Pat was too hurt to mention it.

When Rae went away, looking very smart and grown-up in her leopard coat and a little green hat tipped provocatively over one eye, she kissed Pat good-bye as she did the others but her lips merely brushed Pat's cheek and most of the kiss was expended on air. Pat watched her out of sight with a breaking heart and cried herself to sleep that night. The

loneliness was hideous. She couldn't bear to look at the bed
where Rae had slept or the little old bronze slippers Rae had
danced in so often but thought too worn to take to Guelph.
One of them was lying forlornly under the bureau, the other
under the bed. Pat got up and put them together. They did
not look quite so forlorn and discarded then.

True, there had been no real comradeship between her
and Rae for weeks, though they had shared the same room
and sat at the same table. But now that Rae was gone it
seemed as if hope had gone with her. Pat was too proud and
hurt even to talk it over with Judy. It was the first time she
had not been able to talk a thing over with Judy.

That cold, indifferent good-bye kiss of Rae's! Little Cuddles who used to put her chubby arms about her neck and
love her "so hard!" Pat couldn't bear to think of it. She looked
at her new calendar hanging on the wall . . . a very elaborate
affair which Tillytuck had given her. She had always thought a
new calendar a fascinating thing, yet with something a little
terrible about it. It was rather fun to flip over the leaves and
wonder just what would be happening on this or that day.
Now she hated to see it. There were three months to be lived
through before Rae would come back. And when she did
come would things be any better?

Bold-and-Bad padded into the room and jumped on the
bed. Pat gathered him into her arms. Dear old cat, he was
still left to her anyhow. And Silver Bush! Whatever came and
went, whoever loved or did not love her, there was still Silver
Bush.

Nevertheless Pat looked so haggard and woe-begone at
breakfast that Judy wished things not lawful to be uttered
concerning go-preachers.

During that dreary winter Pat's only real pleasures were
her evenings at the Long House—Suzanne and David were so
kind and understanding . . . especially David. "I always feel so
comfortable with him," thought Pat . . . and her letters from
Hilary. One of his stimulating epistles always heartened her
up. She saved them up to read in the little violet-blue hour
before night came . . . the hour she and Rae had been used to
spend in their room, talking and joking. She always slept
better after a letter from Hilary. And very poorly after a letter
from Rae. For Rae wrote Pat in regular turn . . . flippant little
notes, each seeming just like another turn of the screw. They
were full of college news and jokes, such as she might have

written to any one. But never a word about Silver Bush affairs... no reference to home jokes. Rae kept all that for her letters to mother and Judy. "When I see the evening star over the trees on the campus I always think of Silver Bush," Rae wrote Judy. If Rae had only written that to her, thought Pat.

Pat sent Rae a box of goodies and Rae was quite effusive.

"No doubt it's a youthful taste to be thinking of things to eat," she wrote back, "but how the girls did appreciate your box. It was really awfully kind of you to think of sending it,"..."as if I were some outsider who couldn't be expected to send her a box," thought Pat.... "I hear that Uncle Tom has had the mumps and that Tillytuck is still howling hymns to the moon in the granary. Also that Sid is still dancing attendance on May Binnie. She'll get him yet. The Binnies never let go. Do you suppose North Glen will faint if I appear out in a bright yellow rain coat when I come home? Or one of those long slinky sophisticated evening dresses? Silver Bush must really wake up to the fact that fashions change. I had a letter from Hilary last night. It's odd to think this is his last year in college. He has won another architectural scholarship and is going to locate in British Columbia when he is through. He thinks he will be able to get out here to see me before I leave."

Hilary had not told Pat about any of his plans. The announcement of Mr. Wheeler's marriage was in the paper that day. Judy viciously poked the sheet that bore it into the fire and held it down with the poker.

Two weeks later it was the end of March and Judy was getting her dye-pot ready. And Rae was coming home. Pat found herself dreading it... and broken-hearted because she was dreading it.

"What is the matter with Pat this spring?" Long Alec asked Judy. "She hasn't seemed like herself all winter... and now she's positively moping. Is she in love with anybody?"

Judy snorted.

"Well then, does she need a tonic? I remember you used to dose us all with sulphur and molasses every spring, Judy. Perhaps it might do her good."

Judy did not think sulphur and molasses would help Pat much.

It was a mild day when Rae came home...a day full of the soft languor of early spring when nature is still tired after her wrestle with winter. There had been a light, misty snowfall in the night and Pat went for a walk to the Secret Field in the afternoon to see if she could win from-it a little courage to face Rae's return. It was very lovely in those silent woods with their white-mossed trees. Every step she took revealed some new enchantment as if some ambitious elfin artificer were striving to show just how much could be done with nothing but the white mystery of snow in hands that knew how to make use of it. Such a snowfall, thought Pat, was the finest test of beauty. Whenever there was any ugliness or distortion it showed it mercilessly: but beauty and grace were added unto beauty and grace even as unto him that hath shall be given more abundantly. She wished she had some one to enjoy the loveliness with her...Hilary... Suzanne... David... Rae. Rae! But Rae would be coming home in a few hours' time, artificially cordial, looking at her with bright, indifferent eyes.

"I just can't bear it," thought Pat miserably.

When Pat heard the jingle of sleigh-bells coming up the lane in the "dim" she fled to her room. Every one else was in the kitchen waiting for Rae... mother and Sid and Judy and Tillytuck and the cats. Pat felt she had no part or lot among them.

It had turned colder. There was a thin green sky behind the snowy trees and the silver gladness of an evening star over the birches. Pat heard the noise of laughter and greeting in the kitchen. Well, she supposed she must go down.

There was a sound of flying feet on the stairs. Suddenly it seemed to Pat that there was no air in the room. Rae burst in... a rosy, radiant Rae, her eyes as blue as ever, her mouth like a kissed flower. She engulfed Pat in a fierce leopard-skin hug.

"Patsy darling... why weren't you down? Oh, but it's good to see you again!"

This was the old Rae. Pat was afraid she was going to howl. All at once life was beautiful again. It was as if she had wakened up from a horrible dream and seen a starlit sky.

"Pat, haven't you a word to say to me? You aren't sore at me still, are you? Oh, I wouldn't blame you if you were. I was the world's prize idiot. I realised that very soon after we quarrelled but I was too proud to admit it. And you wrote me such icy, stiff letters while I was away."

"Oh!" Pat began to laugh and cry at once. They got their arms around each other. Everything was all right... beautifully all right again.

It was a wonderful evening. Every one enjoyed Judy's superlative supper, with Rae feeding the cats tid-bits and Tillytuck and Judy outdoing themselves telling stories. Again and again Rae's eyes met Pat's over the table in the old camaraderie. Even King William looked as if sometime he might really get across the Boyne. But the best of all came at bedtime when they settled down for the old delight of talking things over with Bold-and-Bad tensing and flexing his claws on Pat's bed and Popka blinking goldenly on Rae's.

"Isn't it jolly to be good sisters again?" exclaimed Rae. "I feel like that verse in the Bible where all the morning stars sang together. It's just been horrid... horrid. How could I have been such a little fool? I just wallowed in self-pity all the fall and then it seemed as if that outburst had to come. And all over that... that creature! I'm so ashamed of ever dreaming I cared for him. I can't understand how I could have been so... so fantastic. And yet I really did have a terrible case. Of course I knew perfectly well in my heart it could never come to anything. At the very worst of my infatuation... when I was trying to pretend to every one I didn't care a speck... I knew no Silver Bush girl could ever marry a go-preacher. But that didn't prevent me from being crazy about him. It seemed so romantic... a hopeless love, you know. Two fond souls forever sundered by family pride and all that, you know. I just revelled in it... I can see that now. The way he used to look at me across that barn! And once, when he read his text... 'Behold thou art fair, my love, behold thou art fair. Thou hast dove's eyes'... he looked right at me and I nearly died of rapture. He really was in love with me then. You never saw the poem he wrote me, Pat. He was jealous of everything, it seemed... of 'the wind that whispered in my ear'... of 'the sunshine that played on my hair'... of 'the moonbeam that lay on my pillow.' The lines didn't scan very well and the rhymes limped but I thought it was a masterpiece. Can you wonder I was furious when you just stepped in and lifted him under my very nose? By the way, he's married, did you know, Pat?"

"Yes. I saw it in the paper."

"Oh, he sent *me* an announcement," giggled Rae. "You should have seen it. With scrolls of forget-me-nots around the border! If I hadn't been cured before that would have cured me. Pat, why is it written in the stars that girls have to make fools of themselves."

"We were both geese," said Pat.

"Let's blame it all on the moon," said Rae.

They felt very near to each other. And then Judy came in with cups of delicious hot cocoa for them and a "liddle bite" of Bishop's bread and a handful of raisins as if they were children again.

"Just think," said Pat, "to other people this day has been only Wednesday. To me it's the day you came home... home to *me*... back into my life. It may be March still by the calendar but it's April in my heart... April full of spring song."

"Here's to my having more sense in all the years to come," said Rae, waving her cup of cocoa.

"To *our* having more sense," corrected Pat.

"It's lovely to be home again," sighed Rae. "I had a splendid time at Guelph... and I really did learn lots... much more than just nature study. The social side was all right, too. There were some nice boys. We had a gorgeous trip to Niagara. But I am half inclined to agree with you that there is no place like Silver Bush. It must do something to people who live in it. Those darling cats! I really haven't seen a decent cat since I left the Island, Pat... no cat who looked as if he really enjoyed being a cat, you know. I wish we could do some crazy thing to celebrate. Sleep out in the moonlight or something like that. But it's too Marchy. So we must just have a good pi-jaw. Tell me *everything* that has happened since I went away. Your letters were so... so *charitable*. There was no kick in them. Let me tell you once for all, Pat, that a person who always speaks well of every one is a most uninteresting correspondent. I'm sure you must be boiling over with gossip. Have there been any nice juicy scandals? Who has been born... married... engaged? Not you, I hope. Pat, don't go and get married to David. He's far too old for you, darling... he really is."

"Don't be silly, sweetheart. I just want David as a friend."

"The darlints," said Judy happily, as she went downstairs. "I was knowing the good ould Gardiner sinse wud come out on top."

It was wonderful to be too happy to sleep. The very sky through the window looked glad. And when Pat wakened a verse she had heard David read a few days before . . . a verse which had hurt her at the time but now seemed like a friend . . . came to her mind.

> *"Whoever wakens on a day,*
> *Happy to know and be,*
> *To enjoy the air, to love his kind,*
> *To labour and be free,*
> *Already his enraptured soul*
> *Lives in Eternity."*

She repeated the lines to herself as she stood by her window. Rae slipped out of bed and joined her. Judy was crossing the yard, carrying something for the comfort of her hens.

"Pat," said Rae a bit soberly, "does it ever strike you that Judy is growing old?"

"Don't!" Pat winced. "I don't want to think of anything to spoil this happy morning."

But she did know that Judy was growing old, shut her eyes to it as she might. And hadn't Judy said to her rather solemnly one day,

"Patsy darlint, there do be a nightdress wid a croshay yoke all riddy in the top right hand till av me blue chist if I iver tuk ill suddent-like."

"Judy . . . don't you feel well?" Pat had cried in alarm.

"Oh, oh, niver be worrying, darlint. I'm fit as a fiddle. Only I did be rading in the dead list av the paper this morning that ould Maggie Patterson had died in Charlottetown. We were cronies whin I did be coming to the Island at first and she do be only a year older than mesilf. So I just thought I'd mintion the nightdress to ye. The ould lady in Castle McDermott had one av lace and sating she always put on whin she had the doctor."

"I'm so glad you and Rae are as you used to be, Pat," said mother when Pat took her breakfast into her. Pat looked at mother.

"I didn't think you knew we weren't," she said slowly.

Mother smiled.

"You can't hide such things from mothers, darling. We always know. And now I think a little wise forgetfulness is indicated."

Pat stooped and kissed her.

"My precious dear, wasn't it lucky father fell in love with *you*," she breathed.

Rae was in kinks in the hall when Pat went out.

"Oh, Pat, Pat, life *is* worth living. I've just seen Judy making Tillytuck take a dose of castor oil. You'll never know what you've missed."

Yes, life was worth living again. And now Pat felt that she could throw herself into housecleaning plans and spring renovating with a heart at leisure from itself. The days that had seemed so endless wouldn't be half long enough now for all she wanted to crowd into them.

4

David and Suzanne went to England for a trip that spring and the Long House was closed for the summer. Pat missed them terribly but Judy and Rae were consolable.

"That Suzanne has been trying iver since she come to make a match betwane her brother and Patsy," Judy told Cuddles. "I've been fearing lately she'd manage it. And him as'll soon be using hair tonics! Patsy hasn't inny other beau after her just now. The min do be getting discouraged. Somehow the word do be going round she thinks nobody good enough for her."

"And there really isn't a man in the Glens she couldn't have by just crooking her finger," said Rae thoughtfully. "I think it's just that way she has of saying 'I know' sympathetically. And she doesn't mean a thing by it."

"Do ye be thinking, Cuddles, that there is inny chance av Jingle coming home this summer now?"

Rae shook her head.

"I'm afraid not, Judy. He's got a big contract for building a mountain inn in B. C. . . . a splendid chance for a young architect. Besides . . . I think he has grown away from us now. He and Pat will never be anything but good friends. You can't make him jealous . . . I know for I've tried . . . so I'm sure he doesn't care for her except just as she cares for him. Do you know, Judy, I think it would be better if the uncles and aunts...and perhaps all of us...would stop teasing Pat about beaus or their absence. She thinks the whole clan is bent on marrying her off...and it rouses the Gardiner obstinacy. There's a streak of it in us all. If you all hadn't been so contemptuous of poor Larry Wheeler I don't believe I'd ever have given him a second thought."

"Girls do be like that, I'm knowing. But I'd like to see both you and Patsy snug and safe, wid some one to care for ye, afore I die, Cuddles darlint."

Rae laughed.

"Judy, I'm only seventeen. Hardly on the shelf yet. And don't you talk of dying...you'll live to see our grandchildren."

Judy shook her head.

"I can't be polishing off a day's work like I used to, Cuddles dear. Oh, oh, we all have to grow old and ye haven't larned yet how quick time do be passing."

"As for Pat," resumed Rae, "I think perhaps she'll never marry. She loves Silver Bush too much to leave it for any man. The best chance David has is that the Long House is so near Silver Bush that she could still keep an eye on it. Do you know that Norma is to be married this summer?"

"I've been hearing it. Mrs. Brian will be rale aisy in her mind now wid both of her girls well settled. Norma'll niver have to lift a hand. Not that I do be thinking her beau is inny great shakes av a man wid all his money though he comes of a rale aristocratic family. His mother now...she was av the Summerside MacMillans and niver did she be letting her husband forget it. She kipt up all the MacMillan traditions... niver wore the same pair av silk stockings twice and her maid had to be saying, 'Dinner is served, madam,' just like that, afore she cud ate a bite, wid service plates and all the flat silver matching. And in sason and out av sason she did be reminding her husband she was a MacMillan along wid iverybody av inny importance on the Island. It was lucky he had a bit av humour in him or it might have been after being a trifle monotonous. Will I iver be forgetting the story I heard him tell on the madam one cilebration at the Bay Shore? It was whin his b'ys, Jim and Davy, were two liddle chaps and Jim did be coming home from church one day rale earnest and sez he to Davy, 'The minister did be talking av Jesus all the time but he didn't be saying who Jesus was.' 'Why, Jesus MacMillan av coorse,' sez Norma's beau, in just the tone av his mother. Mr. MacMillan did be roaring at it, but yer Aunt

Honor thought it was tarrible irriverint. Innyway, a Gardiner is as good as a MacMillan inny day. And now I must be making a few cookies. Liddle Mary will be coming over for a wake. She do be so like Patsy whin she was small. Sometimes I'm wondering if the clock has turned back. She do be always saying good-night to the wind like Patsy did...and the quistions av her! 'Have I *got* to be good, Judy? Can't I be a liddle bad sometimes whin I'm alone wid you?' And, 'What's the use av washing me face after dark, Judy?' Sure and it's a bit av sunshine whin she comes an I'm thinking the very smallest flower in the garden do be glad, niver to mintion the cats."

Pat was really far more interested in Rae's matrimonial prospects than her own. For Rae seemed to be "swithering," as Judy put it, between two very nice young men. Bruce Madison of South Glen and Peter Alward of Charlottetown were both camping on the doorstep, and were frightfully and romantically jealous of each other, turning, so it was said, quite pale when they met. Life, as Tillytuck said, was dramatic because of it.

Pat had nothing against either of them...except that they meant change...and sometimes it was thought that Rae favoured one and then the other. She discussed them as flippantly as usual with Pat and Judy but both Pat and Judy were agreed that it was highly probable she would eventually decide on one of them. Pat hated the thought, of course. But if Rae had to marry some day...of course it wouldn't be for years yet...it *must* be somebody living near. Pat inclined to like Peter best but Judy favoured Bruce.

"We *would* make an awfully good-looking couple," agreed Rae. "I really like Bruce best in summer but I have a rankling suspicion that Peter would be the best for winter. And he always makes me *feel* beautiful...that's a knack some men never have, you may have noticed. But then...his nose! Have you noticed his nose, Pat? It's not so bad now but in a few years it will be very bony and aristocratic. I can't exactly see myself eating breakfast every morning of my life with it opposite me. And it's terrible to think that my daughters might inherit it. It wouldn't matter so much about the boys...a boy can get away with any kind of a nose because few girls are as sensitive to noses as I am. But the poor girls!"

Judy was horrified but she had no great liking for Peter's nose herself. So Silver Bush had its own fun out of the haunting suitors and the Golden Age seemed to have returned and nobody took anything very seriously until Pat went to a dance at the Bay Shore Hotel and Donald Holmes, as Rae announced at the breakfast table next morning, fell for her with a crash that could be heard for miles. What was more, Pat blushed, actually blushed, when Rae said this. Everybody drew the same conclusion from that blush. Pat had met her fate.

At once everybody in the Gardiner clan sat up and took notice. For the rest of the summer Donald Holmes was a constant visitor at Silver Bush. Rae and her two jealous suitors no longer held the centre of the stage. Everybody approved. The Holmes family had the proper social and political traditions, and Donald himself was the junior partner in a prosperous firm of chartered accountants.

"Oh, oh, that do be something like now," Judy told Tillytuck delightedly. "There's brading there. And he'll wear well. Patsy was in the right be waiting."

"Methinks I smell the fragrance of orange blossoms, symbolically speaking," Tillytuck remarked to Uncle Tom.

"Well, it's about time," said Uncle Tom, who was not given to symbols.

"It's really better luck than she deserves after all her flirtations," said Aunt Edith rather sourly.

Pat herself believed she was in love... really in love. There were weeks of pretty speeches and prettier silences and enchanted moons and stars and kittens... though in her secret soul she suspected him of not caring overmuch about cats. But at least he pretended to like the kittens. One couldn't have everything. He was well-born, well-bred, good-looking and charming, and for the first time since the days of Lester Conroy Pat felt thrills and queer sensations generally.

"I thought I'd left all that behind with seventeen," she told Rae, "but it really seems to have come back."

Rae, who was expecting "one of the men she's engaged to..." *à la* May Binnie... carefully perfumed her throat.

"A plain answer to a plain question, Pat. Do you mean to marry him?"

"I'm not Betty Baxter," said Pat with a twinkle.

"Don't be exasperating. Every one knows he means to ask you. Candidly, Pat, I'd like him very much for a brother-in-law."

Pat looked sober. In imagination she saw the paragraph in the Charlottetown papers announcing her engagement.

"I blush when I hear his step at the door," she said meditatively.

"I've noticed that myself," grinned Rae.

"And I suffer agonies of jealousy if he says a word of admiration for any other girl. On the whole... I haven't quite made up my mind... not quite... but I *think*, Rae, when *he* says, 'Will you please?' *I*'ll say, 'Yes, thank you.'"

Rae got up and hugged Pat chokily.

"I'm glad... I'm glad. And yet I'm on the point of howling."

"Confidence for confidence, Rae. Which, if either, of your young men do you intend to marry?"

Rae pulled an ear of Squedunk, who was sitting on his haunches on her bed, gazing at the girls with his usual limpid, round-eyed look. Gentleman Tom looked as if all the wisdom of the ages was his, Bold-and-Bad looked as if life was one amusing adventure, but Squedunk always looked as if he could be a kitten forever if he wanted to.

"Pat, I wish I knew. I've been horribly flippant about it but that was just to cover up. I really don't know. I do like them both so much... Pat, is it ever possible to be in love with two men? It isn't in books, I know... but in life? Because I *do* love them both. They're both darlings. But, Pat, honestly, the minute I decide I like Bruce best I find I have a mind to Peter. And *vice versa*. That's all I can say yet. Well, Norma's wedding comes off next week. Judy is furious because they are going to rehearse the whole ceremony in the church the night before. 'Nixt thing they'll be rehearsing the funerals,' she says. Judy will be simply mad with delight if you marry Donald. And yet she'll die of sorrow when you go. *When you go*... that turns me cold. Oh, Pat, wouldn't life be nice and simple if people never fell in love? I wish I *could* make up my mind between Bruce and Peter. But I just can't. If I could only marry them both."

The shrieks of an anguished car resounded from the yard and Rae ran down to welcome Bruce... or it may have been Peter.

The next afternoon Pat, as she expressed it, "put off Martha and put on Mary," and hied herself to her Secret Field, although there was apply jelly to make and cucumbers to pickle. She went through the mysterious emerald light of the maple woods, where it seemed as if there must have been silence for a hundred years, and sat down on an old log covered with a mat of green moss in the corner of her field. It had changed so little in all the years. It was still her own and it still held secret understanding with her. But to-day something came between her soul and it. In spite of everything something touched her with unrest . . . the certainty of coming change, perhaps.

She looked up at a splash of crimson in the maple above her head. Another summer almost gone. There was a hint of autumn and decay and change in the air, even the air of Secret Field, with the purples of its bent grasses. Yes, she would marry Donald Holmes. She was quite sure she loved him. Pat stood up and waved a kiss to the Secret Field. When she next saw it she would belong to Donald Holmes.

She had intended to call at Happiness on her way home . . . she had not been there all summer . . . but she did not. Happiness belonged to things that were . . . things that had passed . . . things that could never return.

She was in the birch grove when Donald came to her the next evening. Donald Holmes was really a fine chap and deeply in love with Pat. To him she looked like love incarnate. She had a kitten on her shoulder and her dress was a young leaf green with a scarlet girdle. There was something about her face that made him think of pine woods and upland meadows and gulf breezes. He had come to ask her a certain question and he asked it, simply and confidently, as he had a right to ask it . . . for if any girl had ever encouraged a man Pat had encouraged Donald Holmes that summer.

Pat turned a little away from his flushed, eager face. Through a gap in the trees she saw the dark purple of the woods on Robinson's hill . . . the blue sheen of the gulf . . . the green of the clover aftermath in the Field of the Pool . . . the misty opal sky . . . and Silver Bush!

She turned to Donald and opened her lips to say, "yes." She found herself trembling.

"I'm . . . I'm terribly sorry," was what she said. "I can't marry you. I thought I could but I can't."

5

"I rather think I hope there'll be an earthquake before to-morrow morning," thought Pat when she went to bed that night. The whole world had gone very stale and life seemed greyer than ashes. In a way she was actually disappointed. She would miss Donald horribly. But leave Silver Bush for him? Impossible!

She knew she was in for a terrible time with her clan and she was not mistaken. By the time they got through with her she felt, as she confided to the not overly sympathetic Rae, "like a bargain counter of soiled rayon." Even mother was a little disappointed.

"*Couldn't* you have cared for him, darling?"

"I thought I could... I thought I did... mother, I just can't explain. I'm dreadfully sorry... I'm so ashamed of myself... I deserve everything that is being said of me... but I couldn't."

Everybody was saying plenty. All her relatives took turns heckling her about it. Long Alec gave her a piece of his mind.

"But I didn't love him, father... I really didn't," said poor Pat miserably.

"It's a pity you didn't find that out a little sooner," said Long Alec sourly. "I don't like hearing my daughter called a jilt. No, don't smile at me like that, miss. Let me tell you you trade too much on that smile. *This* is past being a joke."

"You'll go through the woods and pick up a crooked stick yet," warned Aunt Edith darkly.

"There's really been too much of this, Aunt Edith," protested Pat, feeling that any self-respecting worm had to turn some time. "I'm not going to marry anybody just to please the clan."

"What *can* she be wanting in the way of a husband?" moaned Aunt Barbara.

"Heaven knows," said Aunt Edith... but in a tone that sounded very dubious of heaven's knowledge. "She'll never have such a chance again."

"You know you aren't getting any younger, Pat," Uncle Tom objected mildly. "Why couldn't you have cottoned to him?"

Pat was flippant to hide her feelings.

"My English and Scotch blood liked him, Uncle Tom, but the French didn't and I was none too sure about the Irish."

Uncle Tom shook his head.

"If you don't watch out all the men will be grabbed," he

said gloomily. "Beaus aren't found hanging on bushes, you know."

"If they were it would be all right," said Pat, more flippantly than ever. "One needn't pick them then. Just let them hang."

Uncle Tom gave it up. What could you do with a she like that?

Aunt Jessie said that the Selbys were always changeable and Uncle Brian said he could always have told her that Pat was only making a fool of young Holmes for her own amusement and Aunt Helen said Pat had always been different from anybody else.

"A girl who would rather ramble in the woods than go to a dance. Don't tell me she's normal."

Most odious of all was the sympathetic Mrs. Binnie who said when she met her,

"You seem to have bad luck with your beaus, Pat dearie. But never be cast down even if he has slipped through your fingers. There's as good fish in the sea as ever come out of it. And you know, dearie, even if you can't git a husband there's lots of careers open to gals nowadays."

It was hard to take that from a Binnie. As if Donald Holmes had jilted her! And harder still to hear that Donald Holmes' mother was saying that that Gardiner girl had deliberately led her son on . . . kept him dangling all summer and then threw him over.

"But I deserve it, I suppose," thought poor Pat bitterly.

The only person who was not reported as saying anything was Donald Holmes himself, who preserved an unbroken silence and behaved, as Aunt Edith averred, in the most gentlemanly fashion about everything connected with the whole pitiable affair.

Judy was upset at first but soon came round when every one else was blaming her darling and recollected that Donald Holmes had had a very quare sort of great-uncle.

"A bit av a miser and always wint about as shabby as a singed cat. Aven the dogs stopped to look at him, him being that peculiar. And I'm minding there did be a cousin somewhere on the mother's side dressed up in weeds and wint to the church widding av a man who had jilted her. Oh, oh, and it's liable to crop out inny time and that I will declare and maintain."

Sid, too, to Pat's surprise, stood up for her.

"Let her alone. If she doesn't want to marry Donald Holmes she doesn't have to."

Pat lingered late in the garden one night. There was a mirth of windy trees all about Silver Bush and a misty, cloud-blown new moon hanging over it. First the twilight was golden-green, then emerald. Afar off the evening hills were drawing purple hoods about them. In spite of everything Pat felt at peace with her own soul as she had not done for a long time.

"If it's foolish to love Silver Bush better than any man I'll always be a fool," she said to herself. "Why, I *belong* here. What an unbelievable thing that I was just on the point of saying something to Donald that would have cut me off from it forever."

As she turned to leave the garden she said passionately and quite sincerely,

"I hope nobody will ever ask me to marry him again." And then a thought darted quite unbidden into her mind.

"I'm glad I don't have to tell Hilary I'm engaged."

6

There came a grim day in November with nothing at first to distinguish it from other days. But in mid-afternoon Gentleman Tom gravely got down from the cushion of Great-Grandfather Nehemiah's chair and looked all about him. Judy and Pat watched him as they made the cranberry pies and turkey dressing for Thanksgiving. He gave one long look at Judy, as she recalled afterwards, then walked out of the house, across the yard and along the Whispering Lane, with his thin black tail held gallantly in air. They watched him out of sight but did not attach much importance to his going. He often went on such expeditions, returning at nightfall. But the dim changed into darkness on this particular night and Gentleman Tom had not returned. Gentleman Tom never did return. It seemed a positive calamity to the folks at Silver Bush. Many beloved cats of old days had long been hunting mice in the Elysian fields but their places had soon been filled by other small tigerlings. None, it was felt, could fill Gentleman Tom's place. He had been there so long he seemed like one of the family. They really felt that he must go on living forever.

No light was ever thrown on his fate. All enquiries were

vain. Apparently no mortal eye had seen Gentleman Tom after he had gone from Silver Bush. Pat and Rae were mournfully certain that some dire fate had overtaken him but Judy would not have it.

"Gintleman Tom has got the sign and gone to his own place," she said mysteriously. "Don't be asking me where it might be.... Gintleman Tom did be always one to kape his own counsel. Do ye be minding the night we all thought ye were dying, Patsy dear? I'm not denying I'll miss him. A discrate, well-behaved baste he was. All he iver wanted was his own cushion and a bit av mate or a sup av milk betwane times. Gintleman Tom was niver one to cry over spilt milk, was he now?"

Philosophically as Judy tried to take it she was very lonely when she climbed into her bed at nights, with no black guardian at its foot.

"Changes do be coming," she whispered sadly. "Gintleman Tom *knew*. That do be why he wint. He niver liked to be upset. And I'm fearing the luck av Silver Bush do be gone wid him."

The Fifth Year

PAT, coming home from the Long House, where she and David and Suzanne had been reading poetry before the fire all the evening, paused for a moment to gloat over Silver Bush before going in. She always did that when coming home from anywhere. And to-night it seemed especially beautiful, making an incredibly delicate picture with its dark background of silver birches and dim, dreaming winter fields. There were the white, sparkling snows of a recent storm on its roof. Two lace-like powdered firs, that had grown tall in the last few years, were reaching up to the west of it. To the south were two leafless birches and directly between them the round pearl of the moon. A warm golden light was gleaming out of the kitchen window... the light of home. It was fascinating to look at the door and realise that by just opening it one could step into beauty and light and love.

The world seemed all moonlight and silver bush, faintly broken by the music of a wind so uncertain that you hardly knew whether there really was a wind or not. The trees along the Whispering Lane looked as if they had been woven on fairy looms and a beloved pussy cat was stepping daintily through the snow to her.

Pat was very happy. It had been a beautiful winter... one of the happiest winters of her life. None of the changes Judy had foreboded upon the departure of Gentleman Tom had so far come to pass. Winnie and her twinkling children came over often and Little Mary stayed for weeks at a time, though her mother complained that Pat spoiled her so outrageously that there was no doing anything with her when she went home. Mary had once said,

184

"I wish I was an orphan and then I could come and live with Aunt Pat. She lets me do *everysing* I want to."

The only time Mary ever found Aunt Pat cross with her was the day she had taken Tillytuck's hatchet and cut down a little poplar that was just beginning life behind the turkey house. Aunt Pat's eyes did flash then. Mary was packed off home in disgrace and made to feel that if Aunt Pat ever forgave her it would be more than she deserved. Mary really couldn't understand it. It had been such a *little* tree. Aunt Pat hadn't been half so cross when she, Little Mary, had spilled a whole can of molasses on the Little Parlour rug or upset the jug of water on the floor in the Poet's room.

But everybody at Silver Bush spoiled Little Mary because they loved her. She had such a delightful little face. Everything about it laughed . . . her eyes . . . her mouth . . . the corners of her nose . . . the dimples in her cheeks . . . the little curl in front of her ears. Judy vowed she was "the spit and image" of Pat in childhood but she was far prettier than Pat had ever been. Yet she lacked the elfin charm that had been Pat's and sometimes Judy thought it was just as well. Perhaps it was not a good thing to have that strange little spark of difference that set you off by yourself and made a barrier, however slight and airy it might be, between you and your kind. It is quite likely that this lurking idea of Judy's was born of the fact that Pat's beaus no longer came to Silver Bush. Ever since the affair of Donald Holmes the youth of the Glens had left Pat severely alone. To be sure, when Tillytuck commented on this, Judy scornfully remarked that Pat had had them all tied up by the ears at one time or another and no more men were left. But in secret she worried her. It made Judy quite wild to think of Pat ever being an old maid. Even David Kirk didn't seem to be getting anywhere with what the clan persisted in thinking his wooing. When Judy heard that Mrs. Binnie had said that Pat Gardiner was pretty well on the shelf she trembled with wrath.

"Oh, oh, there do be just this difference betwane Madam Binnie and a rattlesnake, Tillytuck . . . the snake can't be talking."

Pat was not worrying over the absence of the men.

"I fall in love but it doesn't last," she told Judy philosophically. "It never has lasted . . . you know that, Judy. I'm constitutionally fickle and that being the case I'm never going to trust my emotions again. It wouldn't matter if it hurt only me... but it hurts other people. There's only one real love in my life, Judy... Silver Bush. I'll always be true to *it*. It satisfies me. Nothing else does. Even when I was craziest about Harris Hynes and Lester Conway and... and Donald Holmes, I always felt there was something wanting. I couldn't tell what but I knew it. So don't worry over me, Judy."

Judy's only comfort was that Hilary's letters still came regularly.

Pat had had a book from him that day... a lovely book in a dull green leather binding with a golden spider-web over it... a book that *belonged* to Pat. Hilary's gifts were like that... something that must have made him say, whenever his eyes lighted on it, "That is Pat's. It couldn't be anybody else's."

If life could just go on forever like this... at least for years, "safe from corroding change." In childhood you thought it would but now you knew it couldn't. Something was always coming up... something you never expected. Only that day she had overheard Judy saying to Tillytuck, "Oh, oh, things do be going too well. We do be going to have an awful wallop before long." Tillytuck had told Judy she needed a liver pill but Pat was afraid there was something in it.

At Silver Bush Rae's love affairs had usurped the place that Pat's used to hold. Rae discussed her two suitors very frankly with Pat and Judy in the talks around the kitchen fire o' nights, often to the unromantic accompaniment of butter-fried eggs or turkey bones. Rae was never of the same heart two nights in succession.

"Don't change your mind so often," Pat said once in exasperation.

"Oh, but it's glorious," laughed Rae. "Think how deadly monotonous it would be to be in love with the same man week in and week out. Of course I mean to make up my mind permanently some day. I feel sure I'll marry one of those boys. They are both good matches."

"Rae! That sounds hatefully mercenary."

"Sister dear, I finished with romance when Larry Wheeler sent me a flower-wreathed announcement of his bridals. That cured me forever. And I'm not mercenary... I'm only through with being a sentimentalist. It's just that I find it hard to decide between two equally nice boys."

"It's hardly fair to them," protested Pat. "And people are talking. They say you're more or less engaged to both of them."

"Well, you know I'm not. Neither of them is by way of being a bit deceived. And, in spite of their jealousy, they're such good sports over it all, too. They are so fearfully polite to each other outwardly. No fear of a duel there even if it wasn't out of date."

"You wouldn't want a man to risk his life for you, would you?" demanded Pat.

"No . . . no." For a moment Rae looked serious. "But I think I'd like to have him *willing* to risk it. I wonder if either Bruce or Peter would be that. However, they are getting no end of thrills out of it. It's a kind of race, you know, and men enjoy that ever so much more than a tame courtship. Sometimes I think I'll decide it by lot . . . I really do. They seem so evenly balanced. If Peter's nose is not all I would fondly dream neither are Bruce's ears. And their names are nice. That's *something*. How awful it would be to marry a man who had one of those terrible names in Dickens! Judy, do you think Bruce will be fat by the time he is forty? I'm afraid I wouldn't love him then. There is no danger of that with Peter. He'll always be thin as a snipe. But he has rosy cheeks. I don't like rosy cheeks in men. I prefer them pale and interesting. And will his mother like me?"

"It wudn't be inny great odds if she didn't, Cuddles dear," said Judy, who was enjoying Rae's "nonsense" immensely. "The woman has no great gumption. I used to be hearing she was one to give her fam'ly b'iling hot soup on a dog-day. Peter do be getting his sinse from his father's side."

"Last night I *almost* told him I'd marry him. But I had sense enough to know it was just the moon. I could be in love with anybody when the moon is just right. Pat, don't look so disapproving. You've no right to. *You*'ve been known to change your mind. I wish I could make up my mind. . . . I really do. It's so wearing. I never thought I could be in such a predicament."

"I don't believe you care a pin for either of them," said Pat impatiently.

"Pat, I do . . . I really do. That is the exasperating part of it . . . the part that doesn't square with books."

"Why not send them both packing and go on with your college course? You used to want to be a doctor."

Rae sighed.

"It costs too much. And besides . . . my ambition seems to have petered out . . . no, that isn't a pun, really it isn't.

We're like that at Silver Bush, it seems, Pat. We're just domestic girls after all and want a home to potter over, with a nice husband and a few nice babies."

"Oh, oh, that's the only sinsible word ye've said to-night, Cuddles darlint," grinned Judy. She knew her Cuddles and did not take her dilemma very seriously. It was all the darlint's fun and added to the gaiety of life at Silver Bush. Some fine day Cuddles would find out which of those nice lads she liked best and there would be a fine wedding and Cuddles would settle down not far from home, as Winnie had done. So Judy hoped in her inveterate match-making old heart. It was only Pat who worried over it. Somehow she could not picture Rae either as Mrs. Bruce Madison or Mrs. Peter Alward. But she asked herself honestly was it because she thought Rae did not care enough for either of them or was it because she hated the change another marriage would bring to Silver Bush?

"Just be letting it alone, Patsy dear," advised Judy. "The Good Man Above do be having things in hand, I'm belaving."

2

It was spring... it was summer... it was September... it was almost another autumn. Pat had come home from a three weeks' visit in Summerside, where Aunt Jessie had been ill and Pat had been keeping house for Uncle Brian. Now she was home again and oh, it was good! Was the sunshine amber or was it gold? How gallant the late hollyhocks looked along the dyke! How alive the air was! What a delightful smell the apple orchard had in September! How adorable were two fat pussy cats rolling in the sun! And the garden welcomed her... *wanted* her.

"Any news, Judy? Tell me everything that's happened while I've been away. Letters never tell half enough... and Rae's have really been sketchy."

"Oh, oh, Rae!" Judy looked rather as if the world were on its last legs, but Pat was too absorbed in Silver Bush generally to notice it. Tillytuck coughed significantly behind his hand and remarked that Cupid had as usual been busy at Silver Bush.

"Oh, Peter and Bruce, I suppose," laughed Pat. "Is Rae

going to keep those poor wretches dangling forever? It's really getting past a joke. Where is she by the way?"

"She did be climbing the haystack in the Mince Pie Field half an hour ago, just after she did be getting home from school," said Judy, frowning at Tillytuck.

Pat betook herself to the Mince Pie Field where a splotch of colour on a half-used haystack betrayed Rae's whereabouts. Pat scrambled up the ladder and Rae grabbed her.

"Darling, I'm so glad you're back. It seems like a hundred years since you went to Summerside. I've just been lying here, letting my thoughts ripen and grow mellow. I think there's a caterpillar on my neck, but it doesn't matter. Even caterpillars have rights."

Pat slipped down beside Rae with a sigh of enjoyment. How blue the sky was, with those great banks of golden cloud in the south! Pat didn't like a cloudless sky... it always seemed to her hard and remote. A few clouds made it friendly... humanised it. How cool and delicious was the gulf breeze blowing round them, bringing with it all kinds of elusive whiffs from all the little dells and slopes of the old farm. The Buttercup Field was a pasture this year. Pat remembered how she and Sid used to play in that field when the buttercup glory came up to their heads.

"Isn't it heavenly just to lie quiet like this and soak yourself in the beauty of the world?" she said dreamily.

Rae did not answer. Pat turned her head and looked at her sister lying in her lithe young slimness on the hay. How very soft and radiant Rae's eyes were! There was something about her...

"Pat darling," said Rae, "I'm engaged."

Pat felt as if a thunderbolt had hit her.

"Rae... let me see your tongue."

"No, I'm not feverish, beloved... really, I'm not."

"Are you serious, Rae?"

"Absolutely. Oh, Pat, I'm just weak and trembly with happiness. I never knew any one could be so happy. It's only three weeks since you went away but everything has changed. Pat, life has just seemed like a story-book these three weeks, and every day an exciting chapter."

Pat had got her second wind but she, too, felt weak and trembly with something that was not exactly happiness.

"Which is it... Bruce or Peter?" she asked a bit drily.

Rae gave a young, delightful laugh.

"Oh, Pat, it's neither of them. It's Brook Hamilton."

Pat felt stunned.

"*Who* is Brook Hamilton?"

Rae laughed again.

"Fancy any one not knowing who Brook Hamilton is. I can't believe I didn't know him myself three weeks ago. I met him the first night you went away at Dot's dance..."

"Rae Gardiner, you don't mean to tell me you're engaged to a man you've known only three weeks!"

"Don't go off the deep end, darling. We're not to be married till he's through college so we'll have lots of time to get acquainted. And he's my man... there's no mistake about that. At nine o'clock that evening I had never seen him. At ten I loved him. Judy says it happens like that once in a thousand years. I never believed in love at first sight before... but now I know it's the only kind."

"Rae... Rae... *I* thought that once, too... I was sure I was madly in love with Lester Conway... and it was nothing but the moon...."

"There wasn't any moon the night of Dot's party, so you can't blame this on the moon."

"I suppose," said Pat sarcastically, "he's extremely handsome and you've fallen for..."

"But he isn't. I think he's ugly really, when I think of his face at all. But it's such a delightful ugliness. And he has such steady blue eyes and such dependable broad shoulders, and such thick black hair... though it always looks as if he'd combed it with a rake. But I like that, too. He wouldn't be Brook if he had sleek hair. Dearest, it's all right... it really is. Mother and dad like him and even Judy approves of him. We're to be married when he's through college and go to China."

"China!"

"Yes. He's going to take charge of the Chinese branch of his father's business there... I forgot to tell you he's one of the Halifax Hamiltons and Dot's cousin."

"But... China!"

"It *does* sound like a long hop. But, really, darling, nothing matters... Indian plains or Lapland snows... so long as I'm with him. I don't talk like this to the others, Pat ... but with you I've just got to let myself go."

"And what about Bruce and Peter?" asked Pat, with a faint smile.

"Pat, it was really comical. Oh, there's so much to tell you. You see, they didn't know anything about Brook, but they told me two weeks ago that I had to make up my mind between them. And I just told them I was engaged to Brook. You should have seen their faces. Then they just faded out of the picture. I don't think they ever really existed."

"And were you engaged *then* . . . a week after you'd met him?"

"Darling, we were engaged three days after we met. I couldn't help it. What would *you* do if Sir Launcelot just rode into your back yard and told you you had to marry him? Because Brook didn't *ask* me, you know. . . he just told me I had to. There wasn't the least use objecting even if I'd wanted to. And . . . oh, Pat, I . . . I *cried*. That's the shameful truth. I haven't the least idea why I did, but I simply howled. It was such a relief . . . I'd been thinking I was just one of the crowd to him . . . and Dot was trying to hint he was after Lenore Madison . . . that freckled, snubnosed thing. You may be sure I didn't ask for any time to consider. Pat, you're not going to cry!"

"No . . . no . . . but this is really a little unexpected, Rae."

For one awful moment Pat had felt as if Rae . . . this Rae . . . were a stranger to her. She had been away from Silver Bush for only three weeks and *this* had happened.

"I know." Rae squeezed Pat's hand. "And I know it must all seem like indecent haste to you. But if you count time by heart-throbs as somebody says you should, it's been a century since I met him. He *isn't* a stranger. He's one of our kind . . . like Hilary . . . knows all our quacks, really he does. You'll understand when you meet him, Pat."

Pat did understand. She couldn't find a single fault with Brook Hamilton. As a brother-in-law he was everything that could be desired. Tall, lean, with intensely blue eyes and straight black brows. Certainly he and Rae made a wonderful-looking young pair in spite of his "rather ugly" face. She couldn't hate him as she had hated Frank, even if he were going to take her sister away. But, mercifully, not for a long time yet. And there was no doubt that Rae loved him.

"I wish I could love somebody like that," said Pat, with a little pang of envy. She sat alone for a long time in her room that evening while the robins whistled outside and the purple night sky looked down on her. So, in the years to come, she would always have to sit alone. For the first time in her life Pat felt *old*... for the first time a little chill of fear for her own future touched her. She almost hated Bold-and-Bad for purring so loudly on the bed. It was outrageous that a cat should be so blatantly happy. Really Bold-and-Bad had no tact.

"I suppose," thought Pat dolefully, "the time will come when I'll have nothing left but a cat." Then she brightened up. "And Silver Bush. That will be enough," she added softly.

At bedtime she knelt by Rae's bed and put her arm across Rae's shoulders.

"Cuddles dear," she said, slipping back to the old nickname, "Brook is a dear... and I think you're both lucky... and I love you... love you... love you."

"Pat, you're the dearest thing in the world. And why didn't you cast the Reverend Wheeler of happy memory up to me and remind me of the time I thought I was in love with him? I really expected you to do it... I don't know how any human being could have resisted doing it."

Judy was only moderately pleased over the engagement because of the prospect of China.

"Oh, oh, I've great opinions of haythens, Patsy dear. They do be all right to sind missionaries to, but not to be living among. And her wid thim looks av hers to go to Chiny! Sure and some ugly girl wud have done for him I'm thinking, since he can't be continted in a civilised country. But I'm not denying he's a fine lad and he can't be hilping his uncle."

"Now, Judy, what about his uncle?"

"Oh, oh, it's an ould tale and better not raked up maybe. Well, if ye will be having it. The Hamiltons may be av Halifax now but the grandfather av thim lived in Charlottetown whin his lads were small. And Brook's uncle was the black shape... if it don't be insulting shape to call him so. Crooked he was as a dog's hind leg. He wint out wist after quarrelling wid his dad and what did he do but write a long account av his being killed whin a train struck his horse and buggy at a crossing and got it published in a liddle newspaper there, one av his wild cronies being editor av it, and sint a marked copy home to the ould folks. It just about broke his poor mother's heart... I'm not saying his dad tuk it so hard and small blame to him... and they had a lot av worry tilligraphing to have the body sint home. And whin they wint to the station wid the hearse and undertaker and all to mate the corpse didn't me fine Dicky Hamilton stip off the train laughing at the joke he'd played on thim!"

"How horrible! But don't tell Rae that, Judy."

"Oh, oh, it's not likely... nor the squeal to it ather. For what do you think, Patsy dear? The young scallywag did be killed the nixt wake in the very same way he'd writ av... he was driving along one avening reckless-like and the train struck him on that crossing on the wist road and that was the ind av him. Niver be telling me it wasn't a jidgmint. But there do be no doubting that Cuddles is over head and heels in love wid Brook. 'Sure and there do be other min in the world, Cuddles darlint,' I sez, be way av tazing her a bit. 'There aren't,' she sez, solemn-like. 'There's simply nobody else in the world, Judy,' sez she. And that being the case we must just be making the bist av it, uncle or no uncle. After all, there do be something rale glamourous about it as Tillytuck wud say."

As a matter of fact, all Tillytuck said was, "Engaged, by gosh!" Such a whirlwind courtship was entirely too much for Tillytuck. He relieved his feeling by playing on his fiddle in the graveyard, seated on Wild Dick's tombstone, much to Judy's horror.

"How do you know Wild Dick doesn't still like to hear the fiddle, Judy?" asked Sid audaciously.

"If Wild Dick do be in heaven he has the angels to be listening to... and if he isn't he do be having other things to think av," was Judy's indignant reply. Tillytuck had to give her his old red flannel shirt for the rose-buds in her new hooked rug before he could make his peace with her. And then nearly wrecked it again by solemnly telling Little Mary, to whom Judy had just been relating a story of some naughty children who had been turned into brooms by a witch... "I was one of them brooms!"

The Sixth Year

FOR a year things went beautifully at Silver Bush. Everybody was happy. Mother was better than she had been for a long time. Sid seemed to have recovered his good spirits and was taking a keen interest in everything again. Gossip no longer coupled his name with any girl's and Pat saw her old dream of living always at Silver Bush with Sid taking vague shape again. It was just like it used to be. They planned and joked and walked in faint blue twilights and Sid told her everything, and together they bullied Long Alec and Tillytuck when any difference of opinion came up. Between them they managed to get Silver Bush repainted, although Long Alec hated any extra expense as long as there was a mortgage on it. But Silver Bush looked beautiful . . . so white and trig and prosperous with its green shutters and trim. It warmed the cockles of Pat's heart just to look at it. And to hear Sid say once, gruffly, on their return one winter evening from a long prowl back to their Secret Field,

"You're a good old scout, Pat. I don't know what I'd have done without you these past two years."

"Oh, Sid!" Pat could only say that as she rubbed her face against his shoulder. This was one of life's good moments. They had had such a wonderful walk. It had been lovely back in the woods. It was after the first snowfall and the woods were at peace in a white transfiguration, placidly still and calm, where the thick ranks of the young saplings were snow-laden and an occasional warm golden shaft of light from the low-hanging sun pierced through, tingeing the dark bronze-green of the spruces and the greyish-green streams of moss with vivid beauty. They had come home by way of Happiness, where Jordan was crooning to itself under the ice. The old pastures, which had been so beautiful and flowery in June, were cold and white now, but Pat loved them, as she loved them in all moods.

She lingered at the gate to taste her happiness after Sid had gone on to the barn. It was going to be a night of frost and silver. To her right the garden was hooding itself in the shadows of dusk. Pat loved to think of all her staunch old flowers under the banks of snow, waiting for spring. Far away a dim hill came out darkly against a winter sunset. Beyond the dyke was a group of old spruces which Long Alec often said should be cut down. But Pat pleaded for them. Seen in daylight they *were* old and uncomely, dead almost to the top, with withered branches. But seen in this enchanted light, against a sky that began by being rosy-saffron and continued in silver green, and ended in crystal blue, they were like tall, slender witch women weaving spells of necromancy in a rune of olden days. Pat felt a stirring of her childish desire to share in their gramarye... to have fellowship in their twilight sorceries.

Off to her left the orchard was white and still, heaped with drifts along the fences. Over it all was a delicate tracery of shadow where the trees stood up lifeless in seeming death and sorrow. But it was only seeming. The life-blood was in their hearts and by and by it would stir and they would clothe themselves in bridal garments of young green leaves and pink blossoms, and lush grass would wave where the snow was now lying and golden buttercups dance among it. Spring always came again... she must never forget that.

Silver Bush looked very beautiful in the faint beginning moonlight... her own dear Silver Bush. It still welcomed her... it was still hers, no matter what changes came and went. Life seemed to have put on a new meaning now that Sid had come back to her in their old companionship. She pulled his love about her like a cloak and felt warm and satisfied.

Rae had settled down to filling a hope chest and writing daily letters of portentous length to Brook Hamilton. She was changed... more gentle, thoughtful, womanly. There was no more pretending to be hard-boiled. Love, Sid told her teasingly, did mellow people remarkably. The old flippancy was gone, though she laughed as much as ever and never had her laughter, thought adoring Pat, been so exquisite.

Pat had resigned herself to the fact of Rae's engagement.

But she would not be getting married for at least three years. They had those years to look forward to... years, dreamed Pat, of companionship and plans and all the dear intimacies of home.

Winter slipped away... spring and summer passed. September wore a golden moon like a ring and again autumn brewed a cup of magic and held it to your lips. Only Tillytuck secretly thought it rather slow. The beaus came no longer, since Rae was known to be bespoken and Pat, so it was said, thought no one good enough for her.

"Life is getting a bit tedious here, Judy," he said, mournfully. "There doesn't seem to be as much glamour, romantically speaking."

Perhaps Judy thought so, too. She sighed... it was not like Judy to sigh. Pat would have another birthday in a week... and not a beau in sight. Even David, Judy had decided, had really no serious intentions, and she hated him for it as sincerely as if she had never disapproved of him. She did not want Pat to marry him, but that was for Pat to decide, not for him. As for Jingle, there never was any word of his coming home for a visit.

"He's grown away from us, Judy. We're only memories to him now. He has his own work and his own ambitions. Even his letters aren't just what they used to be."

Pat hadn't seemed to care. She was more taken up with Silver Bush than ever and she and Sid were "thick as thieves" again. Which was all to the good, as far as it went. To be sure, of late weeks, Sid had taken to gallivanting again. Nobody could find out where he was going although Judy had certain uneasy suspicions she never breathed to any one. Judy sighed again as she clapped her baked beans and bacon in the oven. Then she brightened up. Every one needed a liddle bite once in so often and as long as she, Judy Plum, could provide it there was balm in Gilead.

A week later Judy looked back to that day and wondered if what had happened had been a judgment on her for thinking life had got a bit dull. For Pat's birthday had come and that evening Sid had brought May Binnie in and announced, curtly and defiantly, and yet with such a pitiful, beaten look on his face, that they had been married that day in Charlottetown.

"We thought we'd surprise you," said May, glancing

archly about her out of bold, brilliant eyes. "Birthday surprise for you, Pat."

2

Pat sat up all that night, looking out over the quiet, unchanged fields of the farm, trying to look this hideous fact in the face. She was in the Poet's room and she had locked the door. She would not even have Rae with her.

She could not yet believe that this had happened. At first one cannot believe in a monstrous thing. Can one ever believe it? It was a dream . . . a nightmare. She would waken presently. She must . . . or go mad.

She had been so happy that evening at twilight . . . so unusually, inexplicably happy, as if the gods were going to give her some wonderful gift . . . and now she would never be happy again. Pat was still young enough to think that when a thing like this happened you could never be happy again. Everything . . . *everything* . . . had changed in the twinkling of an eye. Sid was lost to her forever. The very fields she had loved now looked strange and hostile as she gazed on them. "Our inheritance is turned to strangers and our house to aliens." She had read that verse in her Bible chapter two nights ago and shivered over the picture of desolation it presented. And now it had come true in her own life . . . her life that a few hours ago had seemed so full and beautiful and was now so ugly and empty.

It had been such a ghastly hour. Nobody knew what to say or do. Pat's face seemed to wither as she looked at them . . . at May, flushed and triumphant under all her uneasiness, at Sid, sullen and defiant. May tried to carry the situation off brazenly, after the true Binnie fashion.

"Come, Pat, don't look so snooty. *I'm* willing to let bygones be bygones, even if you and I *have* hated each other all our lives."

This was only too true but it was terrible to have the feeling dragged into light as nakedly as this. Pat could not answer. She turned away as if she had neither seen nor heard May and walked blindly out of the room. The only feeling she was keenly conscious of just then was a sick desire to get away from the light into a dark place where no one could see her . . . where she could hide like a wounded animal.

May looked after her and her bold handsome face flushed crimson under Pat's utter disregard. Her black eyes held a flame that was not good to see. But she laughed as she turned to Sid.

"She'll get over it, honey-boy. I never expected a warm welcome from Pat, you know."

Rae alone kept her head. Neither mother nor father must be told till morning, she reflected. As for Judy and Tillytuck, they seemed stricken dumb. Tillytuck slipped off to his granary shaking his head and Judy climbed to her kitchen chamber, feeling, for the time at least, more crushed and cowed than ever in her life before.

"I've felt it coming," she muttered, as she crept into bed forlornly. "I've been hearing he was going wid the bold young hussy. And Gintleman Tom knew it was coming, that he did. That was why he lit out like the knowing baste he was. He knew he cud niver be standing a Binnie. Oh, oh, if I did be knowing as much av magic as me grandmother I'd change her into a toad that I wud. What'll be coming av it the Good Man Above only knows. One does be thinking the world cud be run a bit better. I'm fearing this will break Patsy's heart."

3

All the rest of her life Pat knew she had left girlhood behind her on that dreadful night. Hope seemed to be blotted out entirely. Already the hours that had passed seemed like an eternity and to-morrow . . . all the to-morrows . . . would be just as bad. Her mind went round and round in a miserable circle and got nowhere. May Binnie living at Silver Bush . . . Silver Bush overrun with Binnies . . . they were a clannish crew in their way. Old Mr. Binnie who ate peas with his knife and old Mrs. Binnie who always sopped her bread in her gravy. And all the slangy, loud-voiced crew of them, the kind of people before whom you must always say everything over to yourself beforehand to be sure it was safe. What a crowd for Sid to have got himself mixed up with! No, it could not be faced.

Pat wouldn't go down when morning came . . . couldn't. For the first time in her life she was a shirker. She could hear them talking beneath her at the breakfast-table. She could hear May's desecrating laugh. She clenched her hands in fury and wretchedness. She pulled down the blind and shut out a world that was too glad with its early sunshine and its purple mists.

Presently Rae came in... trim, alert, competent. Her blue eyes showed no traces of the tears she had shed in the night.

"Pat, I left you alone last night because I realised that a thing like this had much better be talked over in the morning."

"What is the use of talking it over any time?" asked Pat listlessly.

"We must talk it over because we have to face the situation, Pat. There is no use in turning our back on it or squinting at it out of the corners of our eyes... or ignoring it. Let's just get down to real things and look to the future."

"But I can't face it... Rae, I *can't*," cried poor Pat desperately. "Talk about the future! There isn't any future! If it had been anybody but May Binnie! I'm not the little fool I once was. I've known for long that Sid would marry sometime. Even when I couldn't help hoping he wouldn't I knew he would. But May Binnie!"

"I know. I know as well as you do that Sid has made a dreadful mistake and will realise it all too clearly some day. I know May is cheap and common and has no background... kitchen-bred, as Judy would say... but..."

"How could he do it? How could he like *her*... after Bets... even after poor Dorothy?"

"May is alluring in her own way, Pat. *We* can't see it but the men do. And she has always meant to get Sid. We've just got to make the best of it and take things as they come."

"I won't," said Pat rebelliously. "They may *have* to come but I haven't got to take them without protest. I'll never reconcile myself to this... never."

> "'To-day that seems so long, so strange, so bitter
> Will soon be some forgotten yesterday,'"

quoted Rae softly.

"It won't," said Pat dismally.

"I've been doing some talking already this morning," went on Rae. "For one thing I broke the news to dad."

"And he... what did he..."

"Oh, there were fireworks. The Gardiner temper flared up. But I know how to manage dad. I told him he had to take a reasonable view of it for mother's sake. When he calmed down he and I worked it out. Sid and May will have to live here for a year or two, until the mortgage is cleared. Then dad will build a house for them on the other place and they can live there."

"And in the meantime," said Pat passionately, "life will be unlivable at Silver Bush . . . you know it will."

"I don't know anything of the sort. Of course it won't be as pleasant as it has been. But, Pat, you know as well as I do that we've got to make the best of it for mother's sake."

"Does she know?"

"Yes. Dad told her. I funked *that*."

"And how . . . how did she take it?"

"How does mother take anything? Just like the gallant lady she is! We mustn't fail her, Pat."

Pat groped out a hand, found Rae's and squeezed it. Somehow their ages seemed reversed. It was as if Rae were the older sister.

"I'll do my best," she choked. "There's a verse in the Bible somewhere . . . 'be of good courage' . . . I've always thought it a wonderful phrase. I suppose it was meant just for times like this. But oh, Rae, how *can* we live with May? Her habits . . . her ideals . . . her point of view about everything . . . are so different from ours."

"She must have some good points," said Rae reasonably. "She's really popular in her own set. Everybody says she is a good worker."

"We have no work for her to do here," said Pat bitterly.

"You know, Pat, nothing is ever quite so dreadful in reality as in anticipation. We must just look *around* this. It's blocking up our view at present because we are too close to it."

"We can never be ourselves . . . our real selves . . . when she is about, Rae."

"Perhaps not. But she won't be always around. And she isn't going to rule here whatever she may think. 'I'm master here,' said dad, at the end of our talk, 'and your mother is mistress of Silver Bush and will remain so.' So that's that. I must be off to school now. You won't have to face May this morning. Sid has taken her home for the day."

Judy, who, for the first time in her life, had been a coward, crept in now and Pat flew to her old arms.

"Judy . . . Judy . . . help me to bear it."

"Oh, oh, bearing is it? We'll bear it together, Patsy darling, to the last turn av the screw, wid a grin for the honour av Silver Bush. And just be remimbering, Patsy, what the Good Book says . . . about happiness being inside av ye and not outside. Thim mayn't just be the words but it's what I'm belaving it manes."

"All very well if things outside would stop poking at you," said Pat, rather less forlornly.

"We've got to be saving Silver Bush from her," said Judy slyly. "She'll be trying to spile it while she do be here and we'll have our liddle bit av fun heading her off, Patsy darlint . . . diplomatic-like and widout ructions for the honour av the fam'ly. Ye'd have had a laugh this morning if ye'd been down, Patsy, to see Bould-and-Bad turning his back on her, aven if she did be making a fuss over him. She's rale fond av the animiles so we nadn't worry over that."

To Pat it was almost another count against May that she was fond of cats. She hated to admit a good point in her.

"How was Sid, Judy?"

"Oh, oh, looking like innything but a happy bridegroom. And just a bit under her thumb already, as I cud be seeing. Her wid her 'honey-boy' and telling av the way his hair curled over his forrid! As if I hadn't been knowing it all his life. But I was as smooth as crame, darlint, and that rispictful ye'd have died and niver did I be aven glancing at her stockings all in rolls round her ankles. Sure and it was a comfort to me to be knowing Long Alec wasn't intinding to hand Silver Bush over to Sid, as the Binnies hoped. Long Alec's not taking off his boots afore he goes to bed. 'You and yer wife can stay here till I can afford to build a house for ye,' sez he . . . and me fine May wasn't liking it. She's been telling round what she would do when she got to Silver Bush. 'I can be getting Sid Gardiner back whin I crook me finger,' sez she. Oh, oh, she's got him, worse luck, but she hasn't got Silver Bush and niver will. A year or two will soon pass, Patsy dear, and thin we'll be free av her. Maybe aven sooner wid a bit av luck."

"She has gone home for the day, Rae said."

"To be getting her boxes and breaking the news to the Binnies. I'm thinking they'll bear up well under it. She did be insisting on washing the dishes first and I did be letting her for pace' sake. She did be making as much commotion as a cat in a fit, finding where iverything shud go, and smashed the ould blue plate be way av showing what she cud do. But I'll not be denying she washed thim clane and didn't be laving a grasey sink."

Pat had always washed the dishes. She began to be sorry she hadn't gone down for breakfast after all. It would have been more dignified... more Silver Bushish.

"Now, come ye down, Patsy darlint, and have a liddle bite," said Judy wheedlingly. "I've been after frying a bit av the new ham and an egg in butter. A cup av tay will restore yer balance like. And we'll be having our liddle laugh now and agin behind her back, Patsy."

Pat pulled up the blind again. There was a little chill at her heart which had never been there before and which she felt would always be there henceforth. But afar the Hill of the Mist was lovely in the September sunshine. When she looked at it it gave her some of its own pride and calm and faint austerity.

She went up to see mother after she had had her breakfast and found her, as always, serene and clear and pale, like a star seen through the rifts of storm-cloud.

"Darling, it's hard, I know. I'm sorry for Sid... he *has* made a great mistake, poor boy. But if we all do our best things will work out somehow. They always do."

Poor brave darling mother!

"We'll be all right when we get our second wind," said Pat staunchly. "I'm going to be decent to May, mother, and there won't be any bickering....I won't have that here. But Silver Bush is going to be saved from the Binnies, mother, and no mistake about it."

Mother laughed.

"Trust you for that, Pat."

The Seventh Year

PAT and Rae felt, in the months of that following winter, that they needed every ounce of philosophy and "diplomacy" that they possessed. The first weeks were very hard. At times adjustment seemed almost impossible. May's quick temper increased the difficulty. Some of the scenes she made always remained in Pat's memory like degrading, vulgar things. Yet her spasms of rage were not so bad, the girls thought, as her little smiles and innuendoes about everything. "I think I have *some* rights surely," she would say to Sid, with a toss of her sleek head. "It's hard to do anything with somebody watching and criticising all the time, isn't it now, honey-boy?" And Sid would look at Pat with defiant and yet appealing eyes that nearly broke her heart.

When May could not get her way she sulked and went round for a day or two "wid a puss on her mouth," according to Judy. Then, finding that nobody paid any attention to her sulks, she would become amiable again. Pat set her teeth and kept her head.

"I *won't* have quarrels at Silver Bush," she said. "Whatever she does or says I won't quarrel with her." And even when May cried passionately, "You've *always* tried to make trouble between me and Sid," Pat would smile and say, "Come, May, be reasonable. We're not children now, you know." Then go up to her room and writhe in secret over the torment and ugliness of it all.

In the long run May succumbed to the inevitable, compromises were made on both sides, and life settled once more into outward calmness at Silver Bush. One thing nobody could deny was that May was a worker; and fortunately she liked outside work better than inside. She took over the care of milk and poultry, Judy making a virtue out of necessity in yielding it to her and never denying that the separator was thoroughly cleaned. "May," Mrs. Binnie said superfluously, "is not a soulless sassiety woman. I brought all *my* gals up to work."

To be sure, May made a frightful racket in everything she did and at Silver Bush, where household ritual had always been performed without noise, this was something of a domestic crime. Pat, suffering too much to be just, told Rae that May made more fuss in ten minutes than any one else could make in a year.

Judy and May had one battle royal as to who was to scrub the kitchen. Judy won. May never attempted to usurp Judy's kitchen privileges again.

Pat found she could get used to being unhappy... and then that she could even be happy again, between the spasms of unhappiness. Of course there were changes everywhere ... little irritating changes which were perhaps harder to bear than some greater dislocation. For one thing, May's friends gave her a "shower," after which Silver Bush was cluttered up with gim-cracks. Pat's especial hatred was a dreadful onyx-topped table. May put it in the hall under the heirloom mirror. It was a desecration. And May's new gay cushions, which made everything else seem faded, were scattered everywhere. But May did not get her own way when it came to moving furniture about. She learned that things were to be left as they were and that a large engraving of Landseer's stag, framed in crimson plush and gilt a foot wide, was *not* going to be hung in the dining room. May, after a scene, carried it off to her own room, where nobody interfered with her arrangements.

"I suppose your ladyship doesn't object to *that*," she remarked to Pat.

"Of course you can do as you like in your own room," said Pat wearily.

Would this petty bickering go on forever? And that very afternoon May had broken the old Bristol-ware vase by stuffing a huge bouquet of 'mums into it. Of course it was cracked... always had been cracked. May said she didn't hold with having cracked things around. She had her own room re-papered... blue roses on a bright pink ground. "So cheerful," Mrs. Binnie said admiringly. "That grey paper in what they call the Pote's room gives me the willies, May dearie."

May brought her dog with her, an animal known by the time-tested name of Rover. He killed the chickens, dug up Pat's bulbs, chewed the clothes on the line . . . Tillytuck had a pitched battle with May because his best shirt was mangled . . . and chased the cats in his spare time. Eventually Just Dog gave him a drubbing which chastened him and Rae, in May's absences, used to spank him so soundly with a stiff folded newspaper that he learned manners after a sort. There were even times when Pat was afraid she was learning to like him. It was hard for Pat not to like a dog if he had any decency at all.

As Pat had foreseen Silver Bush was overrun with the Binnie tribe. May's brothers flicked cigarette ashes all over the house. Her sisters and cousins came in what Judy called "droves," filled the house with shrieks, and listened behind doors. Judy caught them at it. And they were always more or less offended no matter how they were treated. If you were nice to them you were patronising them; if you left them alone you were snubbing them. Olive would bring her whole family.

Olive did not believe in punishing children. "They're going to enjoy their childhood," she said. Perhaps they enjoyed it but nobody else did. They were what Judy called "holy terrors." Judy found a dirty grey velvet elephant in her soup pot one day. Olive's six-year-old had slipped it in "for fun."

Mrs. Binnie came over frequently and spent the after noon in Judy's kitchen, proclaiming to the world that as far as she was concerned all was peace and good-will. She rocked fiercely on the golden-oak rocker May had introduced into the kitchen . . . rather fortunately, Judy thought, for certainly no Silver Bush chair could be counted on to bear up under the strain of Mrs. Binnie's two hundred and thirty-three pounds.

"No, no, two hundred and thirty-six, ma," May would argue.

"I guess I know my own weight, child," Mrs. Binnie would retort breezily. "And I ain't ashamed of it. 'Why don't you diet?' my sister Josephine keeps telling me. 'Not for mine,' I tell her, 'I'm contented to be as God made me!'"

"Oh, oh, I do be thinking God had precious little to do wid it," said Judy to Tillytuck.

Mrs. Binnie had a little button nose and yellowish-white hair screwed up in a tight knot on the crown of her head.

Gossip was her mother-tongue and grammar was her servant, not her master. Also, her "infernal organs" gave her a good deal of trouble. Pat used to wonder how Sid could bear to look at her and think that May would be like her when she was sixty.

"I'd like to give that hair of hers a bluing rinse," Rae would whisper maliciously to Pat, when Mrs. Binnie was laying down the law about something and nodding her head until a hairpin invariably slipped out.

Mrs. Binnie, unlike May, "couldn't abide" cats. They gave her asthma and, as May said, she started gasping if a cat was parked within a mile of her. So when Mrs. Binnie came out went the cats. Even Bold-and-Bad was no exception. Bold-and-Bad, however, did not hold with self pity and made himself at home in Tillytuck's granary.

"But I'd like to have seen ye try it on Gintleman Tom," Judy used to think malevolently.

Generally one or more of "thim rampageous Binnie girls" came with her and they and May talked and argued without cessation. The Binnies were a family with no idea of reticence. Everybody told everything to everybody else... "talking it over," they called it. None of them could ever understand why everything that was thought about couldn't be talked about. They had no comprehension whatever of people who did not think at the tops of their voices and empty out their feelings to the dregs. There were times when the unceasing clack of their tongues drove Tillytuck to the granary even on the coldest winter afternoons for escape and Pat longed despairingly for the beautiful old silences.

There was at least one consolation for Pat and Rae... they still had their evenings undisturbed. May thought it quite awful to sit in the kitchen, "with the servants." Generally she carried Sid off to a dance or show and when they were home they had company of their own in the Little Parlour... which had been tacitly handed over to May and which she called the "living room," much to Judy's amusement.

"Oh, oh, we've only the one living room at Silver Bush and that's me kitchen," she would remark to Tillytuck with a wink. "There do be more living done here than in all the other rooms put together."

"You've said a mouthful," said Tillytuck, just as he had said it to Lady Medchester.

So Pat and Rae and Judy and Tillytuck foregathered as of

old in the kitchen of evenings and forgot for a few hours the shadow that was over Silver Bush. They always had some special little jamboree to take the taste of some particularly hard day out of their mouths...as, for instance, the one on which Pat found May prying into her bureau drawers...or the one when May, who had a trick of acting hostess, assured a fastidious visiting clergyman who had declined a second helping that there was plenty more in the kitchen.

They could even laugh over Mrs. Binnie's malapropisms. It was so delicious when she asked Rae gravely whether "phobias" were annuals or perennials. To be sure, neither Judy nor Tillytuck was very sure just where the point of the joke was but it was heartening to see the girls laughing again as of old. Those evenings were almost the only time it was safe to laugh. If May heard laughter she took it into her head that they were laughing at her and sulked. Once in a while, when May had gone for one of her frequent visits home, Sid would creep in, too, for a bit of the old-time fun and one of Judy's liddle bites. Sid and Pat had had their hour of reconciliation long ere this: Pat couldn't endure to be "out" with Sid. But there were no more rambles and talks and plans together. May resented any such thing. She went with him now on his walks about the farm and expounded her ideas as to what changes should be made. She also aired her views to the whole family. A lot of trees should be cut down...there were entirely too many...it was "messy," especially that aspen poplar by the steps. And the Old Part of the orchard ought to be cleaned out entirely; it was a sheer waste of good ground. She did not go so far as to suggest ploughing up the grave-yard though she said it was horrid having a place like that so near the house and having to pass it every time you went to the barn or the hen-house. When she went to either of these places after dark she averred it made her flesh creep.

"If I were you," she would remark airily to Pat, "I'd make a few changes round here. A front porch is so out of date. And there really should be a wall or two knocked out. The Poet's room and our room together would just make one real nice-sized room. You don't need two spare rooms any more'n a frog needs trousers."

"Silver Bush suits *us* as it is," said Pat stiffly.

"Don't get so excited, child," said May provokingly...and how provoking May could be! "I was only making a sugges-tion. Surely you needn't throw a fit over that."

"She would do nothing but patch and change and tear up if she could have her way here," Pat told Rae viciously.

"Oh, oh, just like her ould grandad," said Judy. "He did be having a mania for tearing down and rebuilding. Innything for a change was *his* motto."

"Judy, last night as I passed the Little Parlour I heard May say to Sid, 'Anyway you'll have Silver Bush when your father dies.' Judy, she did! *When your father dies.*"

Judy chuckled.

"It do be ill waiting for dead men's shoes. Yer dad is good for twinty years yet at the laste. But it's like a Binnie to be saying that same."

2

Sometimes Pat would escape from it all to her fields and woods, at peace in their white loveliness. It carried her through many hard hours to remember that in ten minutes she could, if she must, be in that meadow solitude of her Secret Field, far from babble and confusion. There were yet wonderful ethereal dawns which she and Rae shared together . . . there were yet full moons rising behind snowy hills . . . rose tints over sunset dells . . . slender birches and shadowy nooks . . . winds calling to each other at night . . . apple-green "dims" . . . starry quietudes that soothed your pain . . . April buds in happiness. . . . "Thank God, April still comes to the world" . . . and Silver Bush to be loved and protected and cherished.

And with the spring Joe came home, to be married at last; after every one had concluded, so Mrs. Binnie said, that poor Enid Sutton was never going to get him.

"Many's the time I've said to her, 'Don't be too sure of him. A sailor has a sweetheart in every port. It isn't as if you was still a girl. You never can depend on them sailors. Take Mrs. Rory MacPherson at the Bridge . . . a disappointed woman if ever there was one. *Her* husband was a sailor and she thought he was dead and was going to get married again when he turned up alive and well.'"

There was a big gay wedding at the Suttons and every one thought bronzed Joe remarkably handsome. Pat thought so, too, and was proud of him; but he seemed a stranger now . . . Joe, whose going had once been such a tragedy. She

was even a little glad when all the fuss was over and Joe and
his bride were gone on a wonderful bridal trip around the
world in Joe's new vessel. She could settle down to house-
cleaning and gardening now . . . at least, after Mrs. Binnie had
had her say about the event.

"A grand wedding. Some people don't see how old
Charlie Sutton could afford it but I always say most folks is
only married once and why not make a splurge. I always did
like a wedding. Wasn't May the naughty thing to run off the
way she did, so sly-like? I'll bet you folks here wasn't a bit
more flabbergasted than I was when I heard it. And maybe I
didn't feel upset about her coming in here with you all. But I
always believed it would work out in time and it has. People
said May could never live in peace here, Pat was such a
crank. But I said, 'No, Pat isn't a crank. It's just that you have
to understand her.' And I was right, wasn't I, dearie? May
made up her mind when she come here that she'd get along
with you. 'It takes two to make a quarrel, ma, you know,' she
said. And I said, 'That's the right spirit, dearie. Behave like a
lady whatever you do. You're a Gardiner now and must live
up to their traditions. And you must make allowances.' That's
what I said to her. 'You must make allowances. And don't be
scared. I hope *my* daughter isn't a coward,' I said. It's a
real joy to me to see how well you've got on together,
though I don't deny that Judy Plum has been a hard nut to
crack. May has felt certain things . . . May always did feel
things so deeply. But she just made allowances as I advised
her. 'Judy Plum has been spoiled as every one knows,' I told
her, 'but she's old and breaking up fast and you can afford to
humour her a bit, dearie.' 'Oh, I'm not going to stoop to
argue with a servant,' May says. 'I'm above that.' May always
was so sensible. Well, I'm glad poor Enid Sutton has got
married at last . . . she's gone off terrible these past three
years waiting for Joe and not knowing if he'd ever come. And
what about you, Pat dearie? I can't imagine what the men are
thinking of. Isn't your widower a bit slow?" . . . with a smirk
that had the same effect on Pat as a dig in the ribs. . . . "Folks
think he's trying to back out of it but I tell them, 'no, that'll
be a match yet.' Just you encourage him a little more, dearie
. . . that's all he needs. To be sure, May said to me the other
day, '*I* wouldn't take another woman's leavings, ma.' But
you're not getting any younger, Pat, if you'll excuse my saying
so. *I* was married when I was eighteen and I could have been

married when I was seventeen. My dress was of red velvet and my hat was of black velvet with a green plume. Everyone thought it elegant but I was disappointed. I'd always wanted to be wedded in a sky-blue gown, the hue of God's own heaven."

"One of her poetical flights," whispered Tillytuck to Judy. But Pat and Rae both heard him and almost choked trying not to laugh. Mrs. Binnie, who never dreamed any one could be laughing at her, kept on.

"Is it true the Kirks are putting up a sun-dial in the Long House garden?"

"Yes," said Pat shortly.

"Well now, I never did hold with them modern inventions," said Mrs. Binnie complacently. "An old-fashioned clock is good enough for *me*."

"Never mind," said Rae, when Mrs. Binnie had finally waddled off to the "living room," "it will soon be lilac time."

"With white apple boughs framing a moon," said Pat.

"And violets in the silver bush," said Rae.

"And a new row of lilies to be planted along the dyke," said Pat.

"And great crimson clovers in the Mince Pie Field."

"And blue-eyed grass around the Pool. . . ."

"And pussy-willows in Happiness . . . ."

"And a dance of daisies along Jordan."

"Oh, we've heaps of precious things left yet, Pat—things nobody, not even a Binnie can spoil." Were the days when she could wash her being in the sunrise and feel as blithe as a bird gone forever? Perhaps they would come back when the new house would be built and Silver Bush was all their own again. But that was as yet far in the future. There was Judy coming across the yard, bringing in some drenched little chickens May had forgotten to put in. Was Judy getting bent? Pat shivered.

But still life seemed sadly out of tune, struggle as bravely as one might.

3

"I'll have nothing to do with anything to-day but spring," said Pat . . . even gaily. For May had gone home that morning and they had a whole day to be alone . . . three delightful meals to eat alone when they could sit around the table and talk as long as they liked in the old way. Sometimes Pat and Judy thought those frequent visits of May home were all that saved their reason. Everything seemed different. Judy vowed that the very washing machine ran easier when she was away. Even the house seemed to draw a breath of relief. It had never got used to May.

It had not been an easy spring at Silver Bush despite its beauty. House-cleaning with May was rather a heart-breaking business. She was so full of suggestions.

"Why not do away with that messy old front garden, Pat, and make a real lawn?"... or, "I'd have a window cut there, Pat. This hall is really awfully dark in the afternoons."... or, "The orchard is really trying to get into the house, Pat. Why not have that tree cut down?"

May simply could not or would not get it into her head that Pat was not having trees cut down. In regard to this particular tree, May was not perhaps so far wrong as in some of her suggestions. It really was too close to the house...a young apple tree that had started up of itself and grew so slyly that it was a tree before any one took much notice of it. Now it was pushing its boughs into the very window of the Big Parlour. When May spoke it was a thing of beauty, all starred with tiny red buds just on the point of bursting.

"I think it's lovely having the orchard coming right into the house like this," said Pat.

"You would," said May. It was a favourite retort with her and she always contrived to put a vast amount of contempt into it.

None of her suggestions were adopted and May tearfully told her mother, in Judy's hearing, that she "simply couldn't do a thing in her husband's house." She was determined to have a "herbaceous border" and nagged at Sid until he interceded with Pat and it was decided that it might be made across the bottom of the little lawn, where hitherto nothing but lilies of the valley had grown wildly and thickly. There were plenty of other lilies of the valley about but Pat hated to see those ploughed up and May's iris and delphiniums and what Mrs. Binnie called "concubines," set in their place. Because May really did not care a bit for flowers. She wanted her herbaceous border because Olive had told her they were all the fashion now and every one in town was making one.

"Do you know that May badgered Sid at last into taking her back and showing her the Secret Field?" asked Rae.

Yes, Pat knew it. May had laughed on her return.

"I've seen your famous field, Pat... nothing but a little hole in the woods. And you've been making such a fuss over it all these years."

To Pat it was the ultimate treason that Sid should have showed May the Secret Field... *their* Secret Field. But she could not blame him. He had to do it for peace's sake.

"You love your sister better than your wife," May told him passionately, whenever he refused to do anything Pat didn't want done. He and May had begun to quarrel violently and life at Silver Bush was made bitter all that summer by it. Meal times were the worst. The bickering between them was almost incessant.

"Oh, do let us have one meal without a fight," Long Alec remarked in exasperation one day. Pat, who had been listening in silence to May's sarcasm and Sid's sulky replies, rose and went to her room.

"I can't bear it any longer... I can't," she said wildly. She twitched the shade to pull it down and shut out the insulting sunlight. It escaped her and whizzed wildly to the top, thereby nearly scaring to death Bold-and-Bad, asleep on Rae's bed.

"You don't deserve a cat," said Bold-and-Bad, or words to that effect.

Pat glared at him.

"To think that it has come to this at Silver Bush!"

Rae, coming in a little later with the mail and an armful of blossom, turned the key in the door. That was necessary now. There was no longer the old-time privacy at Silver Bush. May might bounce in on them at any time without the pretence of knocking. She merely laughed at the idea of knocking and called it "Silver Bush airs."

"Pat, darling, don't take it so to heart. I admit there's a time every day when May makes me yearn for the good old days when you could pull peoples' wigs off. But when I feel that way I just reflect what Brook's eyes would make of her... can't you see the twinkle in them?... and she shrinks to her proper perspective. It isn't going to last forever."

"It is... it is," cried Pat wildly. "Rae, May doesn't *want* to have a house built on the other place... she wants to have Silver Bush. I've heard her talking to Sid... I couldn't help hearing... you know what her voice is like when she's angry. 'I'll never go to live on the Adams place... it would be so far out of the world... you can't move all them barns. You told me when you persuaded me to marry you that we would live at Silver Bush. And I'm going to... and it won't be under the thumb of your old-maid sister either. She's nothing but a parasite... living off your father when there's nothing now to prevent her from going away and earning her own living when I'm here to run things.' She's doing her best to set Sid against us all... you know she is. And she attributes some petty motive to everything we do or say... or *don't* say. Remember the scene she made last week because I hadn't taken any notice of her new dress... that awful concoction of cheap radium lace over that sleazy bright blue silk. I thought the kindest thing I could do was *not* to take notice of it. I was ashamed to think any one at Silver Bush could wear such a thing. And she tells Sid we're always laughing at her."

"Well, you *did* laugh last night when she said that thing about the moon," grinned Rae.

"Who could help it? I forgot myself in the delight of seeing that new moon over the crest of that fir in the silver bush and I pointed it out to May. 'How cute!' remarks my sister-in-law. And that creature is... by law... a Gardiner of Silver Bush!"

"Still, the new moon over the fir tree is just as exquisite as it ever was," said Rae softly.

But Pat would listen just then to no comforting.

"Think of dinner. At the best now we never have any real conversation at our meals... and at the worst it is like it was to-day. Rae, at times it simply seems to me that everything sane and sweet and happy has vanished from Silver Bush and only returns for a little while when she is away. Why, she listens on the 'phone... fancy any one at Silver Bush listening on the 'phone!... and gossips over what she hears. I feel dragged in the dust when I hear her. Do you know that she took that gang of her Summerside cousins into our room yesterday... our room!... and showed it to them?"

"Well, she wouldn't find it littered with hair-pins and face powder as hers is," said Rae, looking fondly around at their little immaculate room, engoldened by the light of the new corn-coloured curtains she and Pat had selected that spring. Here, at least, were yet stillness and peace and refreshment whatever might be the state of things elsewhere. "And as for her setting Sid against us, she can't do that, Pat. Sid knows what she is now. And dad will remain master of

Silver Bush. Let's just sit tight and wait. Here's a letter from Hilary I've just brought in from the box. It will cheer you up."

But it hardly did, though Pat wistfully read it over three times in the hope of finding that elusive something Hilary's letters used to possess. It was nice, like all Hilary's letters. But it was the first for quite a long time . . . and it was a little remote, somehow . . . as if he were thinking of something else all the time he was writing it. He was going to Italy and then to the east . . . Egypt . . . India . . . to study architecture. He would be away for a year.

"I want to see the whole world," he wrote. Pat shivered. The "whole world" had a cold, huge sound to her. Yet for the first time the idea came into her head that it might be rather nice to see the world with Hilary or some such congenial companion. Philae against a desert sunset . . . the storied Alhambra . . . the pearl-white wonder of the Taj Mahal by moonlight . . . Petra, that "rose-red city half as old as Time," as Hilary had quoted. It would be wonderful to see them. But it would be more wonderful still to look at Silver Bush and know it for her own again . . . as she was afraid it never would be. Perhaps May was there to stay. She wanted to and she always got what she wanted. She had wanted Sid and she had got him. She would get Silver Bush by hook or crook. Already at times she assumed sly airs of mistress-ship and did the honours of the garden on the strength of her "herbaceous border," explaining ungraciously that the stones around the beds were a whim of old Judy Plum's. "We humour her."

And the place was over-run by her family. Judy used to tell Tillytuck that Silver Bush was crawling wid thim. Sure and wasn't all the Binnie clan that prolific!

That hateful young brother of May's with the weasel eyes was there more than half his time, "helping" Sid and making fun of Judy who revenged herself by hiding tid-bits he coveted away in the pantry and blandly knowing nothing about them.

"Poor old Judy is failing fast," said May. "She puts things away and forgets where she puts them."

May was much in the kitchen now, cooking up what Judy called "messes" for her own friends and leaving all the greasy or doughy pots and pans for Judy to wash. Judy couldn't have told you whether she disliked May more in good humour or in "the sulks." When she was sulky she banged and slammed but her tongue was still; when she was in good humour she never stopped talking. There were few quiet moments at Silver Bush now. Judy in despair took to sitting and knitting on Wild Dick's tombstone. Tillytuck sat there, too, on Weeping Willy's, smoking his pipe. "I like company but not too much," was all he would say. It was all great fun for May. She persisted in assuming that Tillytuck and Judy were "courting" in the graveyard.

"Will I be caring what she says?" said Judy bitterly to Pat. "Oh, oh, she can't run me kitchen. She was be way av hanging up a calendar on me wall yesterday right below King William and Quane Victoria... a picture av a big fat girl wid no clothes at all on. I did be taking it down and throwing it in the fire. 'Sure,' sez I to her, 'that hussy is no fit company for ather a king or a quane,' sez I. And nather was that cousin av hers she had here yesterday in a bathing suit. She come in as bould as brass wid her great bare fat legs and did be setting on yer Great-grandfather Nehemiah's chair, wid thim crossed. And thim not aven a dacent white... sun-tan she did be calling it... more like the colour av skim milk cheese. Tillytuck just took one look and flid to the granary. I cudn't be trating her as I did the calendar but I sez, 'People that fond av showing their legs ought to be dieting a bit,' sez I. 'You quaint thing!' sez she. Oh, oh, it's thanking the Good Man Above I am she didn't call me priceless. It do be her fav'rite ajective. But whin May did be saying that one-pace bathing suits were all the fashion now and did I ixpict people to go bathing in long dresses and crinolines, I sez, 'Oh, oh, far be it from me to be like yer Aunt Ellice, May,' sez I. 'Whin her nace sint her a statue av the Venus av Mily for a Christmas prisent she did be putting a dress on it, rale tasty, afore she showed it to her frinds. I'm not objicting to legs as legs,' sez I, 'spacially at the shore where they do be plinty av background for thim, but whin they're as big and fat as yer lady cousin's,' sez I, 'they do be a bit overpowering in me kitchen.' 'Ivery one thinks that Emma looks stunning in her suit,' sez May. 'Stunning do be the right word,' sez I. 'Ye saw the iffict she had on Tillytuck and he's not a man asily upset,' sez I. 'As for the fashion,' sez I, 'av coorse what one monkey does all the other monkeys will be doing,' sez I. Me fine May sez that I'd insulted her frind and hadn't a word to throw to a dog all day but I'm liking her far better whin she's sulky than whin she's frindly. She did be trying to pump me about Cleaver this morning but I wasn't knowing innything. Do there be innything to know, Patsy dear?"

"Not a thing," said Pat with a smile.

"Oh, oh, I wasn't ixpicting it," said Judy with no smile. She did not know whether to feel relieved or disappointed. She did not quite like Cleaver, who was an honour graduate of McGill and was spending his summer doing research work at the Silverbridge harbour. Pat had got acquainted with him at the Long House and he had dangled a bit round Silver Bush. He was enormously clever and his researches into various elusive bacilli had already put him in the limelight. But poor Cleaver looked rather like a magnified bacillus himself and Judy, try as she would, could not see him as a husband for Pat.

"It'll be the widower yet, I'm fearing," she told Tillytuck in the graveyard. "Spacially if this news we're hearing about Jingle is true. I've always had me own ideas... but I do be only an ould fool and getting no younger, as Mrs. Binnie do be saying ivery once in so long."

"Old Matilda Binnie has a new set of teeth and a new fur coat," said Tillytuck. "Now, if she could get a new set of brains she might do very well for a while." He took a few whiffs at his pipe and then added gravely, "Symbolically speaking."

4

Aunt Edith died very suddenly in August. They all felt the shock of it. None of them had ever loved Aunt Edith very much... she was not a lovable person. But she was part of the established order of things and her passing meant another change. Oddly enough, Judy, who had had a lifelong vendetta with her, seemed to mourn and miss her most. Judy thought life would be almost stodgy when there was no Aunt Edith to horrify and exchange polite, barbed jabs with.

"Whin I think I'll niver see her in me kitchen agin, insulting me, I do be having a very quare faling, Patsy dear."

It was of course May who told Pat, with much relish, that Hilary Gordon was engaged. Some Binnie had had a letter from another Binnie who lived in Vancouver and knew the girl. She and Hilary were to be married when he returned from his year abroad and he was to be taken into the noted firm of architects in which her father was the senior partner.

"He was a beau of yours long ago, wasn't he, when you were a young girl?" asked May in a malicious drawl.

"I think it's true," Rae told Pat that night. "I heard it some time ago. Dot has friends in Vancouver and they wrote it to her. I . . . I didn't know whether to tell you or not."

"Why on earth shouldn't you tell me?" said Pat very coldly.

"Well . . ." Rae hesitated . . . "you and Hilary were always such friends . . ."

"Exactly!" Pat bit the word off and her brook-brown eyes were full of a rather dangerous fire. "We have always been good friends and so I would naturally be interested in hearing any good news about him. All that . . . that hurts me is that he should have left me to hear it from others. Rae Gardiner, what are you looking at me like that for?"

"I've always thought," said Rae, taking her life in her hands, "that you . . . that you cared much more for Hilary than you ever suspected yourself, Pat."

Pat laughed a little unsteadily.

"Rae, don't be a goose. You and Judy have always been a little delirious on the subject of Hilary. I've always loved Hilary and always will. He's just like a dear brother to me. Do you realise how many years it is since I've seen him? Of course we've drifted apart even as friends. It was inevitable. Even our correspondence is dying a natural death. I haven't had a letter from him since he went abroad."

"I was only a child when he went away but I remember how I liked him," said Rae. "I used to think he was the nicest boy in the world."

"So he was," said Pat. "And I hope he's going to marry some one who is nice enough for him."

"He really was in love with you, wasn't he, Pat?"

"He thought he was. I knew he would get over that."

"Well . . ." Rae had been irradiated all day with some secret happiness and now it came out . . . "Brook is coming over for a week before college opens. I do hope Miss Macaulay will have my blue georgette done by that time. And I think I'll have a little jacket of that lovely transparent blue velvet we saw in town to go with it. I feel sure Brook will love me in that dress."

"I thought he loved you in any dress," teased Pat.

"Oh, he does. But there are degrees, Pat."

"And no one," thought Pat a little drearily, "cares how I'm dressed."

She looked out of the window and saw a rising moon . . . and remembered old moonrises she had watched with Hilary . . . "when she was a girl." That phrase of May's rankled. And Mrs. Binnie had been rather odious the other day, assuring her again there were as good fish in the sea as ever came out of it . . . apropos of the announcement of the engagement of a South Glen girl to Donald Holmes.

"You're young enough yet," said Mrs. Binnie soothingly. "And when people say you're beginning to look a bit old-maidish I always tell them, 'Is it any wonder? Think of the responsibility Pat has had for years, with her mother ill and so much on her shoulders. No wonder she's getting old-looking afore her time.'"

Pat had got pretty well into the habit of ignoring Mrs. Binnie but that phrase "young yet" haunted her. She went to the mirror and looked dispassionately at herself. She really did not think she looked old. Her dark brown hair was as glossy as ever . . . her amber eyes as bright . . . her cheeks as smooth and rounded. Perhaps there were a few tiny lines in the corners of her eyes and . . . *what was that?* Pat leaned nearer, her eyes dilating a little. Was it . . . could it be . . . yes, it was! A grey hair!

5

Pat went up to the Long House that night. She walked blithely and springily. She was not going to worry over that grey hair. She would not even pull it out. The Selbys all turned grey young. What did it matter? She would not grow old in heart, no matter what she did in head. She would always keep her banner of youth flying gallantly. Wrinkles might come on her face but there should never be any on her soul. And yet there had been a moment that day when Pat had felt as if she didn't want to be young any longer. Things hurt you too much when you were young. Surely they wouldn't hurt so much when you got old. You wouldn't care so much then . . . things would be settled . . . there wouldn't be so many changes. People you knew wouldn't always be running off to far lands . . . or getting married. Your hair would be *all* grey and it wouldn't matter. You wouldn't be eating your heart out longing for a lost paradise.

Altogether it had not been a pleasant day. May had had a fit of the sulks and had taken it out slamming doors....Rover had eaten a plateful of fudge Pat had set outside to cool....Judy had seemed down-hearted about something...perhaps the news about Hilary though she never referred to it but only muttered occasionally to herself about "strange going-ons." Pat decided that she felt a trifle stodgy and needed something to pep her up a bit. She would find it at the Long House...she always did. Whenever life seemed a bit grey...whenever she felt a passing pang of loneliness over the changes that had been and...worse still...would be, she went up the hill to David and Suzanne. Whenever the door of the Long House clanged behind her it seemed to shut out the world, with its corroding discontents and vexations. Once, Pat thought with a stab of pain, she had felt that way when she went into Silver Bush. That she couldn't feel so any longer was a very bitter thing...a thing she couldn't get used to. But to-night as she and David and Suzanne sat around the fire—it was a cool September night and any excuse served when they wanted to light that fire...and cracked nuts and talked...or didn't talk...the bitterness faded out of Pat's heart as it always did in their company. Suzanne was rather quiet, sitting with Alphonso curled up in her lap: but Pat and David never found themselves lacking for something to say. Pat looked at the motto that ran in quaint, irregular letters around the fireplace.

> *"There be three gentle and goodlie things,*
> *To be here,*
> *To be together,*
> *And to think well of one another."*

That was true: and while it remained true one could bear anything else, no matter what sort of a hole it left in your life. What a dear Suzanne was! And what nice eyes David had...very whimsical when they were not tender and very tender when they were not whimsical. And his voice ...what did his voice always remind her of? She could never tell but she knew it was something that always tugged at her heart. And she knew he liked her very much. It was nice to be liked . . . nice to have such friends to come to whenever you wanted to.

David walked home with her as he always did. Pat had never until to-night stopped to think how very pleasant thôse walks home were. To-night the hills were dreamy under a harvest moon. They went through the close-set spruce grove that always seemed to be guarding so many secrets . . . down the field path under the Watching Pine that still watched . . . for what? . . . over the brook and along the Whispering Lane. At the gate where they always parted they stood in silence for a little while, lost in the beauty of the night. Faint music came to them. It was only Tillytuck playing in his lair but, muted by the distance, it sounded like some fairy melody under a haunted moon. Beyond the trees were great quietudes of sky where burned the stars that never changed . . . the only things that never changed.

David was thinking that silence with Pat was more eloquent than talk with any other woman. He was also wondering what Pat would do or say if he suddenly did what he had always wanted to do . . . put his arm about her and said, "darling." What he did say was almost as shattering to Pat's new-found mood of contentment.

"Has Suzanne told you her little secret yet?"

Suzanne? A secret? There was only one kind of a secret people spoke about in that tone. Pat involuntarily put up her hand as if warding off a blow.

"No . . . o . . . o," she said faintly.

"She probably would have if you had been alone with her to-night. She's very happy. She has made up a quarrel she had before we came here with an old lover . . . and they are engaged."

It was too much . . . it really was. So Suzanne was to be lost to her, too! And she had to be polite and say something nice.

"I . . . I . . . hope she will always be very happy," she gasped.

"I think she will," said David quietly. "She has loved him for years . . . I never knew just what the trouble was. We're a secretive lot, we Kirks. Of course they won't be married till he has finished college. He has had to work his way through. And then . . . what am I to do, Pat?"

"You . . . you'll miss her," said Pat. She knew she was being incredibly stupid.

"You'll have to tell me what to do, Pat," David said, bending a little nearer, his voice taking on a very significant tone.

Was David by any chance proposing to her? And if he were what on earth could she say? She wasn't going to say anything! She had had enough shocks for one day... Hilary engaged... grey hair... Suzanne engaged! Oh, why must life be such an uncertain thing? You never knew where you were... you never had security... you never knew when there might not be some dreadful bolt from the blue. She would just pretend she hadn't heard David's question and go in. Which she did.

But that night she sat in the moonlight in her room for a long while and looked at the two paths she might take in life. Rae was away and the house was silent... and, so it seemed to Pat, lonely. Silver Bush always seemed when night fell to be mourning for its ravished peace. The sky outside was cloudless but a brisk wind was blowing past. "What is the wind in such a hurry for, Aunt Pat?" Little Mary had asked wistfully not long ago. Everything seemed in a hurry... life was in a hurry... it couldn't let you be... it swept you on with it as if you were a leaf in the wind.

Which path should she take? David was going to ask her to marry him... she had known for a long time in the back of her mind that he would ask her if she ever let him. She was terribly fond of David. Life with him would be a very pleasant pilgrimage. Even a grey day was full of colour when David was around. She was always contented in his company. And his eyes were sometimes so sad. She wanted to make them happy. Was that reason enough for marrying a man, even one as nice as David? If she didn't marry him she would lose him out of her life. He would never stay at the Long House after Suzanne had gone. And she couldn't lose any more friends... she just couldn't.

Suppose she didn't take that path? Suppose she just went on living here at Silver Bush... growing into being "Aunt Pat"... helping plan the clan weddings and funerals... her brown hair turning pepper-and-salt. That grey hair popped into her mind. It seemed as if age had just tapped her on the shoulder. But it would be all right if only Silver Bush might be hers to love and plan for and live for, free from all outsiders and intruders. She wouldn't hesitate a second then. But would it be? Would it ever be hers again? She knew what

May's designs were. And she knew Sid didn't want to leave Silver Bush for the other place. Would dad stand out against them . . . could he? No, it would end in May being mistress of Silver Bush some day. That was the secret dread that always haunted Pat. And if it ever came about . . .

A few weeks later David said quietly to her in the garden of the Long House . . . the garden where Bets' ghost sometimes walked even yet for Pat . . .

"Do you think you could marry me, Pat?"

Pat looked afar for a moment of silence to the firry rim of an eastern hill. Then she said just as quietly,

"I think I could."

6

Mother was told first. Mother's face was always serene but it changed a little when Pat told her.

"Darling, do you really love him?"

Pat looked out of the window. There had been a frost the night before and the garden had a blighted look. She had been hoping mother wouldn't ask that question.

"I do really, mother, but perhaps not in just the way you mean."

"There's only the one way," said mother softly.

"Then I'm one of the kind of people who can't love that way. I've tried . . . and I can't."

"It doesn't come by trying either," said mother.

"Mother dear, I'm terribly fond of David. We suit each other . . . our minds click. He loves the same things I do. I'm always happy with him . . . we'll always be good chums."

Mother said no more. She picked up something she was making for Rae's hope chest and went on putting tiny invisible stitches in it. After all perhaps it would work out. It was not what she had wanted for Pat but the child must make her own choices. David Kirk was a nice fellow . . . mother had always liked him. And Pat would not be far from her.

Judy came next and, for one who had always been anxious to see Pat "settled" betrayed no great delight. But she wished Pat well and was careful to say that *Mr.* Kirk had rale brading. Since the engagement was an accomplished fact Judy was not going to say anything against a future member of the family.

"The poor darlint, she don't be as happy as she thinks hersilf," Judy told Bold-and-Bad, regarding him as the only safe confidant. Only she felt that Bold-and-Bad never understood her quite so well as Gentleman Tom had done. "And after all the min she might have had! But I'm hoping the Good Man Above knows what's bist for us all."

To Rae Pat talked more frankly than to any one.

"Pat dear, if you love him . . ."

"Not as you love Brook, Rae. I'm just not capable of that sort of loving . . . or it doesn't last. David *needs* me . . . or will need me when Suzanne goes. We're not going to be married until she is . . . for two years at the least. I wouldn't marry him, Rae . . . I wouldn't marry anybody . . . if I knew I could go on living at Silver Bush. But if May stays here . . . and she means to . . . I can't, especially when you are gone to China. I've always loved the Long House next to Silver Bush. I'll be *near* Silver Bush . . . I can always look down on it and watch over it."

"I believe that's the real reason you're going to marry David Kirk," thought Rae. She looked at the shadow of the vine leaves on the bedroom floor. It looked like a dancing faun. Rae blinked to hide sudden foolish tears. Pat was going to miss something. But aloud she said only,

"I hope you'll be happy, Pat. You deserve to be. You've always been a darling."

Father took it philosophically. He would have liked some one a bit younger. But Kirk was a nice chap and seemed to have enough money to live on. There was something distinguished about him. His war book had been acclaimed by the critics and he was working on a "History of the Maritimes" of which, Long Alec had been told, great things were expected. Pat had always liked those brainy fellows. She had a right to please herself.

The rest of the clan were surprised and amused. Pat sensed that none of them quite approved. Winnie and the Bay Shore aunts said absolutely nothing, but silence can say a great deal sometimes. Only Aunt Barbara said deprecatingly,

"But, Pat, he's *grey*."

"So am I," said Pat, flaunting her one grey hair.

"Let's hope it lasts this time," said Uncle Tom. Pat thought he might have been nicer after the way she had stood by him in the affair of Mrs. Merridew.

May was frankly delighted, though her delight faded a

little when she learned that there was no prospect of an immediate marriage. Mrs. Binnie, rocking fiercely, had her say-so as well.

"So you've hooked the widower at last, Pat? What did I tell you . . . never give up. I've never understood how a gal could bring herself to marry a widower . . . but then any port in a storm. Of course, as I said to Olive, he's a bit on the old side . . ."

"I don't like boys," said Pat coolly. "I get on better with men. And you must admit, Mrs. Binnie, that his ears don't stick out."

"*I* call that flippant, Pat. Marriage is a very serious thing. As I was saying, when I said that to Olive she sez, 'I s'pose it's better to be an old man's darling than a young man's slave. Pat isn't so young as she used to be herself, ma. She'll make a very good wife for David Kirk.' Olive always kind of liked you, Pat. She always said you meant well."

"That was very kind of her."

Pat's amused, remote smile offended Mrs. Binnie. That was the worst of Pat. Always laughing at you in her sleeve. Mebbe she'd find out marrying an old widower was no laughing matter.

Suzanne was wild with delight.

"I've been hoping for it from the first, Pat. You're made for each other. David worries a bit because he's so much older. I tell him he's growing younger every day and you're growing older so you'll soon meet. He's a darling if he *is* my brother. He never dared to hope . . . till lately. He always said he had two rivals."

"Two?"

"Silver Bush . . . and Hilary Gordon."

Pat smiled.

"Silver Bush *was* his rival, I'll admit. But Hilary . . . he might as well call Sid a rival."

Yet her face had changed subtly. Some of the laughter went out of it. She was wondering why there was such a distinct relief in the thought that, since her correspondence with Hilary seemed to have died a natural death, she would not have to write him that she was going to marry David Kirk.

The Eighth Year

It rained Thursday and Friday and then for a change, as Tillytuck said, it rained Saturday. Not the romping, rollicking, laughter-filled rain of spring but the sad, hopeless rain of autumn that seemed like the tears of old sorrows on the window-panes of Silver Bush.

"I love some kinds of rain," said Rae, "but not this kind. Doesn't the garden look forlorn? Nothing but the ghosts of flowers left in it ... and such unkempt ghosts at that. And we had such good times all summer working in that garden, hadn't we, Pat? I wonder if it will be the same next summer? I've a nasty, going-to-happeny feeling this morning that I don't like."

Judy, too, had had some kind of a "sign" in the night and was pessimistic. But nobody at first sight connected these forewarnings with the tall, thin lady who drove up the lane late in the afternoon and tied a spiritless grey nag to the paling of the graveyard.

"One more av thim agents," said Judy, watching her from the kitchen window, as she stalked up the wet walk, a suitcase dangling from the end of one of her long arms. "Sure and I've been pestered wid half a dozen of thim this wake. She don't be looking as if business was inny too prosperous."

"She looks like an angleworm on end," giggled Rae.

"I wouldn't let her in if I was you," said Mrs. Binnie, who seldom let a Saturday afternoon pass without a call at Silver Bush.

Judy had had some such idea herself but that speech of Mrs. Binnie's banished it.

"Oh, oh, we do be more mannerly than that at Silver Bush," she said loftily, and invited the stranger in cordially,

225

offering her a chair near the fire. No Binnie was going to tell Judy who was to be let in or out of *her* kitchen!

"It's a wet day," sighed the caller, as she sank into the chair and let the suit-case drop on the floor with an air of relief. She was remarkably tall and very slight, dressed in shabby black, and with enormous pale blue eyes. They positively drowned out her face and gave you the uncanny impression that she hadn't any features but eyes. Otherwise you might have noticed that her cheek-bones were a shade too high and her thin mouth rather long and new-moonish. She gave Squedunk such a look of disapproval that that astute cat remarked that he would go out and have a look at the weather and stood not upon the order of his going.

"It's a wet day for travelling but I've allowed myself just ten days to do the Island and time is getting on."

"You don't belong to the Island?" said Rae . . . quite superfluously, Judy thought. Sure and cudn't ye be telling *that* niver belonged to the Island!

"No." Another long sigh. "My home is in Novy Scoshy. I've seen better days. But when you haven't a husband to support you you've got to make a living somehow. I was an agent before I was married and so I just took to the road again. Every little helps."

"Sure and it do be hard lines to be a widdy in this could world," said Judy, instantly sympathetic, and hauling forward her pot of soup.

"Oh, I ain't a widdy woman, worse luck." Another sigh. "My husband left me years ago."

"Oh, oh!" Judy pushed the pot back again. If your husband left you there was something wrong somewhere. "And what might ye be selling?"

"All kinds of pills and liniments, tonics and perfumes, face creams and powders," said the caller, opening her suit-case and preparing to display her wares. But at this juncture the porch door opened and Tillytuck appeared in the doorway. He got no further, being apparently frozen in his tracks. As for the lady of the eyes, she clasped her hands and opened and shut her mouth twice. The third time she managed to ejaculate,

"Josiah!"

Tillytuck said something like "Good gosh!" He gazed helplessly around him. "I'm sober . . . I'm sober . . . I can't hope I'm drunk now."

"Oh, oh, so this lady is no stranger to you I'm thinking?" said Judy.

"Stranger!" The lady in question rolled her eyes rapidly, making Rae think of the dogs in the old fairy tale. "He is . . . he was . . . he is my husband."

Judy looked at Tillytuck.

"Is it the truth she do be spaking, *Mr.* Tillytuck?"

Tillytuck tried to brazen it out. He nodded and grinned.

"Oh, oh," said Judy sarcastically, "and isn't the truth refreshing after all the lies we've been hearing!"

"I've always felt," said Tillytuck mournfully, "that you never really believed anything I said. But if this . . . person has been telling you I left her she's been speaking symbolically. I was druv to it. She told me to go."

"Because he didn't . . . and wouldn't . . . believe in predestination," said Mrs. Tillytuck. "He was no better than a modernist. I couldn't live with a man who didn't believe in predestination. Could you?"

"Sure and I've niver tried," said Judy, to whom Mrs. Tillytuck had seemed to appeal. Mrs. Binnie asked what predestination was but nobody answered her.

"She told me to go," repeated Tillytuck, "and I took her at her word. 'There's really been too much of this,' I said . . . and it was all I did say. I appeal to you, Jane Maria, wasn't it all I did say?"

Tears filled Mrs. Tillytuck's eyes. You really felt afraid of drowning in them.

"You're welcome back any time, Josiah," she sobbed. "Any time you believe in predestination you can come home."

Tillytuck said nothing. He turned and went out. Mrs. Tillytuck wiped her eyes while Judy regarded her rather stonily and Pat and Rae tried to keep their faces straight.

"This . . . this has upset me a little," said Mrs. Tillytuck apologetically. "I hope you'll excuse me. I hadn't laid eyes on Josiah for fifteen years. He hasn't changed a particle. Has he been here all that time?"

"No," said Judy shortly. "Only seven years."

"Then you know him pretty well I daresay. Always telling wonderful stories of his adventures I suppose? The yarns I've listened to! And every last one of them crazier than the others."

"Was his grandfather really a pirate?" asked Rae. She had always been curious on that point.

"Listen to her now. His grandfather a pirate! Why, he was only a minister. But isn't that like Josiah? Him and his romances and 'traggedies'! He always had a wild desire for notoriety... always had a craze to be mixed up with any scandal or catastrophe he heard of. Why, that man didn't like funerals because he couldn't pretend to be the corpse. But it wasn't that I minded. After all, his lies were interesting and I like a little frivolous conversation once in a while. He was easy enough to live with, I'll say that for him. And I didn't mind his sly orgies so much though I warned him what happened to my Uncle Asa. Uncle Asa threw himself into a full bath-tub when *he* was full, mistaking it for his bed. He broke his neck first and then he drowned. No, it was Josiah's theology. At first I thought it was just indigestion but when I realized he meant it my conscience wouldn't stand for it. He said there never was an Adam or Eve and he said the doctrine of predestination was blasphemous and abominable. So I told him he had to choose between me and modernism. But I suffered. I loved that man with all his faults. It has preyed on my mind all these years. What is going to become of his immortal soul?"

Nobody, not even Mrs. Binnie, tried to answer this question.

"Well," resumed Mrs. Tillytuck more briskly, "this isn't business. I dunno as I feel very business like just now. My heart don't feel just right. This has been a shock to it. I suffer greatly from a tired heart."

Nobody knew whether this was a physical or an emotional ailment. Mrs. Binnie understood it to be the former and asked quite sympathetically, "Did you ever try a mustard plaster at the pit of your stomach, Mrs. Tillytuck?"

"I fear that wouldn't benefit a weary heart," said Mrs. Tillytuck pathetically. "Possibly, madam, you have never suffered as I have from a weary wounded heart?"

"No, thank goodness my heart is all right," said Mrs. Binnie. "My only trouble is rheumatism in the knee j'ints."

"I have the very thing for that here," said Mrs. Tillytuck briskly. "You try this liniment."

Mrs. Binnie bought the liniment and Mrs. Tillytuck looked appealingly at the others. But Judy said darkly they didn't be wanting inny beautifying messes.

"We do all be handsome enough here widout thim."

"I've never seen anybody so handsome she couldn't be

handsomer," said Mrs. Tillytuck with another sigh as she closed her bag. At the door she turned.

"I s'pose you don't happen to know if Josiah has saved up any money these fifteen years?"

Nobody happened to know.

"Ah well, it isn't likely. A rolling stone gathers no moss. Though he wasn't lazy... I'll say that for him. And you can tell him my parting word was... believe in predestination, Josiah, and you'll be welcome home at any time."

Mrs. Tillytuck was gone. The echo of her steps died away down the walk. Pat and Rae went into their long repressed spasm. Mrs. Binnie said there was always something about Tillytuck that made her think he was married.

Judy was very silent, her only remark being, as she watched Mrs. Tillytuck driving out of the yard,

"A bean-pole like that!"

2

Tillytuck did not show up for supper, having gone on an errand, real or pretended, to Silverbridge. But he slipped into the kitchen at night, when Judy and Rae and Pat were roasting apples around the fire, and slid into his own corner. Judy bustled about to get him a liddle bite and was markedly cordial. Sure and couldn't she be as civil to Tillytuck now as she pleased when nobody could ever again be thinking she was setting her cap for him!

"I suppose you were all a bit surprised to learn I was a family man?" he said, in a tone of mingled sheepishness and bravado.

"Tillytuck, tell us all about it," pleaded Rae. "We're dying of curiosity."

Tillytuck fitted his finger-tips carefully together. "There ain't much to tell," he said... and proceeded to tell it, punctuated by gentle snorts from Judy.

"I've often wondered how I came to do it. It all begun with a moon. You can never trust a moon."

"Oh, oh, we must have something to blame our mistakes on," said Judy, good-humouredly, as she set a large plateful of his favourite cinnamon buns beside him on the corner of the table.

"I'd known her for some time in a kind of a way, but the

first time I really met her was at a friend's house and we sot out on the porch and talked. She was a fine figger of a woman then... some meat on her bones... and them eyes of hers was kind of devastating by moonlight. I won't deny there was a touch of glamour about it. But I didn't really mean to propose to her... honest, I didn't. It *wasn't* a proposal... just a kind of a hint. Partly out of sympathy and partly because of the moon. But she snapped me up so quick I was an engaged man before I knew what had happened to me. Hog-tied, that's what I was. Well, we was married and went to live in her house. It was rather prosy for a man of my romantic temperament but we was well enough for a spell, though the boys called us the long and short of it. I was devoted to that woman, Judy. (Snort.) Many a time I've got up in the middle of the night and made a cup of tea for her. She always liked a cup of tea when she got up in the night. Claimed it was good for her heart. And she was the best wife in the world except for a few things. She sighed too much and she used to get hopping mad if I hung my cap on the wrong hook. Likewise she had an edge to her tongue if I went in without scraping my boots. I ain't denying we had a few surface quarrels but no more than enough to spice life up a bit. It was her theology we went to the mat about finally. I couldn't stomach it and I told her so. She was a fundamentalist... oh, was she a fundamentalist? I was one myself but I wouldn't give her the satisfaction of admitting it, and anyhow I stopped short at predestination. As for my saying there was no Adam or Eve I was only talking poetically but when I saw how she got her dander up over it I pretended to be in earnest. From that on there was no living with her and when she up and told me to go I went as quick as I could get. I was tired of her lumpy gravy anyhow, and the dishwater she called soup. If she'd been a cook like you, Judy, I could have believed in anything."

Tillytuck rumbled and took a large bite out of a cinnamon bun.

"Life would be dull if we hadn't a few traggedies to look back on," he said philosophically.

But three days later the world of Silver Bush temporarily toppled into chaos. Tillytuck had given warning.

Everybody went into a state of consternation. Long Alec and Sid, because they were losing a good man, Judy and Rae and Pat, because they were losing Tillytuck. It did not seem possible. He had been a part of their life so long that it was unthinkable that he could cease to be such. Another change, thought Pat sadly.

"It's just that he feels he's lost face," said Rae. "He would never have thought of going if that horrid woman hadn't come here and given him away. That is his real reason for going, whatever he may say. I'm just going to sit here and hate her hard."

"It do be too bad ye can't be putting up wid us inny longer," said Judy bitterly to him that evening.

"You know it ain't that, Judy. I've stayed longer here than any place I've been in. But I'm getting too contented here. It's always been my motto to move on if I got too contented anywhere. And I'll admit there's been too much Binnie around here of late for my liking. Besides, I'm getting on in years. You can't escape Anno Domini. Farm work on a place like this is a bit hard on me now. I've saved up a little money and me and a friend on the South Shore are going to start up a fox ranch of our own. But I'll never forget you folks here. I'll miss your soup, Judy."

There was a tremble in Tillytuck's voice. Judy was setting the supper-table and trying to make an obstreperous salt-cellar shake. Suddenly she snatched it up and hurled it through the open window.

"I've put up wid that thing for twinty years," she said savagely, "but I'll not be putting up wid it another day."

Tillytuck went away one bleak November evening. He turned in the doorway for a last word.

"May the years be kind to ye all, speaking poetically," he said. "You are as fine a bunch of folks as I ever had the good luck to live among. You understand a man of my calibre. It's a great thing to be understood. Long Alec is the right kind of a man to work for and your mother is a saint if ever there was one. I haven't cried since I was a child but I come near it when she told me good-bye before she went up to bed. If that wild woman of mine ever pays you another call, Judy, for pity's sake don't tell her I believe in predestination now. If she knew it she'd drag me back by hook or crook. I'll send for my radio when I get settled. Ajoo."

He waved his hand with a courtly air, sniffed sadly the aroma of Judy's beans and onions, and turned his back on her cheery domain. They watched him going down the lane in the dim, with his stuffed owl under his arm and the same old fur cap on his head that he had worn upon his arrival. Just

Dog walked close beside him, with a tail that had apparently no wag left in it. A weird moon with a cloud-ribbed face was rising over the Hill of the Mist. The surging of wind in the tree branches was very mournful.

Rae's face crumpled up.

"I...I...think I'd like to cry," she said chokily. "Do you remember the night he came? You sent me to show him the way to the granary and he said 'Good-night, little Cuddles,' as he went up the stair. I felt he was an old friend then."

"Sure and I wish I'd niver found fault wid him for playing his fiddle in the graveyard," said Judy. "Maybe the poor soul will niver get a taste ave dape apple pie again. That wife av his was wondering what wud become av his soul but I'm wondering what's going to happen to his poor body."

"He was a genial old soul," said Mrs. Binnie.

"There was something so quaint about him," whimpered May.

Pat wanted to cry but wouldn't because May was doing it. She slipped an arm about Judy, who, somehow, was looking strangely old.

"Anyway, we've got Silver Bush and you left," she whispered.

Judy poked the fire fiercely.

"Sure and it's a could world and we must all do our bist to bring a liddle warmth into it," she said briskly.

And so passed Josiah Tillytuck from the annals of Silver Bush.

3

Life seemed to change somehow at Silver Bush after Tillytuck's going though it was hard just to put your finger on the change. The evenings in the kitchen didn't seem half so jolly for one thing, lacking the rivalry in tale-telling between Judy and Tillytuck. Tillytuck's place had been taken by young Jim Macaulay from Silverbridge who was efficient as a worker but was only "young Jim Macaulay." He occupied the granary chamber but when evening came he departed on his own social pursuits. He never went on "sprees" and was more amenable to suggestion than Tillytuck had been, so that Long Alec liked him. But Judy said the pinch av salt had been left out of him. Pat was just as well pleased; nobody could ever take Tillytuck's place and it was as well there was nobody to try. She spent more evenings at the Long House that winter than ever before. David sometimes came down but he was always rather a misfit in Judy's kitchen. She Mr. Kirked him so politely and always shut up like a clam. He and Pat were, as Pat frequently told herself, very happy in their engagement. They had such a nice friendly understanding. No nonsense. Just good comradeship and quiet laughter and a kiss or two. Pat did not mind David's kisses at all.

So another winter slipped away... another miracle of spring was worked... another summer brought its treasures to Silver Bush. And one evening Pat read in the paper that the *Ausonia* had arrived at Halifax. The next day the wire came from Hilary. He was coming to the Island for just a day.

Rae found Pat in a kind of trance in their room.

"Rae... Hilary is coming... Hilary! He will be here to-morrow night."

"How jolly!" gasped Rae. "I was just a kid when he went away but I remember him well. Pat, you look funny. Won't you be glad to see him?"

"I would be glad to see the Hilary who went away," said Pat restlessly. "But will he be? He must have changed. We've all changed. Will he think I've got terribly old?"

"Pat, you goose! When you laugh you look about seventeen. Remember he has grown older himself."

But Pat couldn't sleep that night. She re-read the telegram before she went to bed. It meant Hilary... Hilary and the fir-scented Silver Bush... Hilary and the water laughing over the rocks in happiness... Hilary and snacks in Judy's kitchen. But did it... could it? Could the gulf of years be bridged so easily?

"Of course we'll be strangers," thought Pat miserably. But no... no. Hilary and she could never be strangers. To see him again... to hear his voice... she had not been thrilled like this for years. Did his eyes still laugh when they looked at you? With that hint of wistful appeal back of their laughter? And in the back of her mind, thrust out of sight, was a queer relief that David was away. He and Suzanne had gone for a visit to Nova Scotia. Pat would not acknowledge the relief or look at it.

Judy was almost tremulous over the news. She spent the next day making all the things she knew Hilary had liked in the old days and polished everything in the kitchen till it shone. Even the white kittens and King William and Queen Victoria all had their faces washed. May said you would have thought the Prince of Wales was coming.

"I suppose he'll be married as soon as he gets back to Vancouver," she said.

"Oh, oh, that's as the Good Man Above wills," said Judy, "and neither you nor I do be having innything to do wid it."

"Pat always wanted him, didn't she?" said May. "She never took up with David Kirk until she heard Hilary was engaged."

"Pat niver 'wanted' him," retorted Judy. "The shoe was on the other foot intirely. But ye cudn't be understanding."

She muttered under her breath as she went into the pantry, "'Spake not in the ears av a fool.'" May overheard it and shrugged. Who cared what Judy said!

There was a whispering of rain in the air and a growl of thunder when Pat went up to dress for Hilary's coming. She tried on three dresses and tore them off in despair. Finally she slipped on her old marigold chiffon. After all, yellow was her colour. She fluffed out her brown hair and looked at herself with a little bit of exultation such as she had not felt for a long while. The mirror was still a friend. She was flushed with excitement... her gold-brown eyes were starry ... surely Hilary would not think her so very much changed.

She moved restlessly about the room, changing things aimlessly, then changing them back again. What was it David had read to her from a poem the night before he went away?

> *"Nothing in earth or heaven*
> *Comes as it came before."*

It couldn't be the old Hilary who was coming.

"And I can't bear it if he is a stranger... I *can't*," she thought passionately. "It would be better if he never came back if he comes as a stranger."

All at once she did something she couldn't account for. She pulled David's diamond and sapphire ring off her finger and dropped it in a tray on her table. She felt a thrill of shame as she did it... but she *had* to do it. There was some inner compulsion that would not be disobeyed.

Rae came running up.

"Pat, he's here... he's getting out of a car in the yard."

"I simply can't go down to see him," gasped Pat, going momentarily to pieces. "He'll be so changed...."

"Nonsense. There is Judy letting him in. He'll be in the Big Parlour... hurry."

Pat ran blindly downstairs. She collided with somebody in the hall... she never knew who it was. She stood in the doorway for a moment. It was a very poignant moment. Afterwards Pat was sure she had never experienced anything like it. She always maintained she knew exactly what she would feel like on the resurrection morning.

"Jingle!" The old name came spontaneously to her lips. It *was* Jingle... Jingle and no stranger. How could she ever have feared he would be a stranger? He was holding her hands.

"Pat... Pat... I've years of things to say to you... but I'll say them all in one sentence... you haven't changed. Pat, I've been so terribly afraid you would have changed. But it was only yesterday we parted at the bridge over Jordan. But why aren't you laughing, Pat? I've always seen you laughing."

Pat couldn't laugh just then. Next day... next hour she might laugh. But now at this longed-for meeting after so many years she must be quiet for a space.

Yet they had a wonderful evening... just she and Hilary and a rejuvenated Judy... and of course the cats... in the old kitchen. May was luckily away and Rae considerately effaced herself. Outside the whole world might be a welter of wind and flame and water but here was calm and beauty and old delight. It was so enchanting to be shut away from the storm with Hilary... just as of yore... to be drinking amber tea and eating Judy's apple-cake with him and talking of old days and fun and dreams.

He *had* changed a little after all. His delicately cut face was more mature and had lost its boyish curves. His slim figure... so nicely lean... had an added distinction and poise. But his eyes still laughed wistfully and his thin, sensitive lips still parted in the old intriguing smile. She suddenly knew what it was she had always liked in David's smile. It was a little like Hilary's.

Hilary, looking at Pat, saw, as he had always seen, all his fancies, hopes, dreams in a human shape. She, too, had changed a little. More womanly... even more desirable. Her sweet brown face... her quick twisted smile... the witchery of her brown eyes... they were all as he had remembered them. How lovely was the curve of her chin and neck melting into the glow of mellow lamplight behind her! She looked all gold and rose and laughter. And she had the same trick of lifting her eyes which had been wont to set his head spinning long ago . . . a trick all the more effective because it was so wholly unconscious.

How much like old times it was . . . and was not! Time had been kind to the old place. But Gentleman Tom and McGinty had gone and Judy had grown old. She looked at him with all her old affection in her grey-green eyes but the eyes were more sunken than he remembered them and the hair more grizzled. Yet she could still tell a story and she could still produce a gorgeous "liddle bite." Through years of boarding houses Hilary had always remembered Judy's "liddle bites."

"Judy, will you leave me that picture of the white kittens when . . . a hundred years from now I hope . . . you are finished with the things of this planet?"

"Oh, oh, but I will that," Judy promised. "It do be the only picture I've iver owned. I did be bringing it wid me from the ould sod and I wudn't know me kitchen widout it."

"I'll hang it in my study," said Hilary.

"In one of thim wonderful new houses ye'll be building," said Judy slyly. "Sure and ye've got on a bit, haven't ye, Jingle? Oh, oh, will ye be excusing me? I'm knowing I shud be saying Mr. Gordon."

"Don't you know what would happen to you if you called me that, Judy? I love to hear the old nickname. As for getting on . . . yes, I suppose I have. I've got about everything I ever wanted" . . . "except," he added, but only in thought, "the one thing that mattered."

Judy caught his look at Pat and went into the pantry, ostensibly to bring out some new dainty but really to shut the door and relieve her feelings.

"Oh, oh, I'm not wishing *Mr.* Kirk innything but good," she told the soup tureen, "but if he'd just vanish inty thin air I'd be taking it as a kind act av the Good Man Above."

The glow at Pat's heart when she went to sleep was with her when she woke and went with her through the day . . . an exquisite day of sunshine when beauty seemed veritably to shimmer over fields and woods and sea . . . when there were great creamy cloud-mountains with amber valleys beyond the hills . . . when the air was full of the sweet smell of young grasses in early morning. Pat and Hilary went back into the past. Its iridescence was over everything they looked at. They went to the well down which Hilary had once gone to rescue a small cat . . . and Pat, looking down it as she had not looked for a long time, saw the old Pat-of-the-Well with Hilary's face beside her in its calm, fern-fringed depths. They made pilgrimages to the Field of the Pool and the Mince Pie Field and the Buttercup Field and the Field of Farewell Summers. They went to the orchard and saw the little glade among the spruces of the Old Part where all the Silver Bush cats were buried.

"I wonder if the spirits of all the pussy folk and the doggy folk I've loved will meet me with purrs and yaps of gladness at the pearly gates," said Pat whimsically, as they went through the graveyard to McGinty's grave. "We buried him right here, Hilary. He was such a dear little dog. I've never had the heart for a dog since. Dogs come and go . . . Sid always has one for the cows . . . and May's dog isn't so bad as dogs go . . . but I can never let myself really love a dog again."

"I've never had one either. Of course I've never had a place I could keep a dog and do justice to him. Some day . . . perhaps. . . ." Hilary stopped and looked at Judy's whitewashed stones along the graveyard paths and around her "bed" of perennials . . . Judy did not hold with herbaceous borders . . . by the turkey house, where bloomed gallant delphiniums higher than your head. May could never understand why her delphiniums didn't flourish the way Judy's did.

"It's jolly to see these again. I'll have some whitewashed stones . . ." Hilary checked himself again. He gazed about him greedily. "I've seen many wonderful abodes since I went away, Pat . . . palaces and castles galore . . . but I've never seen any place so absolutely *right* as Silver Bush. It's good to be here again and find it so unchanged."

"I've tried to keep it so," said Pat warmly.

"To see the Swallowfield chimney over there" . . . Hilary seemed to be speaking to himself . . . "and the delphiniums . . . and the Field of the Pool . . . and those Lombardies far away on that purple hill. Only there used to be three of them. Even McGinty must be somewhere round, I think. I'm expecting to feel his warm, rough little tongue on my hand any moment. Do you remember the time we lost McGinty and Mary Ann McClenahan found him for us? I really believed she was a witch that night."

Their conversation was punctuated with "do you remembers." "Do you remember the night you found me lost on the Base Line road?"... "Do you remember how you used to signal to me from the garret window?"... "Do you remember the time we were so afraid your father was going out west?"... "Do you remember the time the tide caught us in Tiny Cove?"... "Do you remember the time you almost died of scarlet fever?"... "Do you remember"... this was Pat's question, very tender and gentle... "do you remember Bets?"

"It seems as if your coming had brought her back, too... I feel that she *must* be up there at the Long House and might come lilting down the hill at any moment."

"Yes, I remember her. She was a sweet thing. Who is living in the Long House now?"

"David and Suzanne Kirk... brother and sister... friends of mine... they're away just now." Pat spoke rather jerkily. "Shall we have our walk back to Happiness now, Hilary?"

Our walk back to Happiness! Was it possible to walk back to happiness? At all events they tried it. They went through a golden summer world... through the eternal green twilight of the silver bush... through the field beyond... over the old stone bridge across Jordan.

"We made a good job of that, didn't we?" said Hilary. "There isn't a stone out of place after all these years."

It was all so like the old days. They were boy and girl again. The wind companioned them gallantly and feathery bent-grasses bathed their feet in coolness. On every hand were little green valleys full of loveliness. Everything was wrapped in the light of other days. The dance of sunbeams in the brook shallows was just as it had been so many years ago. And so they came to Happiness and the Haunted Spring again.

"I haven't been here for years," said Pat under her breath. "I couldn't bear to come... alone... somehow. It's as lovely as ever, isn't it?"

"Do you remember," said Hilary slowly, "the day... my mother came... and you burned my letters?"

Pat nodded. She felt like slipping her hand into Hilary's and giving him the old sympathetic squeeze. Something in his tone told her that the pain and disillusionment of that memory was still keen.

"She is dead," said Hilary. "She died last year. She left me... some money. At first I didn't think I could take it.

Then . . . I thought . . . perhaps it would be a slap in her dead face if I didn't. So I took it . . . and had my year in the East. After all . . . I think she loved me once . . . when I was her little Jingle-baby. Afterwards . . . she forgot. *He* made her forget. I mean to try to think of her without bitterness, Pat."

"It doesn't do to hold bitterness," said Pat slowly. "Judy always says that. It . . . it poisons life. I know. I'm trying to put a certain bitterness out of my own life. Oh, Hilary . . . I know it is babyish to long as I do for the old happy days . . . they can never come back, although, now that you are here, they seem to be just around the corner."

In the evening they went through the woods to the Secret Field. Hilary had always understood her love of that field. The woods had a beautiful mood on that evening . . . a friendly mood. They didn't always have it. Sometimes they were aloof . . . wrapped up in their own concerns. Sometimes they even frowned. But she and Hilary were two children again and the woods took them to their heart. They were full of little pockets of sunshine and ferny paths and whispers and clumps of birches that the winds loved . . . wild growths and colours and scents in sweet procession . . . a sunset seen through fir tops . . . great rosy clouds over the Secret Field . . . all the old magic and witchery had come back.

"If this could last," thought Pat.

It was raining moonlight through the poplars when they got back. They went into the old garden, lying fragrant and velvety under the moon. White roses glimmered mysteriously here and there. A little wind brought them the spice of the ferns along the Whispering Lane. Pat was silent. Talk was a commonplace which did not belong to this enchanted hour. It was one of the moments when beauty seemed to flow through her like a river. She surrendered herself utterly to the charm of the time and place. There was no past—no future—nothing but this exquisite present.

Hilary looked at the moonlit brilliance of her eyes and bent a little nearer . . . his lips opened to speak. But a car came whirling into the yard and May got out of it, amid a chorus of howls without words from its other occupants. Pat shivered. May was back. The day of enchantment was over.

May saw them in the garden and came to them. Scent of honeysuckle . . . fragrance of fern . . . breath of tea-roses, were all drowned in the wave of cheap perfume that preceded her. She greeted Hilary very gushingly and looked vicious over his cool courtesy. Hilary had never liked May and he was not going to pretend pleasure over meeting her again. May gave one of her nasty little laughs.

"I suppose I'm a crowd," she remarked. "Isn't it . . . lucky . . . David isn't home, Pat?"

"I don't know what you mean," said Pat icily . . . knowing perfectly.

"Of course Pat has told you of her engagement to David Kirk," May said maliciously, turning to Hilary. "He's really quite a nice old chap, you know. Such a pity you couldn't have met him."

Nobody spoke. May, having gratified her spite, went into the house. Pat shivered again. Everything was spoiled. Suddenly Hilary seemed very remote . . . as remote as those dark firs spiring above the silver birches.

"Is this true, Pat?" he asked in a low tone.

Pat nodded. She could not speak.

Hilary took her hand.

"As an old friend there is no happiness I don't wish you, dear. You know that, don't you?"

"Of course." Pat tried to speak lightly . . . airily. "And I return your good wishes, Hilary. We . . . we heard of your engagement last year."

She thought miserably, "I'm simply not going to let him off with it. I would have told him about David . . . if he had told me. . . ."

"My engagement?" Hilary laughed slightly. "I'm not engaged. Oh, I know there was some silly gossip about me and Anna Loveday. Her brother is a great friend of mine and I'm going into his firm when I go back. Anna's a sweet thing and has her own 'beau' as Judy would say. There's only one girl in my life . . . and you know who she is, Pat. I didn't think there was any hope for me but I felt I must come and see."

"You'll find . . . some one yet. . . ."

"No . . . you've spoiled me for loving any one else. There's only one *you*."

Pat said nothing more . . . there did not seem anything she could say.

They went into the kitchen for a parting hour before Hilary must leave for the boat train. They were all there . . . Judy, Rae, Sid, and Long Alec. Even mother had stayed up late to say good-bye. It should have been a merry evening. Judy was in great fettle and told some of her inimitable tales. Hilary laughed with the others but there was no mirth in his laughter. Pat had one of her dismal moments of feeling that she would never laugh again.

She and Judy stood together at the door and watched Hilary go across the yard to his waiting car.

"Oh, oh, it's a sorryful thing to watch inny one going away by moonlight," said Judy. "I'm thinking, Patsy, I'll never be seeing Jingle again, the dear lad."

"I don't think he will ever come again to Silver Bush," said Pat. Her voice was quiet but her very words seemed tears. "Judy, why must there be so much bitterness in everything... even in what should be a beautiful friendship?"

"I'm not knowing," admitted Judy.

"The scissors are lost *again*," May told them as they re-entered the kitchen, her tone implying that every one at Silver Bush was responsible for their disappearance.

"Oh, oh, if that was all that did be lost!" Judy sighed dismally, as she climbed to her kitchen chamber. Judy was quite unacquainted with Tennyson but she would wholeheartedly have agreed with him that there was something in the world amiss... oh, oh, very much amiss. And she was far from being sure... now... that it would ever be unriddled.

The Ninth Year

HILARY wrote just once to Pat after he went away . . . one of his old delightful letters, full of beautiful little pencil sketches of the houses he was going to design. Just at the last he wrote:

"Don't feel badly, Pat, dear, because I love you and you can't love me. I've always loved you. I can't help it and I wouldn't if I could. If the choice had been mine I would still have chosen to love you. There are people who try to forget a hopeless love. I'm not one of them, Pat. To me the greatest misfortune life could bring would be that I should forget you. I want to remember and love you always. That will be unspeakably better than any happiness that could come through forgetting. My love for you is the best thing . . . always has been the best thing . . . in my life. It hasn't made me poorer. On the contrary it has enriched my whole existence and given me the gift of clear vision for the things that matter; it has been a lamp held before my feet whereby I have avoided many pitfalls of baser passions and unworthy dreams. It will always be so. Therefore don't pity me and don't feel unhappy about me."

But Pat did feel unhappy and the feeling persisted more or less under all the outward happiness of the autumn and winter. For it did seem to be a happy time. Long Alec had definitely stated that in a year from the next spring he hoped to build on the other farm for Sid and May. Every one knew this was final and May, with much pouting and sulking, had to reconcile herself to the fact that she would never be mistress of Silver Bush.

Mother, too, was stronger and better than she had been for years. She said with a laugh that she was having a second youth. She was able to join in the family life again and go about seeing her friends. It seemed like a miracle for they had all accepted the fact for years that mother would always be an invalid, with a "good day" once in a while. Now the good days were the rule rather than the exception. So in spite of May that year was the pleasantest Pat had known for a long time... except for that odd persistent little ache of indefinable longing under everything. It never exactly ceased... though she forgot about it often... when she was gardening... sewing... planning... when Little Mary came to Silver Bush and wanted some of Judy's "malicious toast"... when Bold-and-Bad trounced some upstart kitten for its own good... when she and Suzanne and David sat by the Long House fire... when she and Rae took sweet counsel together over plans and problems... when she wakened early to revel in Silver Bush lying in its misty morning silence... *her* home... her dear, beloved, all-sufficing home ... when Winnie came to Silver Bush, purring over her golden babies. For Winnie had twins... Winnie and Rachel ... babies that looked as if they had been lifted bodily out of a magazine advertisement. When Pat looked at the two absurd, darling, round-faced, blue-eyed mites on the same pillow she always swallowed a little choke of longing.

Rae expected to be married in another year. Her hope chest was full to overflowing and she and Pat were already planning the details of the wedding... a regular clan wedding, of course.

"The last big wedding at Silver Bush," said Pat.

"What about your own?" asked Rae.

"Oh, mine. *It* won't be a smart event. David and I will just slip away some day and be married. There isn't going to be any fuss," said Pat hurriedly... and turned the conversation to something else. She was very, very fond of David but things were nice just as they were. She did not want to think of marrying at all. The thought of leaving Silver Bush was not bearable.

Rae looked at her curiously but said nothing. Rae was very wise in her generation.

"It doesn't do to meddle," she reflected sagely. "I sometimes wish I'd never written Hilary about Pat's various beaus. Perhaps it did more harm than good... if he had come sooner...."

Well, life was full of "ifs." For instance *if* she had not

gone to the dance where she met Brook? She had been within an inch of *not* going. Rae shuddered.

"When Rae is married," Pat told Judy, "I want her to have the loveliest wedding we've ever had at Silver Bush."

"Oh, oh, it ought to be wid a whole year to get riddy in," agreed Judy.

But nothing ever happens just as you imagine it will, as Pat had many times discovered. A week later came the bolt from the blue. Brook wrote that the manager of the Chinese branch had suddenly died. It had become absolutely necessary for him to start for China at once instead of next year. Would Rae go with him?

Of course Rae would go with him. It meant a marriage at three days' notice, but what of that?

"You . . . can't," gasped Pat.

They were sitting in the hay-mow of the church barn, having discovered that it was about the only place where they were safe from May or some prowling Binnie coming down on them. The fragrance of dried clover was around them and an arrogant orange-gold barn cat sat on a rafter and looked at them out of mysterious jewel-like eyes.

"I can and will," said Rae resolutely. "Lily Robinson will take the school and be thankful to get it. We won't bother with a wedding cake. . . ."

"Rae, do you want Judy to drop dead! Of course we'll have a wedding cake. It won't have time to ripen as good wedding cake should but in all else it shall be the weddingest cake ever seen. But what about your dress?"

"Will it be possible to have a white dress, Pat . . . a white satin dress? I'm old-fashioned . . . I'm Victorian . . . I want to be married in a white satin dress. I love satin."

"We'll make it possible," said Pat. Forthwith she and Rae and Judy and mother went into committee on the subject. Pat and Rae hustled off to town for the dress . . . Inez Macaulay came to make it and sewed for dear life. Mother, who hadn't done such a thing for years, declared she would make the cake.

"Oh, oh, and she do be the lady as can do it," said Judy. "All the Bay Shore girls cud make fruit-cake to the quane's taste."

Judy pleaded for "just a liddle wedding." They could have the aunts and uncles and cousins surely. But nobody agreed with her.

"We can't have all the two clans, and since we can't have all we must have none. No, Judy, Brook and I are just going to be married here with you home folks looking on."

Judy had to reconcile herself. But she shook her grizzled head. Times indeed were changed at Silver Bush when one of its daughters could be married off like this.

"Sure and I fale ould and done," said Judy... looking cautiously about, however, to make sure nobody heard her.

"You've taken your own time about telling me," said May with a toss of her head when Pat informed her that Rae was to be married.

"We've only known it for twenty-four hours ourselves," said Pat. May, however, was determined to be sulky. Nevertheless, there were times when Judy surprised a smug look on her face.

"She do be thinking there'll be one more out av her way," reflected Judy scornfully.

"I'm glad to hear you're getting another of your gals married off," Mrs. Binnie told mother patronisingly. "You'll soon be like myself... only one left." A sentimental sigh. "What about you, Pat? Isn't it time you were thinking of leaping the ditch? The men don't seem to be what they were in *my* young days."

Pat fled to her room where Rae had piled all her belongings on the bed.

"Forget Mother Binnie, Pat, and help me pack. I never was any good at packing. Tell me what to take or leave."

The yawning trunk gave Pat a stab. Rae was really going away... going to China! Why couldn't it have been Rae's fortune to settle down near home like Winnie? Yet she remembered that she had thought Winnie's going a tragedy. How life grew around changes until they became a part of it and were changes no more! Winnie coming home with her babies... Winnie's home to visit... why, it was all delightful. But China! And yet Rae was serenely happy over it all. A line of some old-fashioned song Aunt Hazel used to sing long ago came back to Pat, as she folded and packed. *"The one who goes is happier far than the one that's left behind."*

Perhaps it was true. She almost envied Rae her happiness. And yet she felt sorry for her... for Rae, who was leaving Silver Bush. How *could* any one be happy, leaving Silver Bush?

"This time to-morrow I'll be an old married woman,"

said Rae, scrutinising herself in the mirror. "I believe it's high time I was married, Pat. It seems to me that I'm getting a certain school-teacherish look already. Do you know Brook is having the wedding ring specially made. No hand-me-downs for him, he says. I hope I'll get through the ceremony respectably. Mother Binnie will be there, watching me."

"She isn't coming, Rae!"

"She is. May asked me if her mother couldn't come to see me married? I really couldn't say no. So I want everything to go nicely. I'm *not* going to look up at Brook when I'm uttering the final vow. That has got so common... Mrs. Binnie said Olive did it and every one thought it 'so touching.' Anyway, I'd be sure to laugh. Listen to that bluebird out in the orchard, Pat. I suppose they don't have bluebirds in China... or do they? But there'll be cats... surely there'll be cats in China... cats guarding mysterious secrets... cats furry and contented. Only... will they mew in Chinese? If they do! And then, of course, after a while there'll be my children. I want ten."

"Ten? Why stop short of the dozen?" giggled Pat.

"Oh, I'm not greedy. One must leave a few for other people."

"If Aunt Barbara heard you!" said Pat, as she tucked a bag of dried lavender into Rae's trunk... lavender from the Silver Bush garden to sweeten sheets in China.

"But she doesn't. I don't say these things to anybody but you. We've been such chums, haven't we, Pat? We've laughed and cried together... we're *friends* as well as sisters... only for those horrid weeks we never really spoke to each other. That's the memory I'm ashamed of. But I've so many beautiful memories... of home and you and mother and Judy. They'll always light life like a lamp. Can you quote that verse we found the other night and thought so lovely?"

> "'What Love anticipates may die in flower,
> What Love possesses may be thine an hour,
> But redly gleams in Life's unlit Decembers
> What Love remembers.'"

"It's true, isn't it, dear? We'll always have our lovely memories even in our 'late Decembers.' Oh, I'm going to miss you all. I'll often be hungry for Silver Bush. Don't think I don't feel leaving it and you all, Pat. I do. But... but..."

"There's Brook Hamilton," smiled Pat.

"Yes." Rae was very thoughtful. "But the old life I'm leaving will always be very dear to me. And you've been the dearest sister."

"Just don't," said Pat. "You'll have me breaking down and howling. I've made up my mind I won't spoil your wedding with tears."

"And please, darling, don't cry after I'm gone. I can't bear to think of you here, in tears, after I'm gone."

"I'll likely have a little weep," said Pat frankly. "I don't think I can escape that. But I never give way to despair as I used to long ago. Rae, I've learned to accept change even though I can never help dreading it . . . never can understand people who actually seem to like it. There's Lily calling you for your last fitting."

The day before the wedding there was hope at Silver Bush that Mrs. Binnie wouldn't be able to come after all. Her first cousin, old Samuel Cobbledick, had died and the funeral was to be an hour before the time fixed for the ceremony.

"It's a real apostrophe to have him dying at this particular time," Mrs. Binnie grumbled to May. "He's been suffering from general ability for years but he needn't of died till after the wedding. He was always a very tiresome man. It was an infernal hemmeridge finished him off. I'm awful disappointed. I'd set my heart on seeing darling Rae married."

"Oh, oh, I do be hoping the funeral will go off more harmonious than his brother John's did," said Judy. "John did be wanting to make all the arrangements for the funeral himself before he died . . . wanting things done rale stylish and having no confidence in his wife, her being av the second skimmings brand. They did be fighting all their lives but the biggest row they iver had was over his funeral. She didn't be spaking to him agin while he was alive and she wudn't sit among the mourners at all, at all, nor have innything to do wid the doings. It did be kind av spiling the occasion."

"All fam'lies have their little differences," said Mrs. Binnie stiffly. "Poor Sam's widow is feeling blue enough. I've been there all the afternoon condoning with her."

"Ye'll be maning 'condole,'" said Judy innocently. It was not often she bothered correcting Madam Binnie but there were times and seasons.

"I meant what I said," returned Mrs. Binnie, "and I'll

thank you, Miss Plum, not to be putting words in my mouth."

Pat and Rae found it hard to win sleep that last night together. Half a dozen times one of them would say, "Well, let's turn over and go to sleep." They would turn over but they wouldn't go to sleep. Soon they would be talking again.

"I hope it will be fine to-morrow," said Rae. "I want to leave Silver Bush with my last sight of it bathed in sunshine."

"To-morrow?" said Pat. "*Today!* The clock in the Little Parlour has just struck twelve. It's your wedding day, Cuddles."

"Time I was taking the bridal jitters," laughed Rae. "I don't believe I'll have them at all. It all seems so—so *natural* to be marrying Brook, you know."

They must have slept a little for presently Pat was surprised to find herself sitting up in bed looking through the window at a world that lay in a clear, pale, thin dawnlight. It was Rae's wedding day and hereafter when she wakened she must waken alone.

A beautiful sunshiny day as Rae had desired, with mad, happy crickets singing everywhere and sinuous winds making golden shivers in the wheat-fields.

"Really," said Rae, "the weather at Silver Bush isn't like the weather anywhere else, even over at Swallowfield. I've teased you so often, Pat, for thinking things here were different from anywhere else . . . but in my heart I've always known it, too."

"Isn't it a *wonderful* day!" gushed May when they went down.

May rather spoiled the weather for Pat. But then with May everything was always either "wonderful" or "priceless." Those were her pet adjectives. Pat felt that she didn't want May to have anything to do with Rae's wedding day, even to the extent of approving it.

It was a busy morning. Brook arrived at noon. Pat laid and decorated the wedding table. May, too, by way of asserting her rights, set a huge hodge-podge from her herbaceous border in the centre of it after Pat had gone up to dress. Judy carried it ostentatiously out to the kitchen.

"Always taking a bit too much on hersilf," she muttered.

May got square by saying, when Judy appeared in her wine-coloured dress-up dress,

"How well that dress has kept its looks, Judy. It doesn't really look very old-fashioned at all."

2

Upstairs a bride was being dressed.

"Here's a blue garter for luck," whispered Pat.

Rae stood, looking rather wraith-like in her shimmer of satin and tulle. She wore mother's old veil... a bit creamy and a bit old-fashioned... high on the head instead of the modern mob-cap... but Rae's young beauty shone radiantly among its folds. She was so full of happiness that it seemed to spill over and make everything lovely.

"Doesn't she look cute?" said May, who had pushed herself in.

Pat and Rae's eyes met in the last of their many amused, secret exchanges of looks. Pat knew it would be the last... at least for many years.

"I won't... I *won't* cry," she said grimly to herself. "At least not now."

As Rae gathered up her dress to go downstairs Bold-and-Bad saw his opportunity. He had been sitting at the head of the stairs, very sulky and offended because he had been shut out of Pat's room. He pounced and bit... bit Rae right in the fleshy part of her slender leg. Rae gave a little squeal... Bold-and-Bad fled... and Pat examined the damage.

"He hasn't broken the skin... but, darling, the beast has started a run in your stocking. What on earth got into him?"

"It can't be helped now," said Rae, stifling a laugh. "Thank heaven skirts are long. I deserve it... it was I who shut the door in his face. I was afraid he'd get tangled up in my veil. It was no way to treat an old family cat. He did perfectly right to bite me."

The rest all seemed rather dream-like to Pat. The ceremony went off beautifully... though Rae afterwards said she could think of nothing but that run in her stocking the whole time. It would be so awful if Mrs. Binnie caught a glimpse of it somehow in spite of the long skirts... for Mrs. Binnie was there after all, having rushed madly away as soon as dear Samuel's funeral was over. She reached Silver Bush just as the bride came down the stairs.

Mother was pale and sweet and composed and dad, dreaming of youth and his own bridal day, looked very tenderly at this baby of his who had so swiftly and unaccountably

grown up and was being married before he had realised that
she was out of her cradle.

Just as Brook took his bride in his arms to kiss her
Bold-and-Bad stalked in . . . a repentant Bold-and-Bad, carrying a large and juicy rat in his mouth which he laid down at
Rae's feet, with an air of atonement. A moment before
everybody had been on the point of tears . . . but the tension
dissolved in á burst of laughter and Rae's wedding feast was
as jolly as she had wanted it to be.

Nevertheless she found it hard to keep back her own
tears when she turned at the door of her room for a farewell
look. She recalled all the times she had left home before . . . but
always to come back. Now she was going, never to come
back . . . at least as Rae Gardiner. She would go out and shut
the door and never open it again. She had finished with it
and the happy, laughter-filled past that was linked with it.
She clung to Pat.

"Darling, you'll write me every week, won't you? And
I'm sure we'll be home for a visit in three years at the latest."

They were gone.

"I never saw Rae look so sweet and lovely," sobbed Mrs.
Binnie, her fat figure shaking. May was trying to squeeze out
a few tears but Pat did not feel in the least like crying, though
she thought her face would crack if she went on smiling any
longer. She and Judy cleared up the rooms and washed the
dishes and put things away. When Pat crept into the kitchen
at dusk she found Judy sitting by a fire she had kindled.

"Oh, oh, I thought a bit av a fire wudn't be amiss a could
avening like this. The cats do be liking it. Ye know, Patsy, I've
just been wishing poor ould Tillytuck was here, there in his
corner, smoking his pipe. It . . . it wudn't same so lonesome-like."

It was odd to hear Judy talking of being lonesome. Pat
sat down beside her on the floor, resting her head in Judy's
lap and pulling Judy's arm around her. They sat so in silence
for a long time, listening to the pleasant snap of the starting
fire and the vociferous purring of the kitten Judy had snuggled at her side. Judy had always known how to make little
creatures happy.

"Judy, this is the third time we've kept vigil in this old
kitchen after we've seen a bride drive away. Do you remember Aunt Hazel's . . . and Winnie's? . . . how we sat here and
you told me stories to cheer me up? I don't want stories

to-night, Judy. I just want to be quiet . . . and have you baby me a bit. I'm . . . tired."

When Pat had risen and gone to the porch door to let in a pleading Popka Judy sighed and whispered to herself,

"Oh, oh, I'm thinking all me stories do be told. Sure and I'm nothing but a guttering candle now." But she did not let Pat hear her. And before long, when she had been thinking of Mrs. Binnie tearing in red-faced from the funeral, she began to chuckle.

"What is it, Judy?"

"Oh, oh, I didn't mane to be laughing, Patsy, but it did be just coming inty me head what they did be telling once av ould Sam Cobbledick. He was fond av a drop whin he was younger but what wid his wife watching him he niver got much av a chanct to one. He was rale sick wid the flu one time and the doctor lift a liddle whiskey in a bottle for him. Mrs. Cobbledick thought it was only midicine and wint out to church. Thin in drops a neighbour man, ould Lem Morrison, and *he* brings a liddle drop in a bottle, too, sly-like. But ould Sam looks at it in dape disappointment. 'There isn't enough to make us both drunk,' sez he. 'Let's put it together and make one av us drunk,' sez he. 'And let's draw lots to see which'll it be,' sez he. So the lot fell to ould Sam. But ye did be saying ye weren't wanting inny stories to-night."

"I want to hear this one. What happened to old Sam, Judy?"

"Oh, oh, whin Sarah Cobbledick came home her sick man was dancing and singing in the middle av the floor and niver a bit av flu left in him. She didn't be guessing inny av the truth but she tould the doctor his midicines were entirely too strong for a sick man, aven if it cured him that quick. And now, Patsy, darlint, we'll be having a liddle bite. I was noticing ye didn't be ating much supper."

Pat found the night bitter. There seemed such an unearthly stillness over the whole house. She sat at her window for a long time in the darkness. Below in the garden the white phlox glimmered . . . one of the many flowers Bets had given her . . . that sweet-lipped friend of long ago. The pain of Bets' passing had faded out with time as gently as an old, old moon fades out into the sunrise, but it always came back at moments like this. She remembered how she used to lie awake, especially on stormy nights, after Winnie and Joe had gone. She could not bear to look at Rae's little white bed.

But there was a wonderful sunrise the next morning... crimson and warm gold flushing up into the blue. A bird was singing somewhere in the orchard and the borders of the hill field were aflame with golden rod. Dawn still came beautifully... and she still had Silver Bush. Little Mary would often come to occupy Rae's bed. Her spun-gold hair would gleam on that lonely pillow.

And, of course, there was always David... dear old dependable David. She must not forget him.

The Tenth Year

It took Pat a long while to get used to Rae's absence. Sometimes she thought she would never get used to it. The autumn weeks were very hard. Every place... every room ... seemed so full of Rae... even more so than when she had been home. Pat was, somehow, always expecting to see her... glimmering through the birches on moonlit nights... lilting along the Whispering Lane... coming home from school laughing over some jest of the day... wearing her youth like a golden rose. And then the renewed sadness of the realisation that she would not come. For a time it really seemed that Rae had taken the laughter of Silver Bush with her. Then it crept back; again there were jokes and talks in the kitchen o'nights.

Two things helped Pat through the fall and winter... Silver Bush and her evenings with David and Suzanne. Her love for Silver Bush had suffered no abatement... nay, it had seemed to deepen and intensify with the years, as other loves passed out of her life, as other changes came... or threatened to come. For Uncle Tom's big black beard was quite grey now and dad was getting bald and Winnie's gold hair was fading to drab. And... though Pat put the thought fiercely away whenever it came to her... Judy was getting old. It was not all May's malice.

But then mother was so much better... almost well... beginning to take her place in the family life again. It was like a miracle, everybody said. So Pat was happy and contented in spite of certain passing aches of loneliness which made themselves felt on wakeful nights when a grief-possessed wind wailed around the eaves.

Then it seemed that spring touched Silver Bush in the night and winter was over. Drifts of rain softened over the hills that were not yet green . . . it was more as if a faint green shadow had fallen over them. Warm, wet winds blew through the awakening silver bush. Faint mists curled and uncurled in the Field of the Pool. Then came the snow of cherry petals on the walks and the wind in the grasses at morning and the delight of seeing young shoots pop up in the garden.

"I have nothing to do with anything in the world to-day but spring," vowed Pat, the morning after housecleaning was finished. She refused to be cast down even by the fact that the building of the new house on the other place had to be postponed again for financial reasons. She spent the whole day in the garden, planning, discovering, exulting. Judy's clump of bleeding-heart was in bloom. Nothing could be so lovely. But then, to Pat, one flower from the garden of Silver Bush would always be sweeter than a whole florist's window.

"Let's have supper in the orchard to-night, Judy."

They had it . . . just she and mother and Judy and Little Mary, for the men were all away and May had gone home to help her mother houseclean. The Binnies generally got around to housecleaning when every one else was finishing.

Supper under hanging white boughs . . . apple blossoms dropping into your cream-pitcher . . . a dear, gentle evening with the "ancient lyric madness" Carman speaks of loose in the air. A meal like this was a sacrament. Pat was happy . . . mother was happy . . . Little Mary was happy because she was always happy where Aunt Pat was . . . even though the sky was so terribly big. It was one of the secret fears of Little Mary's life, which she had never yet whispered to any one, that the sky was too big. Even Judy, who had been mourning all day because a brood of young turkeys had got their feet wet and died, took heart of grace and thought maybe she was good for many a year yet.

"Life is sweet," thought Pat, looking about her with a gaze of dreamy delight.

A few hours later life handed her one of its surprises.

She went up to the Long House in the twilight . . . past the velvety green of the hill field, through the spruce bush. The perfume of lilacs had not changed and the robins still sang vespers in some lost sweet language of elder days. She found David in the garden by the stone fireplace, where he had kindled a fire . . . "for company," he said. Suzanne had gone to town but Ichabod and Alphonso were sitting beside him. Pat sat down on the bench.

"Any news?" she asked idly.

"Yes. The wild cherry at the south-east corner of the spruce bush is coming into bloom," said David . . . and said nothing more for a long time. Pat did not mind. She liked their long, frequent, friendly silences when you could think of anything you liked.

"Suzanne is going to be married next month," said David suddenly.

Pat lifted a startled face. She had not thought it would be before the fall. And . . . if Suzanne were to be married . . . what about David? He couldn't stay on at the Long House alone. Would his next words say something of the sort? Pat felt her lips and mouth go curiously dry. But of course . . .

What *was* David saying?

"Do you really want to marry me, Pat?"

What an extraordinary question! Hadn't she promised to marry him? Hadn't they been engaged . . . happily, contentedly engaged, for years?

"David! What *do* you mean? Of course . . ."

"Wait." David bent forward and looked her squarely in the face.

"Look into my eyes, Pat . . . don't turn your face away. Tell me the truth."

Under his compelling gaze Pat gasped out,

"I . . . I can't . . . I don't know it. But I think I do, David . . . oh, I really think I do."

"*I* think, dear," said David slowly, "that your attitude, whether you realise it or not, is, 'I'd just as soon be married to you as any one, if I have to be married.' That isn't enough for me, Pat. No, you don't love me, though you've pretended you have . . . pretended beautifully, to yourself as well as me. I won't have you on those terms, Pat."

The garden whirled around Pat . . . jigged up and down . . . steadied itself.

"I . . . I meant to make you happy, David," she said piteously.

"I know. And I don't mind taking chances with my own life . . . but with yours . . . no, I can't risk it."

"You seem to have made up your mind to jilt me, David," Pat was between tears and something like hysterical laughter. "And I do . . . I really do . . . like you so much."

"That isn't enough. I'm not blaming you. I took a chance. I thought I could teach you to love me. I've failed. I'm the kind of man all women like . . . and none love. It . . . it was that way before. I will not have it so again . . . it's too bitter. There's an old couplet—

> "'There's always one who kisses
> And one who turns the cheek.'"

"Not always," murmured Pat.

"No, not always. But often . . . and it's not going to be that way with me a second time. We'll always be good friends, Pat . . . and nothing more."

"You *need* me," said Pat desperately again. After all . . . though she knew in her heart he was right . . . knew he had never been anything but a way out . . . knew that sometimes at three o'clock of night she had wakened and felt that she was a prisoner . . . she could not bear to lose him out of her life.

"Yes, I need you . . . but I can never have *you*. I've known that ever since Hilary Gordon's visit last summer."

"David, what nonsense have you got into your head? Hilary has always been like a dear brother to me. . . ."

"He's twined with the roots of your life, Pat . . . in some way I can never be. I can't brook such a rival."

Pat couldn't have told what she felt like . . . on the surface. The whole experience seemed unreal. Had David really told her he couldn't marry her? But away down under everything she knew she felt *free* . . . curiously free. She was almost a little dizzy with the thought of freedom . . . as if she had drunk some heady, potent wine. Mechanically she began to take his ring off her finger.

"No." David lifted his hand. "Keep it, Pat . . . wear it on some other finger. We've had a wonderful . . . friendship. It was only my blindness that I hoped for more. And don't worry over me. I've been offered the head editorship of the *Weekly Review*. When Suzanne marries I'll take it."

So he would go, too, out of her life. Pat never remembered quite how she got home. But Judy was knitting in the kitchen and Pat sat down opposite her rather grimly.

"Judy . . . I've been jilted."

"Jilted, is it?" Judy said no more. She was suddenly like a watchful terrier.

"Yes . . . in the most bare-faced manner. David Kirk told me to-night that he wouldn't marry me" . . . Pat contrived to give her voice a plaintive twist . . . "that nothing on earth would induce him to marry me."

"Oh, oh, ye didn't be asking him to marry ye, I'm thinking. Did he be giving his rasons?" Judy was still watchful.

"He said I didn't love him . . . enough."

"Oh, oh, and do ye?"

"No," said Pat in a low tone. "No. I've tried, Judy . . . I've tried . . . but I think I've always known. And so have you."

"I'm not be way av being sorry it's all off," said Judy. She went on knitting quietly.

"What will the Binnies say?" said Pat whimsically.

"Oh, oh, I don't think ye've come down to minding what the Binnies say, me jewel."

"No, I don't care a rap what they say. But others . . . oh well, they are used to me by this time. And this is the last of my broken-backed love affairs they'll ever have to worry over. I'll never have any more, Judy."

"Niver do be a long day," said Judy sceptically. Then she added,

"Ye'll be getting the one ye *are* to get. A thing like that don't be left to chance, Patsy."

"Anyway, Judy, we won't talk of this any more. It . . . it isn't pleasant. I'm free once more . . . free to love and live for Silver Bush. That's all that matters. Free! It's a wonderful word."

When Pat had gone out Judy knitted inscrutably for a while. Then she remarked to Bold-and-Bad,

"So that do be the last av the widower, thank the Good Man Above."

2

The breaking of Pat's engagement made but little flurry in the clan. They had given up expecting anything else of this fickle wayward girl. May said she had always looked for it . . . she knew David wasn't really the marrying kind. Dad said nothing . . . what was there to say? Mother understood, as always. In her heart mother was relieved. Suzanne understood, too.

"I'm sorry . . . terribly sorry . . . and bitterly disappointed. But it was just one of the things that had to be."

"It's nice to be able to lay the blame of everything on

predestination," said Pat ruefully. "I feel I've failed you . . . and David . . . and I'm ever so fond of him. . . ."

"That might be enough for some men, but not David," said Suzanne quietly. "I wish it could have been different, Pat dear . . . but it can't be, so we must just put it behind us and go on."

When Suzanne was married and David had gone the Long House was closed and lightless once more. Again it was the Long Lonely House. Some houses are like that . . . they have a doom on them which they can never long escape.

Pat took stock of things. She was at peace. Her whole world had been temporarily wrecked . . . ruined . . . turned upside down, but nothing had really changed in Silver Bush. There was no longer anything to come between her and it . . . never would be again. She was through with love and all its counterfeits. Henceforth Silver Bush would have no rival in her heart. She could live for it alone. There might be some hours of loneliness. But there was something wonderful even in loneliness. At least you belonged to yourself when you were lonely.

Pat flung back her brown head and her brown eyes kindled.

"Freedom is a glad thing," she said.

3

One smoky October evening they found Judy lying unconscious in the stable beside the old white cow. She had not been allowed to do any milking for a long time but she had slipped out in the dim to do it that night, since May was away and she knew "the min" would be tired when they came home from the other place.

They carried her to her bed in the kitchen chamber and sent for Dr. Bentley. Under his ministrations she recovered consciousness but he looked very grave when he came down to the kitchen.

"Her heart is in a very bad condition. I can't understand how she kept up so long."

"Judy hasn't felt well all summer," said Pat heavily. "I've known it . . . though she wouldn't give in that there was anything the matter with her or let me call you. 'Can he be curing old age?' she would say. I know I should have insisted. . . . I knew she was old but I think I never realised it . . . never believed Judy *could* be ill. . . ."

"It wouldn't have mattered. I could have done nothing," said Dr. Bentley. "It's only a question of a week or two."

Pat hated him for his casualness. To him Judy was nothing but an old, worn-out servant. When he had gone she went up to the kitchen chamber where Judy was lying. Pale rays slanted through the clouds above the silver bush and gleamed athwart all Judy's little treasured possessions.

Judy turned her dim old eyes lovingly on Pat's face.

"Don't be faling down, Patsy darlint. I've been sure iver since Gintleman Tom wint away that me own time wasn't far off. And of late I've been faling it drawing nigh just as ye fale snow in the air before it comes. Oh, oh, I'm glad I won't be a bother to inny one long or make inny one much trouble dying."

"Judy. . . Judy. . ."

"Oh, oh, I'm knowing ye wudn't think innything ye cud do for ould Judy a trouble, darlint. But I've always asked the Good Man Above that I wudn't be bed-rid long whin me time came and I've always been hoping I cud die at Silver Bush. It's been me home for long, long years. I've had a happy life here, Patsy, and now death seems rale frindly."

Pat wondered how many people would think that Judy had had a happy life . . . a life spent in what they would think the monotonous drudgery of service on a little farm. Ah well, "the kingdom of heaven is within you," Pat knew Judy had been happy. . . that she asked for nothing but that people should turn to her for help . . . should "want" her. Nothing so dreadful could happen to Judy as not to be wanted.

But was it . . . could it be . . . Judy who was talking so calmly of dying? Judy!

Dr. Bentley had given Judy two weeks but she lived for four. She was very happy and contented. Life, she felt, was ending beautifully for her, here where her heart had always been. There would be no going away from Silver Bush . . . no long lingering in uselessness until people came in time to hate her because she was so helpless and in their way. Everything was just as she would have wished it.

Pat was her constant attendant. May would have nothing to do with waiting on her. . . . "I hate sick people," she announced airily. . . but nobody wanted her to.

"Oh, oh, it's rale nice to be looked after," Judy told Pat with her old smile.

"You've looked after us all long enough, Judy. It's your turn to be waited on now."

"Patsy darlint, if I cud just be having you and nobody else to do for me!"

"I'm with you to the last, dearest Judy."

"I'm knowing ye'll come as far as ye can wid me but ye mustn't be tiring yersilf out, Patsy."

"It doesn't tire me. I'm just going to do nothing for a while but look after you. May is doing the work... to give her her due, Judy, she isn't lazy."

"Oh, oh, but she'll never have the luck wid the young turkeys that I've had," said Judy in a tone of satisfaction.

Bold-and-Bad seldom left Judy. He curled up on the bed beside her where she could stroke him if she wanted to and always purred when she did so. "Looking at me wid his big round eyes, Patsy, as much as to say, 'I cud spare a life or two, Judy, if ye wanted one.' Sure and he's far better company than inny av the Binnies," she added with a grin. Mrs. Binnie thought it her duty to "sit by" Judy frequently and Judy endured it courteously. She wasn't going to forget her pretty manners even on her dying bed. But she always sighed with relief when Mrs. Binnie trundled downstairs.

Yes, it was pleasant to lie easily and think over old days and jokes and triumphs... all the tears and joys of forgotten years... all the pain and beauty of life. "Oh, oh, we've had our frolics," she would think with a little chuckle. Nothing worried her any more.

Pat always sat and talked with her in "the dim." Sometimes Judy seemed so well and natural that wild hopes would spring up in Pat's heart.

"I've been minding mesilf a bit av the ould days, Patsy. It's me way av passing the time. De ye be rimimbering the night yer Aunt Edith caught ye dancing naked in Silver Bush and they sint ye to Coventry? And the time Long Alec shaved his moustache off and bruk yer liddle heart? And the night Pepper fell into the well? Do ye be rimimbering whin liddle Jingle and his dog wud be hanging round? There was something in his face I always did be liking. He had a way wid him. And how ye did be hating to hear him called yer beau! 'That isn't a beau,' sez she, indignant, 'That was just Jingle.' And the two av ye slipping in to ask me for a handful av raisins. Oh, oh, thim was the good ould days. But I'm thinking these days be good, too. There do be always new good coming up to take the place av the old that goes, Patsy. There's Liddle Mary now... she was here this afternoon wid her liddle buttercup head shining like a star in me ould room, and her liddle tongue going nineteen to the dozen. The questions she do be asking. 'Isn't there inny Mrs. God, Judy?' And whin I sez 'no' she did just be looking a look at me, and sez she solemn-like, 'Then is God an ould bachelor, Judy?' Sure and maybe I shudn't have laughed, Patsy, but the darlint wasn't maning inny irriverince and ye'll be knowing I niver cud miss a joke. I'm thinking God himsilf wud have laughed at the face av her. He must be liking a bit av fun, too, Patsy, whin he made us so fond av it. I've been having a long life, Patsy, and minny things to be thankful for but for nothing more than me liddle gift av seeing something to laugh at in almost iverything. And that do be minding me... whin Dr. Bentley was here to-day he did be taking me timperature and I did be thinking av the scare yer Aunt Hazel did be giving us once. She had a rale bad spell av flu and yer Aunt Edith was bound to take her timperature wid her funny liddle ther- mometer. It didn't suit yer Aunt Hazel to be fussed over so whiniver me fine Edith's back was turned Hazel whips the thermometer out av her mouth and sticks it in her hot cup av tay. Whin she heard Edith coming back she sticks it in her mouth agin. And poor Edith just about died av fright whin she looked at it and saw what it rigistered. She flew down- stairs and sint Long Alec for the doctor at the rate av no man's business, being sure Hazel had pewmonia wid a timperature like that. Oh, oh, but we had the laugh on her whin the truth come out. Niver cud ye be saying 'timperature' to Edith agin, poor soul. Her and me niver were be way av being cronies but I'll niver deny she had the bist blood av P. E. Island in her veins."

"Are you sure you're not tiring yourself, Judy?"

"Talking so much, sez she. Oh, oh, Patsy darlint, it rists me... and what do a few hours one way or another be mattering whin ye've come to journey's ind?"

One night Judy talked of the disposal of her few treasures.

"There'll be a bit av money in the bank after me funeral ixpinses do be paid. I've lift it to be divided betwane Winnie and Cuddles and yersilf. Winnie is to hev me autygraph quilt and I promised me blue chist to Siddy years ago. There do be some mats in the garret I put away for ye, Patsy, and the crame cow is yours and me book av Useful Knowledge and all the liddle things in me glory box. And the book wid all me resates in it. Ye'll sind Hilary the white kittens, darlint. I'll be giving me bead pincushion to yer Aunt Barbara for a liddle rimimberance. Her and me always did be hitting it off rale well. And ye'll see that the ould black bottle is destroyed afore inny one sees it. Folks might be misunderstanding it."

"I'll... I'll see to everything, Judy."

"And, Patsy darlint, ye'll see that they bury me out there in the ould graveyard where I won't be far from Silver Bush? There do be a liddle place betwane Waping Willy .and the fince where ye can be squazing me in wid a slip av white lilac at me hid. And I'd like a slab on me grave, too, in place av a standing-up tombstone, so the cats can slape on it. It wud be company-like. And ye'll dress me in me ould dress-up dress... the blue one. I always did be liking it. It won't be as tight as it was at Winnie's widding. Do ye be minding?"

"Judy"... Pat did not often break down but there were times when she could not help it... "however can I... however can Silver Bush get along without you?"

"There'll be a way," said Judy gently. "There always do be a way. There do be only one thing... I'm wondering who'll white-wash the stones and the posts nixt spring. Me fine May won't... she niver hild be it."

"I'll see to that, Judy. Everything is going to be kept at Silver Bush just as you left it."

"It'll be too hard on yer hands, Patsy dear." But Judy was not really worried. She knew the Good Man Above would attend to things.

But it seemed there were one or two things on Judy's conscience.

"Patsy darlint, do ye be minding whin that bit av news about the countess visiting at Silver Bush was put in the paper and ye niver cud find out who did be doing it? Darlint, it was be way av being mesilf. I've been often thinking av owning up to it but niver cud I get up me courage. I did be wanting all the folks to know av it so I 'phoned it in. The editor, he did be touching it up a bit though. Can ye be forgiving me, Patsy?"

"Forgive? Oh, Judy! Why... that was... nothing."

"It wasn't in kaping wid the traditions av Silver Bush and well I knew it. And, Patsy darlint, all thim stories av mine... most av thim happened but maybe I did touch thim up a bit, dramatic-like, now and agin. Me grandmother niver was a witch... but she *cud* see things other folks cudn't. One day I do be minding I was walking wid her, me being a slip av tin or twilve... and we met a man there was talk av. He was alone, saming-like, but me grandmother sez to him, sez she, 'Good day to you and *yer company.*' I've niver forgot his face but whin I asked her what she mint she said to thank God I didn't be knowing and not another word wud she say. He did be hanging himself not long after on his verandah, deliberate-like. And now I've tould ye this I'm not worrying over innything. All will be coming right... I'm knowing it some-how, being death-wise. Love doesn't iver be dying, Patsy. I'd like to have seen ye a bride, darlint. But it's glad I am I'll niver have to live at Silver Bush wid ye gone."

One afternoon Judy wandered a little. She thought she heard Joe's whistle and Rae's laugh. "The Silver Bush girls always had the pretty way av laughing," she murmured. She raked down some one who "didn't be washing the butter properly." Once she said, "If ye'd set a light in the windy, Patsy." Again she was hunting through an imaginary parsley bed for something she couldn't find. "I'm fearing I've lost the knack av finding thim," she sighed.

But when Pat went up to her in the dim she was lying peacefully. Mrs. Binnie had just gone down and had passed Pat on the stairs with an ominous moan.

"Thank the Good Man Above I've seen the last av the Binnie gang," said Judy. "I heard her groaning to you on the stairs. It's bad luck to mate on the stairs as the mouse said whin the cat caught him half way down, but the luck'll be on her. She's been talking av funerals be way av cheering me up. 'Whin me father died,' sez she, 'he had a wonderful funeral. The flowers were grand! And the crowds!' Ye cud be seeing it was a great comfort to the fam'ly."

"Are you feeling any worse, Judy?"

"I niver felt better in me life, darlint. I haven't an ache or a pain. Wud ye be propping me up a bit? I'd like to have a look at the ould silver bush and the clouds having their fun wid the wind over it."

"Can you guess who's been here inquiring for you, Judy? Tillytuck, no less. He came all the way from the South Shore to ask after you."

"Oh, oh, that was very affable av him," said Judy in a gratified tone.

Judy's bed had been moved so that she could see out of the window when propped up. Pat raised her on her pillows and she looked out with a relish on a scene that was for her full of memories. The owls were calling in the silver bush. The patient acres of the old farm were lying in the fitful light of a windy sunset. But the twilight shadows were falling peacefully over the sheltered kitchen garden where Long Alec was burning weeds. Tillytuck, who had asked Long Alec if he might have a few parsnips, was squatted down on his haunches, busily digging, while a stick of some kind which he had thrust into his pants pocket stuck up behind him with a grotesque resemblance to a forked tail.

Judy reached out and clutched Pat's hand.

> "'Did ye iver see the divil
> Wid his liddle wooden shovel
> Digging pittaties in the garden
> Wid his tail cocked up?'"

she quoted, laughing, and fell back on her pillows. Her kind loving eyes closed. Judy, who had laughed so bravely, gaily, gallantly all her life, had died laughing.

4

Silver Bush was made ready to receive death. Judy lay in state in the Big Parlour... Pat had a queer feeling that it should really have been in the kitchen... while outside great flakes of the first snowfall were coming down. Her busy hands were still, quite still, at last. Beautiful flowers had been sent in, but Pat searched her garden and found a few late 'mums and some crimson leaves and berries to put in Judy's hands, folded on the breast of her blue dress-up dress. Judy's face took on a beauty and dignity in death it had never known in life. The funeral was largely attended... Pat couldn't help feeling that Judy would have been proud of it. And then it was over... the house, so terribly still, to be put in order and no Judy to talk it over with in the kitchen afterwards! Pat reflected, with a horrible choke, how Judy would have enjoyed talking over her own funeral... how she would have chuckled over the jokes. For there had been jokes... it seemed that there were jokes everywhere, even at funerals. Old Malcolm Anderson making one of his rare remarks as he looked down on Judy's dead face, "Poor woman, I hope you're as happy as you look,"... mournfully, as if he rather doubted it; and Olive's son yowling because his sisters pushed him away from the window and he couldn't see the flowers being carried out... "Never mind," one of his sisters comforting him, "you'll see the flowers at mother's funeral."

When all was done, Pat, wondering how she could bear the dull, dead ache in her heart, averted her eyes from the spectral winter landscape and went to the kitchen expecting to find it a tragedy of emptiness. But mother was there in Judy's place, with a chairful of cats beside her. Pat buried her head in mother's lap and cried out all the tears she had wanted to cry out since Judy was stricken down.

"Oh, mother... mother... I've nothing but you and Silver Bush left now."

The Eleventh Year

THERE were many times in the year following Judy's death when cold waves of pain went over Pat. At first it seemed literally impossible to carry on without Judy. Life seemed very savourless now that Judy's tales were all told. But Pat found, as others have done, that "we forget because we must." Life began to be livable again and then sweet. Silver Bush seemed to cry to her, "Make me home-like again . . . keep my rooms lighted . . . my heart warmed. Bring young laughter here to keep me from growing old."

Almost every one she had loved was changed or gone . . . the old voices of gladness sounded no more . . . but Silver Bush was still the same.

That first Christmas without Judy was bitter. Winnie wanted them all to go to the Bay Shore for the day but Pat wouldn't hear of it. Leave Silver Bush alone for Christmas? Not she! Every tradition was scrupulously carried out. It was easier because mother could share in things now, and they had a good Christmas Day after all. Uncle Tom and Aunt Barbara and Winnie and Frank and their children came. May went home for the day, so there was no jarring presence. A letter came from Rae with the good news that in two years' time she and Brook would be coming "home" to take charge of the Vancouver branch. Compared to China Vancouver seemed next door. As Judy used to say, there was always something to take the edge off. Nevertheless Pat was glad when the day was over. The first Christmas above a grave can never be a wholly joyous thing. She and mother talked it over in the kitchen afterwards and laughed a little over certain things. The cats purred around them and Uncle Tom and dad played checkers. But once or twice Pat caught herself listening for Judy's step on the back stairs.

By spring hope was her friend again and her delight in Silver Bush was keen and vivid once more. Her love for it kept her young. To be sure, often now came little needlelike reminders of the passing years. Now and again there was another grey hair and she knew the quirk at the corner of her mouth was getting a little more pronounced. "We're all growing old," she thought with a pang. But she really didn't mind it so much for herself. It was the change in others she hated to see. Winnie was getting matronly and Frank... who had just been elected to membership in the Provincial House... was grey above the ears. If other people would only stay young, Pat thought, she wouldn't mind growing old herself. Though it was rather horrid to be told you "looked young," as Uncle Brian once did. She knew the Binnies regarded her as definitely "on the shelf" and that they were calling her among themselves "the single perennial." Even Little Mary once gravely asked her, "Aunt Pat, did *you* ever have any beaus?" It sometimes amused her to reflect that she was really quite a different person to different people. To the Binnies she was a disappointed spinster who had been "crossed in love"... to the Great-aunts at the Bay Shore she was an inexperienced child... to Lester Conway she was a divine, alluring, unobtainable creature. For Lester, who was now a young widower, had tried vainly to warm up the cold soup. Pat would none of him. The time when she had been so wildly in love with him in her Queen's days seemed as far away and unreal as the days of immemorial antiquity. To be sure, he had been slim and romantic and dashing then, whereas he was stout and plump-faced now. And he had once laughed at Silver Bush. Pat had never forgiven him for that... never would forgive him.

In the spring Long Alec again announced that the next year the new house would be built. It had been postponed twice but the mortgage was paid at last and there would be no more postponements. Pat lived on this through the summer. Nevertheless, when the autumn came again it was not just a wholesome time for Pat. Sometimes mother watched her a little anxiously. Pat seemed to have an attack of nerves now and then. She developed a taste for taking lonely walks by herself among the twilight shadows. They seemed to be better company than she found in the sunlight. She came back from them looking as if she were of the band of grey shadows herself. Mother didn't like it. It seemed to her that the child, on those lone rambles, was trying to warm herself by some fire that had died out years ago. She had that look on her face when she came in. Mother wanted Pat to go away for a visit somewhere but Pat only laughed.

"There is nowhere I could go where I would be half as happy as I am at Silver Bush. You know I've died several times of homesickness when I was away. Don't worry over me, sweetheart. I'm fine and dandy... and next year Silver Bush will be *ours* again... and I've a hundred plans for it."

A night came when Pat found herself alone at Silver Bush... absolutely alone for the first time, in that old house where there had been always so many. Mother and father were over at the Bay Shore and would not be back till late. It was wonderful that mother could gad about like that again. Pat thought she wouldn't mind being alone... *could* she be alone with dear Silver Bush?... but some restlessness drove her outside. There was a moan of the autumn wind in the leafless birches and a wonderful display of northern lights. Pat recalled that Judy had always been superstitious about northern lights. They were a "sign." How Judy seemed to come back on a night like this! Dead and gone years seemed to be whispering to themselves all about her. The crisp leaves rustled under her feet as she went along the path to the orchard. She recalled old autumns when she and Sid had raced through the fallen leaves. There were voices in the wind, calling to her out of the past. Many things came back to her... bitter, beautiful, sad, joyous things... crises that had seemed to wreck life and were only dim memories now. She was haunted. This would not do. She must shake this off. She would go in and light up the house. It did not like to be dark and silent. Yet she paused for a moment on the door-step, the prey of a sudden fancy. That shut door was a door of dreams through which she might slip into the Silver Bush of long ago. For a fleeting space she had a curious feeling that Judy and Tillytuck and Hilary and Rae and Winnie and Joe were all in there and if she could only go in quickly and silently enough she would find them. A world utterly passed away might be her universe once more.

"This is nonsense," said Pat, giving herself a shake. "This won't do. These moods are coming too often now."

She flung open the door and went in... lighted a lamp.

There was nobody there except Bold-and-Bad. But Pat could have sworn that Judy had been there a moment before.

She did not sleep for a long time that night. She felt vaguely apprehensive, although she could assign no reason for it. As she said afterwards her soul knew something she did not. Late in the night she fell into a troubled slumber. Thus was passed her last night in that beloved old room where she had dreamed her dreams of girlhood and suffered the heartaches of womanhood, where she had endured her defeats and exulted over her victories. Never again was she to lay her head on its pillow... never again waken to see the morning sunshine gleaming in at her vine-hung window. She had looked from that window on spring blossom and summer greenness, on autumn fields and winter snows. She had seen star-shine and sunrise from it. She had knelt there in keen happiness and bitter sorrow. And now that was all finished. The Angel of the Years turned the page whereon it was writ while she lay in that uneasy slumber... and she knew it not.

It was Sunday and everybody went to church. Pat remembered as she went out of the door that when she was a child she had always been so sorry for Silver Bush when everybody went to church. It must feel lonely. She had always been glad when she was left home because she would be company for it.

Something made her turn her head as the car went down the lane. Silver Bush looked beautiful, even on that dour November day, against its sheltering trees. She felt her heart go out to it as they turned the corner and it was hidden from her sight.

The minister had just announced his text... it was always remarked as a curious coincidence that it was, "Thy house shall become a desolation"... when young Corey Robinson entered the church, hurried up the aisle and whispered a word to Long Alec. Pat heard it... every one in the church heard it in a few moments.

Silver Bush was burning!

Pat seemed to die a thousand deaths on that ride home. Yet when she got there she was curiously numb... terror seemed to have washed her being clean of everything. Even when she saw that terrible fire blazing against the grey November hillside she gave no sign... made no sound.

It seemed as if everybody in both the Glens and Silverbridge and Bay Shore were there... but nothing could

be done . . . nothing but stand helplessly and see a home that
had been a home for generations wiped out. That night Silver
Bush, with all its memories, all its possessions, was in ashes!

2

They all went to Swallowfield until things could be
settled. Pat took no part in the settling. Life had suddenly
become for her like a landscape on the moon. She had the
odd feeling of not belonging to this or any world that she had
felt once or twice after a bad attack of flu. Only . . . this feeling
would never pass. Mother, who bore up wonderfully, watched
her anxiously.

It turned out that May had left the oil stove in the porch
burning when she went to church. It was supposed to have
exploded. Pat was not in the least interested in *how* it had
happened. She was not interested in anything . . . not even in
the finding of Judy's "cream cow" quite unharmed amid the
ashes in the cellar and the old front door with its knocker,
lying on the lawn. Somebody had wrenched it off in a first
vain attempt to enter the blazing house. She did not care
when it was discovered that all the hooked rugs Judy had
stored in the garret for her were safe, Aunt Barbara having
borrowed them to copy the patterns the day before the fire.
When you are horribly, hopelessly tired you can't care about
anything.

The only thing that seemed to be the least bit of comfort
to her was that the white kittens had not been burned. She
had packed the picture up after Judy's death and sent it to
Hilary. He had never even acknowledged it . . . that hurt
her . . . but as she had sent it to his office she felt quite sure
he must have received it. Yes, she was faintly glad Judy's
kittens had not been burned.

At first Long Alec talked of rebuilding Silver Bush. It
was insured. Everybody seemed very pleased about the
insurance . . . but no insurance could restore the old heir-
looms . . . the old associations. And then, four days after the
fire, Great-aunt Frances at the Bay Shore died and it was
found that she had left the Bay Shore farm to mother.

"It's strange how things work out," said Aunt Barbara.

"Very strange," agreed Pat bitterly.

The kaleidoscope shifted again. Long Alec and mother

and Pat would go to live at the Bay Shore. And the new house for Sid and May . . . a house without memories . . . would be built on the old foundation of Silver Bush. It would not be like the old Silver Bush. That was gone and the place thereof would know it no more.

May was openly triumphant. A new house, with all the bay windows she wanted and a colour-scheme kitchen like Olive's! Lovely!

Mother was really pleased at the thought of going back to her old home to live.

"Mother is younger than I am," thought Pat drearily.

She felt horribly old. Her love for Silver Bush had kept her young . . . and now it was gone. Nothing was left . . . there was only a dreadful, unbearable emptiness.

"Life has beaten me," she told herself. She had had enough grief in her life to know that in time even the bitterest fades out into a not unpleasing dearness and sweetness of recollection. But this heart-break could never fade. Everything had fallen into ruins around her. She could never fit into the life at the Bay Shore. She had a terrible feeling that she did not belong anywhere . . . or to anybody . . . in this new sad lonely world.

"I think . . . if I could ever be glad of anything again . . . I'd be glad that Judy died before this happened," she thought. She did not say these things to anybody. Nobody but mother would have understood and she was not going to make things harder for mother. But her heart was like an unlighted room and nothing, she thought she knew, could ever illumine it again.

3

One evening two weeks later Pat slipped away in the twilight and went along the Whispering Lane like a ghost, to where home had been. She had never dared to go before. But something drew her now.

Where Silver Bush had been was only a yawning cellar full of ashes and charred beams. Pat leaned on the old yard gate . . . which had not burned because the wind had blown the flames back against the bush . . . and looked long and quietly about her. She wore her long blue coat and the little dress of crinkled red crepe she had worn to church . . . the only clothes she owned just now. Her head was bare and her face was very pale.

The evening was soft and gentle and almost windless. No living thing stirred near her except a lean adventurous barn cat that picked its way gingerly through the yard. Bold-and-Bad and Popka had been transferred to Swallowfield and Winnie had taken Squedunk.

It hurt Pat worse than anything else to see the dead stark trees of the birch grove. She shuddered as she recalled standing there that fatal Sunday and seeing the flames ravage them. It had seemed to hurt her even more than seeing her home burn... those trees she had always loved... trees that had been akin to her. More than half the bush was killed. The old aspen by the kitchen door was only a charred stump and the maple over the well was an indecency. The hood of the well was burned. May would have a pump put in now. But that didn't matter. Nothing mattered.

All the flower clumps near the house had been burned ... Judy's bleeding-heart... the southernwood... the white lilac. The lawn itself looked like an old yellow blanket. Beyond stretched a russet land of shadows and lonely furrows and woods that stirred faintly in their dreams. Far away, in the direction of Silverbridge, Angus Macaulay must have been working in his forge for she could hear the ring of his anvil, faintly clear, as if some goblin forger were at work among the hills.

"I suppose I can teach," thought Pat. "I have my old licence. They won't need me at the Bay Shore... they've had Anna Palmer there for years to help and she'll stay on. But I can't build up a new life... I'm too tired. I'll just go on existing... withering into unimportance... drifting from one place to another... rootless... living in houses I hate... oh, can it be I standing here looking at the place where Silver Bush was?... that old Bible verse... 'it shall be a heap forever... it shall not be built again'... I wish that were true... I wish no house could ever be built here again... it will be a desecration. Oh, if I could only wake up and find it all a dream!"

"Pat, darling," said a voice from the shadows around her.

She turned... incredulous... amazed...

"Jingle!"

The old name sprang to her lips. The autumn dusk was no longer cold and loveless over the remote hills. Something seemed to have come with him... courage... hope... inspiration... that same dear sense of protection and understanding that had come to her that evening of long ago when he had found her lost in the dark on the Base Line road. She held out both her hands but he caught her in his arms... his lips were seeking hers... a tremor half fear, half delight, shook her. And then that old, old, unacknowledged ache of loneliness she had tried to stifle with Silver Bush vanished forever. His lips were on hers... and she *knew*. It was like a tide turning home.

"I've made you mine forever with that kiss," he said triumphantly. "You can never belong to anyone else. And I've waited long enough for it," he added with his old laugh.

Pat stood quivering with his arms about her. Life was not over after all... it was only beginning.

"I... I don't deserve you, Hilary," she whispered humbly. "It seems... it seems... oh, are you *really* here? I'm not dreaming it, am I?"

"I'm real, sweetheart... joy... delight... wonder! I started as soon as I saw the account of the fire in an Island paper. But I was coming anyway... I had only been waiting to finish our house. I know what this tragedy of Silver Bush must have meant to you... but I've a home for you by another sea, Pat. And in it we'll build up a new life and the old will become just a treasury of dear and sacred memories... of things time cannot destroy. Will you come to it with me?"

"I'll go to the end of the world and back with you, Hilary. I can't understand my not knowing all these years that it was you I loved. Those other men... some of them were so nice... I thought I couldn't marry them because I couldn't leave Silver Bush... but I know now it was because they weren't *you*...."

"Are you really my girl... *my* girl at last, Pat? You remember how furiously you used to deny it? And your eyes are as brown as ever, Pat. I can't see in this dimness but I'm sure they are. And I know you look just as much as ever like a creamy rose with gold in its heart. Do you know, Pat, I never got your letter or Judy's kittens till two months ago? I've been in Japan for over a year, studying Japanese architecture. Letters were forwarded but parcels weren't. And you broke the postal laws shamelessly by tucking your letter inside the parcel. Dearest, let's go into the old graveyard and sit on a slab. I want to have you wholly to myself for an hour before we go back to Swallowfield. There's going to be a moonrise to-night... how long is it since we watched a moonrise together?"

"A moonrise tonight." That was always a magical phrase. Pat was in a maze of happiness as they walked to the old graveyard and sat on Weeping Willy's flat tombstone. She hadn't felt like this for years... had believed she could never feel like this again... as if some supernal musician had swept her very soul with his fingers and evolved some ethereal harmony. Was it possible life could always be so rich... so poignant... so *significant* as this?

"I want to tell you all about the home I have ready for you," said Hilary. "When I came back from Japan and found the picture and your letter I wanted to come east at once. But that very day when I was prowling on the heights above the city I found a spot... a spot I *recognized*, although I had never seen it before... a spot that *wanted* me. There was a spring in the corner with a little brook trickling out... four darling little apple trees in another corner... and a hill of pines behind it, with a river and a mountain within neighborly distance... a faint blue mountain. I don't know its name but we'll call it the Hill of the Mist. That spot was just crying for a house to be built on it. So... I built one. It's waiting for you. It's a dear house, Pat... fat red chimneys... sharp little gables on the side of the roof... a door that says 'come in' and another one that says, 'stay out.' It's painted white and has bottlegreen shutters like Silver Bush."

"It sounds heavenly, Hilary... but I'd live in an igloo in Greenland if you were there."

"There's a lovely jam closet," said Hilary slyly. "I thought you'd want one."

Pat's eyes flickered.

"Of course I want one. While I live and move and have my being I'll want a jam closet," she said decidedly. "And we'll have Judy's rugs on the floor and the old Silver Bush knocker on the door that says 'come in.'"

"The dining-room has a wide, low window opening into the pine wood at the back. We can eat with the sound of the pines in our ears. And from the other window we can see the sunset while we eat our supper. I've built the house, Pat... I've provided the body but you must provide the soul. There's a lovely big fireplace that can hold real logs... I left it all laid ready for lighting... you will light the fire and make the room live."

"Like the old kitchen at Silver Bush. It *will* be home-like."

"You could make any place home-like, Pat. We'll sit there caring only when we want to care for what is outside... wind or rain, mist or moonshine. We'll have a dog that wags his tail when he sees us... more than one. Lots of jolly little dogs and furry kittens. And a Silver Bush cat. I suppose Bold-and-Bad is too old to endure emigration to a far land."

"Yes, he must end his days at Swallowfield. Aunt Barbara loves him. But I'm sure it will be possible to send a kitten by express—it has been done. Hilary, why did you give up writing to me?"

"I thought it wasn't any use. I thought the only decent thing to do was to leave you in peace. Besides, you *were* taking me too much for granted, Pat. You were blinded by our years of friendship. When can we be married, Pat?"

"As soon as you like," said Pat shamelessly. "At least... when I've had time to get a few clothes. I haven't a rag but what I'm wearing."

"We'll spend our honeymoon in a chalet in the Austrian Tyrol, Pat. I picked it out years ago. Then we'll go home... *home*. Listen to me rolling the word under my tongue. I've never had a home, you know. Oh, how tired I am of living in other people's houses! Pat, there is water in the house, of course, but I've made a little well out of the spring in the corner and stoned it up... a delightful little well where we can dip up water under the ferns. And we'll put a saucer of milk there every night for the fairies. Judy's white kittens are already hanging on the wall of our living room and that old china dog with the blue eyes you gave me years ago is squatting on the mantelpiece."

"Hilary, you don't mean to say you've got that yet?"

"Haven't I! It has gone everywhere with me... it's been my mascot. We'll make it a family heirloom. And I have a few things picked up in my wanderings you'll love, Pat."

"Is there a good place for a garden?"

"The best. We'll have a garden, my very own dear... with columbine for the fairies and poppies for dancing shadows and marigolds for laughter. And we'll have the walks picked off with whitewashed stones. Slugs and spiders and blight and mildew will never infest it, I feel sure. You've always been a sort of half-cousin to the fairies and you ought to be able to keep such plagues away."

Delightful nonsense! Was it she, Pat, who was laughing at it . . . she, who had been in such despair an hour ago? Miracles *did* happen. And it was so easy to laugh when Hilary was about. That new, far, unseen home would be as full of laughter as Silver Bush had been.

"And Rae will be somewhere near after two years," thought Pat.

They sat in a trance of happiness, savouring "the unspent joy of all the unborn years" in the moonlight and waving shadows of the ancient graveyard where so many kind old hearts rested. They had been dust for many years but their love lived on. Judy had been right. Love did not . . . could not die.

The moon had risen. The sky was like a great silver bowl pouring down light over the world. A little wind raised and swayed the long hair-like grass growing around the slab on Judy's grave, giving the curious suggestion of something prisoned under it trying to draw a long breath and float upward.

"I wish Judy could have known of this," said Pat softly. "Dear old Judy . . . she always wanted it."

"Judy knew it would come to pass. She sent me this. I got it in Japan after months of delay. I would have started for Silver Bush at the moment if I could have, but it was impossible to arrange. And anyway . . . I thought I might have a better chance if I waited a decent interval."

Hilary had taken a cheap crumpled envelope from his pocket book and extracted a sheet of bluelined paper.

"Dear Jingle," Judy had printed on it in faint, straggling letters, "She has give David Kirk the air. I'm thinking youd have a good chance if youd come back.

> Judy Plum."

"Dear, dear old Judy," said Pat. "She must have written that on her dying bed . . . look how feeble some of the letters are . . . and got somebody to smuggle it out to the mail-box for her."

"Judy knew that would bring me back from the dead," said Hilary with pardonable exaggeration. "She died knowing it. And, Pat," he added quickly, sensing that she was too near tears for a betrothal hour, "will you make soup for me like Judy's when we're married?"

Just as they had admitted they must really return to Swallowfield a grey shadow leaped over the paling, poised for a moment on Judy's slab and then skimmed away.

"Oh, there's Bold-and-Bad," cried Pat. "I must catch him and take him back. He's too old to be left out o'nights."

"This evening belongs to me," said Hilary firmly. "I won't let you go chasing cats . . . not even Bold-and-Bad. He'll follow us back without any chasing. I've found something I once thought I'd lost forever and I won't be cheated out of a single moment."

The old graveyard heard the most charming sound in the world . . . the low yielding laugh of a girl held prisoner by her lover.

ABOUT THE AUTHOR

L. M. MONTGOMERY's fascinating accounts of the lives and romances of Anne, Emily, and other well-loved characters have achieved long-lasting popularity the world over. Born in 1874 in Prince Edward Island, Canada, Lucy Maud showed an early flair for storytelling. She soon began to have her writing published in papers and magazines, and when she died in Toronto in 1942 she had written more than twenty novels and a large number of short stories. Most of her books are set in Prince Edward Island, which she loved very much and wrote of most beautifully. *Anne of Green Gables*, her most popular work, has been translated into thirty-six languages, made into a film twice, and has had continuing success as a stage play. Lucy Maud Montgomery's early home in Cavendish, P.E.I., where she is buried, is a much-visited historic site.

WELCOME TO THE WORLD OF
Lucy Maud Montgomery

If you haven't already met Anne and Emily and the other well-loved characters of Lucy Maud Montgomery, you'll soon know why they've been enchanting readers for generations. These classic books follow the lives and romances of Anne Shirley and the feisty Emily Starr—welcoming you into their magical world—and helping you understand your own.

On Prince Edward Island where Anne of Green Gables grew up, there is a place near the sea called Avonlea. And in this very special place in days not so long ago, lived some very special people.

CHRONICLES OF AVONLEA
In twelve unforgettable stories filled with magic and love, you will laugh as a spinster's clever trick pushes a slow-moving suitor to propose. Or you'll hold your breath in suspense as Old Man Shaw awaits his daughter's return to Avonlea. With each delightful tale your imagination will be stirred with intrigue and wonder.

27534-8 $2.95

ANNE OF GREEN GABLES COOKBOOK
A companion volume to the Anne of Green Gables series, here is a cookbook containing twenty-five recipes, along with the passage from the Anne book that inspired the recipe. By following the simple instructions in this book, you can make Cowcumber Boats (from *Anne of Avonlea*); Miss Ellen's Pound Cake (from *Anne of Windy Poplars*); and Diana Barry's Favourite Raspberry Cordial (from *Anne of Green Gables*). Includes cooking tips, a complete glossary of terms for beginning cooks and charming illustrations.   Trade Paperback 15623-3 $5.95

Don't miss any of the delightful Anne or Emily books!

21313-X	ANNE OF GREEN GABLES	$2.95
21314-8	ANNE OF AVONLEA	$2.95
21317-2	ANNE OF THE ISLAND	$2.95
21316-4	ANNE OF WINDY POPLARS	$2.95
21318-0	ANNE'S HOUSE OF DREAMS	$2.95
21315-6	ANNE OF INGLESIDE	$2.95
23370-X	EMILY OF NEW MOON	$3.50
26214-9	EMILY CLIMBS	$3.50
26493-1	EMILY'S QUEST	$3.50
26921-6	RAINBOW VALLEY	$3.50
26922-4	RILLA OF INGLESIDE	$3.50

Also Available

42163-6	ANNE OF GREEN GABLES DIARY	$9.95
45091-3	ANNE OF GREEN GABLES AUDIO CASSETTE	
	(DOUBLE TAPE)	$14.95

Buy them at your local bookstore or use this page to order.

- -

Bantam Books, Dept. AG4, 414 East Golf Road, Des Plaines, IL 60016

Please send me the items I have checked above. I am enclosing $_____ (please add $2.00 to cover postage and handling). Send check or money order—no cash or C.O.D.s please.

Mr/Ms _____

Address _____

City/State _____ Zip _____

AG4—8/89

Please allow four to six weeks for delivery. This offer expires 2/90.